DEEP SPACE

Compiled & Edited by
Ben Thomas & D Kershaw

Instructed ships shall sail to quick Commerce;

By which remotest Regions are alli'd:

Which makes one City of the Universe,

Where some may gain, and all may be suppli'd.

Then, we upon our Globe's last verge shall go,

And view the Ocean leaning on the sky:

From thence our rolling Neighbours shall we know,

And on the Lunar world securely pry.

Annus Mirabilis, John Dryden, 1666

TABLE OF CONTENTS

AFTERGLOW
By Jacob Baugher

Molly Ramirez sent her daughter to Mars to avoid the apocalypse. Now, she must escape a doomed Earth herself and join her. There's just one problem: Aliens.

> Defenceless under the night
> Our world in stupor lies;
> Yet, dotted everywhere,
> Ironic points of light
> Flash out wherever the Just
> Exchange their messages:
> May I, composed like them
> Of Eros and of dust,
> Beleaguered by the same
> Negation and despair,
> Show an affirming flame.
> —W.H. Auden, September 1, 1939

CHAPTER ONE

Why is it so cold in space, Mama? Why don't the stars twinkle? I can't see Earth anymore. It's just dark outside. Will you be here soon? Auntie Opal says that I'm going to live with her until you and daddy come on the next ship. I hope you come soon. I can't wait to see you and Daddy and Midnight. Please come soon. It's so cold in space. I miss you.

Love, Rachel

—From the Journal of Rachel Ramirez, age 7.

Ten Minutes to Impact

"Life's only worth living if you believe in something." Those were her husband's last words to her. He'd be dead soon, along with the rest of the planet.

All Molly Ramirez really believed in was her handgun, her daughter, and the asteroid that was about to slam into Earth's surface. Oh, and the aliens that were trying to kill her, her squad, Vice President Gard, and also strip the Earth of its water supply.

You know, a typical Cosmic Tuesday.

A month before the Avandii invasion, they lassoed a NEO and hurled it at Los Angeles. Or, rather, they lassoed 433 Eros, a 5-mile-long asteroid, shielded it from nuclear strikes, cloaked it, and sped up its trajectory by about a thousand miles an hour. At least, that's how it'd been explained to Molly. Molly didn't really care about asteroids, she cared about her daughter. So she and her husband, Will, sent her to Mars.

Now, all that stood between Sergeant Molly Ramirez and her daughter were five hundred meters of smoke-filled tunnel and her own commanding officer. And about 34 million miles. Captain Dalton was a complete fuck and had leveraged his way into landing the last spot off Earth. She'd be damned if he made it off the planet and left her to die. Molly couldn't be left behind. She wouldn't allow it. Rachel needed her.

"Go! Go! Go!" Private Evan Davis shouted, whirled, and levelled his M249 SAW down the hallway at the Avandii horde pursuing them. The alpha screamed like an orangutan and leapt twenty feet through the smoke-filled launch hallway. The alien was over two meters tall, had six legs tipped with razor-sharp claws, and was covered in tufty, matted orange fur. It dragged its thick-knuckled, oversized hands on the ground. Its fangs dripped with venom. Oh, and it could release a cloud of spores from its mouth that reanimated fresh corpses and turned them into mindless drones. Fifty or so lurched along at the Avandii's back.

Davis emptied the SAW's entire belt magazine

down the hallway. Gard screamed and clapped his hands to his ears. Purple blood spattered the walls. Molly's helmet cut the gun's sonic impact by 66%. She shoved Gard to the floor, drew her Tek-49 "Sabre" pistol from its holster and dialled it up to 11. It hummed in her hand, more of a vibration than a sound, plasma bolts armed and ready.

She needn't have bothered. It was over in the 14 seconds it took Davis to empty the belt magazine. Screams echoed. Then nothing.

The Tek continued to hum in her hand; the only sound, save for the ringing in her ears. Klaxons blared. Alarms strobed in the acrid black smoke that filled the launch hallway. Red halos reflected against the dull metal walls. She kept one hand on Vice President Gard.

"Clear," Davis said after a moment. He fed another belt into the SAW and slung it over his shoulder.

That's when the alpha got him. Wounded, it dropped from the ceiling, wrapped four of its six legs around Davis' neck and *squelched* its fangs into his skull.

Molly shot them both. A burning blue plasma bolt crackled out of the Tek's muzzle and engulfed the pair of them. Davis screamed. The alpha turned to her, opened its mouth, and let out a bellow like a howler monkey. It staggered toward her and Davis' corpse fell limp from its mouth. Sometimes it sucked being Secret Service.

Molly holstered her Tek, unfastened the M38 incendiary grenade from her belt, armed it, waited for a count of two, and flicked it down the hallway.

Clank, clatter, klaxon, boom. No more monkeys jumping on the secret tunnel to the ultra-secret launchpad to Mars. Warm air rushed down the hallway and tousled the few stray strands of hair that her helmet had missed. The smell of cooking meat hung in the air.

"Come on." She ripped Gard up from the floor, perhaps a little too roughly. "More will be coming." He made a sort of half-moan, half gurgle, but followed her back down the hallway, into the smoke. Almost there.

"Ramirez." Dalton's voice crackled over her earpiece. An explosion rocked the tunnel. Dust trickled down from the ceiling onto the back of her neck. "They're in the tunnels," Captain Dalton shouted in her ear, voice almost lost among the sounds of falling rock and static.

No shit, she thought. But responded, "Understood. Ramirez, out."

Davis wouldn't be the only person she'd kill today.

Gard stumbled along ahead of her, nearly blind in the smoke. Molly reached up and pressed a button on her EVO-Max9 helmet. Glowing blue grid lines sparked to life in the vidscreen, showing her the locations of rocks, debris, and bodies. She grabbed Gard's hand.

"Come on." Their footsteps echoed in the spaces between the klaxon alarms.

The launch chamber had gleaming walls of metal and stone. The carrier shuttle stood on its end in the centre, the same design as every space shuttle since the Columbia in 1981. It would carry them out of Earth's gravity well to the larger, more advanced ship that floated in outer orbit. Mars only had 38% of Earth's gravity. The new ship could escape Mars's orbit just fine if there was a problem.

Captain Dalton was waiting for them, his old .40 Glock 23 in one hand. With the other he helped the President on to the ship. His own Tek-49 was holstered on his belt. Molly released Gard and he hurried up the ramp, leaving her alone with Dalton.

"Davis?" asked the captain.

"Dead," she said.

"Good. Better that way." And then he raised his gun to Molly's forehead and pulled the trigger.

The gun clicked on an empty chamber, the hollow sound bouncing off the metal walls until it faded to nothing.

She raised an eyebrow. Dalton looked at his gun and opened his mouth in disbelief.

Molly shot him in the kneecap. The Tek belched out an electric whirr and blue fire tore the bottom of Dalton's leg off. He crumpled with a howl that echoed against the stone walls. The Tek filled the chamber with that low, buzzing hum as it charged for the next shot.

"Traitor," he snarled. Molly pretended not to hear him. Instead, she put on her best soldier's face, the one she had been working on since boot camp, raised her Tek, and shot Dalton between the eyes.

A lot of being a soldier is pretending.

She pretended not to notice the red mist that hung in the air, that clung to her clothes when she brushed past his body and entered the shuttle. She pretended not to notice when the president and his cabinet gave her sidelong looks, clearly shocked that it was her and not Captain Shane Dalton accompanying them to Mars. No, instead, Molly Ramirez strapped in, pulled the military-grade paracord around her chest and waist, and closed her eyes. Molly was used to pretending.

She shoved down her emotions, locked them away like they had trained her to, in that deep part of her subconscious reserved for regret and darkness and the terrible things that she had done. She imagined that she was a little girl, floating in her uncle's swimming pool.

She thought of that dark, weightless place as her Box of Broken Things. Recently, it'd been stretched to breaking, but she didn't let herself think about it. That was kind of the point of the box; if you thought about the things in the box, they weren't in the box anymore. Molly's Rule #1 was: "Don't open the box in your head." Rule #2 was: "Don't tell your therapist about the box." No one knew about it. Except Will.

While memory's waters sloshed in her ears, beneath her the ship moved. It started with a vibration deep in her chest, a frequency so low that she could feel it in her bones before she heard it. Then came the rumble. Her shoulders strained against the paracord. She squeezed her eyes shut as the pressure intensified, growing from mild discomfort to a burning, buzzing, searing pain in her sinuses. The rumble became a roar, and the vibration, an earthquake. Then nothing.

Molly opened her eyes. Outside the porthole window, the blue sky had faded to midnight black. Her heart beat out a tinny *thumpthump* in the lonely silence. Soft blue light permeated the cabin, cast from the many LEDs recessed into the ship's ceiling and walls, but a harsh orange steadily overtook the tranquillity. She knew what that was...and she made herself look. The spaceship's wing stretched outside her window. Beyond it blazed 433 Eros.

It hurtled past the ship, seeming to just miss its mirrored surface, a mass of molten rock, consumed by indigo flame, that streaked across the sky making the stars pale in comparison. It was primal, dangerous beauty.

When she and Will were newlyweds, they hiked the Colorado Rockies. On the way up Flattop Mountain, they passed a sign that read "Don't get summit fever! The mountain doesn't care about you." The sign was meant to caution hikers to turn back if conditions were bad. If a storm blew up, snow and lightning were often seen in tandem. Mountaineers could freeze, slip and fall off a cliff, or be struck by lightning. To Molly though, the sign meant something different entirely: "The universe doesn't care about you." And from that day it stuck in her brain like a wart. The universe didn't care about her, so she would take care of herself.

Molly shoved that memory back into her Box of Broken Things and forced herself to watch as the Rocky Mountain asteroid plummeted toward Earth. She told herself she wouldn't cry, but she found her face hot and wet with tears anyway. She told herself, when she had entered the labyrinth of tunnels that lead to the launchpad, when she decided to kill Dalton and take the seat for her own, that she wouldn't remember the little house in suburban Ohio with the fenced-in yard and the hardwood floors and the little black corgi. She told herself she wouldn't remember Rachel smiling at her when she first held her, damp with sweat and half-mad with pain from the birth. She told herself she wouldn't remember her husband's tears on her face when she kissed him goodbye for the last time. The scratch of his beard on her chin. The feel of his arms around her. The heat that rose in her chest, in her very soul, that called out to be held, to be kissed, to be loved.

But she did remember. And as the piece of fucking space rock slammed into the Earth's surface, vomiting molten rock and painting the atmosphere bloody crimson, tears flowed hot and fast over her cheeks. And for a moment, Molly Ramirez let herself feel. She tried to picture her husband's face in her mind's eye—tried to tell his memory that she was sorry—but she couldn't. All she could see was 433 Eros and the little house and the little dog dwarfed by the fireball that consumed Earth.

She'd had dreams about this moment. Not about the asteroid exactly, but dreams where blood and tears ran like rivers and she'd wake screaming in the sticky summer nights to the fan buzzing angrily in the window and her husband clutching her arm in that night-terror panic he always got when she woke him abruptly. Dreams that were creeping and ugly and stuck with her no matter how hard she tried to forget them. Dreams where she lost everyone she ever loved in horrible, gruesome ways. Now those dreams had come to fruition.

Rachel was all she had left in the entire universe. She swore to herself (as she had countless times in the seven years since her daughter had been born) that she'd never let anything bad happen to her.

She closed her eyes and shoved the memories back into her Box of Broken Things. Told herself everything would be all right.

But it was just an empty lie.

She was about to turn away from the window when a blinking blue light blazed up in interstellar space. She leaned closer to the window, her breath fogging the glass. She wiped it away. The light travelled in a straight line toward Earth's lifeless husk. Even from this distance, fire burned on its surface and massive arcs of lightning flickered in the crimson sky. The light stopped, hovering, or so she supposed, just outside of Earth's gravity well, as if it were watching. Gard leaned across her and pointed back at the cosmic murk.

"Look."

More blue lights flared. Swarms of them, all blinking out of time with each other. They coloured the vacuum like neon flies and streaked toward Earth's husk.

The Avandii had come for her planet.

CHAPTER TWO

It's so cold in space, Mama. They gave me my own room, but it doesn't have a window. The nice lady next door gave me a little teddy bear and told me it would keep me warm. Her name is Mrs. Mary. I named the bear Mr. Snuffles because his nose is too big. He has brown eyes like you. The captain said we're only a few days away from Mars. Are there trees there? Are there rivers, like home? Will we have a yard for Midnight to play in? I can't wait to see you and Daddy. Please come soon.

Love, Rachel

"Life's only worth living if you believe in something."

Molly believed in her daughter, her gun, and that the universe didn't care about her. It didn't make her feel any better.

It was cold in space. She pulled the shiny plastic emergency blanket tighter over her shoulders. The ship's captain kept the passenger cabins at exactly 65 degrees and 67% humidity to best replicate the projected climate on Earth in Washington, D.C. You know, because the politicians' comfort was more important than everyone else's.

It should have been a balmy fall day. The leaves had

just started to change in Ohio, turning from green to fiery reds and oranges and yellows. They would fall to the ground with each gust of wind, tinged with the barest hint of Erie winter, and stick there against the asphalt until crystalline frost turned them brown, plastered by the patter of cool autumn rain. It would smell sweet in the Cuyahoga River valley; like wet rock and wood smoke and damp earth. If she closed her eyes, tuned out the hum of the ship, the whoosh of the air filter system, she could almost hear the crunch of leaves underfoot, the rustle of wind through the trees. Snapping twigs underfoot on a backwoods trail. Her dog panting next to her. The soft coo of her child's unblemished voice. Her husband's hand in hers.

Almost.

Now, the world seemed to be defined in "almosts."

The hum of the ship; the odourless, too-cold air always brought her back, always ruined the memory and replaced it with the blazing asteroid slamming into Earth. With the swarming Avandii lights spiralling down to her planet's surface like so many hectic leaves.

"Pestilence-stricken multitudes," Percy Shelly said. Will had shown her that poem. He'd read it to her one October night in 2011 as they lay in a hammock on campus. She'd told him it was self-important trash. He'd laughed and kissed her. His lips were soft and warm and drove the early-winter chill from her bones. The beginnings of his stubble scratched her chin and his hands roamed gently around the curve of her hips.

Molly opened her eyes, forsaking the waking dream. The ship was everything that Earth was not: white, cold, and sterile. A bridge, two full wings that housed crew, an entire sub-level for computers and engines and solar panels and, she supposed, the best weaponry money could buy. But the ship's true crowning glory were two slowly spinning compartments. The compartments, while slightly dizzying to be in at first, were the first and only of their kind. The motion generated artificial gravity, keeping their occupants anchored firmly to the floor.

Molly stood in one of these spinning compartments, watching the dark Earth shrink into the black as the stars whirled their hypnotic way about the heavens. Only, it was her that was whirling. Tumbling down, down, down like a maelstrom in clammy bathwater. *The universe doesn't care about you*, the mountain's voice whispered in her head.

The Earth was dark and dead. No lights glimmered on her surface. The blazing stars were harsh and sterile. Even the afterglow of the explosion had faded to nothingness. She supposed that, if it hadn't been an asteroid, it would have been something else. A wandering black hole. A nuclear war. A solar flare. Climate change. If humanity managed not to kill itself, the Milky Way would have collided with the Andromeda galaxy in a few hundred million years, and the supermassive black holes at their cores would have torn Earth apart.

The universe didn't care. The Earth was now just another dead world in a universe of dead worlds. Dead. And with it, her entire life, save Rachel. Everyone that she had loved. Everyone who she had left behind. Molly turned away from the viewport, preparing to lock those thoughts in her Box of Broken Things, but the sounds of laughter interrupted her thoughts.

An aide—at least, he looked like an aide—was playing with a little boy in one of the zero-g rooms adjacent to the observation deck. Every once in a while, the boy would click his heels together and his Star Wars sneakers would light up. He'd giggle, grasp at them, get turned around in the zero-g, and start the whole process over again.

She tried to turn away from them, to finish locking her Box of Broken Things, but she couldn't. And once again, the hollow gap in her chest yawned open. She needed to get to Rachel. Hopefully she was sitting in Aunt Opal's habitation pod, reading a book and waiting for her. That was a nice thought, but Molly knew what the Mars settlement looked like, regardless of what the government wanted her to believe. Rachel would be lucky if she had her own bed, let alone her own room, and books were few and far between on Mars. It's not like Amazon had a distribution centre there or anything.

She shook the thoughts off. It wouldn't help anything to worry about Rachel—she'd be fine. And Molly's sister was there to look after her.

She turned her attention to the aide, just to distract herself. He saw her watching, whispered something to the child, and left him spinning in slow circles in the zero-G, giggling to himself.

"Hi."

"Hi," Molly said automatically. What else *was* there to say? 'Crazy weather we're having. Say, did you *see* the Earth get destroyed?' Not a chance.

"Is that your son?" She blurted the words out before she even knew what she was saying. The boy twisted and spun almost effortlessly as if he were made for the weightless, inhospitable vacuum.

"No, he's not mine. He's Tony's."

"Tony Devon, *Speaker of the House*?" She stressed the title.

"Forgive me," he said. "He prefers us to call him by his first name in private." He trailed off for a moment. "Where's your family?"

Molly glanced back out of the window, toward the now-invisible Earth.

"My daughter is on Mars, waiting for me. My husband...everyone else..." The silence stretched on.

"I'm sorry," he said. And he seemed like he meant it. He reached out and touched her shoulder. His hand was warm in contrast to the cold air. His fingers entwined hers and they both turned to watch the stars through the viewport. The cold air blew. The engines hummed.

"I don't suppose you have a name?"

"Molly," she said. "Molly Ramirez. From Ohio."

He gave her hand a squeeze. "Declan Murdoch. From Maine."

"Where's *your* family, Declan Murdoch from Maine?" The words came out harsher than she'd wanted them to, but there was no use making friends. She'd learned that lesson. Private Davis and Captain Dalton had been her friends and she'd shot them both. She might have to shoot Declan Murdoch from Maine someday, too. He released her hand and stared back at the space where Earth used to be, as if he could will it back into existence.

"My father died when I was eight. My mother...she wouldn't come with me. I offered, of course, but she didn't want to." He turned his head slightly to look at her. "She was religious. Insisted that God wouldn't destroy the Earth again. That he had promised in the Old Testament that, so long as ten people believe in him, he would stay his hand." He let out a long breath and straightened. "I believe she died in St. Louis Church in Portland, Maine. When Eros hit."

"Composed like them of Eros and of dust…"

"What?"

"Nothing. Auden."

He nodded as if he understood. Silence fell between them again. Will had read her that Auden poem, too. She'd liked that one.

"She was a good woman," he continued, "a good mother. And she loved me."

Sometimes simple eulogies were best. The world judged its departed by their capacity to love one another. She wished someone would have explained that to her; before, you know, the apocalypse.

"What about you?" he asked. "Who's kept you staring out the viewport since we broke the atmosphere?"

She was about to tell him, about to open up to him about all she had done—he was a stranger, after all, and willing to listen—so, naturally, she pushed him away and shoved Rachel into the Box of Broken things too.

"No one," she said. "It's not—"

Alarms blared. Ship security swarmed the cabin, armed with stun guns and riot gear, dressed all in white. Molly pushed Declan to the floor, drew her Tek-49, and set it to burn. Power enough to kill, but not enough to puncture the ship's hull.

"Stay down," she shouted, but the aide had already twisted away from her and drawn a small weapon of his own. *An aide, my ass.*

"What?" He looked down at the gun. "Aides are for more than just getting coffee."

She didn't justify that with a response. "Cover my six."

Without waiting to see if he complied, she followed security through the second observation deck. They passed plush couches and pillows and oriental carpets. Hardwood floors, even, were in this pod. The soldiers brushed right past it all and stacked up against a door at the far end of the room. Glowing blue letters above it read BRIDGE in blocky script.

Molly and Declan took cover around a corner, and she tried to get a clear shot of whatever was beyond the door. The captain slammed his ID badge down on the keypad, but it buzzed angrily back at him. He tried again. *Buzz.*

The alarms kept up their whining cry. In the spaces between the near-deafening sirens, she thought she could hear screaming coming from the bridge.

Then, the alarms stopped.

A chill crawled its way up Molly's spine. First one voice, then many, sounded out, muffled from behind the door. All screams. The sounds echoed eerily throughout the weird closeness of the ship, loud and close and raw.

The door bent outward on itself and the distorted *zap, zap, zap* of stun rifles filled the bridge beyond. On Molly's side of the door, however, the officer pounded his fist into the glowing red security console, cursing louder with each buzz that it gave him.

Molly dialled her gun up to eleven. It filled the air with crackles and that low lightsabre hum. She swept past the other guards, grabbed the captain by the shoulder, pulled him back behind the cover of the wall, and opened fire on the door. The gun let out a seismic wail, and a burning arc of lightning erupted from the prongs at the end of her pistol, striking the bridge doors and melting them into slag. Black smoke belched into the hallway, shrouding them in darkness. The smell of burning electrical wire and fire and blood filled her nostrils. Only then did Molly realise that the screaming had stopped.

She checked her six, exchanged a quick look with Declan. His pistol was steady in his hand, and he stared grimly back at her. She knew what that look meant. Fire on a spaceship, even something as small as a lit match, was enough to wreak havoc with the systems. It was the equivalent of shooting off heavy weapons in a submarine a mile under the ocean's surface. With the delicate balance of elements in the air, it could spell the end of their journey in a violent fashion. Also, there was the small issue of fire eating away at the ship's hull and blowing them all halfway to Mars from the sudden release of pressure. She had seen video feed of a breached hull once before. All soldiers had. It was not something she wanted to experience first-hand.

Currently, no emergency fire alarms blared on the bridge, no sprinklers filled with liquid nitrogen splattered the smoking deck. No Kevlar and carbon steel walls sprang up from hidden compartments in the floor. No extinguishing foam fell from the ceiling. The bridge simply smoked and burned and stank of melting plastic and blood. Molly, Declan, and the small squad of security officers huddled behind a corner and waited.

And waited.

Nothing happened: no sound interrupted the softly billowing smoke. Molly shuddered, took a deep breath, and circled her hand in a small motion behind her with three fingers. *On me, switch to comm channel three*, the gesture said. She pulled her helmet out of the small knapsack she always carried with her, and donned it, pulling the black visor over her face.

For a moment, everything looked the same, but then blue lines traced the hallway, the doorway, and past the smoke, into the bridge. Floodlights sprang to life on either side of her visor, and data readouts populated the peripheral of her screen. There was a single fire burning on the bridge, near the centre of the room, at 1100 degrees Celsius. The smoke poured from several consoles lining the walls. There were two life forms in the room—both humanoid—standing at opposite ends of the bridge, facing away from her, most likely staring out the viewports. Her visor informed her that there were other humanoid shapes on the bridge, but they were too cold to be technically classified as "alive."

"Stack up." Her own voice crackled through her earpiece. She dialled her pistol back from "hellfire" to "burn" and advanced into the bridge command centre beyond. The security squad followed. The emergency heavy blast doors slid shut behind her, grinding into place around the twisted mess of metal that used to be the standard bridge doors. Her footsteps seemed to echo loudly in the silence, but she knew it was just her adrenaline. Her HUD registered the fire in the centre of the room and registered that the two glowing humanoid figures on either side of the bridge were motionless. Behind her, the seven security officers formed up, and their steps, their heat at her back made her feel comfortable. Protected. At home.

Together, they pushed through the smoke and up the metal stairs to the bridge observation deck without incident. Molly reached the landing, raised her gun, and her visor screamed at her to take cover. Both glowing figures at either end of the bridge blurred in the infrared display, coming at her with inhuman speed. Molly threw herself to the metal floor, rolled, and came up behind a smouldering console, her gun humming with energy. The security captain behind her wasn't so lucky.

The Avandii pounced on him. The other guardsmen scattered, each clearing the area while the two figures clawed and bit and scratched at the head guardsman's armour. And the fool did the worst thing he could have done; he started to panic-fire.

Molly ducked back down behind her console as buzzing chatter of small arms fire chainsawed around the bridge. She dug at her belt, activated a flash grenade and tossed it over the console. The grenade bounced once, clanging metal on metal, and then there was a small explosion, a bright, burning light, and a boom like—well, like a fucking grenade.

All at once, the ship's systems restored. The alarms blared. Water and foam fell from the ceiling to put out the fires. Turbines sucked smoke from the cabin, and

Molly was finally able to see. The visor had cut the flash-bang's glow by 78% and its sonic impact by 43%, so she wasn't blind and deaf.

She peered over her console and was greeted by a sanguine mass of flesh in a white security uniform. What was left of the captain lay in a red stain spreading across the shiny black bridge floor. His guts, stringy like bloody slugs, hung out of his abdominal cavity.

Dead as a doornail, her mother's singsong voice chirped in her ear.

Except that he wasn't. He was standing tall, as if nothing had happened. Behind him, two other figures also stood, horribly mutilated, intestines spilling out of their gut, throats cut, dozens of burn and bullet wounds. And all three of them were staring at her with dead, empty eyes. She knew those men. The ship's captain and first mate. The Avandii was nowhere to be found.

Molly didn't hesitate. She flicked the dial on her Tek to incinerate and sent three staccato *whumpwhumpwhump* bolts sizzling toward her once-crewmates. Two went wide, melting monitors into piles of scrap. The third connected, and the thing that wasn't the security captain exploded in a dusting of fine spores. Her helmet automatically filtered the spores free of her nostrils, and they passed over her without incident. Across the room, another cloud of dust rose up as Declan dispatched another. And then all was silent, save for the sound of coughing. Molly waited for the third creature to reveal itself. Nothing.

"Status report," Molly barked.

No answer.

"Status report!"

"Here," Declan said weakly. He emerged from the cloud, soon to be swept away by the turbines working overdrive to clear the air.

Hacking coughs filled the cabin. Molly rolled from behind the console to check her surroundings. The crew lay strewn out across the floor. Sporadically, security officers lay bleeding. None of them had helmets, and all of them were coughing.

"Take a minute," Molly said, turning toward the ship's navigation system. Declan joined her, smacking the emergency button as he passed it. Immediately, the alarms silenced. He wore his own helmet, similar to hers.

The navigation console was one of the few undamaged, luckily for them, and it was locked on to Mars's trajectory.

"It's set to auto-pilot," Declan said. Molly glanced up at the ceiling where dust swirled among the many blue fluorescent lights.

"How far are we from Mars?"

Declan ran his fingers through his hair, seemed to

realise that he was wearing a helmet, and stopped himself mid-motion. "We just lost optical visual on Earth," he said. "Days, maybe a week, depending on how fast the ship is."

"And I don't suppose we can override the system to keep the ship on autopilot?"

"No, you would have to reauthorize it every eight hours."

"Of course," Molly sighed. "That would be too easy."

She turned and took in the bridge. Dust still swirled around the blue LED lights in the ceiling, making everything look like one of those vintage 1990s laser tag games with too many fog machines.

"I guess we'll just have to fly it," she said, and made to sit down in the captain's chair.

Before she could, Declan caught her arm.

"Wait," he said. "Listen."

She did. The fans blew. The engines hummed. The stench of fire extinguisher foam filled her nose. But besides that…

"Listen to what?" she asked. But then it dawned on her. The coughing had stopped. The sounds of movement, groans of pain, rustling fabric had stopped. Molly turned, raised her gun, and froze.

The seven security officers and the entirety of the

ship's bridge crew stood behind them. All in white uniforms stained with red. All with dead, black eyes. All with blood pouring from their eye sockets. All with guts hanging out of their stomachs. Behind them, an Avandii alpha loomed, muscles rippling under orange fur, claws extended, fangs dripping sizzling venom onto the bridge floor.

"Run," she whispered to Declan. "Run!" She fired three rapid shots into the crowd of crew members and sprinted for the door. The floor was wet and slick with blood. Molly grabbed the railing and vaulted over the stairs. Declan was already at the end of the hall, waiting by the blast doors, hand hovering over the emergency "lock" mechanism.

She redoubled her pace. Behind her, a stampede of boots followed, all in discord with one another. She glanced over her shoulder. They were gaining on her.

The nearest lunged and snagged her leg. She tumbled, her ankle *popped* and seared with pain, and suddenly they were on her, tearing at her clothing, drawing thin, burning lines across her skin. Her head smacked back against the floor. Stars filled her vision. Her mind began to drift, distancing itself from the experience. But something in her railed against that, some deep, dark part of her soul cried out in fear. The universe didn't care about her, but Molly Ramirez sure as hell cared about her daughter. And so, she raised her arm and started shooting.

The thrall atop her—a midshipman or ensign—vaporised into dust, only to be replaced by another. Molly kicked and fought and clawed her way to her feet. Her gun grew hot in her hand, and yet still more crewmen came at her, clawing at her stomach and chest with bloody fingernails. Behind her, Declan called her name and began picking off the thralls with his own weapon, but there were too many.

The ship's crew, the security force, members of the presidential cabinet, ranked naval officers all swarmed around her like so many overripe beetles. Too many. She crawled backwards under Declan's cover fire until he stood between her and the thralls.

They kept coming, swarming up over the fallen. Soon, Dalton's clip would run dry and they'd overtake him, and then her. She couldn't let that happen, couldn't leave Rachel to fend for herself on Mars. She steeled herself. She'd done worse things.

Molly shot him in the back. The thralls swarmed onto his body and started ripping at his body armour. Declan screamed.

Molly levelled her gun again, only this time she aimed it at the tempered glass viewports far down the hallway on the bridge and emptied the clip. The Tek hummed and seven brilliant balls of blue exploded from the barrel, screamed down the hallway, and cracked the viewport glass. She popped another clip into the Tek and then fired three rapid shots down the hallway, hitting the spiderwebbed glass on the bridge.

It shattered. The cold vacuum of space sucked dead crewmen out into the void. Bodies hurled against navigation consoles and weapons interfaces. Another alarm blared somewhere behind her and the ship's systems shuttered the broken window with steel.

And still the monsters kept coming. At their head, the Avandii alpha roared his challenge and bared his fangs. Molly reached up, groped at the console, and punched the "close" function on the blast doors. They slammed home, leaving her in silence, save for her ragged breathing. She holstered the TEK and tried to push herself to her feet. The world spun, soft blue lights swirling like… *Like balloons*, she thought. Why would they hang balloons in a spaceship?

Boom.

Something rocked the blast doors, tenting a fist-sized dent in their centre. Molly reached for her Tek again, whirled around, and her ankle gave out from under her. She collapsed again.

"Fuck." It just wasn't fair.

Boom. The dent widened, then was followed by

several smaller impacts and the sounds of shrieking metal. She needed to get away from these monsters, re-group, and devise a strategy to get back to the bridge. She looked back as they hit the blast doors again. They wouldn't hold much longer. Whoever thought humanity would be destroyed by super-intelligent, super-strong monkey-aliens? Eat your heart out, Charles Darwin.

She dragged herself down the hallway, back toward the centre pods. Ahead, a utility closet door was hanging open. She awkward-crab-crawled inside it, shut and locked the door, and collapsed in the darkness. She had no illusions that they couldn't tear through the door if they wanted to, but, if she were quiet, they might move past her and search the rest of the ship, giving her time to catch her breath.

She lay back against the cool floor and stared up into the dark, letting her eyes adjust in that blossoming red firework way that they always did since she was a child. *Fireworks.* The red ones danced alone for a while until they were joined by green and blue, like on the 4th of July. They took Rachel to a Fourth of July celebration once.

Molly watched the fireworks reflected in her daughter's wide blue eyes. Rachel hadn't been scared, she just watched the explosions, blinking at every crack and boom that echoed across Gorge Metropark. She studied them like she was trying to figure them out, eyebrows knitted together, upper lip stuck out, eyes scrunched. She'd sat in Molly's lap. Will held her hand.

That had been before, when the world was still living in blissful ignorance of their impending doom. All that had mattered to her in that very moment was Rachel, Will, and the little life they'd built together. Now their life was over, Will was dead, and Rachel was all that mattered.

Molly watched the fireworks a little longer, until they blurred and blinked and their colours faded. Eventually, darkness crept into their edges, and then to their cores.

CHAPTER THREE

It's so loud here, Mama. We landed an hour ago and everyone's been shouting. They were going to let us off the ship but then they told us to go back to our rooms. I don't know what to do. I'm just sitting on my cot with Mr. Snuffles. Why did you send me here by myself? I'm afraid everyone's forgotten about me. There's just so much yelling.

Please come soon.

Love, Rachel

Luminous balloons glowed overhead. Molly tried to reach them. Reds and greens and blinking oranges all floated and spun and twisted to the wind's every whim. They reminded her of a trip to Baltimore's Inner Harbour that her parents had taken her on when she was a girl. "Sailabration," her parents had called it. She hadn't understood the pun at the time, but there were ships there. Molly loved ships. Submarines and Naval Battleships and old replica pirate vessels all bobbed and swayed on the Chesapeake Bay, and all of them had balloons of every colour tied to mainsails and communications arrays and masts. They bobbed in salty sea air like tethered birds in the wind blowing off the Inner Harbour. It was full of people and life and culture, she supposed, but Little Molly—the Molly in her memory—was only concerned with ships and balloons and ice cream.

The balloons in front of her now were glowing electric blue, and some of them were blinking in the sky. She had never seen a blinking balloon before. She thought back to watching the Naval pilots perform tricks in their fighter jets over the water, to eating funnel cakes and seeing fireworks over Fort McHenry. She remembered tugging on her father's blue jeans when she wanted a balloon from a red-nosed clown. None of those balloons glowed.

"Stay close, Molly," he would say. "I can't lose you, Molly. Molly. Molly."

"Um, Ms. Molly?" Someone was shining a flashlight in her

eyes and poking her cheek. "Ms. Molly?"

She sat up. The voice gasped, and the sound of clattering broomsticks and mop buckets came from a corner of the room. Little blue lights flashed in little shoe shapes near the floor.

Molly almost shot at them. "Quiet," she hissed. "They'll hear."

"Sorry," someone squeaked out from the corner. Then, small, muffled sobs emanated from that same corner. A child's voice. She sighed, fished around in her pack for a light, and clicked it on. Sure enough, a young boy, no more than eight or nine, huddled in bloodied clothes with light-up Star Wars shoes pressed up against boxes of floor cleaner. *Tony's kid? Had to be. Same shoes.* There were tear tracks in the blood that covered his face.

"How did you know my name?"

The kid made a choking noise, then coughed out, "Mr. Murdoch told me."

Molly pushed herself up to comfort the boy. The world swayed and whirled, but not nearly as badly as it had before. She was able to cross the room with only minor pain in her ankle. She crouched down next to the kid and put an arm around him.

He buried his face in her chest and let out those long, wracking, hyperventilating sobs that only kids seemed to be able to do. Molly squeezed him close to her.

"Hey," she said, "It'll be okay."

"They killed my daddy." The boy shook and cried his silent tears. "They killed my daddy." Molly found herself crying with the kid. He kept repeating the same words over and over and over. "They killed my daddy, they killed my daddy, they killed my daddy," in a higher and higher pitch until the words passed out of intelligible speech and into a continuous, sobbing moan. All at once, Molly's Box of Broken Things burst open, and all the ugly, sad, dark truths came boiling out.

"I'm so sorry." Her own tears were coming hot and thick. They mingled on the utility room floor. "They killed my daddy too."

CHAPTER FOUR

I'm so scared, Mama. There's a monster here. They let us off the ship but the alarms went off. Everyone started screaming. Mrs. Mary pushed me into a cleaning closet and shut the door. It's so dark. I started praying to Jesus like we used to and eventually the screaming stopped. Maybe He sent a guardian angel to fight the monster. It's been quiet for a while now, so me and Mr. Snuffles are going to go outside and find Mrs. Mary. I'm trying to be brave like you taught me, but please come soon.

Love, Rachel.

Molly believed in her gun, in violence, in revenge, and in Rachel. Also, she found herself believing in the little kid. She'd get them both out of here, if not for her sake, then for his. So Molly began to lock things back away in her Box of Broken Things. She locked away her memory of the Earth dying; all the ugly, horrible words she and her husband had said to each other in anger, countless family secrets that had hurt her, that she'd promised not to tell anyone, then immediately had told Will anyway. Her father's cancer diagnosis. The fact that he'd beaten it, fallen into alcoholism, beaten that, and then died a fiery death with every other person who had fought and struggled and triumphed and failed. Even stupid, small pains she locked back away: the fact that her dog had died in the fireball too. That she hadn't just lost her home, her husband, and her world, but every physical copy of memory that she and her ancestors had ever produced. Photos, heirlooms, everything. She locked away Declan Murdoch from Maine. She locked them all back up in her Box of Broken Things and shoved them away until she'd achieved that cold apex of clarity that she'd so carefully cultivated. The world didn't care about her. But she damn well cared about her world.

So, she gave the little kid one last hug and got to her feet.

"What's your name, kid?"

"Jack," came the reply.

"Okay, Jack, we're going to get out of here." She stripped off her pack and dug in it. Three clips, an incendiary grenade, a flashbang, and a knife. In the outside pocket she had three rations packs. She clipped the flashlight overhead so it illuminated a little pale orange orb on the floor. She emptied her pack onto it.

"Right," she said. She handed Jack the knife. "Do you know how to use one of these?"

He nodded.

"Good." She handed him a ration pack and tore open one of her own. "Eat. We have time now."

They ate. Molly explained the plan. If they could kill the Avandii leader, get on the bridge and close the blast doors, the crew wouldn't be able to breach the doors. That would leave them free to fly to Mars and let whoever was in charge there clean up the remainder of the thralls. They finished and set the wrappers aside. Molly unholstered her gun, explained it to Jack, then explained the incendiary grenade and the flashbang. She stowed them back in her pack.

"Right," she said. "Ready?" He nodded and looked very small in the dim light of the utility closet.

"Kill the leader, run like heck."

"Right. On three, I'll open the door and we'll make

for the bridge." He nodded again and flung his arms around her. She allowed herself to hold him there for just a second or two and then brushed him off, stood up, and readied her gun.

"One." Jack gritted his teeth.

"Two." She put her hand on the door.

"Thr—"

The Avandii burst through the closet door, fangs dripping venom. Molly was ready for it. She already had her gun raised. She pulled the trigger in three staccato *thwackthwackthwacks*. The bolts impacted on the alien's chest, pushed it out of the doorway (and made the room smell like hell). Molly drove her shoulder into it and rode it to the ground, firing the Tek the whole way.

"Run!"

Jack ran. The gun clicked empty. She reversed her grip on it and pistol-whipped the monster over the head.

The Avandii wasn't fazed. It curled, taking the blows, got its clawed feet between them and kicked her halfway down the hallway. She bounced, skidded, rolled, and came up running, heading toward the bridge. Jack was already there, his hand on the blast door controls. She dived, knocked him out of the monster's path and slammed a new clip home in the Tek.

She never got the chance to fire it. The Avandii

pounced, covered the last 20 meters of the hallway, and tackled her into a metal railing. Something popped in her back and icy cold washed down her legs. It got its hands around her throat, lifted her up and squeezed.

The fireworks came back. The balloons came back. Rachel's face came back. The Avandii squeezed and, as the world started to fade to darkness, Molly pushed away all those other things and focused on her daughter's face. She kicked feebly at the Avandii's gorilla stomach, but they were the frantic, powerless kicks of captured prey. Her vision started to dim, and she wondered what it would be like to die. Even now, the darkness was creeping into her vision. She expected there to be a white light and, yes, there it was.

She waited to see what would happen next, but the pressure on her neck was suddenly gone, airway clear. She blinked. The white light was fading, leaving the ship's bridge in its place. The Avandii was on its back. Jack stood over it, her Tek in one hand. The other was a bloody stump. From somewhere, a thought welled up: *that brilliant little jerk stole one of my flashbangs.*

The gun wavered in Jack's hands.

"Jack," she croaked, "The dial."

The kid fumbled with the gun, hissing in pain as it touched the stump of his left hand, and dropped it. The alien shook itself, raised its head and kicked Jack's legs out from under him. He screamed, dived for the gun, pinned it to the ground with his bloody wrist, twisted the dial to "incinerate" and shoved it into the Avandii's knee.

The Tek belched indigo flame that caught on the monster's hair and set it ablaze. The alien bellowed its howler monkey cry and crashed back to the floor. Jack followed it, Star Wars shoes lighting up with each step.

He emptied the clip directly into the Avandii's eye.

The monster convulsed, twitched, and went still. Flames burned on its fur. The ship's fire suppression system blared on and doused the corpse in liquid nitrogen. Molly got to her feet, shut the blast doors, and crossed to the kid.

"They killed my daddy," he whispered over and over again. Blood dripped from his finger stumps. "They killed my daddy."

Molly said nothing, just ejected the burning hot clip from the Tek and pressed it into the kid's wrist. It sizzled, cauterising the wound. Jack didn't make any indication that he'd felt it. Molly held him for another moment to make sure he was steady on his feet, then released him and set a course for Mars.

"They killed my daddy."

She held Jack the rest of the way and thought about Rachel.

CHAPTER FIVE

Mama, Mama, Mama, please come soon. The monster got me. I love you so much. I love you. There's so much blood. Why didn't you come with me? The monster got me. There's so much blood. He killed Mr. Snuffles. I prayed to Jesus but he didn't come either. I can't stay awake. It's getting so dark. Why is it so dark? Please, please, please come soon. I'm so afraid. It's so dark and you're not here. Where are you? You promised you'd be here. I love—

"Omega-1 to Mars outpost-5, do you copy?"

Silence from the comm. The remaining thralls beat against the blast doors with weak, sickly *thunks*, but the doors held. The red planet hung in their viewscreen, a little dusty ball of earth. How could such a desert support the remainder of humanity? She couldn't imagine starting a new life here, with nothing green, no water.

"Maybe they can't hear us?" Jack looked out the window, picking at the cast that covered his left hand.

"Stop that," Molly said. He did, but gave her a little broken smile that just about broke her heart. She didn't think she could live with herself if Rachel ever gave her that smile.

"Our communications relay is still functional according to the sensors." She tapped one of the only glowing blue terminals that hadn't been burned or melted into slag metal. "It must be a problem on their end."

Jack sat back in his seat and stared out of the viewport. He started picking at his cast again. She let him; she'd already ripped hangnails off her thumb and chewed her fingernails bloody.

"I hope they're all right."

Me too, kid. "Come on." She pushed on the ship's thrusters and began their descent.

The ship lurched and sputtered but obeyed. Fortunately, the autopilot hadn't been disabled. The ship essentially flew itself, she just controlled *when* it did what it did. The sensor array locked on to Mars-5 and the ship spiralled its way down to the dead, dusty planet.

No one greeted them when the ship touched down in the hangar and red sand cascaded down the viewport. No one hailed them on the sensor relay. The hangar doors ground shut, sound muffled in the cockpit. Lights flickered on outside, and the climate-control kicked into gear with a low hum. The hangar was empty. Molly and Jack sat in their seats and listened to the silence. Behind them, the thralls jostled against the blast doors. The wet sounds of their lurching limbs tapped out a demented rhythm.

"Where is everyone?"

Molly unstrapped herself from the pilot's chair and unholstered her Tek. She made sure her emotions were locked away in her Box of Broken Things. She grabbed a spare jacket from under the pilot's chair. Rachel would probably be cold. It was cold in space, after all.

"Come on," she said, and took one last look out at the hangar, full of ghosts and bare metal.

"What's out there?" Jack said.

"Nothing." She crossed to the crew's exit hatch and punched the button. Her fingers twitched on the Tek. The door hissed open and the ramp lowered.

It was cold in the hangar. Her footsteps echoed on the ship's ramp and then crunched on the red sand. Jack's footsteps followed behind her. They reached the hangar doors. The access panel glowed blue in the dim light. Molly's hand twitched on her gun again. Somewhere, in a place she'd buried deeper than her Box of Broken Things, she knew what lay beyond. She pressed her hand to the access panel.

Death filled the spaceport. The stench hit her first. Sickly-sweet, ripe, rotting flesh. Molly and Jack stood in the doorway. His little hand found hers, and together they walked into the carnage. Molly took in the cold details. Bodies littered the room, eviscerated. The Avandii had already been here. She turned in a slow circle. Her hand twitched on her Tek again. Annoyed, she looked down at it and found that both her hands were shaking. Jack stood next to her, silent tears streaming down his face, clutching on to her other hand. He pointed across the room, at the far wall.

The words "SURVIVORS TO IO" was scrawled there in bloody spray paint. A fluttering piece of paper was taped below it. And beneath it...

She sprinted through the spaceport, tripped over a dead arm and went sprawling. She rolled, smacked her head against the floor, and Molly's Box of Broken Things shattered. A low, moaning sob bubbled out from her throat. She crawled the rest of the way to the tiny, broken body. She cradled her daughter's head in her lap, kissed her forehead, wiped the blood from her nose. Her wispy blonde hair was matted with blood. She clutched a small, headless teddy bear in one hand, holding it close to her chest. The other held a tiny notebook.

"I'm sorry," Molly whispered between sobs. "I'm sorry, baby." And a hundred fragmented memories rushed through her mind. Rachel's first skinned knee, crying as Molly poured peroxide on the wound. Her first wobbling baby steps, squealing as she tottered into a wall and grabbed the dog for balance. Her first birthday. Fistfuls of cake. Out-of-tune *Happy Birthday* songs. Nursing her quietly in the back of Mass when she and Will had still gone to church. The first kiss her daughter had planted on her cheek and then ran away giggling. How, when she was tired, she'd toddle up to Molly, plop her head down on her chest, and sigh.

All gone. All gone.

"I'm sorry, I'm sorry, I'm sorry." What good was a mother who couldn't protect her child? What good was she to anyone?

What good was the world without her daughter in it? What good was life with nothing to live for? Her Tek lay on the ground next to her daughter's bloody sneakers. *Her feet. They cut her little feet.* Tears flowed anew. She reached for the gun. *The world doesn't care about you*, the mountain's voice echoed in her head. *The world doesn't care.* Her hand closed around the Tek. She held her daughter close to her chest. She closed her eyes. *I'm so sorry, baby.*

"Ms. Molly?" Jack's voice was high and excited. "Ms. Molly!" Halting footsteps. A small hand on her shoulder. Paper rustled between them. She pulled herself away from Rachel, dropped the gun, wiped tears from her eyes.

"What you got there, buddy?" Her voice echoed, seemingly lonely in the cavernous room. Her hands shook.

Jack's blue eyes were wide with excitement. He shoved the paper with the list of survivors on it at her. It crinkled in her shaking hands. He pointed to a name.

"My mom." Tears filled his wide blue eyes. "My mom."

She nodded, folded it up, and put it in her pocket. Molly had nothing to live for, but Jack still had hope. She holstered her Tek.

She gathered up Rachel's body, wrapped it in the spare jacket that she'd grabbed, and laid her down under the scrawled message. She folded her daughter's arms over her chest and nestled the teddy bear in them. She tucked the bear into the jacket and made sure Rachel's feet were covered. It was cold in space after all. She gave her daughter one last hug, kissed her clammy forehead, and took the notebook from her tiny hand.

CHAPTER SIX

Baby,
It's so cold without you. I love you. I miss you. I'm sorry.
Love,
Mommy

The smell of gasoline filled Molly's nostrils. The gas can sloshed and fuel spattered on the ground. She'd drenched the hangar. She finished up by running a trail to Omega-1's ramp. Jack was there, waiting for her with a small lighter they'd found on one of the security staff's corpses.

She reached down and grasped Jack's tiny hand in her own. He squeezed it, let go, flicked the lighter to life with his good hand, and dropped it on the trail of gasoline. Mars-5 blazed up in the night. They both turned their backs on the crackling flames and boarded the ship.

Molly secured the cabin, punched in the coordinates for Io and started the take-off sequence. The ship shuddered. The hangar doors opened, and the night sky whirled above them with dizzying numbers of stars. They lifted off, Mars's burning surface spiralling away far below them. The ship made a wide, slow turn, exited the atmosphere and faced the black.

Molly Ramirez believed in her gun, her ship, and Jack. She believed in her daughter's memory, in Will's memory, in violence, and revenge. But most importantly, she believed in hope. The ship accelerated to cruising speed. The engines hummed, and Molly and Jack sped toward Io. His hand crept over from the co-pilot's chair and squeezed hers again. She squeezed back. Jack smiled a wide, little kid's smile and faced the stars as if to say, "Hold on, Mom, I'm coming." After all, life's not worth living unless you believe in something.

"All I have is a voice
To undo the folded lie,
The romantic lie in the brain
Of the sensual man-in-the-street
And the lie of Authority
Whose buildings grope the sky:
There is no such thing as the State
And no one exists alone;
Hunger allows no choice
To the citizen or the police;
We must love one another or die."
—WH Auden, September 1, 1939.

JACOB BAUGHER teaches Creative Writing at Franciscan University of Steubenville. When he's not teaching or coaching the track team, he can be found in the Cuyahoga Valley hiking with his wife and son or brewing beer on his front porch. He's received honourable mentions for his work in the Writers of the Future contest and he co-edits a series of Fantasy and Science Fiction anthologies titled Continuum.

Bibliography

ANGELS, Black Hare Press, 2019
BEYOND, Black Hare Press, 2019
Continuum: Chaos Theory, 2014
Continuum: Fables of the Fallen, 2012
Continuum: Impetus, 2017
Continuum: Until Dawn, 2013
Deep Space, Black Hare Press, 2019
Storming Area 51, Black Hare Press, 2019
WORLDS, Black Hare Press, 2019

DREADLOCK
By Stephen Herczeg

After years in exile, known terrorist leader and xeno-biologist, Professor Aaron Black, resurfaces after the hijacking of a military vessel. Cybernetically enhanced trooper Dared Locke (codename Dreadlock) and his team are sent in to bring Black to justice. Nothing's ever easy, and Dreadlock's team is attacked by creatures beyond imagination that lead them to a final confrontation with Black and his plans for domination.

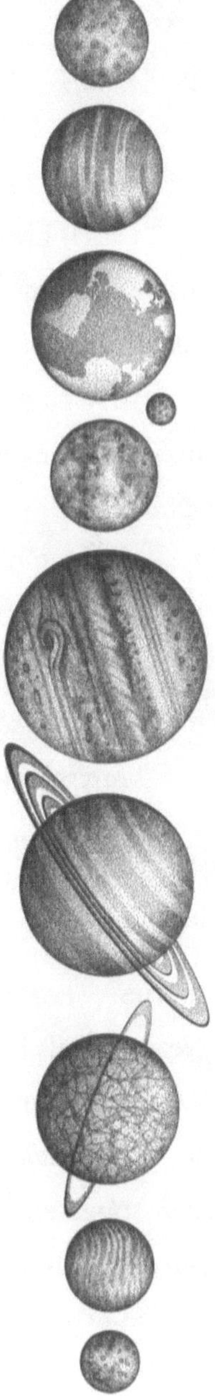

The shuttle dropped out of the pre-dawn light and flew low over the thick canopy of jungle before slowing down to hover above a wide clearing.

At a metre above the ground, the rear door slid open and several men, dressed in combat fatigues and carrying automatic weapons, jumped down and took up positions in a wide circle around the ship. The door immediately slid shut and the ship rose into the sky.

Dared Locke, call-sign Dreadlock, stood in the middle and surveyed the dense forest around them. His head snapped towards movement to his left. A slight whirring noise emanated from the cybernetic implant over his right eye. In his eyesight, the world turned black with slight splotches of yellow and red. He focused on the movement. A small patch of red faded to black. His implant returned to the visible spectrum.

Butch Magee, a career warhorse of a soldier, his face a mess of battle scars, stepped up next to him.

"Anything?"

Dreadlock shook his head.

"No. Just an animal. According to reports, this planet has a varied fauna level, with a single superior hominid species. They operate around the same level as Terran Neanderthals did. Should be no problem unless cornered. We leave them alone, they'll leave us alone."

Butch held up his left wrist. A topographical map of the area appeared, floating above his arm. The troopers were shown as flashing red triangles, a large rectangular shape sat on the edge of the map. With his right hand he pointed towards a thick copse of trees.

"Black's compound is one klick north-west. Nothing but dense forest between us."

The map zoomed in on the building. A set of doors was highlighted.

"This is the most likely entrance. South side of the building, close to the forest line. Intelligence says there are no security protocols except a simple fence."

Dreadlock nodded. Something in the back of his mind nagged at him. He dismissed it, pointed North-West, and spoke to the men.

"Move out. Smith, Danvers, on point."

Two troopers nodded and moved forwards. The rest dropped into a formation of pairs behind them, then headed into the forest.

A path led from the clearing through the forest, wide enough for the men to stick to their formation. As they walked, Butch kept a check on their progress.

"This seems strange," he said to Dreadlock, "This pathway is a little too convenient, it's leading us straight to the compound."

"This whole thing seems strange, but the pathway would be used to move supplies," he returned, "I'll be much happier when we find Black and get the hell off this rock."

"Agreed."

Within ten minutes, they broke from the forest and were confronted by a three-metre-high steel fence surrounding the compound. A large gate stood before them, and in the middle of the compound sat a tall, solid-concrete building. Its plain façade showed it to be functional but boring. A muddy service road ran around the building, but no vehicles could be seen.

Butch and Dreadlock looked along the length of the fence.

"No cameras or any other security," Butch said.

"Intelligence said Black was the only human on the planet. The fence would stop any animals or hominids getting into the compound, and he wouldn't be expecting anybody like us. Doesn't mean we should get complacent," Dreadlock said.

He turned to the rest of the men.

"Smith, Davison, check along the fence that way," he said, pointing to his right. He turned and looked at Danvers and Connor, then pointed left, "You two, that way. Back here in five."

The troopers left—Logan, Johnston, and Evans—took up positions around their leaders. Butch and Dreadlock stepped up to the gate to examine the lock.

"Simple code lock," Butch said. He brought his wrist computer up to the keypad and pressed the screen. A light scanned across the keypad for several seconds, then a numeric code flashed up on the screen. Butch reached a finger forwards. Dreadlock stopped his hand.

"Wait for the men to return."

Butch nodded.

Within minutes, both teams returned.

"The compound goes for about three hundred metres to the north. The warehouse is about two hundred long, and the outside area is full of crates and containers. Place is huge, but we didn't see a soul," Davison reported.

Dreadlock turned towards Danvers.

"Same story on the other side, Sir," he said.

Dreadlock pursed his lips and grimaced, he looked at Butch and spoke. "They were sure he was here, right?"

Butch nodded and smiled.

"Just because they're called Intelligence, doesn't mean they've got any," he said.

Dreadlock nodded, "Crack the lock, let's do this."

Butch moved back to the gate, and within seconds had it open. The squad moved into the compound and headed for the exterior door opposite.

Dreadlock held up his left arm. The scanner showed only the troopers outside of the building. Beyond the wall remained black.

He adjusted the scanner and aimed it at the wall.

"Lead lined. Rare. Black's hiding something from

prying eyes," he said.

Butch moved up to the door and had the simple keypad lock cracked in seconds.

"But why such crap security?" he said. Dreadlock shrugged and pushed the door open.

Connor led the way into the building, the others following in single file. Johnston remained outside to guard their backs.

Dreadlock's eyes adjusted quickly to the darkened interior. The area ahead of them was stacked high with wooden packing crates, a strange hangover from the distant past, but used widely in this and the nearby solar systems. Forests grew thick on many of the habitable planets, and wood was a handy substitute for oil-based plastics when making simple items such as furniture and transport packaging.

Butch noticed the arrangement of the crates and scanned with his wrist computer.

"Check this out," he said to Dreadlock. They both looked down at the ad hoc arrangement of the towers of crates. No two passages ran parallel for any length, and many turned in alternating directions and wound back around on themselves.

"It's a maze," said Dreadlock, staring up towards the towering roof. He lifted his gun in readiness.

"This isn't a warehouse, it's a training ground," he said.

Suddenly, the crack of gunfire erupted from the gloom. Evans seemed to dance as a volley of bullets smacked into his body. He dropped to the ground and lay in a spreading pool of blood.

Dreadlock ducked to his left and took shelter behind a wall of crates. The others raced to join him.

Behind them, the door opened revealing Johnston silhouetted by blinding sunlight. He stepped inside and squinted in the gloom.

Dreadlock turned and waved him away. "Get out," he shouted.

"What hap—" Johnston started to say as a fresh volley of bullets slammed him into the wall and cut off any further speech.

"Shit," said Butch.

A hail of bullets smacked into the wooden crates showering Dreadlock and his team with woodchips and splinters. Dreadlock waited for the firing to cease then peered along the row of packing crates. They were blocked at one end with the only exit being the way they'd come in.

"Stupid," he said under his breath.

He looked up. The walls on each side rose a good three metres above the floor. Easy to scale but not with the firepower currently aimed at them.

If we can climb it, so can they.

Butch moved in closer and peered up.

"You want me to go up?" he whispered.

Dreadlock shook his head and reached into a small pouch on his belt. He pulled out a transparent sphere. He put a finger to his lips to keep Butch quiet, pressed a red dot on the side, stepped away from the wall of crates and threw it over the top.

It flew through the air for a while, then a blinding light flashed out of it followed by a shrieking siren. The light and sound was immediately met with a volley of bullets. Dreadlock stepped back and edged up against the wall.

"You'd be dead before you got halfway across."

Butch nodded then shrugged.

Dreadlock pulled a grenade from his belt. He moved a small dial on the side and clicked a red button on the top. The letters "EMP" flashed up on a small screen built into the surface.

Butch nodded again, immediately shouldered his rifle and slipped a long bowie knife from a thigh sheath. He turned to the group of men pressed against the crates and clicked his fingers. Every head turned as one. They all saw Butch's knife and copied him, shouldering guns and sliding out their knives. Each man pulled down their helmet visor, ready to switch to infra-red.

Butch turned back to Dreadlock and winked.

Dreadlock shouldered his own gun and smiled.

He brought up his right hand, a hand that owed its creation to a machine shop rather than Mother Nature. Dreadlock flexed the metallic fingers. Small servo motors powered the digits silently as interlocking components and tiny pulleys and wires served as replacement tendons and joints and mimicked the workings of a functional human hand.

Dreadlock closed his fist and immediately three blades slid out of their hiding places. One on either side of his wrist and one pointing straight out the top of his fist. The blades slid back inside, and Dreadlock placed the EMP grenade in his right palm.

He pressed the button on top, stepped back and threw. The grenade sailed over the top of the wall of crates and, after a couple of seconds, let out a muted *whump.* The lights throughout the warehouse went out, plunging the team into abject darkness. The green lights on each of the men's rifles flickered and died.

The stuttered noise of gunfire ceased as soon as the electro-magnetic pulse erupted. The enemy were using electronically controlled weaponry the same as Dreadlock's men. Several squeals erupted from deep in the warehouse, followed by the clattering of rifles hitting the floor.

"They'll be back on-line in about ten minutes, go, now," Dreadlock shouted.

The men didn't wait for further orders. As one they ran from the alleyway and turned left. Straight ahead the passageway ended in a T-junction. Three turned left, Butch and the other two turned right. It was a standard flanking technique that Dreadlock's team had used before. Butch would lead his three-man team back around; they would split up and come in from different angles on the enemy's right. The others would head around to their left.

Dreadlock looked towards the top of the wall of crates before him. That was his job. Come at them from straight ahead. Usually it was level ground, but after being cornered he had to improvise.

The wall of crates was laced with hand and footholds. He concentrated for a moment and the cybernetic ocular implant whirred as it changed from the visual spectrum to infrared.

He grabbed the first handhold and managed to climb up quickly, scrambled over the top and belly crawled across. He stopped at the edge and surveyed the area below him. The only movement was his own men, the enemy was either well-hidden or had retreated beyond his sight line.

Bugger.

He looked across the expanse of the warehouse and the ocular implant buzzed slightly and moved out. The feed into Dreadlock's brain showed the area zoomed in by a factor of three. He scanned every inch searching for any movement. Still nothing.

His eye caught sight of one of his men, Davo, moving slowly along a low corridor of palettes off to the right. Davo held his knife up and scanned left to right as he moved.

Dreadlock spoke into his radio, "Davo, all clear around you. Continue on." Davo gave a thumbs up to Dreadlock and moved out of sight.

Davo turned a corner and scanned ahead. Nothing. No movement. No bright images in his viewfinder. He looked down another aisle leading between two towering rows of packing crates. Again, no movement. He slowly made his way along the corridor, scanning all around.

Behind, a ripple of a shadow slithered down the side of the packing crate wall. The dark shape gained its feet and stepped up behind him. His visor glowed bright green for a moment as the figure's hot, fetid breath blew past his shoulder.

There was no time to react. No time to turn as a long taloned claw was clamped across his mouth, stopping any screams, and another plunged into his back, bursting out through his chest. The concrete floor received a spray of blood and organs.

Davo's knife dropped to the floor with a metallic clatter, and a muffled cry followed by a thick ooze of blood came from his mouth. His legs buckled but he stayed upright against all nature until the creature removed its claw and let him crumple to the ground.

Dreadlock's head snapped around in the direction of the knife clatter. He realised it came from where he'd seen Davo heading. He jumped down from his viewing position and quickly moved to the start of the passageway. He peered around the corner. It was empty. He stepped into the opening and moved along the line of crates. His boot hit something on the floor and sent it skittering away.

He looked down and saw a combat knife slowly spinning a few feet away. He moved over, picked it up and stared at the weapon. Slight hints of brighter green showed on the handle where someone had held it.

Dreadlock searched the area for the owner. Still nothing. He took another step and his foot shot out from under him. His right hand lashed out and grabbed the nearby crate, crushing the wood but stopping him from falling. He dropped to his knee and checked the floor. A large puddle of sticky liquid spread out before him. He touched it and sniffed his finger.

Blood.

Less than ten metres away, Logan and Smith moved slowly down a parallel aisle. Logan had taken the lead and scanned from side to side as they crept along. Every step that Smith took was met with a distinct squeak from his boots.

"Dude, what's with the noise?" Logan asked in a whisper.

"New boots. Should have worn them in before we came on the mission," Smith replied.

"Damn straight you should have. Now try and walk without making a sound, okay?"

Logan's question was met with a strangled cry and the sound of Smith's boots clattering up the palette wall next to him.

"The fuck was that?" Logan asked as he turned to look at Smith. He scanned around for his teammate with no luck.

"Smith?"

As Logan turned back, his visor was filled with an

image from hell. A great bulbous head appeared before him. Its slit-like mouth slowly opened, revealing sharp, pointed teeth, then shot forwards. Logan had time for a small cry before darkness and pain took him.

Dreadlock heard both cries and the clamour of boots on wood. He hurried around the towering heap of crates and checked down the next aisle. It was empty. He scanned across the passage and along the top of the crate wall. No movement. He started to move away when something caught his attention.

Hurrying down the aisle, he noticed small hot patches showing up on his infra-red sensor. He knelt down to investigate and realised they were spots of cooling blood.

Again?

He spoke into his communicator, "Alpha team report in." The replies came quickly.

"Butch here."

"Danvers here."

Then silence.

"Connor, report in," Dreadlock said.

Silence again.

Damn.

"Beta team, report in."

Nothing but silence.

He turned his wrist over and looked at the display panel. A rectangle showing the warehouse floor appeared with three red triangles scattered across it. Four other triangles were lined up against a far wall.

"Butch, Danvers, meet at my location."

Both came back with, "Roger that."

Dreadlock scanned the immediate area. Nothing showed up on the infrared through his implant or the naked eye next to it. He checked the wrist display. The two red triangles were edging their way towards him.

Suddenly, a scream erupted into the stillness of the warehouse. Dreadlock's head shot up in the direction of the sound.

"Butch?" he asked into the communicator. His first instincts were to ask about his closest friend.

The reply came back from directly behind him.

"It was Danvers."

Dreadlock turned and saw Butch standing behind him.

"Have you seen anything?" he asked.

"Nothing. Whoever they are, they're good. Seem to be almost invisible. We're sitting ducks if we don't move."

Dreadlock nodded. He held out his wrist map.

Danvers's triangle was rapidly moving towards the others.

"We head towards the other men. That's where the enemy will be." They both moved off.

Dreadlock's implant flipped through several spectrums. Infra-red, ultra-violet, heat, even X-ray. Nothing showed. The enemy was either imperceptible or holed up with the bodies of his teammates. He stayed on the infra-red setting and looked across at Butch to make sure it was working. His friend showed up as a bright green figure. Suddenly, Butch stopped dead still and pointed. Dreadlock looked in the direction.

Ahead of them, at the end of the passageway, a tall, slender figure with a huge bulbous head stood staring back.

"What the fuck is that?" said Butch.

"I have no idea. I've never seen anything like it bef—" Dreadlock's voice trailed off. A flash went off in his head as a suppressed memory flooded his brain.

Two suns shine down on a planet covered in a palette of greens and blues.

On a wide-open plain of the largest continent, the wind blows long strands of grass and bends them to its will. They move like the waves on an ocean and crash against the trunks of trees in the bordering wood. A sublimely serene environment that any adult would trade their front teeth for.

But war is afoot.

Amidst the tranquillity, a lone figure rises from the long grass. Tall, well-built, wearing jungle fatigues and carrying a semi-automatic rifle with sniper scope attached. A label with the name "LOCKE" is stitched on his left breast.

He brings a pair of binoculars up to his eyes and scans the edge of the forest. There is no movement as far as his sight can penetrate. He puts the binoculars down and raises a fist. He quickly opens his hand and splays his fingers. Ten men materialise from the grass and fan out around him. Dreadlock unslings his rifle and starts forwards. The men follow.

A soldier edges up besides Dreadlock. Harris, new to the team. Dreadlock nods in his direction then returns his attention to scouring the forest before him.

A high-pitched whine erupts out of the silence. Harris is thrown backwards.

"Down," came a shout.

The chattering of automatic fire from the depths of the forest follows.

Dreadlock ducks and crawls back to Harris. The

huge hole in the man's forehead tells him all he needs to know. He taps his left ear and speaks into his radio.

"Get to cover. Try to get to the flanks but stay low," he shouts.

Dreadlock combat crawls into the nearby tree line. A continual hum of bullets sprays over him. Several hit the ground nearby, spitting up dirt and stone chips. He manages to edge up to a thick trunked tree and sits with his back to it. The muted thud of several bullets smacking the other side of the tree flows through to him.

He grabs a small camera built into his helmet and pulls. A long flexible cable draws out of its holder. He manipulates it until the camera is pointing behind him and moves his head slightly. His wrist communicator shows the dark forest behind him. He taps a panel and the darkness lights up a blaring palette of greens and blacks as it goes to infrared.

The trees show up dark, with several bright shapes moving behind them.

He taps his ear again.

"There are seven of them, just behind the trees on the other side of the clearing."

A loud crack blasts out from his left. One of the bright figures falls down. A loud cheer follows.

"Make that six. Good work, Butch."

Dreadlock pulls the camera back and replaces it. He

edges to his left and looks across at Butch who sits behind a tree with a huge smile on his face. Butch gives Dreadlock the thumbs up then stands and points his rifle around the tree. He looks through his extensible sniper scope which curves around at a ninety-degree angle.

Another whine and a silver dart-shaped projectile buries itself in the other side of Butch's tree. Without thinking Dreadlock breaks cover and sprints towards Butch. Several bullets smack into the ground in his wake. He reaches Butch, dives and grabs his friend in mid-flight. They both hit the ground and tumble just as the tree behind them explodes.

Without stopping, Dreadlock rolls over, regains his feet and sprints towards the enemy line. A pale figure breaks cover and lowers a long cylindrical-shaped weapon at him. Dreadlock ducks to his right just as the figure fires. Another silver lancet passes close to Dreadlock's helmet and smacks into a tree behind him.

Just as the tree explodes, Dreadlock jumps and launches himself at the enemy. He tackles him in mid-air and they both land heavily with Dreadlock on top. He straddles the enemy soldier, pulls his boot knife ready to slam it into the man's chest but stops, the weapon still raised.

Dreadlock's first good view of the enemy soldier stuns him into inaction.

The creature below him is unlike anything he has ever seen in his life. It is naked and covered in pale, shiny skin. Its head is large and bulbous, with thin slits for eyes and nose, and a large mouth filled with sharp teeth. Its long-fingered hands are clutched to its chest.

The creature turns its head and looks up at Dreadlock. Its mouth extends in a mimicry of a smile and it seems to chuckle to itself.

The reason becomes obvious as it unfolds its long taloned hands to reveal a pulsing thermal grenade.

Dreadlock cries out and starts to back away. Too late. The detonation throws him several metres away from the creature to land heavily on his back and burst the breath from his lungs.

The last vestiges of his memory are the concerned faces of several soldiers as they crowd around his broken body. He sees Butch mouthing his name.

"Dared, Dared," he says but there is only the ringing deafness from the grenade.

Then there is only pain, and finally darkness.

The creature sprinted to a nearby packing crate wall, scampered to the top and ran off. Dreadlock watched it disappear then looked down at his cybernetic hand. He flexed it several times and winced as the phantom pain returned for the first time in years. Pain shot up his arm and joined the agony in his head. His brain reminded him of his former fully human self when flesh grew where the cybernetic implants now reside.

At the time, his imminent death had seemed inevitable. The quick thinking of Butch and the team of doctors back at base had saved his life, but it had left him a broken man. It wasn't until he came to the attention of Thurston Drake, a recruitment specialist with X-Com—a provider of covert paramilitary operatives across the galaxy—that he was resurrected and given a second life. Fitted with cybernetics, reinforced titanium bone implants, and hard-wired into the X-Com network, he became the first of a new type of soldier.

Butch and the remaining members of his old team were easily coerced into joining X-Com; their innate abilities and talents lend themselves to a quick initiation into the life of for-hire operatives.

X-Com was the go-to specialists for most of the galaxy's military requirements. Rather than train and maintain a covert military force, they engaged companies like X-Com instead.

A month ago, Terran command had commissioned X-Com to investigate the genocide of an entire city on Arcturus, a planet in the alpha quadrant. The team had entered under cover of darkness and found every member of the local militia torn apart, their weapons unfired and the rest of the population executed like cattle.

The weapons used on the citizens pointed to a recent deep space hi-jacking of a military cargo vessel. The modus operandi pointed to a terrorist organisation that disappeared ten years previously. Not long after Dreadlock's encounter with the grenade.

That organisation had been headed up by Aaron Black, once Professor of Xenobiology at the University of Altair IV. He had been a specialist in the splicing of organisms from different ecosystems. His final crime had been to cross human DNA with that of an alien hominid species. Even the open minds of the Galactic Science Federation couldn't accede to such experiments and drummed him out of the University.

His location was lost until now.

X-Com believed Black was operating on a small remote planet deep in unexplored space. His recent operations were interpreted as a way to gather resources for more unconventional experimentation.

The Galactic Council had sanctioned Black's termination and the gathering of all intellectual property associated with his work.

Thurston Drake had been handed the assignment and had ordered Dreadlock's team to make landfall on the planet, investigate and enact the sanction.

Butch moved up next to Dreadlock and continued to stare at the spot where the creature had disappeared.

"We've seen those things before."

Dreadlock nodded and held up his metal fist.

"Yep," he said.

Butch looked at his friend's hand.

"You okay?"

A beep from his shoulder interrupted his reply. He unslung his rifle. The light glowed green again. He pulled the magazine out, checked for bullets and slapped it back in again.

"I will be when we kill these fuckers and Black is dead."

He pulled the slide on his weapon and fingered the trigger to slam it back into place.

Butch and Dreadlock moved on, side by side. They came to the spot where they'd seen the creature and scanned both sides of the junction. Dreadlock indicated to his left.

"It went that way. We follow."

Butch nodded and they moved again. Their heads looked up as the light relays snapped back into action. The arc lights flared then dimmed.

"Lights will take a few minutes to brighten. Keep infra-red on for now."

They looked back down the alleyway, and one of the creatures came into view. They brought their guns up, expecting it to run off. It simply stood, eyeing them through the slits in its face.

"What's it doing?" asked Butch.

Dreadlock watched it for a moment. A nagging thought started in the back of his mind. He looked up and spied a bright green flash coming towards them along the top of the crates at high speed.

"It's bait."

He trained his gun upwards and fired off a volley of shots. A loud squeal was followed by the creature crashing into the crates above. Butch kept firing, his bullets shredding the wood above. Dreadlock dropped his gaze and noticed motion behind Butch. He brought his rifle down towards Butch.

"Drop," he yelled.

Butch looked at him and saw the rifle. Without hesitation, he dropped to his belly and reached the ground as a Dreadlock fired over him. The creature running at them down the passage was stopped dead in its tracks by a face full of lead.

Butch got to his knees and smiled at Dreadlock.

"Thanks."

"No problems," Dreadlock replied as he shouldered his rifle and started to climb the wall. At the top, he found the other creature lying on its back and gasping for breath.

He stood up and studied it for a moment. It was similar to the creature from the war—the one that robbed him of his arm and eye—but the skin was slightly mottled, the arms and legs longer and more muscular, and the head more bulbous and alien-looking.

It opened its slit-eyes and stared at him for a moment. Even on such a foreign-looking face, pain and fear were evident. A touch of sympathy flashed in Dreadlock's mind but was immediately replaced by the knowledge that this thing and its kind had likely killed seven of his team and tried to kill him and Butch.

He reached down to his leg holster and withdrew his pistol. He fired off a shot, and the creature's brains blew out over the wooden crate. He gave the beast one last look then scurried back down to where Butch stood.

Butch smiled slightly, "Feel better?"

"Not really."

He unshouldered his rifle and moved on. Butch scampered after him.

"Hold up, man."

They moved down another dark alleyway towards a large solid wall at the end. Just as they reached the junction, the lights dimmed then flared fully on. They both closed their eyes and looked away as their infra-red vision flashed bright green for a moment. Butch flipped his visor up. Dreadlock's implant switched back to normal vision.

"Should make it easier," Butch said.

Dreadlock nodded as they moved on. He reached the corner first and moved to the right. Butch turned left and stopped.

"Holy Mother of God," he said.

Dreadlock spun in his direction to see what was wrong. He looked up, and anger boiled in his mind.

Before him was a long, plain wooden wall with a single door at the bottom. The creatures had killed his men and brought them here. Good men. Men that he'd known and worked with for years.

Each man had been crucified to the wooden walls of the building. Their chests had exploded from the impact of the creatures' claws and, to add to the carnage, each man's eyes had been torn out. Their bloodied visages stared down at the floor where their lifeblood had pooled and was drying.

"What the fuck are we dealing with here?" Butch said.

"No idea."

Butch tensed and brought his gun up. Dreadlock spun in the same direction and raised his own weapon. One of the creatures stood at the end of the passage.

Another pincer movement.

Dreadlock didn't hesitate this time. He fired. The creature squealed and ducked off to its right.

"Watch my back," he said and ran after it. Butch followed a few metres behind. He scanned around, searching for any more surprises.

Dreadlock disappeared around the corner and continued on. Butch arrived a moment later and found him standing before the creature as it leant against a shipping container. He stepped towards the two, keeping an eye out for any others.

"Are there any more of you?" Dreadlock asked the beast, "We've killed two of you already. Are you the last one?"

The creature looked at him. It held its hands over a wound in its side. A thin line of blood ran down from its mouth. It coughed and spat a gob of blood-soaked mucus to the ground. It shook its head then looked up at Dreadlock.

Its head tilted slightly upwards.

Alarmed, Dreadlock spun and brought the gun up. A pale blur leapt from above and fell towards him. Butch's gun spat molten death moments before the creature collided with Dreadlock, sending them both to the ground.

Dreadlock rolled the creature's body off him and regained his feet. Anger lit up his face. He stepped over to the injured beast and pushed the barrel against its temple. It dropped to its knees.

"I'll ask again. Are there any more?"

The creature shook its head.

"Last one," it croaked, "don't kill. Please."

Dreadlock lowered the rifle.

"Stay here. You move and I'll be back," he said.

The creature nodded and stayed crouched. Dreadlock turned and stepped away. A sudden sound made him spin and move sideways. The injured creature sprung at him, its taloned fingers extended. Dreadlock ducked sideways and knocked the hands away. His right fist came up with the blade extended. He punched the creature in the head. Blood burst from the impact. He punched twice more to make sure. The creature stopped moving and slid to the floor.

"Idiot," he said.

He retracted the blade, turned and walked around the corner. Butch hurried to catch up.

Dreadlock pushed the door open. The corridor beyond lit up as if triggered by their arrival. He stopped and studied it.

Butch looked at the wrist map.

"This leads into another multi-room area. Laboratories, admin, or possibly Black's personal rooms," he said.

The passage was stark white with a severe sterility bordering on hospital level cleanliness. At the far end lay the only obvious exit, another metal door that led into some inner sanctum.

They stepped into the corridor and closed the metal door with a muffled clang. With barely enough room to stand side by side, they moved slowly towards the far end of the corridor. Their heavy footfalls echoed up and down the passage with every step. The tattoo they beat out reverberated around Dreadlock's skull giving him the beginning of a massive headache.

"This room has all the hallmarks of a sanity test," Butch quipped.

A noise above the corridor stopped them in their tracks. They pressed themselves flat against the wall and trained their guns on the source of the noise. Suddenly a hatchway in the roof slid open and a pale hairless figure dropped to the floor on all fours. It unfurled itself and stood erect to its full height of two metres. It was bigger and stronger than the previous beasts.

Dreadlock didn't wait. His rifle spat fire within seconds, but the creature propelled itself vertically, flipped over and clung to the ceiling. Butch sprayed death towards the creature but it took off, sprinting across the ceiling straight towards them, avoiding the bullets with every stride.

Butch switched to shotgun mode. Several booms erupted. The walls and ceiling behind the creature disintegrated under the concentrated firepower of the gun.

A few metres from them, the creature let go of the ceiling, spun in mid-air, and slammed into Dreadlock with all its weight. He was knocked backwards and slid for a few metres before coming to a complete stop.

The creature stood up on its two rear legs and backhanded Butch before he could bring his gun around. He went flying backwards and slid to a halt halfway down the corridor and lay still.

The pale figure raised itself to full height and held its arms out to the side. It flicked its hands open. The digits extended out from the hands and immediately grew long, serrated nails. It took two long steps forwards then sprang into the air, heading straight towards Dreadlock with arms stretched out in front.

Dreadlock leapt to his knees and thrust his fist

upwards as the creature reached him. Its vicious nails raked across his face and optical implant before sailing over him and crashing to the floor behind.

Dreadlock picked himself up and moved to the prone figure. He prodded it with his boot, but the beast wasn't a problem anymore. The blades had opened its chest up and sheared its heart in two.

"I've had enough of this crap," he said to himself.

"I'm with you there, brother," a groggy Butch replied from further down the corridor as he wearily sat up. Dreadlock slammed a fresh magazine into his rifle and moved to help Butch get to his feet.

They made their way to the far end of the corridor and stood before the metal door. Dreadlock checked the white corridor behind. Nothing moved. Nothing else could be seen except for the dead creature slowly cooling at the other end. He turned back to the door and grabbed the handle. Butch readied his rifle and nodded.

Dreadlock tried the handle.

It turned easily. The door swung away from him revealing a sumptuously decorated room beyond. He pushed the door with his boot swinging it all the way open. Butch looked down his gun sights and swept it across the visible area inside the door.

A voice called out to them.

"Mr. Locke, Mr. Magee, there's no need for that.

You can lower your rifles. Come in. Join me."

Dreadlock stepped through and swept his rifle around the entire room. The voice had come from a small figure sitting behind a large desk at the far end of the room. He lowered his weapon and scanned the room once more, Butch followed suit. Dreadlock found no creatures lurking anywhere and was finally able to take in the details of the room.

It was pure luxury. Red velvet walls. Lush red plush pile carpet. Wooden furniture in the form of a large desk, bookcases, chairs, armchairs, a fireplace and display cabinets.

Finally, he stared back at the man behind the desk.

"Nice place you've got here, Mr. Black. Strange location, but nice place."

"Why, thank you, Mr. Locke. I so seldom have unannounced guests...or guests of any kind for that matter."

The bald man behind the desk looked back at the pair and smiled. He picked up a nearby bottle of amber coloured liquid, poured some into three glasses before him, and pushed two across the table.

"Scotch? My research says it's your favourite drink. One shared by your whole team, am I right?"

Butch bristled at the mention of his dead teammates. He started to bring his weapon up. Dreadlock placed a hand on the barrel and pushed it down. He shook his head slightly as if to say, *Not yet.* Butch nodded and looked back at Black, a sneer prominent on his lips.

Dreadlock glanced around once more; his mind raced, unable to justify the amicable nature of his target with the situation he found himself in. Seeing Dreadlock's nervousness, Black picked up his glass, toasted the mercenaries and downed his drink. Dreadlock watched Black for a moment and, when there was no reaction to the Scotch, he looked down at his own proffered glass and shrugged.

He placed his rifle down against the desk and took a seat in the chair opposite Black. Still wary, Butch did the same. He picked up the glass and considered the Scotch for a moment.

"It's one I've been saving for a special occasion. It's very nice, a twenty-one-year-old single malt. Smooth. Peaty, but not too much. Enjoy."

Dreadlock smiled and downed his drink. The liquor spread warmth through his innards and sparked a brightness in his mind. Butch watched Dreadlock for a moment then slammed his home. His eyebrows rose at the delicate flavour of the liquor.

"Very, very nice," he said.

He placed the glass back down on the desk then turned his attention back to Black. Dreadlock spoke up.

"I'm happy to drink your expensive Scotch all night, Mr. Black, but that's not why we're here, is it?"

"No, it's not, Mr. Locke. No, it's not."

"You took out the contract with X-Com on yourself. Am I right?"

Butch's eyes lit up in surprise. Black brought his hands together and cradled his fingers. A smile grew across his face. He eyed Dreadlock with an intense stare but coupled with a high level of admiration.

"Well done. When did you figure it out?"

"The white passage. You only had one of those creatures as your final defence. You wanted us to get through or else you would have sent another whole squad. The only question I have is why?"

"The answer to that one is simple. You. I need you. Mr. Magee's presence is a bonus, but ultimately, I wanted you. But first I had to test you. I had to see if you were everything that my researchers tell me you are."

"What do you need me for? You've got protection. Those creatures. I don't know where you get them or who created them, but they are almost perfect."

"Ah, but that's where you are wrong. They aren't perfect. They still have flaws. You would have seen it. When they get hurt, they become useless. They fear pain, plus they revert back to a savage brutality my behavioural scientists cannot remove. Hence the strange treatment of your comrades."

Butch started to rise. Dreadlock looked at him and shook his head. Black continued.

"That's where you come in. Pain, fear, anger are alien to you. It's in your very nature to ignore emotions. To keep going. To push through the pain and finish the job. Only when you are comfortable that things are done do you allow yourself to rest, to feel, to recover. I need that. I need to build that resilience into my creatures."

"How?"

Black smiled broadly. His face showed so much joy at the act of explaining to Dreadlock and hopefully bringing him into the fold.

"Your DNA. My creatures are the product of cloning experiments carried out in this facility. I use the local hominid population as a base, then splice their genes with others. Some human, some alien. We've started to crack the ability for the body to control itself on a cellular level. We've experimented with the ability to extend their fingers and arms, to control body heat and colouring. It's all still in the development stage but getting there. But we need to control this," he tapped his temple before continuing, "They are virtually useless when injured. In this planetary environment, they are the top of the food chain—they have no natural predators—so that weakness is ingrained in their psyche.

We've tried to control it through training to some degree, but their nature returns in the end and makes them unusable."

"Let me get this straight. You took out a contract on yourself. You tailored it to bring me and my team here. You unleashed your creatures on us. They decimated my team but, because I managed to survive and make it here, you now want to take my DNA and merge it with your creations."

"Yes, yes, that is exactly it. My creatures are the future of warfare. The future of mercenaries. In a few months, your teammates would have been out of a job anyway. They knew the risks they were taking. In this case, they were just collateral dam—"

Black's head exploded in a shower of blood, bone and brains. His body was thrown backwards, and he crashed to the lush carpet. Dreadlock turned his head slightly.

Butch stood next to him. A small trail of smoke curled from the barrel of his sidearm. He re-holstered it and looked down at Dreadlock.

"Those men were my friends," he said, a look of fury still on his face.

Dreadlock smiled and said, "Contract fulfilled, I think."

On the edge of Black's desk, a small screen flickered

to life. A message—PROTOCOL 101 ENGAGED—flashed up for a moment before fading away.

Dreadlock stepped around the desk and bent to examine Black's body.

"That dude is dead, man," said Butch craning to look over the desk.

Dreadlock picked up the man's hand and pressed his index finger to the screen on his wrist communicator. The scanner flickered to life and took an imprint of the finger. Black's name flashed up for a moment.

The noise of a door opening off in the distance grabbed Butch's attention. He spun, bringing up his pistol in one fluid motion, and pointed it in the direction of the sound. Dreadlock unholstered his own gun and moved around the desk.

A figure stepped out of the darkness at the far end of the room. It held up both hands in supplication as it came forwards.

"Mr. Magee, please don't shoot me again. Let me finish what I was about to say. I want to make an offer for your services. Both of you."

Dreadlock almost dropped his pistol in surprise as Aaron Black stepped into the light. He turned and looked behind him to check that the bald man's corpse was still lying there.

"What the fuck?" asked Butch.

"Yes. That was me, and this is me."

Dreadlock turned back. The man standing before them was a perfect replica of the dead man behind.

"How?" Dreadlock asked.

"Surely, you shouldn't be that surprised that I have a fail-safe system in place. If I die, I have clone bodies waiting to replace me. My memories are downloaded continually and uploaded to the next clone. It does have its downside—I haven't left this building in years—but I can continue to live indefinitely."

Black looked at the guns.

"Can you put those down so we can talk terms, please?"

Butch peered at Dreadlock, a look of suspicion played across his face. Dreadlock nodded and they both lowered their weapons. Black dropped his hands and continued to talk; his words aimed more at Dreadlock than Butch.

"I look at you and see a man who has seen much too much in the way of fighting, war, death, and pain. If you help me then I can help you. I can give you more money than you will ever make in your job and I can give you back your humanity. I can replace your lost arm. Your lost eye. You can be whole again."

Dreadlock pondered the offer for a moment.

"What about the others in my team? Can you bring

them back?"

Black shook his head.

"No, I'm sorry, it's been too long for them. To clone someone, you need to harvest their DNA within a few minutes of death, otherwise it starts to degrade and become useless."

"Then no."

Dreadlock raised the gun and fired straight at Black's chest. His body was thrown back and crashed into a small table covered with priceless antique glassware. Dreadlock stepped forwards and fired again to make sure. Black's corpse jumped as the bullet smashed into its head.

"God, I hope that does it," said Butch.

Dreadlock stared at the shattered corpse for a moment before answering, "Don't bet on it."

Immediately, the panel on Black's desk flashed to life with the message: PROTOCOL 101 ENGAGED.

Dreadlock stepped away from the fresh corpse and tapped his wrist panel. He bent forwards and spoke into it.

"X-Com, this is Locke. Contract target eliminated. Seven team members lost to security forces. Over."

"Come again. How many lost?"

"Seven, only Butch and I remain."

"Ah, bugger. Complete the secondary objective, secure all intel and return to the pickup point. Dropship is on its way. Over."

Dreadlock moved behind Black's desk and studied the computer panels built into it. He placed his pistol to one side and touched one of the panels. A password screen popped up.

"Damn."

Butch followed him over and stood looking down at the computer array before him.

"Is that a fingerprint scanner?" He pointed at a small touch panel to the side, "You could use his—"

A shot rang out of the silence cutting Butch off in mid-sentence. Dreadlock looked up into his friend's face.

"Butch?"

Butch stared at him, anguish and pain spread across his face. He mouthed a few words, but no sound came out, just a dribble of blood. A patch of red appeared on the front of his shirt and quickly spread. He peered down at the stain then gazed back up at Dreadlock, a questioning look on his face. Butch tried to speak again but dropped to his knees and collapsed to the floor.

"Butch!" Dreadlock shouted, craning to see over the edge of the desk. He started to move, but a voice from the dark stopped him.

"I didn't need him. I'm even surprised he made it this far."

A dark shape stepped slowly out of the darkness.

The light shone onto a younger version of Aaron Black's face, complete with a full head of hair. He carried an automatic rifle and aimed it straight at Dreadlock. A burst of fire smashed into the desk. Dreadlock dropped just in time as the bullets smashed into the woodwork spraying him with chips from the desk, chair and floor.

Everything went quiet for a moment until Black broke the silence.

"Are you dead?" he said and waited for a reply before continuing, "I don't want you dead, but I don't actually need you alive. We can extract viable DNA from your lifeless corpse as long as we are quick, but I wanted you alive so we could use the expertise locked in that brain of yours. But you and that idiot killed me twice, so I don't care anymore. It's personal now."

Dreadlock watched as the scientist's feet stepped forwards. He reached for his leg holster but found it empty. He pictured the gun lying on the desk just above his head. He'd lose a hand reaching up. Out of the corner of his eye, he spied his rifle lying in front of the desk.

He cautiously edged forwards and reached for it. The slight noise it made as he slid the rifle towards him was as loud in his mind as nails down a blackboard.

Black shifted as the scraping noise of the rifle reached him and raised his own gun. In one swift move, Dreadlock picked up the rifle in his left hand and fired at

Black while reaching out with his cybernetic hand. A hidden piton shot out from his palm and slammed into the wooden panelling across the room. A thin black rope trailed out across to Dreadlock. A winch inside his wrist quickly wound the rope in and dragged Dreadlock across the floor away from Black's stream of bullets.

Dreadlock's aim was true.

Black's head shot back as the first bullet smacked into him. His body rocked backwards as the next few hit him in the chest. His rifle sprayed bullets into the ceiling as he was knocked onto his back.

Dreadlock waited a few seconds, watching the new corpse for movement, then stood up. He extended a blade, cut the rope free and dropped it to the floor. Switching the rifle to his right hand he walked over and examined the new body. The skin and muscle tone suggested a man about ten years younger than the version of Aaron Black that Dreadlock first met.

Gotta stop this.

Dreadlock moved into the darkened end of the room. A rack of weapons stood inside a cupboard next to the wall. He stepped towards the weapons rack and a hidden door slid open. The hum of refrigerator equipment and other machinery drifted towards him.

He stepped through into a dimly lit room beyond and looked around. A line of glass tanks stood along the far wall, each with a naked body floating in them. Dreadlock realised they were all clones of Aaron Black but at different stages in the aging process.

Lights blazed over the very last tank. A small screen above it showed the message: PROTOCOL 101 ENABLED. The lights blinked a few times then the liquid in the tank started to drain out. The message changed to read: PROTOCOL 101 FINISHED. Then: TARGET CLONE VIABLE. When the liquid had finished draining, the door at the front of the tank opened with a hiss and a cloud of frost blew out veiling the clone from view for a moment.

As the cloud dispersed, the clone stepped out and stood on unsteady legs. It blinked its eyes a few times then stared at Dreadlock.

It raised its right arm and pointed at Dreadlock and croaked, "You."

Dreadlock raised his rifle and said, "Not again."

He fired into the clone's head, knocking it back into the tank where it crashed to the floor and lay still. He turned and repeated the action, ending the life of every Aaron Black clone in the room.

That should do it.

The lights in the room started flashing red, a large screen embedded in the far wall lit up with the message: EMERGENCY PROTOCOL 201 ENGAGED. The whining and grinding of machinery echoed through the chamber but nothing moved. Dreadlock scanned the room then moved around, searching for the source of the noise. After a couple of minutes of frantic searching, he stopped to gather his thoughts.

The noises died off and the large screen changed to "EMERGENCY PROTOCOL 201 FINISHED".

Dreadlock's senses snapped into overdrive. He brought the rifle up and sighted along the barrel ready to shoot at a moment's notice. He examined every inch of the room for potential threats and edged his way towards the entrance when a noise from behind spun him around.

A hidden door slid open at the far end of the room, spilling a cloud of vapour into the main cloning room. Dreadlock trained the gun on the doorway and moved slowly forwards.

A tiny silhouette appeared. Its hands were held up before it.

"I mean you no harm, Mr. Locke. In fact, I have no way of harming you now. All I ask is to be allowed to live."

The figure stepped into the dim light of the main room. Dreadlock's mouth dropped open in shock to be replaced by a sudden fit of laughter.

The figure spoke again, "As you can see, you have

reduced me to this." The figure standing before him was a six-year-old version of Aaron Black. Dreadlock gathered himself and stepped forwards. He raised the rifle and put the barrel against the child clone's forehead.

"I don't go in for killing kids, but for you I'd be happy to make an exception. Give me one reason why I shouldn't."

The child's eyes welled up with tears. It dropped to its knees and stared up at Black with huge doe-like eyes.

"I can give you all the research and documents about our cloning technology."

Dreadlock shifted the gun down and took a more assertive stance.

"I was going to take those anyway. What more you got?"

"Your friends. I can give you back your friends."

Dreadlock sneered. "You said they were dead. Their DNA was useless."

"Of course I did, but I wasn't going to let the DNA of a team of trained mercenaries go to waste. My creatures took samples as soon as they killed each man. They are stored in freezers deep in the complex. We can have them revived within a matter of weeks."

Dreadlock realised, "The eyes, right? And Butch?"

"Yes, yes, if we are quick and gather his DNA, he will be fine. The cloning technique saves the personality and memories from the moment of death. Within weeks he will be as good as new."

Dreadlock smiled and moved the gun away.

"You just brought yourself a new life. I think you'll find the facilities at X-Com might not be up to your expectations, but pretty soon you'll call it home."

The child's face dropped in shock.

"No, I need to stay here. I need to repair the cloning facility. I can't leave."

Dreadlock chuckled, "Oh, you're leaving alright. You've been a bad boy, and I think you need a timeout."

STEPHEN HERCZEG is an IT Geek, writer, actor, film maker and Taekwondo Black Belt based in Canberra Australia. He has been writing for over twenty years and has completed a couple of dodgy novels, sixteen feature length screenplays, and dozens of short stories and scripts.

Stephen's scripts, TITAN, Dark are the Woods, Control and Death Spores have found success in international screenwriting competitions with a win, two runner-up and two top ten finishes. His stories have been published in Sproutlings; Hells Bells; Anemone Enemy; Below the Stairs; Trickster's Treats #1 & #2; Shades of Santa #1; Behind the Mask; Petrified Punks; Beyond the Infinite; Beginnings; Beside the Seaside; and Sea of Secrets.

His Sherlock Holmes pastiches have appeared in Sherlock Holmes: In the Realms of H.G. Wells; Sherlock Holmes: Beyond the Canon; The MX Book of New Sherlock Holmes Stories - Vol 11 & Vol 13; The New Adventures of Solar Pons; and Sherlock Holmes in the Realms of Steampunk. He has had a large number of his drabbles accepted and published in Worlds; Angels; Monsters; Beyond; Unravel; Apocalypse; Curses and Cauldrons; Elemental Drabbles - #1 & #2 and Guilty Pleasures. Later this year his newer works will appear in A Tribute to H.G. Wells; Journeys; Capricorn; Aquarius; Demonic Carnival; Through Death's Door; Sanitarium Magazine; Eerie Christmas; Coffins & Dragons; Trickster's Treats #3; The Necronomicon of Solar Pons and The MX Book of New Sherlock Holmes Stories – Vols 17 and 19.

Connect
Amazon: amazon.com/-/e/B07916SQQS
Facebook: @stephenherczegauthor

FIELD OF QUAY
By Shelly Jarvis

A Magic Door, a bit of smuggling, and a little luck are the only things Finley and Oscar need to move from petty criminals to men of means. Unfortunately for them, luck has never been on their side. When they meet a woman in a hole-in-the-wall bar on the edge of nowhere, will her claims of knowing a Door's location pan out, or are they doomed to repeat the mistakes of the past?

CHAPTER ONE

There are two facts universally accepted about Magic Doors: the first is that they never stay exactly where you put them, and the second is that, be they inside or out, they can only be seen after it rains.

Garret Finley was thinking on these facts, and Magic Doors in general, when from the corner of his eye, he was certain he spied the Duke of Islington walking past.

Duke Reginalt MacReoch XII of Islington, referred to as the Dark Duke in impolite society (which, of course, was a perfect descriptor of Finley), was unlikely to be in a place of ill repute such as this. He ruled an outlying planet, sure, but even the poorest of the system's planet-keepers were rich, though maybe not respected. Anything he could want was at his disposal or could be purchased and brought to him at the press of the button on his credit-comm. Yet he was here, in the same hole-in-the-wall as Finley, rubbing shoulders with all the wrong folks.

Finley took a sip of his electric-blue helio-vodka. The menu called it a *Turpain Stunner*, but the only thing stunning about it was how violently drunk it made you after about three sips. Quick, effective, and most importantly, cheap. Perhaps that was why he saw it in the hands of nearly everyone in the bar.

Finley turned towards where he'd seen the Dark Duke, checking to see what he was drinking. Red, fizzy, with black bubbles clinging to the bottom. Not a poor man's drink. Something with cloves, anise, or some other useless herb imported from beyond Door Three.

Finley wondered what it was called and hated his own curiosity.

He sneered. He hated the Dark Duke, too. For his stupid drink (why couldn't the bastard just order a get-drunk-quick item with the noxious liquor overpowered by a strong fruit), his filthy rich-ness, and a petromic assload of other reasons. Why in the four hells of Hectron was the Duke in the Tuscorion Tavern in the first place? And how had he *walked* past when Finley was absolutely certain the Duke of Islington had no legs?

Finley's thoughts were kindly interrupted when a dark-skinned man stumbled against the table, gripping the edge with his long fingers. He was tall, well-built, and had an air of mystery about him.

Finley smiled up at him, struck yet again by how handsome Oscar Temiteo was. Finley watched as Oscar sat down. He looked into his strange eyes—white, glowing orbs without pupils. The lack of colour was a defect from Oscar's techplant, but the tech itself was still functional and the weird eyes made him stand out and blend in simultaneously; most found it easy to forget everything else about him. Not Finley. He drank in each of Oscar's movements as he stored them into his mind with a million other small moments they'd shared.

Oscar pulled a stubby from his shirt pocket. He lit it, took a puff, and said, "Loo was full. Pissed in the alley."

"Oscar," Finley sighed, "didn't you learn from the incident on Purdri? These Regency fucks are obsessed with where you pull out your dick. Don't get yourself arrested on another shit planet."

"Can't promise. Shit planets are my bread and butter," Oscar said with a smirk. He tipped his head towards the Dark Duke and asked, "MacReoch in the corner?"

Finley nodded.

"Where'd he get the legs?"

"Dunno," Finley said, taking his second sip of the *Turpain Stunner*. With a shrug, he said, "Maybe that's why he's here."

Oscar took another drag, exhaled slowly, and narrowed his eyes at the Duke. "Nah. Coulda got 'em closer to home and had 'em covered in gems or some such shit. Or wired up into his nervous system as to be useful. But them's not special-made. Don't even look like they fit him proper. More like trash metal if I'm bein' truthy."

Finley nodded. "Maybe he's on a rendezvous."

Oscar said, "Doubtful. Both his husband and wife are beauteous things. Why would he downgrade to that lot?"

Finley studied the people at the Duke's table. There were no great beauties among them, sure, but perhaps they were overflowing with personality. Finley was about to remark as much when a waitress leaned over their table.

"What can I get you?"

Finley pointed to his drink. "Probably nothing. I'm already at two sips."

"Lightweight, eh?" She smirked and asked, "If you change your mind, the Charpot '112E is particularly flavourful."

Finley took a hard look at the waitress. She had thick blonde hair pulled into a ponytail. She was tall and slender, but definitely hiding a bit of muscle under the uniform. She certainly wasn't like the usual townie messenger, but there was no mistake about it: she had given the code word.

Now the transaction began. Every word between them meant something else, a thousand other things, and his life might depend on whether or not he could decipher them. He scrubbed a hand through his curly brown hair, hoping to the high hells this woman wasn't as bad as the last one had been.

"Charpot is acceptable," he replied, confirming his understanding.

"Lightyear for me," Oscar added. "Twist o' lime."

The girl nodded and walked back to the counter. Finley turned back to his partner. Oscar was running diagnostics behind his eyes. Most people wouldn't notice, but Finley could see the change. The corner of Oscar's eyes took on a slight blue hue, blended so well into the white that it was nearly invisible.

"Whaddya got?" he asked, running his finger over the rim of his glass. He wanted to take a swig, but knew he'd be wasted with that third sip.

"Two of his companions have records," Oscar said. "The one with the ponytail and the man with the serpent on his thigh." Finley began to turn towards their table, but Oscar grabbed his hand and whispered, "Don't look. The woman with the shaved head is surveying the room. She might have ears."

Finley put his hand over Oscar's and laughed. "Oh, honey, that's hilarious."

The waitress reappeared with their drinks. "Here you go, boys."

"Thanks," Finley said.

"Shit, shit, shit," Oscar mumbled

"You wanna pay up now or keep a credit open?" she asked, as if nothing was out of the ordinary.

"We'll pay now," Finley said. He leaned his arm towards the waitress and pulled up his sleeve so she could access his credit-comm. She hovered over him for a moment and Finley used her as a shield to ask, "What's wrong?"

The waitress cut in, saying, "Four hundred and eighty-seven credits, and a nice tip if you wanna be a sweetheart. Some gib over there only left me a thirty-seven credit. Can you believe that? After working a double shift like this, almost makes me regret my career choice."

Finley and Oscar looked at each other, both acutely aware of the waitress' number choice. Their ship was docked at 37.2, and apparently there was a problem. Finley saw Oscar's eyes tinge blue again. He turned to the waitress and said, "Double shift, eh? What time you get off?"

"Whenever I want."

She purred in a way that made Finley think of sex. He felt heat creep up his collar. This girl was damn good at playing her part. Too good for a shithole post like this. Townies were just supposed to relay intel, and they were guaranteed to screw it up one way or another, but she seemed to know exactly what to say and how to say it.

She leaned over the table and her breasts practically fell out of her uniform. Finley turned away so fast his neck cracked. But the woman didn't seem to notice his embarrassment. Or she didn't care. Finley turned tentatively back towards her. She hadn't moved an inch. She was either wildly confident or the gesture was completely non-sexual. *Probably both*, Finley thought. *I'm shit at reading people.*

The woman smirked, finally acknowledging the discomfort in Finley's disposition. She said, "Supposed to be off at four if you're interested in hanging around. But if I have to stay over it may be closer to five."

Finley glanced past her to the Duke's table. Another man with a violent scowl had joined them, taking their party from four to five. She was good all right.

Oscar's eyes cleared and he seemed to just now realise the waitress was still here. She gave him a nod and asked, "Anything else for you?"

"One last thing," Oscar said, emptying his Lightyear in one gulp. "We're looking for some odd jobs while we're around this system. Any idea where we could pick some up?"

"Not right off," she said, pretending to think. "Maybe Old Ethel could help you out. He's up on Mrathi in sector-4, right on the main drag, big gold sign out front."

"Thanks," Oscar said.

The girl walked away, checking on some other customers and collecting empty glasses as she went. As Finley watched her walk away, he asked, "How do you wanna play it?"

"Easy," Oscar said. "But the girl with the ears are Regency, so it's probably gonna get rough."

"Hold steady," Finley replied. "The waitress is

delivering their drinks. Maybe she'll give us a distraction."

Finley watched the woman glide towards the table, a tray balanced on one arm. She set the drinks down and talked to the newest arrival.

"Wait, that's not her," Finley whispered.

"How can you tell? All these blondes look the same."

Finley shrugged, his eyes roaming the tavern. "So, where is our girl?"

Before the words were out of his mouth, one of the Duke's companions erupted into a coughing fit and fell against the table gasping for air. Taking their cue, Finley and Oscar jumped from their table and made a mad dash for the door. Finley turned as he reached it to see the others shove the waitress aside, pull their weapons, and head after them.

Finley followed Oscar through the narrow streets, their feet banging against the rickety planks of the boardwalk. He heard the Duke's people behind them, shoving townies out of their way. Once or twice he heard a splash as someone was pushed into the murky water beside the floating town. Oscar must've heard the splashes as well because he ducked between two domed buildings into an alley that led away from the main drag. Finley hoped they could avoid getting a bunch of townies stuck in the middle of a firefight. Again.

Oscar was attempting to direct them to their ship, but in his effort to keep away from innocent bystanders, he'd inadvertently led them into a dead end. They turned around as soon as they realised their mistake, only to find themselves facing the business end of three blasters.

The Duke was nowhere in sight.

"Put your weapons down and keep your hands where I can see 'em," the woman with the shaved head said.

Finley and Oscar did as they were told.

Clearly the leader of the group, she sent one of the others to grab the weapons from the ground. She had an air about her, as if she was used to having flunkies do her bidding, and she seemed to enjoy her limited power. She wore a tight-fitting leather jumper that bulged over her muscular arms and robust belly. The jumper was old (older than her, if she was natch and not a freezer-rebirth) and impractical for the smothering humidity of Nim-6.

"Well, well," she said, her oily voice causing an immediate squirming reaction from Finley. "Didn't expect to find a couple of Door Riders all the way out here. Thought it was a joke when the orders came through."

"Whose orders were they, anyway?" Finley asked.

Old Suit laughed, her flunkies joining in. She smirked and said, "Stun 'em and let's get off this miserable globe."

Before the stunners were out of their holsters, both of the goons fell forwards onto the grimy alley. Old Suit spun around to find a .103-Pulser mere inches from her face.

"Hi there," the waitress said, as if she were there to take the woman's drink order. "One breath out of place and I'll pulse your brains out of your head."

Old suit seemed to gather her courage before she took a deep breath, then spat in the waitress' face. She reached for her blaster, but her hand didn't make it an inch before the waitress' finger twitched on the trigger.

The force of the pulse blew Finley and Oscar back against the alley walls. Flying through the air, Finley thought, *Huh. Her brains really did pulse right out the back of her head.*

The waitress wiped the spit from her face, then stepped over old suit's body. She stood with her hands on her hips, staring at the men as they clambered to their feet.

"I told you 37.2 was no longer an option," she said. "Why did you come this way?"

"We forgot," Finley said.

She sighed. "Well, running for your lives will do that to you. Grab your guns and follow me."

She turned around and walked back out the way

they had come, Finley and Oscar following wordlessly behind her. Finley noted the grace and ease with which the waitress seemed to take in her surroundings as she checked for danger. He furrowed his brows and asked, "You're a townie?"

She glanced over her shoulder. "Like none you've ever seen."

The woman led them out of the city to an airstrip, long deserted because of its insistence on sinking into the swamp.

"Blasters ready, boys," she whispered back as they made their way into the hangar.

They edged around the corner and behind some boxes. There was a small freighter-class ship in the hangar, a huge tarp trying to camouflage it from prying eyes. Around the ship, Finley saw a dozen figures, all carrying huge weapons.

"We'll never be able to take them all," Oscar whispered.

"We don't need to," the waitress said, smiling.

She stepped around the boxes and waved to the closest man. The man aimed his gun at her chest and called another man to him. Finley watched as the waitress headed straight towards the men with guns pointed at her, astonished by her reckless bravado.

"Doc," she said as she reached the older of the two men. "Good to see you."

The man lowered his weapon and pulled her into a hug. "Good to see you, too. We weren't sure you'd make it."

"Wouldn't miss it," she said.

The other man had turned back to his post, leaving her with the grey-haired leader. She waved for Finley and Oscar to join her, which they reluctantly did.

"We've got everything prepped and ready for you, Quay," the man said. "The guy from the bar is already onboard, detained in your quarters."

"Right," Quay said. "Did you relieve him of his coughing?"

"Kimby gave him a dotal strip when he picked him up from the club, but he'll need another in four hours. His throat will be raw for a few days, but he'll be well enough for interrogation by tomorrow."

"Good. I want to know who he's working for before we hit the Door."

"Come on, Quay, you already know."

"No," she said, "not for sure. These guys weren't there for me, Doc, they were there to catch these Riders."

"What about the Duke?" Finley piped up.

Doc put his hands on his hips and looked him over. Finley felt like a hanrius being appraised for slaughter. Finally, Doc growled, "Let him go. Not much we could do with a planet-keeper. Regent would be on us in an instant."

Doc pointed to the ship and the camo netting was removed. The engines were purring softly, barely audible even at such close range. Doc and Quay headed towards the ramp, Finley and Oscar following behind.

"You boys ready to go?" she asked.

"Where?" Finley asked.

"Door Nine."

"Nine?" Finley asked. "There is no Door Nine. And we're looking for Six, anyway. That's the whole point of us being out here."

"You're not gonna find Six out here," Quay laughed.

"We heard a rumour—"

Quay cut him off and said. "Just get on the fucking ship."

"We have our own ship," Oscar said.

"Not anymore," Doc replied. "It blew up about an hour ago."

"Blew up?" Oscar asked, shock and fear fighting for control of his voice. Their ship was his pride and joy, and Finley had a feeling the idea of being without it had never entered his mind.

"The bounty hunters who were chasing you must've contacted the Regent because there were troops around that ship within ten minutes of your dock and departure. They sent a full troop inside, probably looking for information on the Doors."

"Damn it," Finley said.

"Wait," Oscar said. "If the troops were inside looking for information, how did it get blown up?"

The old man looked a bit sheepish. "Well, we couldn't let them have what they were looking for, could we?"

"You blew up my ship? YOU BLEW UP MY SHIP!"

Finley grabbed Oscar as he reached for his blaster, but it was pointless. One of the other guards had already stunned him. Oscar slumped towards the floor, Finley barely catching him before his body hit the ground.

"Pick him up. We've gotta go," Quay said. "We've wasted enough time already."

Finley hoisted Oscar over his shoulder and climbed the ramp. Without a ship, they didn't have a choice. They could go with this psycho waitress and her crew or become townies like the rest of the stranded nobodies on Nim-6,

"There are bunks to the left," Quay said, nodding

towards a cabin. "I'll need you up front when you're finished."

Finley put Oscar on a bunk and headed towards the cockpit. "Where's the rest of your crew?"

"Not coming with us. They've got business elsewhere. You know how to pilot?"

Finley smirked. "Enough."

"Good. You've got about thirty seconds until we're spaceborne."

He familiarised himself with the craft. The controls of most ships were straightforward once you'd flown a few, so Finley had no trouble adjusting to the new ship's layout.

"Prepare hyperdrive," Quay said. "I want to hit it as soon as we clear orbit."

"Right," Finley said. "Calculations?"

"Unnecessary," she replied. "They're completed and locked. Just be ready to hit the switch when I tell you."

Finley bit back his response. He was the one who normally gave commands, but after being rescued by this woman more than once today, he didn't feel like he should be arguing. Besides, he'd been looking for Door Six for two years without success. If this woman could take him to it, after he helped her not find her imaginary Door Nine, all the better for him.

CHAPTER TWO

"We've got incoming," Quay said, breaking into Finley's thoughts. "Two Regency HFPs on our tail and it looks like there's a full IPT waiting just outside of orbit."

Finley looked at the monitor. "Nim-6 is closing their shield."

"Damn it. Regent must've told 'em to lock us in."

"You've got about fifteen seconds before it closes," he said.

"Hold on. It's going to be a tight squeeze."

Quay adjusted the yoke, pitching the ship to fit through the closing shield. She kicked the power up as high as she could. Finley's teeth rattled inside his head and he felt himself being pushed against the seat. The noise of the craft was a cacophony around them; hums and rattles, beeps and screeches sang through the ship.

"Oh shit, oh shit, oh shit," he mumbled as he squeezed his eyes shut.

The silence was like a smack in the face. It engulfed them, the nothingness vibrating through the air. Finley opened one eye. They were through the shield. He opened the other eye and stared at the massive transfer ship hovering ahead of them. The laser cannons on the side shifted towards them.

He glanced at the radar and felt a slight relief. "The

HFPs are locked in the shield."

"That IPT isn't," Quay replied as lasers sprayed their starboard side. She flipped a couple of switches on the control board and said, "Hyper drive on my mark: three, two, one."

Finley punched the hyper drive and watched the pinpoints of stars become star lines, and the star lines become blackness. It was a familiar and comforting sight, especially after the trouble they'd somehow just escaped. Quay still stared at the monitors, checking for any sign of pursuit. After a moment, she sighed and switched the ship to autopilot.

"That was fun," she said, a genuine smile on her face.

"Most fun I've had all week," Finley replied.

She reached her hand towards him and said, "Perian Quay, Dunner's Mark."

"Garret Finley, Hofstarn. My parents are originally from Dunner's Mark though."

"No shit? Small galaxy. Related to Jack Finley, by chance?" she asked, brows furrowed.

"I am. You know him?"

"Oh yeah," she said, her lips curving up.

"Were you a student of his?" Finley asked.

A look of confusion crossed Quay's face for a moment before she said, "I guess you could say that, though I like to think I taught him a few things." She saw a grimace on Finley's face and cleared her throat, saying, "Everybody knows Jack. He's a force, ya know? You his kid brother or something?"

"Jack Finley is my dad."

Quay laughed. "Couldn't be. Jack's what, twenty-six or so?"

"We must be talking about different people," Finley said. "Dad is from Ebriton on DM."

"So is my Jack."

"He's fifty-six. Married to Esme Patur."

"Esme Patur?" Quay asked, her face colouring in anger. "That little bitch. I *knew* she was after Jack."

"Hey, whoa. I dunno what you're on about, but you can't talk about my mom like that."

Quay ground her teeth together and stared hard into Finley's eyes. "Are you fucking with me? About Jack and Esme?"

"No, I'm truthy hundred," Finley replied. "But I don't know why you're upset about a wedding that happened twenty-eight years ago."

Quay turned and looked out into the blackness of space, staring at nothing for several moments. When she turned back to Finley, her face was deadly serious.

"I need you to tie me up."

"Excuse me?"

"Look at me, Finley. How old am I?"

"Uh, I don't know, mid-twenties?"

"Twenty-five," she said, her voice controlled, "or at least I was when I took this gig. But you just told me that someone who I was in Flight School with, someone who I trained beside, someone I was engaged to, has been married for twenty-eight years."

Finley stared into her olive eyes and saw the turmoil within, and fear began to grip him as well. "You've been gone twenty-eight years?"

"I've been gone for nine months, Finley. At least, that's all I remember."

"This is crazy. It's impossible."

"Maybe," she said. "Maybe not."

"How?"

"I don't know. There are a lot of scenarios playing out in my head right now, but nothing makes sense. Just do us both a favour and tie me up," she said. "At least until we figure out what's going on."

"Quay, you just saved us from Regency capture. Clearly we're on the same side."

"I hope so," she said. "But until you can get me into Medical and find out where my life went, you can't take the chance that we aren't. They could've done anything to me: sleeper agent, doppelganger, maybe they filled me with a disease to spread to the rebels..."

She trailed off, her jaw sharp as a knife as she clenched against the fear rising in her. Finley said, "Okay, I'll take care of it."

She nodded. There was nothing else to say.

"Hey, babe," Oscar said as he slipped into the co-pilot's seat. "I gave the prisoner the second dotal strip and his coughing is chilled."

Finley nodded. "What about Quay?"

"She's dosed and locked in the bunks."

Finley sighed. "I don't know if the sedation is really necessary."

"She thinks so."

"Either way, thanks for taking care of it."

Oscar put his hand on Finley's shoulder. "S'okay. I know you're a little squeamish. Besides, it gave me a chance to check some things." Oscar's smile melted to a grimace as he said, "I need to tell you something, and you're not gonna like it."

"I don't like a lot of things right now, so it can just mix in with the rest."

"Quay is truthy, far as I can see."

"You went digging?" Finley asked.

"Little. She's chipped, one of the oldies that don't

keep a meshed log, but it still had some info."

"If it wasn't fully integrated, maybe it was faked," Finley said.

Oscar shook his head. "Nah. Even a primo hackbot couldn't match it so perfecto with the ship's logs."

"What did the ship say?"

"When I linked up, it was scattered. Thought it was thirty years ago and kept trying to update my software to its time. Then it could only give me nine months of data."

"You're hundred it couldn't have been altered?"

Oscar nodded. "There would be traces somewhere. One or other off by a nanosecond. But no, her chip matches the ship down to the tiniest snatch o' second. I'm hundred."

"I just don't see how it could be true."

Oscar shrugged. "I don't neither. Weird things, babe. Not the weirdest we've seen though, eh?"

Finley stared at Oscar, brows raised. "Yeah, mate, I think it is the weirdest. Some rando townie who used to fuck my dad shows up after missing the last however-long, saves us from Regency bounty hunters, then asks us to knock her out in case she's a sleeper agent—and you don't think that's the weirdest shit we've seen?"

Oscar shrugged. "'Member the rodeo on Panlucia?"

Finley flinched. "Okay, so this is the second weirdest. And we promised we wouldn't mention the rodeo ever again."

"Right, right," Oscar said. He looked at the passing blackness for a moment, seemingly lost in thought. Finally, he shook his head and said, "I can't believe I didn't see it before. Fuck me, the rodeo saves us again."

"What are you talking about?"

"The brother-mucking Cloud Race, Fin. It's that all over again."

"Oscar, you're not making sense. Could you have caught a virus from the ship's computer?"

Oscar jerked back, offended. "This ship don't have the balls to try it. Knows my tech would scramble it perma."

"Then what are you saying?"

"I'm goin' in deep. Down to the day this ole heap o' metal was birthy."

"Anything I can do to help?"

Oscar stood and planted a kiss on Finley's forehead. "Check on me in an hour." He turned and stepped out of the cockpit. Before he turned around the hall's corner he yelled, "And make me a sandwich."

Oscar was digging for eleven hours. Finley checked on him every hour, brought him food and water, but the food sat uneaten and the drinks still full. He tried talking to him too, but Oscar was deep and couldn't hear him.

He went to Quay's room to check on her instead. She was out cold, sleeping through the sedation she'd demanded. Finley brushed the hair off her face and stared down at the strange woman, unsure what to make of her. It'd been less than a day, but he felt some sort of strange kinship with her. It wasn't attraction (at least he hoped it wasn't—that would put a strain on him, considering he'd never been attracted to a woman before), but it was some *need* to be around her, to help her, to love her.

"Blerg shit," he said, nearly jumping from the bed. *Love.*

What a strange word to enter his head. He felt like he had a good grasp on the things around him, his feet grounded in reality. She flipped everything upside down. He walked to the door, but couldn't stop himself from turning back to look at her again. She wasn't there. "What the—"

His words were choked off as an arm caught him around the throat. He pawed at the arm, but it held tight against him, closing off his air supply.

Quay's voice growled in his ear. "Who are you? How did you get on my ship?"

Despite her questions, she didn't ease up on her grip.

Finley couldn't answer, could barely find a breath. Darkness closed in around the edges of his vision.

He slammed back against the wall, crushing her against it. Her grip tightened. He pounded against the wall, again and again. Quay wrapped her legs around him and strengthened her grip. Finley felt himself growing weaker, fell to his hands and knees on the ground.

Blessed air filled his lungs as her grip finally gave way. He sucked it in with great gulps, like a man with a bad spacesuit pulled inside just in time. He stared into Quay's green eyes as she lay on the floor beside him, a needle sticking from her neck. When his senses returned in full, he realised he had no idea what had happened.

Finley hated not knowing something. Made his brain itch.

He moved to get up and felt strong arms behind him, lifting him to his feet. Oscar spun him around, running hands over Finley's face and neck and hair before pulling him against his chest.

"I'm okay," Finley croaked. His voice was raw. He smiled, unable to stop himself. He sounded like one of those rugged cowboys on the movies his grandma liked (they were old when *she* was young).

"Only 'cause I came up when I did. If I'd stayed digging any longer, who knows?"

Finley pulled back a little, pressed his forehead against Oscar's. "But you didn't, and I'm okay. What about her?"

"Dosed her good. She'll be down a few hours."

"Thanks," Finley said. "Any idea what triggered her?"

Oscar frowned. "Sedatives? It's my only guess, though it doesn't make sense yet."

Finley slipped from Oscar's arms and they worked to tie her up. This time, they checked her for sharp objects she could use to cut her ropes.

They headed towards the cockpit, Finley rubbing his sore neck the whole way. When they sat down, he asked, "Find anything from *The Quarrel*?"

A grin tore across Oscar's face. "It was buried, but yeah, I did. She might not remember the last twenty-seven years, but *The Quarrel* sure does."

"So, the records are just sitting there?"

"Under layers of Regency security."

Finley drew a sharp breath. "Regency? Are you sure?"

Oscar shrugged. "Well, not exactly, but who else would it have been?"

Finley's mind raced, searching for an answer. The Regent was a fucker, no doubt about it, and his control of the planets made things difficult for the less than scrupulous (i.e. him and Oscar), but there was still plenty of life to be had under the radar. His control of the inner eight planets was tight; the planet-keepers who carried out his bidding had their own forces and were regularly reinforced with Regency troops, holding tightly to the requirements of the regime. But he wasn't as strict on the outer five. There were still keepers, sure (like that bastard, Duke MacReoch), and they were still richer than a Garovium mine on a warm day (when the Garovium was nice and melty and you could scoop it up with no effort, no machines, and no wasted fuel). Those outer keepers though, they let shit slide if it didn't suit them. And much of it didn't.

So why would the Regent, with all the control he already had, want to take some random woman and steal her life away? How did it benefit him to have Quay under his control? Was she a rebel? She certainly wasn't Regency...at least, not before she was captured thirty years ago. But she knew Finley's parents. How did they play into this?

Finley scrubbed a hand over his face, the questions too taxing to think about in that moment. He said, "I don't know, but we need to find out. She didn't even remember me from a few hours ago. What else is she not remembering?"

"This ole trash pile's been flying around the whole time, even if she doesn't remember. The logs don't lie. Well, after you dig 'em up, anyway."

"So, where has she been?"

"If she was with the ship, a whole lotta places. Through Doors that don't exist."

"Door Nine?"

Oscar nodded. "And ten, eleven, and twelve. Not to mention thirteen through twenty."

"Twenty?" Finley said, eyes widening.

"I thought it a mistake, so I double-checked. And tripled. The coordinates are there."

"Holy shit," Finley whispered. "Twenty Doors. The Regent would *kill* for that intel."

"So would the rebels."

They stared at one another a moment, the words hanging in the air. Oscar was right. Anyone who discovered Quay's secret became a threat. The Regent would desire the Door coordinates to control trade in and out and to make his volatile empire stronger. The rebels (and their dangerous, do-whatever-it-takes leader, Corelia Copal—great-granddaughter of the overthrown original Regent) would use them to siphon control from the Regent as they had been trying, bit-by-bit, to do for the last hundred years.

After a moment, Finley looked up and said, "We're fucked."

Oscar nodded. "Well and truthy."

CHAPTER THREE

Finley watched the pale red planet grow in his vision. It was a nowhere-place, out beyond the invisible marker that divided the galaxy worth fighting for and the galaxy where neither Regent nor rebels gave two shits.

Streams of green swirled through the atmosphere, reminding him of the gas pools on Islington they had visited for their anniversary (a fun trip, until Oscar got arrested and Finley had his first run-in with the Dark Duke).

Oscar had erased every trace of what he'd found from the ship, after saving to his own tech, of course. There had been a fight about that. Finley had lost, obviously; Oscar was in charge of his own body, and despite Finley's objections because of the dangers, Oscar was going to do what he damned well pleased.

After the heated debate, followed by a furious make-up session, Finley found himself alone, staring at a planet he'd never thought to visit, looking for a Door he'd never known existed.

Footsteps rattled across the floor behind him and he heard Oscar let out a low whistle. "Foxy, in't she?"

"Why is it a she?"

Oscar shrugged. "Just is. Look at 'er."

Finley was. He'd been looking at her for a quarter of an hour as they made a slow approach into the atmosphere. No one had radioed, scans hadn't found anything, and she appeared empty. The planet seemed altogether perfect. Too much so.

"You think the prisoner would know anything?" Finley asked for the third time that hour.

Oscar sighed. "We've been over this."

"I know," Finley shrugged. "He's probably just a small-time bounty hunter hoping to make some credits by busting a couple Riders. But what if he isn't?"

"Whaddya thinkin'?"

"Maybe we were led to Nim-6 by those rumours as a way to draw out Quay."

"If she's Regency, why would they need to draw her out?"

Finley bit his bottom lip. "I don't know."

"And why us?" Oscar asked. "We're nobodies."

"She knew my dad. That's no coincidence."

Oscar shrugged. "Dunno. Seems like a few too many unknowns to make sense. Best we can do is get through Door Nine, like she wants. It's the one the ship logged more than any other. I just hope she don't kill us before we get there."

"Me too, Oscar. Me too."

The air on Kyorl wasn't breathable. The ground (what little they could find) was too soft to land on and kept eroding almost as soon as they found it. Water— or whatever the liquid was—swished back and forth under them, though neither could figure out what was controlling the ebb and flow.

Finley put the ship on auto and headed to the quarters. He wanted answers.

The coughing bounty hunter (who was also a certified heartthrob now that Finley could see him in proper lighting) they'd nabbed from the tavern was lying on the bed, black hair askew. His dark eyes opened lazily as Finley entered and a smirk passed across his lips, gone as quick as it came.

"I wondered when you'd come," he said.

"Don't be a gib," Finley said, rolling his eyes. "I'm not in the mood for it."

The man said, "What's wrong? Your other prisoner giving you trouble?" When Finley didn't respond, he asked, "She is your prisoner, right? Please tell me you're smart enough to figure that much out."

"What can you tell me about Magic Doors?" Finley asked, ignoring the man's jibes.

"Nothing you don't already know. Quay's the expert."

"What were you doing in the tavern?"

"Looking for my wife."

Finley blinked. It wasn't the answer he'd expected. "Your wife?"

"Yeah," the guy said. "I've been tracking her for months, got a lead she was there."

"But why was the Dark Duke there?"

"Hell if I know. I was there to see Shasta."

"Shasta."

The man raised his brows. "Tall, ponytail, probably dead now? Not ringing any bells?"

Finley remembered the crew in the alley. Quay *had* shot someone with a ponytail. "I remember."

The man lifted his tied hands from his lap as he talked. "Yeah, well, didn't really need Shasta when I saw Quay serving drinks. But then she poisoned me, so, there's that."

The pieces clicked together in Finley's head. "You're Quay's husband?"

He nodded. "I guess so. Is there a certain number of times a person has to try to kill you before you stop being their spouse?"

Finley floundered for a moment. "Uh, twelve?"

"Twelve? Hmmm. Is that for real or did you make it up?"

"Pretty sure it's twelve," Finley said, though he knew full well it was one.

"Damn. Guess I'm outta luck."

Finley put his hands on his cheeks and pressed until his lips puckered. Through fish-lips, he said, "I'm so fucking lost."

The man chuckled. "Gets me now and then, too. Even when you know all the parts, it'll make your brain hurt. Has she tried to kill you yet?"

Finley nodded, and the man nodded along with him commiseratingly.

After a minute, Finley said, "So, you uh, wanna get a drink?"

Adger Olifeld was a ghost. At least, that's what Oscar's records said. But he had an explanation for that: he was from a different galaxy.

"He's fork-feeding us a load of blerg shit," Oscar said.

They were outside the circular kitchen in the centre of the ship. The door was open. Finley looked in to see Adger smiling at him and waving the plastic spoon they'd finally agreed to give him (after a heated debate on how likely it was he could kill them with it, including the death stats Oscar pulled up to use for his side of the argument), so he could eat his engorged protein pack (made with REAL air!).

Finley shrugged. "I dunno. I think I believe him. Call it a hunch."

"A hunch in your pants, maybe. Pretty boy fills your ears with crazy and you lap it up."

Oscar was right, he was pretty. His skin was a pale olive, his features dark. He had just the right amount of stubble to be sexy without looking sloppy (a feat Finley had been trying—and failing—to master for years). He smiled when he should be angry, smirked when he knew he was right, and Finley could tell there was trouble brewing behind those dark eyes if he really wanted to let the storm go.

He didn't try to deny it. "He might heat the water, but it still boils at home."

Oscar rolled his eyes. He had never been the jealous type. He said, "Just try not to fuck up, k? Don't trust him, do not untie him, at least until we know more."

Finley nodded. "Speaking of, I should probably check on Quay and see if she can help sort some of this out."

"Good luck," Adger scoffed, confirming he was listening to the whole conversation.

"We can get them on their way and get back to siphoning from the rich, eh? Maybe we'll find some rare goods to smuggle from one of these Doors, make an assload of credits, and take a big vacation?"

Oscar frowned as Finley nudged him. Finally he said, "I want the whole thing this time. Flashy. No work while we're there."

Finley nodded. "As long as *you* promise not to get arrested this time."

Oscar smiled. He passed Finley and headed back towards the cockpit. "You know I can't promise."

Finley shook his head and sighed. He hoped he could deliver on a payload to get them away from this dangerous life.

But until then, he had the husband-and-wife-sized pain in his ass to deal with. He looked into the kitchen again. Adger gave him a wry smile and a wink.

Quay was awake when Finley entered the room. She was sitting on the bed, her eyes rimmed in red. Finley's heart hurt seeing her like this.

"Jack!" she yelled, jumping to her feet. She threw her tied hands around Finley's neck and kissed him hard on the mouth. When she pulled away, she was smiling. "I knew you'd rescue me. Thank Daya and her vengeful angels you're here."

Finley stared, mouth ajar. "I'm, uh, not Jack."

She pulled back and looked at him, her smile falling just a bit. "What are you saying? Of course you are. I'd know those eyes anywhere."

Finley pulled her arms up and off his neck. "Jack is my dad. I'm Garret."

Quay put her hands on top of her head. "It's happening again, isn't it?"

"What is?"

"Lonnia. Robert, then Jack. Now you."

"Lonnia and Robert?" Finley asked. "Robert Finley?"

She nodded.

"Please don't tell me you fucked my grandpa, too." She didn't respond, but Garret took it for a yes.

He pulled her arms from above her head and walked her to the kitchen. Adger was still there, spooning up the last of his food. "Hi, honey."

"No, no," she said, backing into Finley.

"What's wrong?" Finley asked.

"He's gonna take me back. He's gonna wipe it all out and take me back. I don't want to go."

Finley looked to Adger, who continued to smile up at Quay as she backed behind Finley. Finley asked, "What's she talking about?"

Adger shrugged. "She's been through a lot. I don't

know how long she's been off her medicine. If we can get some into her, we might be able to make sense of it all."

"What medicine?"

"It's in my front pocket," Adger said. He pointed his chest towards Finley, offering the medicine to him.

Finley took two steps towards him, but Oscar's voice caught his attention and he stopped. He turned, trying to make out the words Oscar was yelling through the ship. Rope slid around his neck as something sharp jabbed into his side. Adger pulled the object out and Finley glimpsed the end of a plastic spoon chewed into a shiv.

Fuck me, he thought. *Now I'll have to tell Oscar he was right.*

Adger didn't stab him again. Instead, he threw Finley to the side and tore off after Quay. Oscar came around the corner a moment later, a grin on his face. "It's raining. The Door should show—what the hell?"

"Get to Quay," Finley said. He was already applying pressure to the wound on his side. He wasn't bleeding bad enough to die, as long as Oscar could patch him up soon, but he wasn't sure what Adger wanted with Quay. And they couldn't afford to find out.

"You're bleeding," Oscar said.

"He's trying to drug her. I dunno why. Save her. I can wait."

Oscar pressed his lips together and Finley knew he didn't want to leave him. But he did. Oscar always did what was right. Finley watched him leave the kitchen, heard the clatter of running feet, felt the shock of a pulse blaster going off. *Who was on the receiving end?*

He looked up through the small window in the kitchen's ceiling, blinking away tears and the ragged breaths that wouldn't stop. He could see the faint outline of a Door forming: darkness leaked out the edges, black as Arphilus ink, but inside was a comet-tail of colours arcing round and round, spinning so feverishly it was hypnotic.

Finley watched the colours spin and swirl, expand and contract, as they drew closer, pulled by the field of the Door. He watched until he forgot about the others, forgot the blood pouring from his side, forgot his own name. He watched until the tears he was crying were from keeping his eyes open too long until Oscar was a memory and Quay was a dream.

Then the blood loss (more than he had expected, actually) got the better of him and he passed out on the cold metal floor.

CHAPTER FOUR

"I know you don't understand," Adger said.

Finley turned his eyes towards the voice as he came awake. Adger was sitting in the pilot seat of *The Quarrel*, staring out into whatever was beyond. Finley straightened, adjusting in the co-pilot seat he was strapped to. It hurt to move, hurt to think through the fog in his brain, and it took him a moment to remember that he didn't like Adger.

Finley blinked a few times, trying to shake loose his thoughts. He said, "I understand. Mostly."

Adger scoffed. "Then maybe you can clear some of it up for me. Because there are parts I still don't get."

"Why are you after Quay?"

"I told you. She's my wife."

"Doesn't seem like she wants to be."

"Of course not," Adger said. "You're a Finley."

Garret furrowed his brows. "And?"

"She always loses her shit when she's around one of you. Some kind of marker in your blood, I think. Makes her chip malfunction and sends her spiralling."

"Okay, maybe I understand less than I thought," Finley said. He grunted as he tried to straighten up in his restraints.

"Sorry about the whole stabbing thing," Adger said.

"I patched you up a bit. I didn't want to hurt you."

"Strange way to seal our friendship."

Finley's thoughts turned to Oscar. His head swivelled, looking for him, but he wasn't in the pit. The pulse that had gone off...

"I locked him up, but he's fine. Nearly pulsed my head off though," Adger said, rubbing his fingers through his thick hair.

They sat in silence a few minutes, staring off into the world below them. There were clouds, fluffy and golden, glowing under the double suns above them.

"Where are we?" Finley asked.

"Fosh," Adger said. "It's the second planet on the other side of Door Nine."

"This is what Quay was looking for."

"Yeah, I figured. She comes here just before the end."

As they descended, Finley watched a flock of purple and silver birds fly under the ship. They were thick necked with large heads and spindly wings that seemed to struggle to support them. Sink, swoop, repeat. Like people. They were beautiful.

"So, she's what? A sleeper agent? A clone? Regency?"

"Yes. Damn, I didn't think you'd know all that. Makes it easier on me, honestly."

"Wait, what? She's all of them?"

Adger shrugged as if in apology, then flew below the clouds. Finley's eyes grew wide as he stared at rows and rows of...*something*. Glowing *something* for miles in each direction. With streams of black and pulsating green between them. Cables of some kind, he realised, as they got closer.

And then they were circling close enough for Finley to see bodies in the glowing *somethings*. Freezer-birth chambers, that's what they were.

Quay was in each one.

They landed on a small hill in the centre of the fields of Quay. Finley followed Adger out of the ship. The air was breathable during the day, Adger told him, but at night noxious gases released from the flora. Finley didn't see any flora, but Adger assured him it was there, hiding from the sun for the next few hours.

"She hates it here," Adger said as they walked through rows of Quay's forever-young face.

"But she was trying to get here."

Adger nods. "Something in her knows when the time is coming."

"The time?"

"To switch bodies," Adger said. He chuckled. "I

guess this is where it gets complicated."

Finley stood over a Quay as she looked up through sightless eyes. "What is she?"

"She's Perian Quay, the love of my life. She's also on the fourth version of that woman."

"Why is she like this?"

"She sought immortality and her lead scientist provided it."

"So, she *is* Regency."

"She's not just Regency," Adger said, "she's the Regent. The original that started it all. That's why the current Regent is so desperate to find her. If she remembered everything, she could destroy him."

"I'm lost," Finley said. "It's too fucking much."

Adger nodded. "Tell me about it. Try being married to her."

"So, she was the first regent from a hundred and some years ago. She made herself immortal by switching into a new body when the old…what? Wears out? But at the cost of her memory."

"Kinda. She remembers the most when she first wakes. That's always the best for us. We can go home and enjoy life for a few years. But after a while, she starts to forget things. Little things, at first. Then me," Adger said, his voice cracking.

Finley winced. He couldn't imagine what it would

be like to lose Oscar over and over and still be trying to keep it together. "I'm sorry."

"It's fine. I mean, it's not, but you know. Do what you have to for the one you love."

"What happens after, you know, she forgets?"

"She goes looking for a Finley."

Garret squinted, confused. "But why?"

"You're what she remembers from before me, and she goes retracing her steps. She forgets about the clones and who she was, and searches for the last thing she knew before the gap in her memory."

"My grandpa?"

"Great-grandpa," Adger says, smirking. "Rutger Finley was the one she loved before she was Regent. When she went haywire the first time, long before I knew her, she went looking for Rutger and found his daughter, Lonnia, instead. She loved her, too. Your grandpa Robert was the third Finley, then your dad, last time, and now you."

"You said it was a marker in our bloodline?"

Adger shrugged. "It's just a guess. Something keeps pulling her back. She can somehow find you, no matter where you are."

Finley sighed. Part of him felt like he could understand what Adger was saying. He'd felt pulled to Quay from the moment he saw her. There was a need in him to protect her, and it wasn't something he understood or knew how to explain. How did you tell her husband you loved her, even though you'd just met? How did you explain it to yourself? Oscar would understand—it wasn't the same as the love he had for him, after all, it was more rooted, like he'd always had it buried inside him but didn't know until he saw her.

He turned to look at the ship in the distance, realising how far they'd walked. He turned back to Adger to ask where they were going, but found Adger pointing a blaster at him instead.

Adger motioned for Finley to raise his hands as he said, "I'm really sorry about this, fella. It wasn't the plan."

Finley got a sick feeling in the pit of his stomach. "Oscar isn't in quarters, is he?"

Adger swallowed, shook his head almost imperceptibly. "I'm truly sorry about that, Finley."

That was it then. Without Oscar, there wasn't much point to life. Smuggling and outrunning the Regency? It was boring without that white-eyed wonder by his side.

"What happens now?" Finley asked. "You gonna fly off with a new Quay?"

Adger shook his head. "Nah, I think I'm done with that life."

"You're just going to let her die?"

"No, of course not. I'm going to turn her in."

Finley's jaw dropped. This man claimed to love her, but he knew with every fibre of his being that he would've done anything to save Oscar, to spare him from pain. Love wouldn't allow him to turn Quay in to the Regency, so clearly he didn't love her.

"Don't give me that look," Adger said. "Sad eyes aren't gonna sway me. I'm too tired of racing around the Doors for a woman who will always forget me."

Adger backed away from Finley, still pointing the blaster at his chest. As he went, he began pressing buttons on a gadget on his wrist. All around them, birther pods began to open. The Quays inside didn't move, still asleep without the chip that held Quay's memories and personality.

"The gas," Finley said, his mouth going dry. "You're going to kill her."

"She's already dead," Adger said. "These are just copies."

Finley took a step towards him and Adger fired a warning shot at his feet. "Don't move again. I don't want to shoot you."

Finley laughed. "Go ahead. You've already taken away the only thing I've ever loved. And you're leaving me here to die anyway!"

"Good point," Adger said.

His finger pressed the trigger. A jet of red shot Finley

in the chest and he dropped to the ground. He listened as the remaining pods opened, as Adger's footsteps faded away, as he started up the ship. He saw the craft pass overhead, followed by a flock of birds, dark spots against the twilight sky.

The suns had set, leaving Finley in the dark of Fosh. He heard a rustle and turned his head to the left. Pushing up through the ground was a vibrant green plant with shimmery white veins.

"Aren't you foxy?" Finley mumbled.

He heard a hiss and saw the air above him alight with sparkling particles floating towards the ground. A cough tickled his throat as he closed his eyes.

SHELLY JARVIS began working on young adult fiction thanks to a writing assignment in Mrs. Burger's eleventh grade English class, but her passion for writing developed at seven when she wrote a Halloween tale about a witch and a ghost who became best friends.

An avid science fiction and fantasy reader, Shelly spends a large portion of each day dwelling in other worlds. She gives credit to Madeleine L'Engle with her introduction to the genre, J.R.R Tolkien for expanding her view, and Patrick Rothfuss, George R.R. Martin, and J.K. Rowling for blowing her mind. Shelly enjoys spending time with her wacky husband, Joe, her wonderful family, and her rescue pups, Gimli, Butters, Fergus, and Pickles. She currently resides in West Virginia, in the wild and wonderful mountains that have her heart.

Bibliography

ANGELS, Black Hare Press, 2019
BEYOND, Black Hare Press, 2019
Black Sea Bright Song, 2019
MONSTERS, Black Hare Press, 2019
Rise of the Chosen, 2018
Storming Area 51, Black Hare Press, 2019
The Dreamwalker, 2015
WORLDS, Black Hare Press, 2019

Connect
Website: www.ShellyJarvis.com
Twitter: @shellyjarvis
Amazon: amazon.com/-/e/B006H8NJZ2

ECHOES OF LIVES GONE BY
By Carole de Monclin

In my eyes, Malalaya excels in all she does. But that's only because I'm human. She sees things differently. She's a disabled alien, and I've been chosen to be her pet companion. By chosen, I mean abducted. Other humans preceded me here. They left traces behind. Why have they been replaced? Will I meet the same fate?

Her hands flew over the keys, gentle, precise, and swift. She played effortlessly when only a handful of pianists could do justice to this dark, almost hallucinatory, piano solo. The notes rose, ricocheted, and flowed, woven in intricate patterns.

As she reached the third

movement of "Gaspard de la Nuit"—by far the most difficult—the music became frenetic, exploding in tumultuous staccatos. Her virtuosity brought me to tears. I wiped them furtively with the back of my hand before she could notice.

Showing weakness was dangerous.

As the last chord faded, she unfolded the sixth finger on both hands—she kept them tucked away when she played human music—and turned towards me. She couldn't physically smile, but I recognised her happiness and sensed her pride in this accomplishment.

However, the modicum of peace it afforded me would be short-lived. New demands would arise soon.

Her name was Malalaya, and I was her pet companion.

With one wave of her hand, the piano disappeared, leaving the room bare for a few seconds before she summoned a circle of floor pillows covered with elaborate patterns. I'd taught her Mandalas yesterday, so today she toyed with designs. Three oval windows appeared, letting warm light slant inside the room as we settled on the cushions. I expected she'd ask what to explore next, what new skill to take on, what knowledge she could suck out of me.

I was wrong.

"They're thinking of replacing you," Malalaya spoke

the words so quickly I barely understood them. Usually, she took her time, enjoying forming almost perfect approximations of the sounds that made up the human language.

Shock rendered me mute, but I finally managed to ask, "Have I done anything to displease them?"

"No." The flat answer didn't give any indication as to her feelings.

I'd learnt early on my questions rarely deserved an answer, but I pressed on, clasping my hands together to hold them steady, "Then why?"

"You've served your purpose. They believe I need someone more intelligent, more educated, more skilled."

"Have I not been a good companion?"

"You've tried your best."

The words felt like a blow. Since I'd first understood the rules of my captivity, her satisfaction had been the only goal filling my days. I'd tried to resist at first but only met with the Pain.

There was no other way to name the agony that came from nowhere but shattered every nerve in your body. I learnt to fear those who inflicted the Pain, her Kin.

"Do you agree?" I asked.

"My opinion doesn't matter." She didn't try to hide

the irritation in her voice.

"Are you sure?" I insisted.

"They know what's best. Not me."

What would happen to me? Instinct screamed my fate—never so much as alluded to—would be their equivalent of flushing the goldfish down the toilet.

"I disagree."

"Must we have that discussion again?" Her fingers drummed on the red pillow she cradled in her lap.

"Yes," I inhaled deeply as I stepped onto a treacherous path by contradicting her. Since I'd submitted, no threats had ever been issued, or physical mistreatments inflicted, but something always lurked just below the surface, "I think you're perfectly capable of making decisions for yourself."

Her silent compliance suffocated me. She could speak up when I couldn't. As much as my guts boiled every day, urging me to scream at her, at my circumstances, at fate, I stifled the feeling every night.

"I'm stupid," Malalaya shouted, her words slightly distorted because she didn't master talking at such volume, "I'm mentally impaired!"

"Not to me."

She threw the red pillow away. In mid-air, it disappeared into oblivion. She hated being reminded of her condition. A condition I still struggled to make sense of. She played the piano or painted like only a handful of humans in all of history. She discussed quantum physics, biochemistry, or astronomy better than any professor.

But all this amounted to nothing. To her Kin, those accomplishments constituted barely more than cave paintings hidden deep inside a long-forgotten cavern.

When I spoke next, my voice was soft and gentle, "Do you regard me as stupid?"

"You're human," she tossed another pillow that met the same fate as the first one. "Things are different for you. You can't understand the way my Kin reason."

I couldn't deny the workings of her mind eluded me. She could be the most brilliant being I'd ever seen one second, and the next seem surprised I existed when she wasn't around. If I couldn't grasp her mind, what hope did I have to understand her Kin?

"Maybe. But if you like the way things are, tell them."

Malalaya's long fingers grabbed another pillow, but she didn't throw it this time. Tilting her head to the side, she studied me with large strange eyes, and I felt the heavy pressure of her pity on my chest, making it difficult to breathe.

"Not long after my Kin gifted you to me, you spoke about your dog."

"I don't want to talk about Max," my words came

out harsher than was prudent.

Under normal circumstances, recalling my past brought pure misery. Now, it became torture.

"I shouldn't have shared this with you," I whispered when Malalaya stayed silent.

"Why not?"

I wanted to explain she was never entitled to my memories. Discussing human culture didn't pain me anymore. Anything not tied to a memory could remain a pure concept. I'd learnt to keep things abstract and devoid of any emotion. But specifics about my life conjured up looks, words, touches, and feelings better left buried.

"You loved Max, didn't you?" she asked.

I nodded. We rescued Max, a German Shepherd, when he was six. I hadn't wanted such a big dog, but my husband cajoled me into accepting.

"Despite the love you felt, discussing nuclear fusion with him would have been impossible."

"Max was a dog."

What became of Max would remain a mystery, but I used the past tense. It hurt a little less if I stuck to the past tense.

Malalaya hugged the pillow between her powerful arms, "My point is you loved Max despite his limitations, despite the fact he could never rise to your level."

I tried to push away images of Max running in the yard, jumping in greeting, cuddling next to me. They were already inviting more hurtful images. Smiles, laughs, and strong arms around me. I wouldn't think about my husband.

"You wouldn't have trusted Max to make a decision about himself," Malalaya paused, "They feel the same way. As much as they love me, my relationship with them can never go beyond a certain level."

"You're no animal. You're their child."

"I don't know if your dog realised his limitations. Maybe he did. I certainly understand mine, as painful as they are. Only humans can match my intelligence. You've no idea how that feels, nor should you."

All the pillows vanished, and I found myself sitting on the ground. My gaze darted to the windows for a last glimpse at the warm light. They disappeared next leaving me in that cursed shadowless semidarkness. Malalaya had gone without a word of goodbye or explanation. She'd come back whenever the fancy took her. In an hour or maybe a day. I'd got accustomed to such incertitude, but today her departure raised a different question, not the habitual "when," but instead a "what if." What if she never came back?

"They're going to replace me," I whispered to the silence.

I walked to the bed in my private corner of the room. I grabbed the thin mattress and pulled it onto the floor with the covers still on, freeing the bed base. With practiced ease, I flipped the frame. Its material seemed like a hybrid between wood and plastic.

Unlike the other objects in the room, my possessions—mainly a bed, a side table with some writing material, some books and clothes, sheet music, a shower, and a toilet—were permanent. They never changed shape, colour, or disappeared. All the tools we used for Malalaya lessons she summoned from the void, I assumed from a giant database of sorts.

My belongings were mine only. Painfully Earth-like in their design, they offered a sense of durability the rest of my world was utterly devoid of. But even more precious than this, they were a link to those who came before.

As I had many times before, I slowly ran my finger along the carvings etched in the slats. He was an MIT professor, but I didn't know his name. He forgot to write it down, or maybe he intentionally didn't. He made a different choice, one I'd considered myself in the beginning. Although I changed my mind, his decision remained a perfectly valid one in our situation.

He killed himself.

At least, he wrote he was going to, then nothing

after that. I had no way of knowing if he followed through.

There were clues a third person was here too, engravings of a different nature, running deeper into the material, rougher, angrier, but they didn't form words. So, no information regarding this third companion in misery reached me. Maybe others shared my fate but didn't leave any trace behind.

Malalaya always refused to speak about the ones that came before. Questions annoyed her unless she was the one asking them. How many were there? Did they get replaced? Or commit suicide?

I caught myself humming notes from "Le Gibet," the second movement from "Gaspard de la Nuit." It meant the gallows. I stopped, then realising how fitting it was in my situation, I resumed louder, wondering if I would carve a few words today.

The professor wrote on the bottom of the slats, so I used the top. My first attempts turned out pitiful, but I'd improved with practice. It helped I wasn't sobbing anymore while I carved. Tears didn't come so easily now. The agony dulled, and the brain adjusted to the new reality however skewed.

My first entry read, "I'm Rebecca." No last name needed.

My carvings were no work of art, but I could identify

periods.

First came despair.

"I miss you."

"I love you."

"I'll never see you again."

"Do you think of me?"

The litany went on.

It hurt too much, so I'd decided to stop writing to him and entered my cynical period.

"Resisting will get you nowhere."

"Complying will get you nowhere."

"Abandon hope all ye who enter here."

I realised it wouldn't help those who'd come after prompting a transition to my obliging period.

"Don't ask questions."

"Space out your knowledge."

There weren't as many entries in this phase. Not much to say in the end.

I moved to the apathetic period which consisted of carving nothing but a few useless words.

Today marked the beginning of a new period, but I didn't want to name it. I took a pen, and while I continued humming, I used the tip to etch, "I'm afraid."

"They're thinking of replacing me," I repeated.

"Will it even be a human?" I wondered.

Despite our differences, I could still relate to

Malalaya's motivations and feelings, but her Kin transcended my understanding. Their minds seemed to exist in a different realm. Her analogy described the way I felt both times I interacted with them perfectly: a dog trying to understand nuclear fusion. They were by no mean all powerful otherwise they'd have healed Malalaya, and I'd have continued my life oblivious of their existence.

I was nothing to those creatures. Maybe they should have been called parents, but I didn't know how many they were, or how they reproduced. So, I preferred Kin. When I asked Malalaya if she was female—something about her said female—she replied, "It's more complicated than that," and wouldn't share anything more.

"What are you doing?"

I glanced up from the bed base startled to find Malalaya standing over me, a puzzled look on her face. She'd never come back so quickly.

Lying wouldn't help, "I'm carving for the person who'll replace me."

"Why?"

"I don't know…" I shrugged as I peered down at the unfinished words before I added, "Support, relief."

She chuckled, "Humans say such strange things. I want to learn more music."

"If they replace me, what will happen to me?" I couldn't believe I spent so much time with her, and she appeared ready to discard me like a toy she'd have outgrown. She'd been my sole companion for months, the only voice other than my own to fill the silence. If solely for that, I couldn't hate her. I wished I could call her monster, sometimes I did, but she was just a child. I thought offspring was a fitting name.

"I don't know." Her voice was toneless.

"What happened to the ones before me?"

"I don't know."

"You didn't ask?" I wanted to scream, but that would only scare her off.

"I want to play music. Chopin maybe?"

Despite her dislike for questions, I couldn't help asking the one that had been on my mind from the start, but had avoided acknowledging, "Is there a chance they'll bring me back home?"

Emotions were speaking, not reason. I knew enough about space travel to understand nothing awaited on Earth.

At first, I'd tried to imagine maybe this wasn't real, but a simulation for some sick entertainment. I'd also tried to cling to the idea our knowledge of physics was flawed, or limited and I could be reunited with my husband somehow.

I'd killed hope long ago. There was only this: this room and the monstrosity who sucked my knowledge as if I were an ink cartridge she used to write the pages of her existence. Empty cartridges ended up in the trash.

But if one wasn't careful hope tried to rise from its ashes like a phoenix, prompting you to reopen wounds better left alone.

"Don't be ridiculous. It'd be such a waste of energy. What about Liszt?" Malalaya stared, waiting for an answer, and when I failed to give her one, she ventured, "Chopin, Liszt, or Ravel?"

Malalaya's fingers danced again on the piano keys. The music must have been exquisite but only induced nausea in me.

Three days. She'd left me alone for three entire days. Three days of not knowing if suddenly I'd be grabbed and…I had no idea what. I'd run a lot of options in my head; sent to the farm, put out to pasture… My favourite was I might just disappear like a damn floor cushion. Those three days of silence almost drove me mad. Even madder than I already was.

"Why didn't you visit?" I asked over the music.

"I was busy."

I stared at her blankly, but she didn't look up from the keyboard. Malalaya finished the piece and turned to me. After scrutinising my face, she said, "We're going to see a friend today. She's like me."

Her voice modulated unusually, and it was the first time I heard her use the word "friend." What form could a friend take in her case?

"I didn't know there were others."

She stood and walked about the room. "Of course, there are. Although we're only a handful on the planet," she said absentmindedly as she prepared for her guest. Multicolour pillows appeared boasting patterns even more intricate than last time and forming three perfect concentric circles. The grand piano remained in the centre of the room, but its lines became more delicate, sleeker while it turned bright red.

Malalaya never gave any information. I'd been here for about half a year now—I kept track by etching small bars in the bed frame. Cliché, but effective. Although I had no idea how long the days stretched on this world, and no object tracked the time. Only the rhythm of meals marked the passage of time.

Malalaya had never alluded to us being on a planet. Self-evident as it sounded, for all I knew, it might as well have been a spaceship. I saw what felt like sunlight, but since I never went outside, I'd never seen the sun nor the sky. Windows were always frosted in some way.

Now I knew of those others, I added another possibility to my list. They might give me instead of disposing of me, hand me down like used clothes.

The prospect of meeting a being other than Malalaya was exhilarating. Her obvious enthusiasm for her visitor emboldened me, "Tell me more about your condition."

Her hand stopped mid-air, and the process turning the windows to stained glass halted. She considered me before saying, "My brain can't connect."

"Connect to what?"

"Neurocore would be an approximate translation."

"What is it?"

"A global synthetic neural network. This isolation precludes me from reaching a superconscious state. The others surf multiple streams of consciousness when I'm condemned to stoop to the level of inferior creatures and mould my mind to their crude intelligence."

She finished the windows, but the patterns of the stained-glass wound up duller than the pillows scattered on the floor. I knew better than to press her. It was more than I got in months. She added tables, and the colours she used became vibrant again.

"They're here," Malalaya said, then disappeared. Before I had time to process the significance of the plural pronoun, she reappeared with her guest.

The stack of sheet music I'd been holding fell to the ground, my trembling hands hanging by my side. I made no effort to pick up the pages. All I could do was gawk.

Malalaya's friend looked just like her, if not for the difference in size—Malalaya was taller—I wouldn't have been to tell one from the other. But that was irrelevant. What mattered was who stood next to them.

The guest had a pet companion.

I was gaping at her, a woman younger than I, carrying a large tray with a cake in the middle. She smiled, appearing nowhere as surprised as I was to see her. She calmly stepped towards me.

"Bonjour," the blue-eyed girl said.

Long wavy brown hair framed her freckled face. Her light skin contrasted with my dark one. I used to brag about taking French in College, but in truth I barely remembered a few words, most of them utterly irrelevant to my present predicament. Knowing how to ask where the library was wouldn't help.

"Je suis Américaine," I managed to reply in a breath.

"Hi. My name is Manon," the woman switched to English unfazed.

I wanted to say how happy I was to see her, how amazing it felt to see another human face after so long, but all I managed to blurt was hello.

My body shook. I almost reached out to touch her face, but the tray in her hands created a barrier between us. Others preceded me with Malalaya, so the fact there were other humans around somewhere shouldn't have come as a surprise.

I was struck by my luck. What if Manon couldn't speak English? What if the professor had been Japanese? Then all his carvings would have been lost on me. Did the successive companions always talk the same language?

An eerie voice filled the room, "Manon, tu peux apporter le gâteau, s'il te plait?"

"Tout de suite, Sananawa," Manon replied lightly as she padded towards the offsprings.

She put the tray on a low table and expertly transferred slices onto small plates. Her hands were steady, and the smile she gave Sananawa when she offered her a plate seemed genuine, "Remember our hosts do not speak French."

Manon then picked up a plate and offered it to me. Was she a better actress than I was?

"C'est vrai. Sorry. I forgot," Sananawa made eye contact, and boasted, "I made this cake without Manon's help."

I had trouble understanding her. Like the slice of cake sitting on the plate balanced in my hand,

Sananawa's accent had two thick layers, one alien and one French, creating an unlikely mix, but her tone held a certain softness.

Staring at the spoon on my plate, I hesitated before I picked it up. The food here tasted deprived. Deprived of taste, colour or texture. I was afraid of the memories this cake might bring back, but its rich, creamy flavour was unlike anything I'd tried before.

Manon went back to the offsprings to offer a second serving. When she came back to my side, she sat swiftly on a blue cushion. Her demeanour changed the second the offsprings stopped paying attention to us. Worry scrunched her face, "How long have you been here?"

"Six months, I think. You?"

"Five and a half years."

"That long?"

She nodded, and a small smile graced her lips as if she were talking about something pleasant. But when she spoke next, the smile vanished, "How has Malalaya treated you?"

"She…I don't know."

"Malalaya is different. She doesn't…" Manon intertwined the fingers of her splayed hands, trying to convey with a gesture the word she couldn't find, "…bond," she finally said, "Malalaya can't bond."

"And Sananawa?"

"She's been good to me," a small sigh escaped Manon's lips. "So far."

"Have you met other humans?"

"Seventeen. Well, with you that's eighteen."

"Malalaya said they're thinking of replacing me," I whispered.

"Replacing you?"

"Rebecca," Malalaya's voice interrupted with an imperiousness I'd never heard from her, "Please bring my music and turn the pages."

My eyes stayed on Manon, but she stared at Malalaya, frozen.

"Please," Malalaya repeated, and I had no other choice but to comply. The pages still lay on the floor where I'd abandoned them. I slowly picked them up hoping in vain Manon would whisper something more.

Malalaya sat next to me on the piano bench, and the first notes of "Grande Valse Brilliante" by Chopin soared. Their cheerfulness felt like a betrayal, but the light and airy music tamed the chaos in my head. On Earth, I used to lose myself in music, here I dissolved into the melodies to forget.

Sananawa's strange voice brought me back to reality, "That was fantastic."

"I still need to perfect it," Malalaya's body language belied her demure tone. Casually resting on the keys, her hands were shivering in pleasure at the praise.

A heavy silence fell. I wanted to break it in a million pieces and ask Manon all the questions that burnt my tongue. But Sananawa was the one who spoke, "I'd like to invite you to join us next time we hike up the three peaks."

My gaze darted to Manon's face but found no surprise in her features. Malalaya emitted a small rasping noise then moved closer to Sananawa and spoke in a low voice I couldn't understand, presumably their language.

"A hike?" I whispered.

"The sunset over the peaks is quite the view."

"I've never left this room."

Manon's eyes widened, "Never?"

I shook my head slowly. The pity I read in her eyes, those wonderful human eyes, made me hate her for a second.

"I knew Mike," Manon murmured.

"Mike?"

"The guy before you."

The professor.

"What happened to him?" I asked for confirmation.

"He talked about suicide. I tried to dissuade him, but... I'm not sure," she trailed off.

Manon grabbed my hand, but I didn't have time to enjoy the contact of her warm skin, because she went on hastily, "Don't trust—"

Malalaya announced loudly, "Please excuse me, but I'm not feeling very well."

The offsprings exchanged a few words, and before I even had time to say goodbye Sananawa and Manon vanished. Right before she disappeared, Manon mouthed, "Be careful."

Malalaya's gaze lingered on me, but I couldn't read her expression. The colourful cushions disappeared. In a Pavlovian response, my eyes instantly rushed for one last desperate glance at the windows. Too soon I lost their light. Malalaya remained for a few seconds more, and then she was gone.

With the room reverted back to its barren state, I could have dragged myself to bed, but instead, I crumbled onto the floor. My world had changed almost as drastically as the day I woke up here.

Even in hell, I'd found a way to be doomed among the damned.

When Manon looked at Sananawa, I'd seen no fear or hatred, only quiet contentment. She'd talked about bonds between the offsprings and their companions. Nothing could be further from my reality.

Ignorance had made my condition easier to accept. Knowledge could be a cruel friend, but I'd understood that already. Knowledge was the source of my slavery.

Had I been a mediocre musician, I would have been sleeping in my bed tonight.

More than anything, the memory of Manon's expression when I told her I was going to be replaced petrified me. I wished I could cry, but my eyes stayed dry.

When I woke up after an uneasy rest, I realised the piano still presided over the room. Had I been so upset I'd failed to register it, or had it reappeared while I slept? The sheet music still sat on the music rack. I decided to try my hand at "Gaspard de la Nuit." My fingers weren't agile enough. I had to slow down in a few places, and hit the wrong keys several times, but I kept playing.

A mind focused on a single complex task didn't wander towards dark shores. No thoughts about the future, privileges, or the sky. No wondering if Malalaya would ask her Kin to keep me. Nothing but the music.

"I play it better," Malalaya's voice came from behind.

My hands lifted from the keyboard hastily.

"Yesterday was a success," Malalaya said, sitting on pillows that hadn't been there a moment before.

"Will they be coming back?" I asked.

"I suppose."

I didn't hesitate, "Do you have any news?"

Malalaya cocked her head, "About what?"

The subject was foremost on my mind, but apparently not in hers.

"About me."

"You?"

"About if or when I'm going to be replaced?"

"No," she stared, and for once I didn't look away. "But the way things progress, I'm afraid it might be soon."

What things? Something in her demeanour bothered me. It wasn't really a change in her expression, but more about the way she carried herself, about how her hands shivered a little, just like when she'd just mastered a challenging piece.

"Will we go to the three peaks?"

"No," the refusal held a hint of steel. After the briefest pause, she went on, "Enough questions. I want to play some Beethoven. Find the Fifth Symphony."

"No."

"No?"

"Find your own damn music."

I stood up from the piano and walked to the back of the room, farthest away from her.

"You've never said no before."

Her tone was more curious than reproachful. Months of self-control, and now I needed it the most it failed me. I shuddered under her scrutiny, but I was determined to not back down, even if the Pain came. I noticed the slight shivers of her hands again. This time I understood.

She was enjoying herself.

"Are you sure this is wise?" she asked.

"No."

The trembling got more pronounced, but she didn't say anything more. She took the seat I'd just vacated, slowly, deliberately, then proceeded to fish the music from among the pages on the piano and placed it neatly on the rack. Her fingers were poised on the keys, but she didn't start to play.

I couldn't take it anymore. I had to fill the silence, "I need to know what's going to happen to me."

"Why? You can't change it."

The music swelled. The four-note opening motif mirrored my emotions, then the notes swirled around me, cascading like the thoughts whirling in my head.

Meeting another human, a content one, came as a cruel coincidence just after Malalaya had dropped her "you might be replaced" bomb. The contrast between the French girl and I only heightened my precariousness.

As I watched her fingers move in a frenzy, I realised Malalaya wouldn't have acted differently if she'd wanted to torture me. I'd always assumed her Kin had inflicted the Pain without Malalaya's involvement. I'd never ascribed her any malicious intent. Insensitivity, dismissiveness, lack of empathy, for sure, but nothing deliberate.

Until now.

Malalaya fed off my emotions the same way she fed off my knowledge.

Before the end of the first movement, I'd schooled my features into an expressionless mask. I sat on a cushion, leg crossed, back straight, hands loosely resting on my thighs.

The music stopped. Malalaya drummed her six fingers on the piano's frame, but I ignored the exasperating noise. Finally she disappeared. I didn't move. Not when the pillow vanished, not when my food materialised, and after a while dematerialised. My eyes closed, I had emptied my mind of any emotion. It was the only freedom I had left.

Time stretched out without goal.

Until I felt she was back. It wasn't scent or movements that betrayed her presence, but the sensation the air just thickened.

"What are you doing?" Her voice sounded the same, but my heart beat faster.

"Meditating," I replied without opening my eyes.

"Meditating?"

I heard a shuffling of limbs.

"Useless," she whispered in my ear.

She rarely approached this close, let alone touched

me, as if an invisible barrier existed between us. My eyes opened in surprise when something grazed my skin. The contact intensified. Positioned in a circle, the tips of Malalaya's six fingers bit down onto my face with such force if I hadn't been sitting down she'd be forcing me to kneel. I couldn't see past the palm that loomed close to my eyes.

"You belong to me," she hissed.

"I know." I tried my best to keep my voice level. I didn't want to offer her my fear.

"No, you don't really know what that means. You're the only thing in my life over which I have total control. Every little comfort you have is because of me."

She increased the pressure, and I struggled not to move or beg.

"Every little comfort you don't have is also because of me. You'd love to leave this room, talk with that other human, but we can't have that, can we?"

Claw-like nails dug into my skin.

"If I shifted my fingers just a little, I could gouge your eyes out. I'd like to see tears of blood running down your cheeks for a change."

A finger from her other hand scratched down my face, from eye to jaw, and I tasted blood trickling at the corner of my mouth.

"Did you know I watch when you're alone? Your

tears are few and far between now. Your useless carvings diverted me for some time, but I'm growing tired of them. I enjoyed the stories you used to share, but you stopped telling them. You don't even touch yourself anymore," Malalaya tsk-tsked. "I was expecting more of a reaction when I told you about your replacement, but you've been quite boring. Where's the pleading, the grovelling, the breakdown? I've tried to tempt you with a human, the outside, but all you've given me is more apathy. So dull." The fingers dug deeper. "I've seen better."

Was she talking about the professor? The other carver? Someone else?

"I enjoyed learning the music, but you taught me well. I don't need you anymore. Maybe I'll ask for someone who can help me pick up sculpture next. I'm definitely not baking any stupid cakes."

One finger traced my other cheek, and I couldn't help the tremors that shook my whole body.

She sighed, "My Kin, as you call them, won't like it when they find out."

"Why do it then?" My voice came out like a squeak.

"Because I can."

Were her Kin aware of what she was about to do? If it wasn't the first time—I was convinced it wasn't—maybe they didn't care. Perhaps to them, it was like a sadistic kid who killed the guinea pig. As the fingers thrust into my skin, I had one last thought. My husband's smile.

But oblivion didn't come.

It happened so fast I didn't even have time to react. The pressure on my face faded away. The suffering too.

Absolute darkness surrounded me, but I was still conscious. And alone. I tried to wipe the blood from my face, but my fingertips found none. A voice filled the space as if coming from everywhere at the same time, "We observe/analyse/intervene."

Malalaya's Kin hadn't spoken to me since my third day in this room when they'd explained docility would stop the Pain. I recognised the disembodied quality, unable to guess if one or several talked simultaneously.

"This course of events is disturbing/dissatisfying/disappointing. The implications for Malalaya's future/rectification/cure need to be contemplated/explored/assessed."

I dreaded they'd inflict the Pain. But instead, I perceived feelings even if they were not voiced. Annoyance at having to deal with the situation. Sadness it had come down to that. Compassion towards me, in a detached way, but it was there.

"What will happen to me?" I asked.

They'd made no mention of me, my role and my future. And here I was thinking in threes, like them.

"We learn/improve/provide."

A light breeze caressed my skin, enveloping me for a few brief seconds before a dim grey light gradually dawned around me. I was surprised to find myself in a different room, minuscule and completely bare. I should have felt trapped, but instead felt protected. Nothing seemed to be able to get to me here. No Malalaya, no Pain.

They'd volunteered little, but it was no use trying to talk to them. I shrugged because I couldn't make myself care. The safety provided by this small space made the rest inconsequential. No matter what awaited me, it couldn't be worse than what I'd just left. If a sliver a doubt crept into my mind, I made it fizzle out. I was content just waiting.

Without warning, the light went out again. This time a stronger wind blew, although as brief as before. I opened my eyes to a large space, much bigger than the one I used to occupy. The human quarters took up a greater portion and looked nothing like mine. Shelves burst out with books. Plush armchairs surrounded an elegant coffee table. A bed at least twice the size of mine caught my eyes. I spotted a TV, a game console, sound speakers, to say nothing of the deep bathtub. I'd have killed for a hot bath.

I trailed my fingers along the spines of the books as I took everything in. I didn't dare to open the drawers to see what treasures they held. I couldn't bear to invade the privacy of another. For all the extreme tidiness and cleanliness of those quarters, they belonged to someone.

An open book had been forgotten spine up on a side table near an armchair. From where I stood it seemed to be a door-stopper. He or she must be quite the reader. Padding forwards, I peeked at the title nestled in the crease in the spine. "Crime and Punishment."

That was when I noticed a folded piece of paper on a pillow. I'd have left it where it lay except for the fact my name spread across it in my own hand. I took a deep breath against the eerie sensation gripping me and picked up the note, unfolding it carefully.

"Welcome to your new home

I'm Lususuna

I think two days alone will be enough to acclimate to your new environment

If not, write on the board to let me know

Should you need anything for your comfort, don't hesitate to use the board

I can't wait to meet you."

A new home? These books were mine? The bed, the bathtub? It sounded too good to be true. I glanced around and found the board on the wall.

More important than material possessions, I had a new owner, one willing to give me time to myself. However, of greatest significance was her gift of something I hadn't known for so long.

A choice. Multiple ones even.

"If you need anything," the note said. How far could it go? On the small ledge at the bottom of the board, I found a stylus. I tapped the object against my cheek in thought and finally wrote with care, "Can I have some chocolate ice cream, please?"

"Of course."

The words flashed briefly on the board in my hand, but it didn't feel as unsettling as reading the note. When they faded away a white bowl with two scoops appeared on the coffee table complete with a silver spoon.

That easy... I took a bite, closed my eyes, and moaned in pleasure. I placed the bowl back on the table and walked back to the board. Ice cream was good, but I had more essential needs.

"Can I have a window, please?"

I hastily added before the request could be granted, "No frosted glass."

Then I scribbled another "please."

"Of course," appeared again.

I held my breath as I watched the words fade. A large window materialised, its panes so transparent they might as well have not been there. A giant red sun was disappearing behind three rugged peaks in the distance. Two bright spots already shined in the dusk. Were those stars or other planets in this system? Still faint against the purple sky, a myriad of dots was scattered across the heavens, a promise of starry wonders to come.

I watched the night fall. The darkness engulfed the expanse of land that stretched in the direction of the mountains before I could make sense of the shapes inhabiting it. Mineral, animal, vegetal, or none of the above. For tonight, it didn't matter.

I spent the next day indulging, ordering all the food I'd craved. I soaked in the tub for hours. I slept. I selected a stack of books for later perusal but didn't play any video or music. I enjoyed the silence too much to spoil it with anything more than muffled sounds.

All that had happened in the last few days, in the last few months, started to feel unreal. A respite was welcome. I wouldn't have been able to face an offspring right away. This thoughtfulness from Lususuna hopefully boded well.

Surrounded by all those reminders of the past, I didn't want to think about him. He was gone. Here and now it seemed I might have something for myself, something bearable.

On the second day, I searched every inch of my new quarters but to my disappointment found no vestiges left behind. No carving on any piece of furniture, no writing in the margins of books or tucked away between two pages.

Maybe it was a good sign.

When sunset came, the last thing I wanted was for my seclusion to end. After hours spent watching out of my window, I still didn't know what to make of the strange shapes. The room was perched too high to distinguish details, but I was satisfied just to continue drinking in the sky for now.

Later, I picked up "Crime and punishment." I hadn't touched the book before now. It had felt like intruding on somebody else. Also, Russian literature never appealed to me. Too long, slow, and tortured. But as I sat back into the welcoming armchair, I decided to give it a try since it was obviously somebody's favourite.

It started better than expected, but something strange became quickly distracting. At first, there were only one or two every page. They looked like small stains, and I hardly gave them a second thought. But the frequency increased.

There were tiny black dots, almost imperceptible, under some of the letters. So many it had to be deliberate. Was that it? The link I'd been looking for?

The letters on the page I was reading, assuming they went from left to right, and top to bottom, formed:

pymemor

Not much of a word.

ycans was the word on the following page.

egoodhap the one on the previous one.

I wrote the three words on a piece of paper.

Egoodhap pymemor ycans

I wrote them again, linking them all together this time.

egoodhappymemorycans

Aha, I saw them now. Words in the chain of letters. In the case of these three pages: "e good happy memory can s." The e was the last letter of a word starting on a previous page. The s the first letter of one continuing on a following one. Fairly simple.

I went back to the beginning of the book and started reading the message between the lines. Identifying the words proved more difficult than I expected. The lack of punctuation or capital letters didn't help. However, the absence of contractions simplified the task somewhat.

The message was meant to stay hidden, so I didn't write more of it down.

"My name is James Williams from Oxford UK. I am forty-five, divorced. One kid, Vanessa. I teach philosophy. I love Locke, Sartre, fishing, and tennis. In this new world, do all those things still define me? The man I used to be feels like a mental construct now, but I know one good memory can sustain you for a long time…"

He called his offspring "it"—when he wrote about her, which wasn't often—and never used her name. He'd spent at least two years with his offspring, met all the other humans, explored outside. He seemed satisfied with his lot, but the text felt guarded.

"Rebecca," a voice said softly.

I dropped the book and scurried away, putting the

armchair between me and the apparition.

"I didn't mean to startle you. I'm Lususuna."

Of course she was, but in my panic, I saw Malalaya come to torture me again. Even now looking into her large eyes, I still didn't see the difference between their alien faces.

"Two days weren't enough," she said, "I'll leave you now."

I was alone again, and grateful for it. The paradigm shift gave me vertigo. She saw to my comfort both material and emotional. I'd seen proofs of it before, in the setting, in the possibility to make requests, but I hadn't really believed it. My doubts started to dissolve in this newfound kindness, and a hope I'd thought dead had just hatched.

Perhaps all would be well, and I was no longer doomed among the damned. It wouldn't be the life I wanted or was supposed to live, but it'd be a life.

Lususuna left me after another long day outside. I'd been her companion for three weeks now. That was how I called myself now, companion. Not pet.

With a sigh, I sunk into my favourite armchair. I'd order my food in a moment. "Crime and punishment" still lay on the side table next to me. I hadn't had time to finish it yet. James' story that was. I got better at deciphering it, but after a while, it started running in circles. I didn't know most of the authors he referenced. Besides, the need for a link wasn't as strong as it used to be.

I picked up the book, found my place and started reading. I wasn't that far from where the dots stopped. It was more of the same, but then I read:

"This book is the only way I found to record my thoughts without It reading them. It has invariably searched my things looking for writings and found everything I tried to hide. It uses…my own thoughts to find new underhanded ways to torment me. I think this book has escaped its notice so far. My time has run out. It said It needs the room for another. I will be removed once I tidy up. I can only speculate what removed means. Do not trust the façade. Under the veneer, there is only rot."

I rushed to decipher the last words, then hurled the book wishing I could just annihilate it mid-flight.

"Stupid, naive, idiot," I screamed at myself.

Maybe the cage shone brighter, but I was still trapped in the same cold hell, only worse because of the mirage of hope.

James' last words echoed in the silence, "You are nothing, a mere toy to be tortured in endless new ways. Farewell."

CAROLE DE MONCLIN travels both the real world and imaginary ones.

She's lived in France, Australia, and the USA; visited 25+ countries; and explored Mars, Ceres, and many distant planets.

She writes to invite people on a journey.

Stories have found her for as long as she can remember, be it in a cave in Victoria, the smile of a baby in Paris, or a museum in Florida.

She thought writing would be a solitary adventure. She couldn't have been more wrong. Along the way, she met amazing writers in Australia and the USA. She's very thankful for their help and support. This story wouldn't be what it is without them.

Bibliography
ANGELS, Black Hare Press, 2019
BEYOND, Black Hare Press, 2019
Deep Space, Black Hare Press, 2019
MONSTERS, Black Hare Press, 2019
WORLDS, Black Hare Press, 2019

Connect
Website: CaroledeMonclin.com
Amazon: amazon.com/-/e/B07SW7DNP5

UNBEKNOWNST
By K.R. Monin

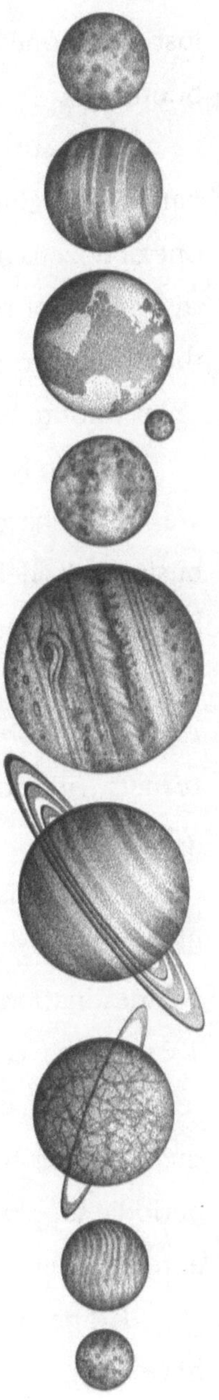

Earth is disintegrating, but Sirja was never able to call the planet home. A translator on the only exploratory spacecraft funded by a reality TV show, she dodges the constant cameras while her crewmates grind the gossip gears. Sirja, however, spends the one-way trip piecing together the secret of their destination, finding more than the answer to her life-long search for belonging.

"They say we have enough raw materials to land on a new planet and found a sustainable town the size of Ligonier, Pennsylvania, in less than five years. Because of course, we all know how big that is." Calvert winks at no one in particular. The small town he's just mentioned is about to experience an economic boom.

"And, cut!" Akeeno, our ship's superfluously titled narrative engineer, strikes the nearest livestream sensor, one of dozens on the ship. The strings of red lights lining the ceiling of the corridor fade. I sense tension leaving the bodies on board now Earth no longer can see us. "You want to be in the next scene, Sirja?" he asks.

Captain Keeylah would want me to, despite the fact we both share disdainful opinions of this mission's business model. I shake my head. I signed up to find a home on a planet that isn't disintegrating, not become famous among the human masses. *There are thousands of space companies looking to find new home planets…why did I commit to the one funded by a reality TV series?*

Our ship is stocked with seeds and pairs of animals like the Ark of old, but we know next to nothing about our destination. As an extra incentive to produce good TV on this one-way trip, the network continues to remind our Captain—and she continues to remind us— the higher ratings, the more money will flow to our periodic supply shipments. Leave it to humans to expect entertainment to save them.

"Come on," Akeeno presses me. "Do the scene. I have a great idea for a narrative arc where you wake up from pod hibernation and you can't get this dream out of your head. The only good listener aboard is Calvert, so you tell him—"

Calvert cuts him off when my stony expression doesn't change. "Do you think you're too good for it, or not good enough?" he asks me.

"Neither, thank you." I stand to leave before the scenario evolves into more fodder for Earth's number one show. I don't trust that the cameras are ever truly disabled. If I were running this ship, they would be set to Constant Capture, with background AI feeding Akeeno the steamiest, most conflict-ridden footage. He'd do anything to win an award for the first reality show in space. I've spent most of this trip safe-guarding my secrets from cheap exposure. *But would it be a relief for Earth-dwellers to finally recognise I am not one of them?* I wonder.

History says no, it would be deadly.

I find a new window seat to resume my studies, an ancient language text draped across my lap, but I can't shake the silent distraction of millions of prying eyes potentially staring at me. I've never considered myself vain, but I'm suddenly so aware of every mole, every ounce of fat, every stray hair and every unsightly sneeze. Even when I stare out the window, trying to lose myself in the darkness between pinpricks, I catch myself staring at my own reflection. I've caught many of my crewmates doing the same. After space swallowed the azure seas and golden rim of Earth, most of us are looking at ourselves instead of the stars.

I close my eyes, trying to imagine what's waiting for us at the end of this long voyage. Even with the clues I've found scattered across Earth's most ancient records, written in stone and in dark, secret places, it's difficult to imagine what we will find. It's more difficult to imagine how I will be received—not to mention this ship full of fame-drunk humans.

Calvert, plops down next to me, so close and so sudden he jostles the tome from my lap and onto the floor. Our ships star, pun intended, has become too comfortable due to my crewmates' invitations to invade their personal space. "You'll warm up to being on TV, Sirja, don't worry." He settles his arm around me. Akeeno is leaning against the wall, staring at his nails as if they'd caught up some dirt, though I doubt he's ventured into the agricultural bay for some time. His vest glints with another camera lens.

A strong reaction will only encourage them, so I sigh and lean over to scoop up my fallen text, wishing we were funded by a public trust or philanthropic billionaire. But this mission is too far-fetched for such entities. "Remember, it's a one-way trip," Calvert continues to cajole. "Have you ever gone skinny dipping? Cheated? Had a little too much fun in a cantina? There must be something you've always wanted to share with the world when you'd suffer little or no consequences."

I remain silent. The surest way to discourage them is to remain boring. Last time they cornered me, I launched into a monotone recount of my academic achievements.

But his nagging is starting to wear off on me. The daughter of generations of secrets, this desire for publicity is foreign. I remind myself again that the simplistic empathy and shallow affirmation from millions of faceless humans will accomplish nothing.

My brother, Elias, learned less than a century ago that a spilled secret means a slit throat to our kind. I thought we would live our centuries-long lives together, waiting for a quiet death—the end of our lives and, possibly, the end of our race and its secrets. But when I was barely an adult, I felt his death from our home in Stockholm. I experienced his torment first hand, through the mental-emotional link shared by everyone of Marman descent. His last thoughts were incoherent, shredded by fear, before he flickered and flashed out like an exploding bulb. He'd been in the U.S., I found out later, near their capital. He must have told their government about his dream—the same dream I started to have a few years later.

"See?" Calvert is pulling me into his sweating armpit, the scent of his intoxicating cologne still heavy around me. "You're so far away, your mind's caught on that secret right now, isn't it?"

I stand, letting his arm fall back against the glass. I imagine him tipping backwards, out into the breathless expanse of space, never to annoy anyone again.

"We've got a long voyage ahead," I say. "I'll process it and we can add it to your script, okay?" I look at Akeeno, who nods with child-like eagerness. Here, there is nowhere to hide except in a lie, and I'll need some time to spin one.

But I won't make the same mistake, I promise Elias' soul, drifting somewhere past the distant stars outside. *I won't trust a single human, even if it means bearing the weight of our secret forever.*

"You know," the filmmaker says as he adjusts his equipment vest. "If you gave me access to your Chiron, I could get some good inspiration, find an arc that fits you naturally."

I resist the urge to cup a protective hand over the device on my temple. One of humanity's more recent inventions, Chiron clips to the skull to translate the firing of synapses into transmittable signals. If I give my crewmembers' counterpart devices access to my own, we would share an intuitive-seeming connection, the ability to sense each other's primal emotions. The connection is ideal for quick, nonverbal commands needed to run the ship, but the experience is hauntingly similar to the telepathic link shared by Marman descendants. I resist most requests to access my Chiron, including this one. "I'll let you know."

I collect my things to leave the crew's lounge as Akeeno launches into improvising another scene. He snags his next victim easily, a female crewmember who's likely been lurking, hoping she'd be asked. "Dr. Locklear, just sit there and say whatever comes to you, like you're telling Calvert a secret—or let him tell you one!"

The red livestream lights come on overhead. "Oh, Doctor," Calvert is smooth as pomade in front of the camera. "I just love when shooting stars fly by. I hope they make kids back home think of us, like a little flash of hope. Space is beautiful. Also, I don't think I've had the chance to tell you, *you're* beautiful."

The doctor, some Johns Hopkins hussy, is devouring his knavish grin. "Thanks, I hope the lifeforms at our destination are genetically compatible so I can find an equally attractive match." She's playing hard to get, hoping for more screen time. Even when you can't hear the roar of the crowd, fame is more addictive than any drug.

Calvert doesn't miss the opportunity to pump his own ego. "I'm sure you'll find a few lookers. If not, I'm sure your offspring well. We'll have a handful of handsome spacelings after a few generations of my genes." Akeeno must have scripted that line for him.

I turn my back, disgusted. To them, this is their big break in entertainment. To me and the other seven crewmembers, this is a dark horse bid to save our respective races.

The automatic bay doors ahead of me slide open, and I nearly collide with Captain Keelah. I'd been too preoccupied to recognise her Chiron signal approaching, but she understood mine too clearly. She gestures for me to follow her back into the corridor and I oblige, letting the doors slide shut to block out the red livestream lights glowing in the crew's lounge behind us.

"I can't tell from your signals whether you want to mack on him or murder him," she says. She's one of the few crewmembers I've allowed to access my neurotransmitter.

I know she means Calvert. "If it were the latter, we could rip some of these gaudy panels off the walls," I point out. Most ships are designed with a utilitarian philosophy, but ours is polished to appear more aesthetic. The garish lights and gleaming surfaces match humanity's sleek, romantic vision of the future—creating many inconveniences for our crew. Every detail of this mission is oriented towards one priority: keeping the love and money from our Earthly patrons flowing.

"We're on time, on target, and once we land we might even get some Heineken in our first supply shipment," she reassures me, though I know from our Chiron transmission she shares my sentiments. I know Keeylah can sense my unease about our telepathic Chiron connection, but doubt she will press me on its sources. In truth, this sharing of emotional signals is the closest I've felt to kinship since Elias' death. Centuries of secrecy and infighting drove our secret Marman communities apart. After our parent's death, he was the last Marman I knew.

The signals I am receiving from Keeylah match the general attitude of severity she exudes, one that is embodied in her gaze. I've concluded from the points of her boots and her bright gele she's adopted intimidation as her brand.

I like her. But I don't trust her. *I can't trust her. She's human.*

"If you want more viewers, both death and love would get screen time," I point out.

"At first," she smiles, a genuine expression Chiron

informs me to be a mask. "But I want those beers, Sirja. And I want to survive. We can't run the show or the ship without Calvert. I need you to keep him happy. And yes," she agrees, translating my incensed reaction. "I wish our courage and noble mission was enough. But we must sell ourselves every step of the way. Did you join this ship in search of comfort or greatness?" She nods, accepting my nonverbal answer. "Good. Don't jeopardise us."

I sigh. "What kind of world mandates A-list sex appeal, an inflated story arc, and an aesthetic setting to make saving humanity worthwhile?"

"A world weaned on beautiful white heroes and happy endings." This time, the shallow nature of her smile is betrayed on her face. "Let's go, we need you in the receiving room. We have just received a message from the same source as the original signal."

I take a long breath, my hope finally feeling concrete once again.

She motions in the direction we must take, back through the crew's lounge. "Don't say anything to them. Once we know what the message says, we'll frame it for filming."

As we pick our way through the unfolding scene, I force my features not to react to Calvert's semi-scripted remarks. "Half the success of this mission will be colonisation! You know, I was looking at the inventory request for the next supply launch, and I didn't see condoms mentioned."

The receiving room is dark, open on nearly every side to the star-spattered void. I am struck by it for a moment. I often struggle to contemplate space. Its void is greater than the godless holes in our hearts—a sensation all humans should experience when they look up and remember celestial beings are not coming to save them from the ruin they inflicted on Earth's atmosphere.

"Here, Sirja." Keeylah's voice draws me back into the receiving room. Colourless glows emanate from countless screens. Digits, graphs, and holograms lurk wherever they fit, vanishing and reappearing across arms, walls, windows, or anywhere they can be projected. Our captain is indicating the only blank surface available, the floor. She flicks her wrist like she's casting a spell. A flowing script snakes across, just missing the toes of my boots. The two crewmembers present, our physicist and our navigator, step back with habitual urgency. The navigator's Chiron signal, one of the few currently tuned to mine, is abuzz with activity. I can barely guess at the nature of her tasks, how she's broken down this complex scientific mission into something manageable and viable.

But my presence changes her. The current of activity in her brain slows until her attention swirls around me, thirsty for new information. As the ship's anthropologist and translator, this is my duty. When an amateur space station received the first transmission, I was the only linguist on Earth able to translate the coordinates it contained. The information was written off as risky at best and a hoax at worst by many national entities. Only a small, private production company took interest—and here we are. Though my identity is unbeknownst to the humans, those who are not starstruck recognise me as the reason this ship took off, the reason we might find a new, habitable planet.

I maintain that I can decode the cryptic messages we receive due to my lifelong study of ancient dialects. The reverse is true. I first learned to read and write with these symbols, as many men did centuries ago. From dusty graffiti beneath volcanic ash and painstakingly preserved papyrus, all the way up to social media posts, Marman glyphs are the root of all written human language. My ancestors also taught humans how to put stones on top of one another, and how to design waterways and agricultural systems. Without the evolutionary jumpstart, humans might still be in the trees.

"Is it a reply to our previous message?" the physicist asks, her question a hiss like she knows she's interrupting.

I shake my head. It's the truth, though I had not shared in full what my last digital transmission to Marma had been. It mirrored the one I stretched out in my dreams. *We are coming. We have launched a small ship, with shipments of supplies to follow. I am the only Marman.*

The last phrase of my message hangs on me, the full weight of my secret. *I am alone.* I've studied ancient texts and cultures, looking for others like me, looking for hints of the world I might call home. But for all my secrets, I barely know more about Marma than the humans aboard.

I let a few moments hang, studying the glyphs on the floor as if I'm still trying to decipher them. I'm no attention whore, no Calvert, but I can't let this appear too easy.

At last I say, "This message is vague, but it's welcoming. Their lack of suspicion indicates maybe we will not be the first foreign vessel to land there. We should reach out again. We're still so far out, we may even receive a reply before we come into orbit."

"But what does it say *exactly*," Keeylah presses me. She's flexing her fingers like she's been gripping something heavy. Perhaps she wants to touch her gun.

"There's no exact translation, I'd be making assumptions," I say, an attempt to keep from lying more than I have to. In truth, the closest translation of the message reads: *Come home, daughter. You are greatly needed. You are part of the dawn of prosperity.*

I release a heavy breath. The emotional signals of longing, confusion, wonder, and fear must be emanating from my Chiron device. At least these are authentic, hardly suspicious. Keeylah's signals do not indicate she suspects anything. I feel no guilt next to my secret. These women and the other crewmembers accepted the danger in this mission when they signed their contracts. We are bound together by a tiny slice of hope, a bond reinforced by Chiron. This, I imagine, is only a taste of what community is like on Marma.

When I return to the glamorised corridor, I sense Keeylah's intensity behind me. I turn to see her following. Though I performed the correct protocol before stepping back into the livestream area, her long, dark finger beckons me back into a secure conference room. *Does she suspect?* I follow her into the room.

She motions for the glass door to shut just as I notice Akeeno approaching, his step light in the reduced gravity. Either he's patrolling to collect B-roll with his camera-decked vest, or he is prying to see if Keeylah had summoned me for disciplinary action. I try to signal for the glass to frost and give us some privacy, but nothing happens. I'm not sure how to ask my commanding officer to keep this short. If she sees him, she gives no indication.

"Were you feeling anxious, Sirja?" her voice is level, as if she could overcome any scenario with only her presence. "I sensed you were uneasy just then."

"I think we all are." I try to keep my emotions level so Chiron won't betray me. "We have a lot on our shoulders."

"I wanted to say," Keeylah's gaze holds mine, "I think you're doing really well. I know you loved the sense of community in that moment. I did, too. Everyone needs community, especially out here. I know I barely had community on Earth, and I think you were the same. Don't feel the need to explain anything to me, or to anyone. But don't feel the need to keep secrets, either."

I'm not sure how to speak past the nodule in my throat. "I don't have much experience responding to comments like this," I nearly apologise. My first instinct is to resist her, to resist vulnerability.

"There's no need," she says.

She must sense my inner turmoil. *I'm going home,* I tell myself. *Do not risk trusting a human now. They're waiting for you on Marma.*

But I don't know Marma. I have no idea what it will be like, whether I will be welcomed or treated like an outcast. I've grown up on Earth, surrounded by humans who perceived me as young due to my slow ageing. Next to humans, the Marman of old were god-like geniuses. *Should I stand next to a true Marman, would I seem slow and stupid, like a human?*

I smother my vulnerability and look my captain in the eye, offering as honest an answer as I dare. "I've never felt at home," I say. "I'm not sure I will ever be able to find one, even when we land."

"I understand." Her embrace is business-like, but genuine. "We will have to make one. Together."

I want to push her away, to resist a gesture I don't know how to receive, but Akeeno is still standing on the other side of the glass door. When Keeylah looks up to follow my gaze, he retreats. Chiron projects her disdain. "Perhaps if we were rivals, it would better match his narrative."

At the end of our shift, the crew sets the ship for hyperspeed and we prepare for hibernation.

There's something abnormally calm about the violet light in the suspension room. Human-sized pods like polished eggs line the walls. I ignore Calvert, who's artfully removing his clothing to the giddy joy of the doctor and the agricultural engineer further down—not to mention half the population of Earth.

I slip off my own jumpsuit and fold it loosely next to my pod. I press Chiron and feel the gentle release of pressure like escaping steam as its needles retract and the device relaxes away from my skull. I click it to the outside of my pod, which lifts open like a hatch. Within the hour, all ten of us will have exercised the same routine, our bodies resting as the ship catapults us closer to our destination.

The water doesn't quite feel warm, but it isn't cool. Sensors in the pod are picking up my body temperature, adjusting to match. When all but my narrow nose is submerged in the saline solution, the hatch of the pod descends with a gentle hiss. For an immeasurable moment, I am nearly nothing. I feel, hear, see, smell, nothing, but I know gas is filling the empty space in my pod to put me under.

Just before I dive into unconsciousness, I sense a presence.

Is there someone near this tank, on this ship, sharing a telepathic connection? Without Chiron or the confines of my body, my mind is free to roam and look for others. I am not alone. *Could I be mistaken?*

I slip into a dream more vivid than my memories, the same dream I have been having since Elias' death. The places change, but the words are the same.

I'm standing in a cave, the sound of the tide gradually smothering the exit, the indigenous people shouting as they pull their boats up from the waves. Sand and broken shells bite the soles of my feet. I'm staring at the message smeared onto the wall. Only I notice the script buried in the shorthand of countless signals and stories left by the native tribe. This is a place from my past, one of the many locations I've discovered over the course of my long life, where Marman glyphs are preserved. When I first read this message, it was one of welcome, a hailing to a god. Now, in my dream, the message is quite different.

The dream changes. I'm crouched in a cavernous hallway inside a temple south of the Equator, columns disappearing past me in either direction, devouring both vanishing points. Only when I stand in a certain spot and achieve a certain vantage can I see the glyphs I decoded once before, though they, too, are different in my dream.

I'm huddled in a tunnel in a remote, Northern tundra, reading words inscribed with animal blood.

I'm daring to touch hieroglyphics in a tomb.

I've found a mural in a hidden pocket at the base of a mesa.

In my dream, each message from every place I

remember now reads the same. *We are calling you home, daughter. Come, bring prosperity.*

I wake from the dream. I stretch my face upwards and take a breath, as much air as I can suck in from the humid atmosphere. The dream shakes me. When it had been Elias who experienced it, he tried to convey to me its urgency, the great sense of purpose it gave him. "The Marman are communicating with me. We need to do something, to reach them somehow!" But even with our emotional connection, I never understood until I felt it myself. Only when I began to have the dream did I begin to forgive the brashness that got him killed. The pod does not open right away. The others must still be in hibernation. "How early did I wake?" I ask the pod.

Less than five minutes, it chirps in an androgynous tone, reading the countdown on the wall in the suspension room beyond.

I could leave the pod's confines and dress first, but I take the spare moments to calm myself instead. I close my eyes despite the pressing dark. Part of me curses my Marman relatives for their enigmatic nature. *I don't want to guess anymore. I don't want to keep secrets. I don't want to masquerade, I don't want to hide. I need the truth.*

I resolve, once more, to wait. *I cannot trust the humans.*

I wish Elias were here. He'd reassure me of the things I told myself but couldn't believe. *All things happen for a purpose*, he would say. *In some way, all humans are good.* I wonder what he would say now, after they killed him, after I had to change my name and leave our home, smothered by secrecy.

As my body stews in the salt of the pod, my heart and mind stew in bitterness for humans. In a way, after our race helped shape and build their early world, it does seem they owe us a debt.

I signal to the pod that I am ready. I can rise and dress before the cameras turn on. I'm an old soul, more than a century and a half, and have not adapted to the past few decades' fondness for nudity. I take a moment to savour the silence of the violet room as every other pod continues to sleep. Beyond my own heartbeat, the only sound I sense is the faint hum of the sleep-inducing machines. I wonder what true silence is, out there in the void of space.

But this room is not a void. I am not alone. Just as I reach for the Chiron device still linked to my pod, I feel someone once more. From the opposite end of the room I sense longing, different from my own. The emptiness is filled with a pain I've only associated with death. But this soul doesn't hurt for death—it hurts for love, having never known it.

As I focus on it, the telepathic link becomes stronger, much clearer than any formed by Chiron. *A Marman?*

The room's floral hues make it difficult to distinguish, but I see the last pod near the door is open. On the wall above, the clock, its bright numbers meant to countdown the time until our next shift, races towards zero. Days and minutes have passed—there are only seconds left. I approach the pod, droplets crawling down my legs, jumpsuit in one hand, towel and modesty forgotten.

While I'm several meters away, a spiky, dripping head pokes from beneath the lid of the pod like a mammal emerging from its hole. "Akeeno? Are you there?" Calvert calls.

Over the next few phases of our shift, I look for a way to confront Calvert, a task made impossible by the omnipresent cameras. I don't dare approach him in a setting as casual as the mess or crew's lounge. These spaces are always a flurry of activity, and Akeeno is constantly hovering while my intimacy-starved crewmates bid for their turn in the spotlight.

I could join the mob of hopefuls, I realise, but I don't like to imagine the wonderful new story arc material

Akeeno would glean from my interest.

But our ship is small. My hovering and staring betray me before I can develop a strategy.

I look up during a meal and realise Calvert is coming at me between the glistening rows of benches and tables. His little cohort scurries to match his stride. He slides onto the seat next to me and spits some of his semi-scripted wit. "Hello Sirja, I've seen your side-eye recently. What made you warm up?" Akeeno stops in front of me. I stare straight into the camera mounted on his chest, a dark cyclops betraying my face to countless eyes countless kilometres away. Overhead, the livestream lights glow scarlet. I wonder if one of the crew struck one of the random sensors when they saw the conflict unfolding, or if Akeeno and Calvert planned this ambush. I feel naked.

My first instinct is to limit the violations to my privacy. Though few can access my channel, I reach up and remove Chiron.

Nearly the whole ship is watching. This is quickly becoming more than a confrontation. It's everything they want. Romance, conflict, drama. "Oh, I guess you'd rather put into words how you feel?" Calvert coaxes. "There's no need to be shy, it's not like you're the only one. There's *literally* a club you can join!"

For a moment, his smile is so wide and genuine I

can't help but wonder, *Did he sense it too, outside the pods? Does he know we're both Marman?* But if he does, he wouldn't try to address me like this. *But maybe he has no other way,* I realise. *He's been carrying the same secret in plain sight—in the spotlight.*

"Another time," I attempt to diffuse. I wish he would remove his Chiron so I could send him a mental signal. The device appears to be blocking out natural connection.

He leans in like he's going to tell me a secret. My instinct is to take a step back, to tell him he's crazy to try to talk about it in front of the crew, in front of the entirety of humanity. So close, I notice how clean his teeth are, how his breath smells of cinnamon candy. When he grabs my hand, the sweet spice sinks into my skin. His sultry tone can be heard by half the people and all of the microphones in the room. "Why later? We've got time."

My slap sends the hard candy he'd been sucking flying from his mouth and snapping off Akeeno's camera lens. The discipline alarm screams before Calvert can figure out what happened to his face. Someone, I think the doctor, Locklear, snags me by both arms. The room is full of confusion. Akeeno has already found and flourished a napkin to Calvert's red cheek. Our star looks horrified, staring at his filmmaker, eyes begging, *Was that live?*

I half hope and half fear it was. If I were a bystander I would have savoured the moment, but deep down I'm shaken. *What's he going to do to me?* His presumption and the blasé tone he had used spoke of power he had no qualms asserting.

Keeylah appears. She looks at me, then Calvert, and turns to leave without a word. Though Chiron is still clutched in my hand, I understand the command to follow. "Disengage all cameras," she orders over her shoulder. Akeeno cowers and obeys as the door grinds closed behind us.

In the corridor, Keeylah removes her Chiron and meets us both with her steel gaze. Calvert removes his device as well, pivoting his gaze between us as though he's uncertain what to expect. With both our devices disabled, I can sense his consciousness, but he's too much in shock to realise mine. He's desperate, an empty hole that cannot be filled—even by millions of expressions of devotion. *That's why he's on this mission to save the humans*, I realised. *He needs their love.*

"Out there," Keeylah says with an intonation that implies she could rip us apart, but chooses not to, "you keep up your masquerade. Pretend it's a lover's quarrel, it's a rivalry, whatever his writer says." She points at Calvert. "But when the cameras are off, you shake hands. You keep your shit together. You keep this ship moving. Understand?"

I give her a single affirmative nod. Calvert doesn't move. I once more resolve to find a way to pin him in a corner.

I force my way through the last three Earth days of the shift. I've lived as long as a biblical patriarch—such a short span should seem trivial, but it feels as though every step leads me through a maze of unseen judgement, harsh glances, and uncomfortable banter.

My slap, it seemed, had been broadcast.

Akeeno is playing the scene off as the finale for this season of the series. The next season will feature my "tell-all" as its first episode, to be filmed during our next shift. He gives me a fiendish grin every time we cross paths, swearing he won't drop hints about what he's putting in my script, trying to goad me into asking.

From the social chatter transmissions we receive, it seems a large portion of our audience back on Earth, mainly women, supports me. Others believe it was staged. Akeeno films a series of interviews as a teaser for the next season, trying to turn crewmembers against each other in a debate on the topic. I watch some of the filming unfold, but it's difficult to tell whose feelings are genuine.

I don't care about any of it—I don't care who is on my side, either onboard or on Earth. All this mess has only made it more difficult to get to Calvert.

Finally, I can take it no longer. When my chance to address him does not present itself, I create it. I can think of only one time when we are not wearing our Chiron devices: when we end our shifts and prepare to re-enter our pods.

Lucky for me, Calvert likes to linger outside and crawl in last, soaking up the moment to bid his adoring fans farewell. Before anyone else enters, I slip down the half-dry floor to his pod, the last one before the door. The egg-like capsule is smeared with cheeky lipstick stains like the tomb of a sex star. It's disgusting. Doctor Locklear should have been more thoroughly vetted. Or perhaps this is what the showrunners want.

A few moments later, I strip and take refuge in my own pod just as the first of my crewmates wander in to remove their clothes. I leave my lid ajar, floating in the treated water, careful to keep my ears above the surface. Even with the light commotion outside, the wet dark brings me dangerously close to a natural sleep.

Finally, all grows quiet. I sit up and hoist the lid of my pod open all the way. I hear a faint, frustrated struggle. A muffled curse. I sense a flood of frustration, raw and unfiltered in my brain, as if it were my own.

"Hey, my pod won't close?" He's shouting as he crouches on the rubber mat. "Come help?"

I all but slide down the aisle and catch him by the wrist as he reaches out to struggle with the container's latch, which I'd jammed. "Hey!" He sees my face and tries to wrestle his arm away, "Get off me!"

But I'm much more determined than he. I push him backwards and he stumbles into the unoccupied toilet behind him. I give him an extra shove then step inside and pull the door shut, engaging the lock.

He stares at me in horror like I'm about to force myself on him, but I am shameless, even in my pale nakedness. I see the recognition creep into his expression as he finally processes our mental connection, then my command for him to speak first.

"Yes, yes," he allows for some strange combination of shaking and nodding his head, breaking our eye contact. "Yes, I am Marman. I guess you are too. What of it? What good has it done me?"

"How old are you?" I ask.

"Not yet one hundred," he says, cracking his neck like he's comfortable with his youth. "But I'm sharp for my age. It wasn't easy, dropping into the entertainment world without a full social media backstory. I didn't know how long I'd be able to live in the spotlight until someone found an old picture of me on the internet and started to ask questions. I have a whole Doppelganger PR package ready, can you believe it? Plus, plastic surgeons work miracles these days, but I can't stay young and claim to be human forever. So I thought, hell with it all, let's take this one-way ticket to space, go out with a bang."

"Let's go home, you mean."

"Home?" I sense his sudden apprehension.

"Marma."

"That's where we're going?" He's not relieved. He's not celebrating. He's nervous. Guilty?

I nod.

He releases a breath and attempts to crack his neck again. His taut muscles and well-groomed chest arouse a physiological attraction. I smother it before he can sense.

"On Marma, we might make it," I say. "Not just you and I, but the humans too. Earth's atmosphere is so thin, the planet has less than a century left. At best." What I don't say is that I am becoming less and less inclined to save humanity, but it's certainly important to him.

"Helping with that issue does boost my popularity," he admits. I taste the longing in his heart again, a longing for devotion he can never satisfy. He's been filling that longing with sex and attention, but the pit grows deeper with every brush with satisfaction.

"Of course," I let my lip curl with sarcasm. "That's

our top priority." I don't ask what created this black hole in him. I don't care. He's wondering why I'm here, but he doesn't say it aloud. Perhaps he's not used to showing interest in other people. "I'm ready to finally be somewhere I belong," I say. "I just want to be at home and to be done with secrets. I don't need the credit for it, I don't care about standing out."

"Didn't seem like that the other day."

"You singled me out."

"And you dragged me naked into a bathroom. How's this going to look for you?"

I shake my head. "It won't matter. Once we reach Marma, I don't care what anyone thinks or knows. I've been looking for home for as long as I can remember. We're so close. We need to think about what we're going to do when we get there. We need to help the humans understand the Marman."

"Oh, so we're a team now?" I can tell he's sizing up the door behind me, wondering how difficult it would be to push past. "What makes you think I won't go flip the cameras on now and parrot your whole story to the world? I won't even put my pants on first."

"My brother was killed," I say.

"Why?" he challenges. His chin, its perfect stubble, is set with a resolve that says he knows his flaws and has destroyed his sense of shame long ago.

"Why? Because he was Marman! He told U.S. federal officials our race was calling us home. If you reveal anything before we land, we don't know how the others would react, or if they would turn around—"

He interrupts me with anger. "Why," he says with stressed pronunciation, "are they calling you home?"

"I'm not sure," I'm not ashamed to admit. "I'm worried they need help somehow. But so do humans. Perhaps we must help one another."

"They didn't call me for help. Why would they only signal to you? Or your brother? My parents were proud Marman. To be honest, I thought they were the last. We never heard a thing."

"I've looked for clues everywhere, in cave paintings, ancient texts, art and architecture. I've transcribed as much oral history and tradition as I could. I still don't understand them—us—but I will. As soon as I get home, I'm going to learn it all."

He's not sure how to answer, not sure how to compare his long life to my own.

"The cameras, the fame. There must be some way we can use them," I insist. "When we land, I want to tell the truth. We don't have to be alone, Calvert. I can send a message to the Marman through the receiving room next chance I get. I'll tell them you're here. We need as much support as possible. I'll say it out loud: I'm afraid.

I'm bridging worlds. I don't want to do it alone. Will you help me?"

"These people," he responds, thinking not just of the crew, but of the souls behind every watching lens. He keeps his gaze turned down at his bare toes, but I still read him. "They love me. I can't let them know I've been lying."

"But we *know* you," I insist. "We *understand* you."

He stands, slightly shorter than me, but sturdy, angry. "Bullshit."

He pushes past. I don't stop him, though our damp, warm flesh chafes as he forces his way back into the violet light.

"There he is!" My luck. Akeeno has not yet entered his pod. He must have been waiting just outside the door to disengage the live stream switch from the panel outside.

"No thank you!" Calvert yells back at me as he slams the toilet door, keeping up his charade. "You have to wait in line like everyone else!"

I open my eyes to dark. I try to remember the echoes of my dreams, the songs from my ancestors summoning me towards distant loved ones I've never met. I sit up and strike my head against the lid of the pod. It occurs to me only then that I have not drifted from an intentionally designed unconsciousness. The first time since I've entered the ship, I realise I am waking from natural sleep.

Sleep is deadly. Sleep only happens if the pods turn off, when the gas recedes and comas set in.

I fumble, command the pod to open, sensing a stillness unlikely from a ship hurtling through the stars.

I emerge to a room no longer coloured violet. The skylights above are open to streaming white light, as if we have already landed and are staring up through an atmosphere. The ship is quiet. I look down the length of the pods, all the way to the door. The countdown clock that predicts the start of our next shift is frozen, thirteen days, two hours, twelve minutes, four seconds and thirty-two milliseconds still left. Only one pod is open near the door. Not Calvert's. It might be Keeylah's, I can't quite remember the order.

I sense, once again, that I am not alone. I am not wearing Chiron. I slipped from my pod and zip my clammy skin into my jumpsuit. *Is anyone there?* I reach out with my senses and emotions.

"Hello?" I cry with my words. "Keeylah?" A figure appears. I sense confidence, an air of command. In one arm, the figure holds a bright, red gele.

Mind groggy from sleep, I realise there's a sound

wandering down the corridor, a message leaping and distorting across the puddles and smooth surfaces. Only one word is clear. "*Warning.*"

"Keeylah?" I call out again. The figure comes closer. Not Keeylah. The skin is too fair, the stance too easy, the shoulders too broad.

"Hello sister. My name is Iry-Hor. Welcome home." I've never heard the words aloud before, but I know them by instinct. The mystery figure is not a woman, I realise, but a man with a soft face, sweeping hair, and a gentle smile. His words reach me just after his emotions. His gratitude is overwhelming.

"Come, your brethren want to thank you. We are grateful for the seeds and stories on the ship you brought us," he says. His face is young, but greying curls ring his face. "We are most grateful for your gifts. This is a dawn of prosperity." When he reaches me, I let him wrap his arms around me in a hug tighter than the last embrace I shared with my brother. I share in his rush of joy as he leads me past the silent pods, but my own emotions are grey, queasy.

"You must forgive us, you're malnourished," he tells me. "As your ship came closer, we issued a program to put you all to sleep and drew you in. You've been out for so long; you must be ill."

"*Warning.*" I hear the sound again as we draw closer

to the sliver of synthetic light slicing across the floor, marking the partially open door. *"The ship has been breached. Warning. Report to your posts."*

He can sense my hesitation and grips my hand as if to dispel any suspicion. "Grateful," he says aloud again, but I stop him. We've reached the open pod. Placid bubbles creep to the otherwise still surface of the water within. Just above my knee, Keeylah's Chiron is still clipped to the pod, its normally blinking lights dark.

I look at Iry-Hor, whose eyes and mental signals betray nothing. "Where is she?" I ask.

"Your captain?" he replies, not to clarify, rather to accuse, as if I have been bowing down to a false goddess.

She's dead, I presume. I'm not certain how to process the realisation.

"We are grateful for the life you have brought us, sister. Our usual system of receiving resource tributes from settled planets was beginning to falter. We thought we'd have to send a collection committee soon. Anyone will admit, we expected Earth to pay off the least, considering the humans' slow rate of evolution. But you came through! Your ships and your following train of supplies will do wonders for our stores and crops, not to mention our morale. You are truly the fruit of your forefathers."

I step from the dim room and emerge into the

corridor amidst a burst of applause. Ageless faces, clean and beautiful, rush around me. I am greeted with warm embraces more sincere than I've ever felt. I put out my arm to hold them back, desperate for a breath. I'm caught, disoriented, my heart crushed between belonging and confusion. Iry-Hor speaks with a baritone that belies his build. "Take steps back, give her breath to make her own remarks."

"*Warning. Report to your posts.*" The alarm commands again. Following Iry-Hor's words the Marman fall back against the glass along the far side of the corridor. Outside, where I once saw the expanse of space, I now see foliage comprised of wide, waxy leaves in gorgeous shades of deep green.

Most of the Marman align in perfect rows, some still showering the air with their scattered applause. Off to one side, there is an awkward shuffle. They're making way around an obstacle at their feet like a fish parting around a stone.

It's not Keeylah, but Calvert who lies on the floor, his sculpted lips slack, tasting his own blood as it pools around his throat.

"*Warning. The ship has been breached.*"

Iry-Hor is behind me, hovering over my damp shoulder to whisper so that none of the others can hear. "He's no true son of the Marman. Maybe in his body, but not in his heart. Without us, humans would not be able to write, to remember, to reach the stars as they have. Think of them as little more than cattle. We do not need them the way he did."

My stomach churns, but I think of Elias. Trapped. Tortured. Murdered. Deep down, a part of me agrees with Iry-Hor.

Each of my brethren, I realise, is holding a knife, crude instruments of stone I've seen at museums and dig sites, tools they taught men to make. The Marman file past me into the suspension room, each taking a moment to look into my eyes, touch my hand, or stroke my hair in gratitude. I keep my post outside the door, my fingers only inches away from the control panel, my body surging with confusion. There are so many buttons I could press. Iry-Hor continues to speak to me in a voice meant to calm and soothe, but I am no longer focusing on his words. Despite my chosen convictions, I'm imagining how simple it would be, with a flick of my hand, to crush the next one, any of them, in the door as they enter the suspension room. *But they're my family. They're accepting me. Why do I still feel allegiance to the humans?*

I have no love for the inhabitants of Earth, not enough to join Calvert on the floor, facing a death far from home.

But Earth is not home.

The Marman move together, synchronised through their mental links. They reach for the emergency latches beside the blinking Chiron devices to open the pods, revealing my sleeping crewmembers. They raise their knives.

Is this what I meant to call home?

I brace myself for the slaughter.

I don't have a home. I've never had a home.

Keeylah's bare body lunges from the same bathroom where I'd hidden with Calvert. She wraps her hands around Iry-Hor's neck, fingers like claws.

I move to interfere, but stop. *Who should I save? Both? Neither?*

I should choose Iry-Hor, I realise. *The Marman won't spare Keeylah.* But I don't move. I take a step back. One Marman is racing forwards to save his brother, but I take a step forwards into his path. We collide. As we both struggle to rise, I hear Iry-Hor's neck snap.

In the next instant, stone knives descend upon Keeylah.

"Sirja!" With her dying words she screams my name. "Stop them! Save them!" Her cries shake me to my spine.

When the carnage is over and the last human is dead, my brethren close in on Iry-Hor's corpse, their pain tangible. I sink to my knees as well, resigned. Together, we mourn. I turn to my brother, the one I tripped, and beg his forgiveness for my clumsiness. He gives it. This is the last lie I will tell.

Each Marman places a finger on Iry-Hor's cooling skin. "Should we host a celebration in his honour?" One suggests. We all agree.

"We should wait several cycles and leave his body where it can be venerated," another adds. "Let's celebrate his life when the first supply shipment from Earth arrives."

We agree once more. I trust the Marmans. I am one of their own. I know they will love me, even when the shipment does not come.

I have done everything I can. I am not a soldier, or a spy, or a genius—either by Marman standards or human. I am both alone and not alone in this new world, a world that is both familiar and strange.

We hoist Iry-Hor's body, and I turn to take my first steps on Marman soil. Above us, the red lights of the livestream I initiated from the door panel glow with silent judgment. Perhaps Akeeno will receive his award posthumously.

I don't love humans, but I don't hate them. I leave them behind with two gifts: Keeylah's revenge and my truth.

K. R. MONIN writes near-future sci-fi and speculative fiction. She lives in Pittsburgh, identifies as a beer snob, and thrives on wanderlust.

Bibliography
ANGELS, Black Hare Press, 2019
Deep Space, Black Hare Press, 2019
MONSTERS, Black Hare Press, 2019
WORLDS, Black Hare Press, 2019

Connect
Twitter: @kunderscoremons
Website: krmonin.com

THE LUCKY ONE

By Gregg Cunningham

Conscripted to work on board the decommissioned USSS *MacGyver*, her colony's last hope for survival, Cadet Sydney Brown must overcome her tragic loss, and endure the extremities of cargo hauling in deep space, or suffer the same fate as her unlucky crew mates.

The prehistoric groaning from the rusting pipes inside the Deep Space Hauler *MacGyver* woke Sydney, signalling yet another crisis down in the ship's engine room. The tannoy alert would be next, followed by the alarm indicator on her wrist. If she were lucky, she would get another ten minutes lying on her bug-infested mattress, before she was called into action.

"All blue shift personnel report to their section Elders on B deck immediately." The ship's ageing tannoy system crackled, then repeated itself, followed by a high-pitched alert tone.

"Scrud it!" Sydney felt her wrist locator vibrate and it lit up brightly as she rolled the greasy pillow onto her face and screamed.

Another week like this and she would be fit for nothing but shovelling the Stalker shit in the cargo hold. And those cattle cats could pile the shit high. Real high.

"You hear that, Syd?" The static crackled on her wrist com and she sighed.

"Un-scruddin-fortunately, yes!" she replied with a yawn.

"Raincheck on the meet up tonight then?" the crackling voice responded.

"Sure, Vince. Just like last week, and the week before!"

"Drop by when you got a break then, Scrudwad!" Vince laughed, his voice fading out with another static crunch.

She reached down and grabbed her engineer boots, fumbling under her bunk in the blue glow of her wrist communicator as the *MacGyver* shuddered again, making another tight evasive manoeuvre.

"Stinking scrud suckin' Scrudders!" Sydney muttered under the tones of the tannoy as another shudder knocked her backwards onto her bunk.

This was the fourth attack by what remained of the Founders in as many shifts, and with no Raven escort frigates to protect the hauler back to the colony planet, it had become a game of cat and mouse.

Another twelve hours repairing fuel pipes with the cattle scrudders on B deck was just what she needed.

No wonder her father looked so old; he had been doing this kind of shit all his adult life. Sydney, on the other hand, had just been recruited from the colony last year when she turned sixteen.

One of the lucky ones, apparently.

Sydney tied up her boots and left the bunk for the next shift, with twelve hours of dripping fuel pipes in the dark tunnels in the bowels of the ship to look forward to.

She zipped up her boiler suit, then made the bed, softly smoothing out the creases and fluffing the pillows. Her father would be in from his shift soon, probably even more tired than she was. She pressed her bracelet up to the calorie dispenser and waited for the pills to fall into the tray, a selection of multi-coloured uppers designed to perk the body up for the shift ahead.

Sydney smiled and selected the red Dexiflex pill from the tray, placing it on the smooth, warm pillow, then swallowed the rest. It wasn't a chocolate love-heart wrapped in shiny foil like her father had told her they once put on the pillows on Earth, but a Dexiflex pill meant the same thing to her, letting her father know she was still thinking of him, and his arthritic pains.

Sixteen hours later, Sydney kicked off her damp work boots with a sigh. They fell to the thread-worn hessian carpet with two individual thuds, then rolled their separate ways under the bunk.

Another scruddy shift over.

Falling back onto the sagging flea-ridden mattress, exhausted, she pressed the dispenser button above the bed for her calories. It seemed the same routine for as long as Sydney could remember on the trip, the twelve-hour long shift within the rusting space tankers engine room, numbing her thoughts and dreams until they faded into one long monotonous journey into hell. The constant running repairs to the crumbling pipes, and the leaking hydraulic rods. The round-the-clock patching up of the panel damage from random attacks by the hit and run Corporation fighters as they tried to find a way to steal their precious livestock cargo.

The bed she fell back onto stank of her father's

sweat. As always, he had already vacated the small crew bunk by the time she returned, avoiding another of her many lectures of having his dry shower *before* he got into bed. She wouldn't complain about the journey, the bunk sharing, the tiny, dimly lit cramped quarters that only a few of the elders could acquire.

Others weren't so fortunate and had to use the barrack quarters. So at least they had one to share, and as she slowly unzipped her boiler suit, she soon forgot about his rank odour and began to wipe the dry skin from the exposed sheets onto the floor without so much as a sneer of contempt.

He gets my pills on his pillow, while I get his toe jam on my sheets!

The dull grey cell of a room stank of diesel, and the rusting orange walls ran wet with condensation. On the wall was a cork pinboard hanging askew, filled with photographs of a younger Sydney and her friends, happy and carefree under the hazy sun of the new colony's chosen planet, Big Red.

Good luck messages and *come back safe* drawings hung on scraps of paper next to fading pictures of smiling children.

One picture was framed, an image of her and Vince from red shift. They were smiling together in an embrace back on the Earth Moon just three weeks before the

Founders attacked Colony Hill. He was now just another friend she rarely saw these days due to the overrunning of the shift patterns. But they managed to talk on the communicators every now and then when the outdated communicators worked that is.

Sydney dialled in Vince's channel and left him a crackled message, then reset her blue shift bracelet on her wrist as her head hit the stained pillow.

"Enjoy your shift, Scrud-breath."

She watched the light flicker onto the leaky pipes along the low ceiling as she pulled up the tattered army issue brown blanket. The dim light cast long shadows over her bed and up to the cork pinboard that decorated the empty cramped cabin.

Apart from her photographs, she realised she had few possessions with her on this resupply trip. As she cast her exhausted gaze over the pictures above her discarded clothes that hung over the chair, her heavy eyes soon closed. And like the four nights before, she was asleep before the power ration timer could click off and plunge her into darkness. Even the battered calorie dispenser that allocated her the daily intake of rations was met with the silver catch tray and not Sydney's eager, grabbing, grubby hand.

The Elders in command of the *MacGyver* were pushing them hard and they knew the constant workload was beginning to take its toll on the weaker ones. The Founders, now just a remnant of a once great empire, were persistent, attacking in waves to weaken the hulking great Space Hauler convoy. They were relentless in their attack of the lumbering relics of the past that carried the 350 volunteers who had taken the journey from the Earth's first moon colony to find and trade for livestock to breed back on their new colony. But the ancient cargo vessels were taking more and more damage as they neared their colony planet. Hopes were fading for a successful trip now they had been separated from the HMASS *Jackman*—Australia's last remaining relic—which was nothing more than an interplanetary sheep transporter these days with outdated fighters and a few rusting gun turrets.

Sydney tried to keep the faith but was slowly giving up, with little left in her tank to give. Maybe another day or two, three at the most, but any longer and she too would have to give up her post for a healthier candidate, not that there were many left anymore. If they did, it would surely mean giving up their bunk and having to return to B deck.

No, she didn't want to think about that dark place below crammed with the alien cattle known as Stalkers, huge creatures grown and cloned centuries ago in the moon's laboratories.

Sydney drifted off to thoughts of the enemy fighters buzzing the cargo ship and stealing the creatures below, but she was just too exhausted to care about corporate pirates tonight.

Maybe tomorrow she would catch up with Vince.

"Syd! Get your shit together, you're late!" Her father shook her roughly, his greying hair hanging wet with sweat over the bed.

"Syd, get up. One more and we lose the bunk...MOVE IT!" Tom pulled back the brown blanket and pulled her from the thin stained mattress as her shift bracelet blinked blue light onto the floor.

Her small toned body looked pale against her father's muscled torso as Sydney hung limply in his arms, and he saw her arm was covered in more red bites from the bugs nesting within the mattress springs. She was sick. Too sick to make her shift tonight. He cursed softly to himself and laid her back down carefully, noting her calorie pills still sitting in the silver dispenser tray.

Tom scooped them out, held her head, and fed each of the pills gently inside her mouth. Then he pressed his red bracelet on the sensor of the dispenser and waited as it burred and clunked before dispensing *his* daily quota into the empty tray. Tom scooped them up as well, pushing one of the Dexiflex capsules into his own mouth, then paused for a second. He looked down at his daughter lying there and sighed, wiping her hair from her sweaty brow. Then he pushed the rest of his calories into her dry mouth without hesitation, unscrewing his water canister and taking a long mouthful before he placed the canister upon the bed.

Tom stooped, rubbed the bridge of his nose, and then leant over to take Syd's shift bracelet from her limp wrist. He snapped it onto his wrist, above his own red blinking one. Pausing, he looked down at his own red blinking bracelet, deciding whether or not this was a good thing to do, then released the catch, the blue band now flashing faster, indicating the imminent shift change.

He placed his red bracelet on her arm, and then clunked the two together like beer glasses to transfer details across. His was bulkier, and as an Elder, had several keys and charms hanging from it that rattled as he fastened it.

He reached over for his water canister and took a long drink.

"You owe me, my little star…don't lose it, or I'll be down in the hanger, cleaning the cattle shit with you." He smiled, poured some liquid into her mouth, and then pulled the blanket back up around her. She opened her eyes and saw his unshaven face beaded in sweat.

"Take a shower…you stink, Dad!" she croaked with a confused smiled, clutching his water canister. "Any sign of the Ravens or the *Jackman*?"

He kissed her on the cheek as she smiled, and he smiled back, stroking her matted black hair lovingly. "No, we haven't seen them on the scans since we were separated. But we haven't given up. We'll join them soon."

The Ravens or R.A.V.E.N.S were the last line of defence, consisting of 12 Rapid Attack Vessel and Evasive Navigational Support frigates assigned to protect both the *MacGyver* and the *Jackman*. But during the last raid, they had been separated from the convoy by the Founder fighters, and now the *MacGyver* was alone and vulnerable.

"How far are we away from home now?" she asked.

"Not far now, two days perhaps, if we can keep her moving at this speed we'll catch up with the *Jackman*." He ruffled her hair then stood. "Sleep well, Syd. I'll see you in the morning… get some rest." He walked over to the door and stopped. "Your mother is going to kill me when she sees the state of her little twinkling star."

"Yeh well, she'll go supernova when sees that grotty beard too!"

He laughed, stroking his whiskers as he walked away and through the door, turning down towards the engine room before the blue shift handover monitors could notice her bracelet marker missing from the engine room.

It would be the last time he ever saw Sydney.

The first shudder broke Sydney's slumber, but it did not wake her fully. It was the second explosion that sent her spilling from her bed and crashing to the floor.

The hull of the *MacGyver* was being violently torn apart as the volley of rockets destroyed the last of the battered outer panelling plates that had protected the engines for decades.

They had no chance of catching up with the *Jackman* now.

All the months of running from the Founder attack ships had been pointless. Now their crippled ship would drift helplessly in the void between worlds, left to be torn apart for its parts, just like all the other supply ships attacked and left to drift for eternity, never returning to their loved ones in the new frontier colonies.

Sydney rolled to her bare feet, dazed, searching the darkness for her boots and her overalls and finding only the latter with a curse. She sat on the balding carpet and quickly slid into her oily suit that she pulled from the chair as the general alarm sounded briefly, then went silent as another blast shook the deck.

"Scruddin pirates!" she swore as another explosion rocked the ship.

The metal cabin door was blown open, flying off its hinges, and she was swept under the bed along with the debris as the emergency light flickered briefly before going out.

Sydney found one of her boots tucked under her body, then the other as the air around her began to be sucked back out into the madness in the corridor. She pulled herself from under the bed. The glass and debris crunched under her shuffling knees as the sucking air pulled Sydney along and she had trouble holding back, only just managing to steady her balance by holding onto the broken door frame.

Outside, in the corridor, one of the large mechanoid labour units clunked past her, cradling an injured blue shift colleague in its arms who turned, waved to get her attention.

"We got to head for the evac suite. The engines have gone, Syd!"

If the engines were damaged, shouldn't they be down with the shift trying to fix them?

"How bad is it down there?" she shouted as the ship buckled and groaned.

The young man turned back over the shoulder of the tall strutting Floyd unit, his bloodied hair flapping over his face.

"How bad? Shit, Syd…they're all gone…blue shift are all gone!" he shouted back as his robotic saviour continued down the corridor.

Sydney called after the robot medic carrying the man, "Have you seen my father?"

Blue shift…gone, she thought as she watched him shake his head slowly.

She paused, chewing on her lip, then turned back towards the engines. Surely it couldn't be *that* bad. They had fought off the void pirates before, there was always notice before they struck.

Another blast, this time in the direction of the front of the ship, and the blast shook her to her knees. She grabbed on tightly to the handrail and watched as the debris changed course and was sucked the other way, along with some stragglers following the young man who had just spoken to her.

What in High Digits sake do I do now? She turned and began fighting against the vacuum, heading for the engine room. There were choices she could make from that end, several emergency evacuation shelters that people could survive in, and besides, she knew more of that side of the ship than the Elders quarters down the other way. Her father always insisted she made her way to the shift shelter if she ever got lost. He would find her there.

He always had done before.

Her greasy black hair flapped around her face as she fought the vacuum's pull, ducking whenever anything came tumbling her way. At one corridor corner, she found the broken body of another of the robotic Floyd units, this one pinned against the floor by a jagged section of the ceiling that had collapsed on top of it. Small electrical sparks smouldered from the war mech's gyros. The robot lifted up the twisted remains of the support girder for Sydney to pass herself through, and she did, thanking the ancient mechanoid. The faded pink-armoured robot nodded as she passed, lowering the joist, while staring out from emotionless blue eye globes.

More explosions, this time she could see the debris from the porthole, floating past outside in large, buckled, twisted, chunks. Sydney kept moving forwards, trying not to imagine the view from the fighter ships destroying the *MacGyver*. If the Ravens had been there, they could have shot the bastards up, gave the *MacGyver* a fighting chance, but they had been lost, scattered by the last attack as they defended the floundering *Jackman*.

Outside, several dismembered bodies wearing blinking blue bracelet lights floated past the portholes, and she turned her head away in horror.

The young cadet in the corridor was right, the compartment seal was breached. Sydney could see the warped bulk plate twisting and groaning before her.

Is it all gone behind there? she wondered, then immediately her thoughts changed back to her father.

Was he behind the plate when it came down? Did he make it to the shelter? Or was he wearing one of the blinking bracelets outside…but he wore red, not blue.

Sydney felt sick as her stomach tightened. She lifted her hand to her mouth and saw the shift bracelet, the red blinking light that her father obeyed.

He swapped… He took my shift!

Guilt rushed over her and filled her heart as another four blasts rattled the dying cargo hauler. Only this wasn't directed at the *MacGyver*, this time it was *their* cannons blasting the attackers. She peered out of the nearest porthole into the darkness of space and watched as one of the smaller attacking vessels took a direct hit, exploding in a glorious fireball. The two ships next to the scuttled vessel thrust away, deciding to chase the escaping pods ejecting from the *MacGyver.* They fired out grappling hook attachments into the floating debris, catching one unlucky survivor as she watched.

Another ship fired its thrusters, edging closer, possibly to avoid detection of the lone gunner in the cannon, but its tethered hook became tangled around the debris of the floating Terra priming equipment. The ship seemed to be trying to recover its hook as it spun out of control, firing its thrusters again, and Sydney watched as the craft collided against the outer panels of the *MacGyver* and was speared through the cockpit by its unwanted catch of the day. She watched as the tangled mess caught up on the jagged panels of the hull, dragging the ship behind it like seaweed caught on a rudder. The pilot of the enemy ship ejected the cockpit canopy. His bloodied body slowly slid from the front of the cockpit as he clutched his helmet, contorting awkwardly as he tried to stem the oxygen escaping from the shattered visor. He convulsed and shook violently, before stiffening and floating from his ship. She watched with strange satisfaction as he died, drifting slowly toward the broken hull of the *MacGyver.* Sydney told herself she was the lucky one to be alive. Quickly, she turned and continued along the corridor.

"Syd. Syd…" She heard the static blast from the wrist comm and replied.

"Dad, is that you?" she shouted back.

"Syd…help…" Vince was screaming through the static, but she could make no sense of the message as another crunch of static screaming erupted in a high shrill into her ear.

"VINCE!"

Another static burst erupted in a mash of screams and explosions over both the intercom and her wrist comm before falling silent again.

"Hello, anyone. Hello… Hello? Scrud!"

She reached the emergency crew shelter and saw the outer door was wide open; the blue shift crew hadn't even had the time to evacuate to the safety of the shelter. She slid herself inside and pulled the door shut. Then she staggered over to the protective cover of the emergency door seal lever by the hanging ancient pressure suits, and hesitated.

What if he is still on his way? What if more come…what if someone survived and I lock them out? She hesitated again as the canons of the *MacGyver* blasted out a final volley in response to more tearing shudders along the hull, and then both sides fell silent.

"Vince? Dad? I'm waiting on C deck." She flicked her wrist comm, but only static replied.

She waited.

"Vince! I'm keeping the door open…"

Sydney waited until her head went dizzy, but no one knocked. Nobody came.

"Vince…you there? Please talk to me?"

Nobody else has survived.

She wondered if the young man who warned her to go to the escape pods was in one of the pods that were snatched from the void by the raiders. *What was his name?* She knew him, a promoted cadet from the outbound journey, but just couldn't think.

"Vince…are you okay?"

The air continued to vent as she held onto the hope that her father would slide open the door and take her into his arms. But he did not show.

"Vinny…can you hear me?"

No one else showed. Time passed. She could wait no longer, and her fading consciousness, let the sagging weight of her body fall onto the emergency lever.

She heard the grinding doors seal her inside.

"I'm…so sorry…Vince." She faded.

Alone but safe.

One of the lucky ones.

Sydney had no idea how long she lay unconscious by the door of the emergency shelter but, judging by her growling stomach, she reckoned maybe one shift pattern had passed. The black lighting lit the chamber in an eerie purple glow. She pushed herself up and knelt on the floor, wiping the drool from her cheek. She rose from the metal grid floor, rubbing her neck as she got to her feet..

This room had been commandeered by one of the Raven pilot crews, their jumpsuits left hanging on the hooks behind Perspex glass and musty smelling flight boots scattered the floor. They were bathed in dark purple light from above, shrouding the room in unsettling silence. Flight plans and shift patterns for the *Jackman* were stuck to the wall, maintenance manuals and photographs of loved ones strewn across desks. Flight paths between moon colonies and enemy locations hung from map boards. She saw team boards with pilot head shots, courageous leathery-looking men and women who had fought and died in the Great War to free themselves from the tyranny on the Moon Colony.

No alarm alerted her anymore, no canon blasts shattered her eardrums and no commotion could be heard outside in the corridor. For now, Sydney was totally isolated in the purple emergency lights of the crew shelter.

Lucky to be alive.

She walked over to the decompression door handle, still dazed, and rested her hand on the manual release lever, then backed off when she heard what she thought was Vince's voice.

Stupid girl, what is lesson one? Stay put. Wait for help to come to you.

She backed away and rubbed her cold arms vigorously.

"Vince?"

It's getting cold in here.

Sydney realised that too, blowing into her cupped hands.

Don't you get it, kid? Lesson two…stay warm…deep space is a cold place!

She cursed Vince's Yoda voice lessons in her head and looked around the cramped area for the emergency lockers.

The red lights on each of the doors meant she knew they would all be locked, her lessons drummed that into her daily routine; only senior shift and monitors had been allocated clearance to unlock supply units, no junior had access or authority to unlock any ration box or door for that matter. She walked over to the blinking access panel that opened the lockers and slapped the monitor key.

"Hello, anyone there?" Silence greeted her. Another curse left her mouth as her shin bone struck the dry ration box below the bench, and she fell onto the wooden seat that followed around the contours of the back wall.

Wake up, Sydney, for the love of High Digit! Sort yourself out or you're going to end up like the rest of blue shift.

She thumped her fist down hard on the bench and screamed out, "Enough, Vince!"

The voices stopped, and she reached down for her boots, slowly untying the laces. "Enough!" She sobbed again, letting her matted black hair fall over her young face.

She thought of her cadet friends in blue shift, now just frozen bodies floating around outside the *MacGyver,* all her friends spiralling away from the ship, frozen by the void of space, destined to float forever in the vast nothingness between the Colony planets.

They're all dead, Dave. The sick thought was quickly cast aside.

They were supposed to be taking the lead from the Elders on the cargo haul so they could one day continue the supply run for their colony, for a time when the elders could no longer make the journey. Now it looked like the colony was destined to fail. Thoughts of her mother left stranded in the Colony with little livestock or supplies to survive on scared Sydney.

"Enough…please…enough!" she sobbed, trying to rid herself of the images of the dead as she tried to get her numbing feet warm again.

Her hands were shaking, the cold inside the emergency shelter biting now, and she looked around for something to pry open the supply boxes above. She found nothing.

Sydney sat on the dirty bench for a while, clutching her face, while her breath panted out in frosty clouds, drifting and lingering above her, and she cursed again. Even the ancient spacesuits on the far wall were behind glass, out of reach to juniors such as Sydney.

She sat and listened to the groaning ship as it twisted aimlessly, but with no engines propelling it, she supposed it would just stop. Momentum might keep it moving for a while, but with no rudder, it would just go on whatever course it wanted.

She wondered about her father and Vince, where their bodies were, how they had perished. Had anybody else made for the shelters, she knew of three sites in the rear of the ship.

How many of the elders had stayed with the ship as it went down?

Did they all abandon ship?

Were the Founder raiders still outside, already picking the *MacGyver's* bones for its cargo, or had they filled their quota?

"Enough, Sydney. Don't do this to yourself...please!" Sydney tried the lockers again, but none opened when she tried to pull at them with her freezing fingers. And once more she screamed out in frustration.

"Scrud you, Digit. Thanks for nothing you…you…turd muncher!" She lifted her first and began pounding it against the lockers as she screamed.

"You can't leave me here to die like this, it's not fair, you stupid turd eaters!" She pounded and pounded until the muscles in her arms burned, realising she had to keep moving, keep the limbs moving or they would freeze up.

Sydney began to jog on the spot, flapping her arms up and down and clapping them in wide applause, watching the red light on her shift bracelet make lazy loops as it passed under the dark light from above. Then she stopped and stared at it.

I have senior clearance.

"I have senior clearance!" She laughed maniacally. Running over to the access panel, she raised her father's shift bracelet to the reader and waited.

"Access granted; Senior shift Engineer Thomas Brown, First Class."

The lockers clicked, then each of the lights turned green, as did the space suit portal that unlocked and rolled open. Sydney yelped in joy as she ran over to the supply locker and grabbed the first suit at hand and wriggled inside.

There was precious little to smile about Sydney realised very quickly, apart from the suits hanging in the chamber. Most of the lockers were empty, some had only empty wrappers hidden inside them, others only had discarded calorie beans left behind by a thief with a conscience. "Thieving scruds, the lot of them!" she fumed, expecting nothing more from the Elders who looked after themselves on the journey. The only thing worth salvaging from the lockers was the water canisters that had been left. And they were left only because they were probably foul-tasting.

The green footlocker held little of appeal either, apart from an old tartan engineer hat with ear flaps that Sydney dusted down and stuck on her head, a little happier. Most of the emergency oxygen mask bottles had corroded and read empty, but she did find six that indicated that each was full and capable of 4 hours regulated breathing. She stacked them on the bench and continued searching.

In all, she found three water flasks, a handful of calorie beans, a flat battery torch, a rusted wrench, and the oxygen masks.

So much for a safe house. What did I expect from a ship over one hundred and twenty years old? Anything of value was bound to have been swiped a long time ago. And who do you actually think was going to replenish the stores?

She slammed the footlocker lid shut and looked around her prison cell. The low air was making her dizzy again and she realised the room was venting too quickly to replenish itself.

Now what? Do I eat the beans first and choke on the chalky barf...or do I swallow them and puke myself empty drinking the water from these death canisters?

She laughed out loud, picking up the large rusted wrench, "Maybe I just beat myself over the head with the wrench until my brains fill my oxygen mask!"

"Or I could go and look for Vinny down on D deck."

She realised there was little to debate.

So, that was the predicament private Sydney Brown, Third Class, found herself in at the tender age of 16. Fatherless, crewless, and powerless, cast adrift by the Founder Pirates lurking outside. *The Vikings of the Void.* Deep space's answer to the buccaneers of the high seas, and thieves of anything with nutritional value. Scruds, as Sydney put it, of the highest order.

No doubt the alien eight-legged cattle below had been emptied and corralled onto their cargo longboats by now, and the remaining fighters would be escorting their bounty back to wherever they hide. But the scruds would be back to finish the salvage soon enough.

Sydney ate some of the chalky beans; they crumbled in her mouth and tasted of little but she drank the water down to clean her pallet all the same. After sorting through the space suits, she found a flight suit, the nametag across the chest patch read,

R.A.V.E.N 5: COMMANDER REDUX 3760

Sydney stepped out of her boiler suit, deciding it best to relieve herself before climbing into the all in one suit. It was a loose fit, with plenty of room to move inside. She had to drag the footlocker over to the suits in order to reach the shelf with the helmets on, managing to knock three of them to the floor and crack two of the visors in the process.

I really hope that the helmet for this suit is not one of those on the floor. She prayed to High Digit, as she pulled the last one off, sighing with relief when the faded name and number matched her suit.

She found the backpack marked REDUX, his panel repair gun tools and a reel of safety line were inside. Sydney hauled it down and rummaged in all the side pockets for something to eat.

Among the bits and pieces, she found a protein bar.

She took the helmet and bag over to the bench and began inspecting the helmet as best as she could, checking the oxygen hose dangling from the side, but found no obvious damage. Then she picked up one of the full oxygen canisters and clicked the bayonet connector from the oxygen canister to the hose and listened for the air hiss. There was a hissing at first, but then it fizzled out. Alarmingly the indicator still said FULL she discarded that one, struggling with the connection, then tried another. This time the air hissed freely, and she smiled.

Sydney filled the backpack with her findings, sticking the remaining untrustworthy oxygen canisters around the outside pockets, and buckled down the straps. She slid on the helmet and clicked it tight, breathing in the fresh venting air. The canisters fit neatly into the front pouch and she fumbled with the buckle through her steamed-up flight visor.

The only thing now was to open the door and test the suit hadn't been compromised. She slid the backpack over her shoulders and picked up the wrench to use as protection from any screwheads still hanging about outside looking for anything that was of value.

"Okay, Vinny Boy. Sit tight, I'm on my way!" she mumbled, taking a deep breath, then backed up against the wall and pulled the lever upright.

The chamber quickly decompressed, all that was not secured flipped and bounced outside into the corridor,

Sydney held on tight as the remaining silver space suits escaped, flapping through the doorway. When she began floating, weightless, she pulled herself out into the corridor.

"High Digit, have mercy!" she gasped.

She froze as she drifted, staring at the sight that confronted her.

The whole side of the *MacGyver* was gone, with the hull plating torn from the ship like an opened tin lid pulled from a tomato can. Drifting off in the other direction, floating off into the horizon of deep space, was the back end of the ship, the buckled remains of the huge ion engine among the twisted burnt out panelling that spun freely into the darkness.

So, the scruds did beat us, finally!

Sydney pushed off carefully and clutched the remains of the walkway, slowly floating up the corridor towards the darkened side of the crippled ship, making sure she had a firm grip of the handrail. Below her, there was nothing but empty space.

The thought of losing her grip and tumbling out into space like the pilot she had witnessed earlier, filled her with dread. Even more dread than the other thought of how little breathing oxygen she had left to…*to do what?*

What am I going to do with less than a day's supply of oxygen canisters? I can't fly the ship on my own, ignoring the fact that the engines are now halfway to Big Red's spinning gas clouds.

If there were any escape pods left, she doubted that anyone other than the bloody creepers outside would pick her up anyway. So that left what exactly? Finding other survivors and having a group hug until the air ran out?

Just get to Vince's bunk. He's waiting for me.

She looked down as vertigo struck and quickly closed her eyes as she began to hyperventilate.

Enough, Sydney, we will think of something. You'll see!

This gave her little comfort, but she was able to open her eyes again and pull herself over the empty void and over into the enclosed part of the ship's corridor. She breathed a sigh of relief as her feet landed on the remains of the metal grated walkway and she had to turn around to see the damage from the new perspective.

It was an awesome sight. At least half of the rear of the ship was gone, torn off, leaving nothing but jagged ripped panelling that protruded into the void like fingers reaching up to touch the stars. The enemy fighter, snagged up on its own metal tension rope, spun around behind the *MacGyver* like a kite being dragged along the ground behind an eager child.

Her sanctuary had been the last section reprieved from the total break-up of the ship, and she saw how close she came to, waking up on the other side of the ship, staring back at the side she now stood on.

Is anybody standing there now, looking back at me filled with the same dread and emptiness? I hope not for their sake, at least I have a suit! I'm one of the lucky ones!

She stared at the scene for a while before turning and heading up the corridor towards the Elders' quarters and the helm. If anyone did survive, that's where they would be, huddled in the darkness behind the protection of the emergency doors like she had been, waiting for rescue.

The long corridor to D deck had been purged—nothing was left to obstruct her spacewalk—and she made quick progress to the first airtight sealed hatch. This was a manual door seal of old, like the old submarine doors, blocking the walkway and separating it from the next, should the pressure be breached in one of the connecting corridors. The ancient turning handles were easy to access, and isolated from any electrical seals, although maintenance had been lacking on this trip. The rusted bulk door was labelled 5, and she reached out for the wheel, hoping it would turn easily. It did not.

It took her ten minutes to decide to use the large wrench as a lever, jamming it into the spokes and heaving it upwards. It eased, then gave up with a screeching of the hinges. The small gloomy interior separating the next corridor was empty, and she slid inside, then closed the door behind herself. The darkness was full, the blinking red light from her bracelet was hidden under the suit, and she began to panic.

Easy, Sydney, easy...just breathe slowly.

She turned the door handle without the use of the wrench and turned to face the next door. Again, she needed the wrench to jimmy the seal, but it eased without too much fight. Sydney braced herself, then spun the wheel the rest of the way, and opened the door.

It was not like the corridor previously; this one was pitch black with blinking pinpricks of light from the floating bodies and discarded personal items. The blinking shift bracelet lights illuminated the walls where they passed, and Sydney could see that most of them wore red.

As she pushed off and moved closer, she bumped into the first two contorted faces of the floating dead, illuminated by their bracelets, and realised that they had suffocated, the air stolen from their lungs as the oxygen was sucked from the corridor.

She pushed them away as they floated towards her, their frozen grasping hands reaching out for her as she passed. One body was still clasping an oxygen mask to their face with both hands, as if still trying to suck out the last, final breath before the canister read EMPTY.

Why Sydney checked the reading on the dead man's canister she did not know, but she did anyway…and it read FULL.

She shook her head, unconsciously wondering how many of the canisters *she* had would read FULL as she sucked on the empty hosepipe for one dying breath that wasn't there.

She moved faster through the darkness as it closed in around her, her thoughts filled with fear of the salvagers from the Founders ships, fear of them snatching her from any of the open rooms she passed.

Vince's bunk was close, and she held her breath as she neared his door.

Something flickered from a room ahead, and she froze again as the beam scanned the corridor.

The scruds are here, ransacking the dead and

stealing what's left.

Cautiously she approached, gripping the wrench for security, stopping before the open door to a bunk where the beam of light suddenly arced out again.

"Vince, you there, buddy? Vinny?"

The torch beam scanned the corridor wall, then flickered behind the door, and she yelped in fright. Taking a deep breath, she raised her wrench, not realising that trying to bring it down on anyone's skull with force would be impossible in zero gravity. The light slowly passed again, like a prison camp guard scanning the fence line, and she peered inside.

The torch was in the clutches of a kid not much older than Sydney. His blue, shimmering, lifeless body spun freely among the sheets and the calorie beans.

She let out a pitiful sigh and whimpered slightly, reaching for the torch in his frozen death grip, but could not release it from his grasp. She raised her wrench to shatter his grip, confirming who the boy was.

"Vincent…oh no!" she sighed.

They had played together as children in the colony, spent days together in the creek with the other kids. They had chased the Stalker cattle into the herding pens together, and fled the Founders mechanoid warriors on Earth's Terraformed moon together. They were as close as you could be without being siblings.

"I'm so sorry, Vince!" She wiped the frost from his brow, staring into his glazed eyes, a look of terror still etched on them, as they floated together, her hugging his body tightly as they spun among the debris, her soft sobbing muffled in her helmet.

She couldn't smash the torch from his grasp, destroy the closest thing she had to a brother. And she couldn't just leave him there to float beside his dirty laundry.

So, she did the next best thing.

They floated out together, like they had done on the creek, lighting up the corridor for Sydney to float unhindered. She pushed him ahead as if he was a surfboard on the sea, it sickened her at first, but it was either that or smash the frozen hand that gripped the torch. And she wasn't going to do that just yet if she could help it.

Vince and Sydney floated through the corridor of the dead together, Sydney humming a long-forgotten tune that just popped into her head as she stared down at his frozen corpse navigating the next of the bulky air-tight doors.

"Do you remember the time old Scrudface caught us stealing apples his terraforming wagon?" She smiled through the glass at Vince.

"Remember him locking us in the back and taking

us all the way to the citadel to lodge a complaint with the lawman?" She started laughing. "And we ate about twenty more of his stock just because we wanted to make the theft worthwhile!" She rubbed her belly. "Yeh well, I feel as sick as that now, Vinny. My belly is cramping up something bad!"

She looked down at his dead frozen face.

"I wish I was back in the back of that wagon with you now, Vincent, so that I could tell you that I was scared…and that I loved you." She began to sob again, wrapping her arms around his torso as they floated down the darkened corridor together, lost in her insecurity for once in her life.

The corridor ahead was split open, a huge hole torn through the glass ports allowed a view of the planets out in the darkness of space.

The red one far off to the left was their home, Big Red, but they were so far away from the colony now.

Sydney realised they wouldn't be able to pass like this. She blinked away the tears in her eyes and sniffed away the self-pity, laughing, embarrassed at the revelation.

"Thanks for that, Vinny, but I'm real sorry. I'm going to need that light." She sighed, staring at his frozen features one more time.

I can't…I can't do this, she thought, turning back

and seeing all the floating bodies, suspended like objects on a macabre child's mobile.

They floated effortlessly between the dead children, bumping into one another as their momentum spun them against the darkness of the metal corridor. Sydney looked down at her frozen friend's clutching fingers wrapped around the torch and gulped hard. She couldn't bring herself to mutilate his cold corpse, and she knew she could not continue her search pushing his body through each pressured bow door, like some novelty shop signpost. So, reluctantly, Sydney let him drift away, out into the void of space, the torch beam falling across nothing, while she sobbed quietly.

"See you in the next world, Vince!"

The next corridor was the same and the next…and the next.

More dead faces that she recognised. More dead bodies floating in her path with terror frozen on their young faces. Their last thoughts, utter helplessness, as they fled like rats to the escape pods.

Sydney cursed, unable to wipe the tears rolling down her face, clumsily banging her heavy glove on the visor as she tried. Then she regained her composure, pushed herself off in the zero gravity, and headed back through the bodies.

So much darkness.

As she passed the dead, she had an idea. She reached out for their blinking wrist bracelets, unclipping as many as she could and snapping each of them on her own arms until she had five up each suited forearm. Then she clipped another 6 around each of her legs and floated there like some sort of blinking, illuminated decoration.

She inspected the new look and smiled,

The human torch!

Now the walls next to her glowed with a mixture of red and blue lights, and she was able to see obstacles in her path as they approached. Sydney pushed away again and headed back down the corridor.

This time, as she unlocked the bulk door, she lit up the interior and felt a little easier about sliding inside the pressurised compartment and closing the door shut behind her. The door sealed, and she began unwinding the next wheel. The door moved with ease and as it unlocked, the seal hissed as the pressure purged inside, allowing Sydney to push it open, and gaze out into yet another darkened room.

This hall seemed empty of bodies, but there were

still objects floating around her, and as she floated down, she saw the bodies had all massed at the other end of the long walkway, plugging a large blast hole.

Sydney moved down the corridor like some flashing deep-sea fish scouring for prey, lighting up the uncharted depths of the ocean. This was the third level corridor, the one next to the Elders quarters and the life pods. After this corridor was the restricted area, senior access only, so she was not sure what to expect. All she knew was that any survivors would be more than likely secured behind the bulkheads in the control area.

The bleeping on her helmet signalled the end of the air supply and panic set in. She needed to change the canister soon or her eyes would dry up, and she would become disorientated fast.

"Oh, scrud!"

It was inevitable, Sydney lurched inside her helmet, and pushed away.

In my helmet. Shit, really? Only cadets made that kind of rookie mistake. She cursed herself as the bile dribbled down her chin and soaked inside her tunic collar. She gagged again, this time on the foul air inside her helmet with little time to change the canister. She had to do it as soon as she could now, or she would be joining the bodies as they floated from the ship out into the void.

Her eyes could not stop staring at the shifting bodies drifting outside, like frozen performers cartwheeling and shimmering in a circus show. Some looked like they were in mid-dive, performing eternal twists for the judges waiting for the splash that would never come.

She noticed movement from farther away, almost beyond the planet referred to as 'Big Red'. A rogue ship perhaps, breaking the atmosphere to return for what was left of her ship?

No, this one was more familiar. This one was one of the Ravens from the lead convoy, and her eyes beamed wide with hope as the radio static crackled in her helmet.

"This is Commander Redux from Raven 5. Over."

"*Jackman*. Go ahead, Sir. Over."

"Yeh, dammit. I got a visual of the *MacGyver*. She's gone! Over."

"Affirmative. Digits mercy. Don't hang about. Over."

"We'll do a quick sweep then head back. Out."

Sydney reached for her comm link.

"No! Don't go… Help…can you hear me?" She watched as the Raven tore through the darkness, followed quickly by two other menacing vessels.

Her air canister continued its death bleep, dousing

her hopes of rescue, and Sydney began to hyperventilate as she floated by the airlock door. The bile in her helmet lapped at her chin in sloppy, sticky waves as her thoughts became blurred. She had to try and focus, put some sort of order into the confusing thoughts pouring into her head.

"Hello, Raven crew… Help… Do you have visual?" She was dizzy from the carbon monoxide building up inside the suit now, but realised the vessels following the Raven were that of the Founders fleet. Two arrowhead fighters gaining on the lead ship as it neared the wreckage.

A splash of bile entered her mouth and she choked, scrambling for the spare canister in the pack. The movement was swift, and she took a deep breath, then unscrewed the canister lock, untwisted the bayonet connection. As the old discarded canister floated away, she swung the new canister from the rucksack into the helmet's slot and tried to find the bayonet dock.

For a moment she could feel the panic rising again, fumbling with the damn thing as it just plain refused to click into place. Glancing from the corridor window she saw the fleeting view of Big Red. But to her shock, she watched the approaching Raven changing its course, its search beams now focussing elsewhere along the other piece of the scuttled *MacGyver* now spinning far from her broken piece of the hauler. It seemed unaware of the two vessels quickly sneaking up behind.

She watched the Raven's searchlight as it adjusted its heading and thrust towards the rear end of the *MacGyver*, the part now heading to whichever planet's gravity it was now destined for.

"Oh Scrud, you better know what you're doing guys."

Her movements were becoming frantic now, the canister was still not locked into place, and because she had no grip on the ship, she was beginning to spin again. The bile in her helmet washed over her face as she closed her eyes and held onto the last dying breath inside her helmet. But she refused to let the panic cloud her judgement, and the bayonet finally clicked into place with a flick of her wrist. She took a gulp of the hissing air as it entered the helmet, blinking the sloppy ooze from her eyes, but to her horror, it too began to bleep almost immediately.

This is a nightmare.

Sydney could only fill her lungs with thick nauseous air from the canister for two more inhalations before she became dizzy again and it actually registered that she would have to change that one over as well.

She watched the tracer rounds firing from the Founder ships strafe the space between their craft and the Raven, and prayed that the Raven had seen the danger.

They had, and the Raven quickly shot off in the opposite direction, away from the *MacGyver* wreckage.

"NO…I'm here…I am over here!" Sydney felt her heart sink as the Raven disappeared from view behind the bulkhead. But as she struggled with the spare air canisters her arm caught the drifting body of one of the dead and the canisters were pitched from her grasp like toppling juggling balls.

Scrud!

This was chaos, slow motion madness, and the more swipes she made for the canisters, the further away they spun from her grasp. She lost sight of one of them as it twisted away among the debris, instead focussing on the other as it made its way to the gaping hole in the hull that was packed with the frozen bodies.

The two Founder ships separated, one going over her head as the other streaked towards her, spraying the side of the *MacGyver* in more deadly, penetrating gunfire.

She heard nothing as she ducked down, only feeling the dull explosive thuds of the rounds as they penetrated the hull, the sonic blasts vibrating through her entire body as the fighter blasted past her faster than any other ship she had ever seen. Her body shook as she watched the Fighter barrel roll up and then disappear over the broken hull.

She had to break position and grab the air canisters, or she was going to suffocate in her helmet. But if she chased after them, she would surely be risking her life again as the Gatling guns peppered the hull casing once more.

The decision was made instantly, and she swiped the bodies aside, kicking off in pursuit of the air canister, praying to Almighty Digit that it had more air inside than the one she had just changed.

Sydney was all out of choices.

The canister floated slowly through the blasted hole in the hull and spun out into the frozen void, and she followed the equipment, wide-eyed and without thinking of anything but her survival. When she finally snatched it, she was outside the ship, twenty feet from the *MacGyver*, gasping for air once more. She was like a manic space-coke junky after her daily fix as she twisted the canister from bayoneted groove and then fumbled with the other, twisting it on. This time she got it the first time, and breathed in lungfuls of the fresh air, watching the *MacGyver* below her, dumbstruck as the distance grew to fifty feet, then one hundred, then two hundred.

Then her eyes widened to the spectacle playing out

in front of her. Front row tickets to the most impressive dog fight in progress behind the *MacGyver* she had ever witnessed. The three ships were performing some kind of beautiful ballet routine, each one barrel rolling and twisting away from the other as they outmanoeuvred the tracer fire exploding around them.

The Raven was being out classed at every twist, but the pilot was good. He was very good, managing to avoid everything the enemy fighters were launching his way. Rocket after rocket sliced past each wing of the Raven as he barrel-roll after barrel-rolled, twisting and turning like a crocodile in a death roll.

Sydney watched on in silence, there was no soundtrack to this spectacle. Only silent explosions as the ships entwined in gut wrenching dives, each one flying closer to the debris field to gain the upper hand on the other.

But it was the Raven who was now doing the chasing, picking off one of the fighters in an amazing stunt that saw the pilot lift his ship's nose and loop back around until he faced the oncoming fighter, then open up both wing guns.

The fighter tried to copy the manoeuvre, but was cut in half by the missiles, erupting in a ball of light as it twisted away and exploded against the *MacGyver's* heavy shield plating.

The shock waves sent Sydney tumbling further from the fighting arena as the two remaining ships streaked her way, blasting past her like two nineteen fifties teenage drag racers playing a game of chicken. The concussion blast ruptured one of her eardrums, and blood trickled down her neck as her teeth rattled in her gums. Her ears rang out as she yelled in pain, the duelling ships already out of her sight.

And then there was nothing.

She spun around, searching the empty heavens for the ships, but they had gone, streaking off towards Big Red and leaving her floating alone again, with only the *MacGyver* and her dead crew for company.

Then the pieces of the *MacGyver* just seemed to drift away in silence. Flickering lights on several decks spluttered, then faded like the sinking Titanic as Sydney floated away from her home of eight months. The huge hulking mass deserting her, deserting the dozens of dead crewmates floating around in the wake of the dog fighting arena. Roaming bodies tumbled in the debris field next to her, each in their own silent death waltz, some knocking into each other like billiard balls, appendages simply snapping off and shattering as they floated away.

"Hello...can you hear me?" Sydney tried her helmet again. But there was just silence.

No screaming, no tantrums, only utter bewilderment as she watched the huge broken ship from between her legs, twisting like a great harpooned whale, dying in the vast emptiness of the tranquil sea of space. *The Great Void Ocean. The Gulf of Nowhere. The Dead Sea.* The titles just rolled from her unbelieving brain.

They're all dead, Dave.

It was all so futile, the scrambling for air, the pursuit of survival. All her hard work was for this. Floating in space among the dead, gasping for the next cannister to prolong her agony, suffering each and every death shroud of her friends as they passed her.

Sydney watched her dead crewmates for a while, her breathing becoming more of a panicked hyperventilated pant.

She could watch no more.

It's okay, any moment now the Raven will return. Any scrudding moment now…

She cast her eyes over the silent expanse. First left, then right. Up, then down, but nothing approached, only the twisting arc of light from Vince's torch could be seen spinning away from the *MacGyver.* No one heard her. No one came for her. She just drifted further away, tumbling into the darkness as she counted down her last hour of air.

That's when Sydney realised it…her luck was out. It was the dead who were the lucky ones, not her.

The dead didn't have to watch this madness anymore. The dead didn't have to choke on contaminated air canisters and fight their way through a nightmare. The dead didn't have to say goodbye to all their friends, watch them shatter into a million frozen pieces and float away.

Sydney fought back the tears, slowly reaching up for her helmet commlink with trembling fingers, her eyes pleading for intervention to arrive as the tears eventually rolled down her cheeks.

"Please… Commander…can you hear me?" Her earpiece crackled, then silenced.

Sydney floated further on, like the other hundred lost souls drifting in the darkness, drifting away into the void of deep space.

"Anybody…?"

The radio static woke her, breaking Sydney's sleep-like trance, and as she opened her eyes to the silence again, the laboured sound of her breathing filling her helmet.

Sydney blinked away the pain and peered out into

the darkness through the foggy condensation dripping from the helmet visor. She had no time left. She had come to the end of her fight and was now just another twinkling beacon among the never-ending backdrop. A red and blue twinkling star.

She sighed, thoughts of her loved ones filling her head.

Well, at least Vince would have a laugh if he saw the state of me now!

She snorted a pitiful laugh as the radio link suddenly crackled to life again.

"*Jackman*, I have a visual…"

GREGG CUNNINGHAM, 48, is a short story writer from Western Australia who has contributed to various genre anthology books published by 559 Publishing 13 Bites volume 3,4,5, Plan 559 from Outer space volume 2 and 3, Other Realms, Heard It on The Radio, 559 Ways to Die.

He has had several short stories publishing by Zombie Pirate Publishing in anthology books such as Relationship add Vice, Full Metal Horror, Phuket Tattoo, World War four and Flash Fiction Addiction, with their Grievous Bodily Harm thriller due later in the year.

He hopes to one day dust down and edit the huge manuscript under his bed and get it out to the Sci-Fi community.

Bibliography
ANGELS, Black Hare Press, 2019
BEYOND, Black Hare Press, 2019
Deep Space, Black Hare Press, 2019
MONSTERS, Black Hare Press, 2019
Storming Area 51, Black Hare Press, 2019
WORLDS, Black Hare Press, 2019

Connect
Twitter: @GGGcunningham
Website: cortlandsdogs.wordpress.com
Amazon: amazon.com/-/e/B016OTHX0K

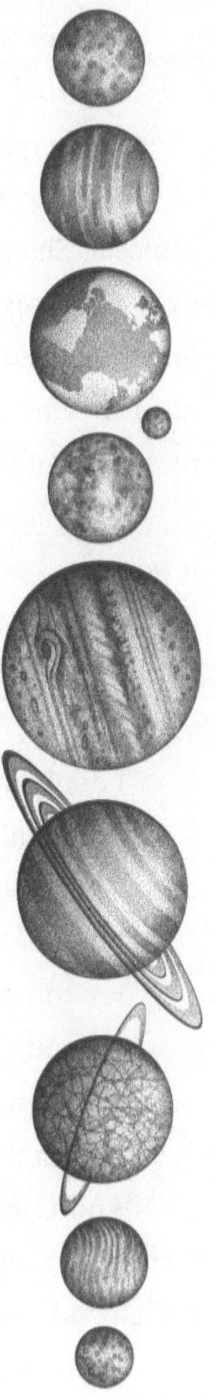

TRUTH TO POWER
By Joel R. Hunt

As an author and academic, Shah inherited the brains of her family, but she has always lived in the shadow of her celebrity brother Raz - the Jester from Jupiter, the Ganymedian Comedian, the Man with a Million Masks. In the run-up to the election of the next Galactic President, Raz invites her to take part in his latest prank, yet the more she discovers about it, the more concerned she becomes. Shah must choose which she would rather risk: her brother's career or her own integrity.

The two drinks that Raz slammed onto the table were almost as green as his hair. Shah couldn't help but grimace.

"What's that?" she asked.

"If I told you, you wouldn't drink it," said Raz, "Just hold your nose and open your gullet."

With a hesitance usually reserved for bomb disposal, Shah raised the drink to her lips, closed her eyes and threw the liquid down her throat. Apple and lime exploded in her mouth, before giving way to a distinct aftertaste of chemicals. It wasn't exactly pleasant, but it wasn't half as foul as she'd expected.

Then again, nothing with Raz was ever quite what it seemed.

He raised his own glass and took a delicate sip.

"What did you think of last night's show?" he asked.

"I don't know," said Shah, "I never watch it."

"You don't watch your own brother's show?" Raz cried with mock horror.

"You don't read my books."

"I'm too stupid to understand your books."

"I'm too smart to understand your comedy."

Raz laughed and raised his glass.

"A toast then," he said, "to stupid academics."

"And unfunny comedians," Shah added, clinking their glasses together. Raz finished off his mystery drink and tapped out an order for two more. Then he began to study her with his startlingly green eyes.

"What?" asked Shah.

"I know that look," said Raz, "Something's bothering you."

"You mean other than you?"

Raz snorted a laugh.

"I don't know," said Shah, "I've just been thinking a lot about Xavier Norman."

"Ah yes, our future glorious leader."

"Don't even joke about it," said Shah, cringing, "I used to think he was some extremist bigot scraped up from the sewers. But I've been watching the polls. He's outstripped all the moderates, and now he's catching up to Aja-Zepeda. I genuinely think he might have a chance. Every time he says something hateful or stupid, I keep hoping it'll tank his campaign, but it's as if he's living in a different world! He seems to be entirely immune to the normal rules, able to get away with saying things we wouldn't even dream of uttering. And it's frightening to think how many people buy into his rhetoric. I know a lot of them are only being duped by his charisma, but then I don't know whether I'd rather have a galaxy of bigots or a galaxy of idiots. Did you hear what he said yester— Why are you smirking?"

Raz pushed his glass aside and leaned across the table, an impish glee in his eyes.

"I bet you'd set him straight if you had the chance,

right?" he asked. Shah scoffed.

"Oh, there's plenty I'd like to say to him," she said.

"Do you want to?"

Shah frowned. She tried to peel back the layers of her brother's expression, but she'd never had his skill at reading people.

"What are you getting at?" she asked.

"I happen to know where Xavier is right now," Raz said, "and if you'd like, I can arrange a face-to-face meeting. Tonight. Just say the word."

"How could you sort out a meeting like that?"

Raz waved his fingers like a discount magician.

"All will be revealed," he said, "but this is a limited time offer, Shah. He's a busy man, he has places to be and lies to peddle. This may well be your only chance to meet him. And who knows, you might be able to change his mind on a few things."

"This isn't one of your big jokes?" Shah asked.

Raz laughed.

"I can genuinely take you to see Xavier Norman, if that's what you mean. But I can't promise there won't be jokes on the way."

Shah tapped a knuckle as she mulled over the proposition. She doubted it was as simple as Raz was making it seem, but she had been dreaming of confronting that fascist for months. She couldn't throw that chance away, however slim it might be.

"Alright," she said, "let's go."

When the taxi finally landed, Shah didn't recognise the dark compound they found themselves in. It was only when they turned a corner and she saw her brother's twenty-foot face beaming down at her that she realised where they were. Raz's personal studio.

Security drones flew over to meet them, scanned Raz's face and then left, but otherwise there were no signs of activity anywhere. The buildings were in shadow, the carpark was empty, and the only lights were focussed on posters and screens advertising her brother's show. There was nothing to indicate the presence of a Presidential hopeful.

"What on Jupiter would Xavier Norman be doing here?" Shah asked.

"He hangs out sometimes," said Raz, "Hey, don't pull that face at me, he does! I know it's hard for you to believe, but some people actually enjoy my company."

"For the life of me, I can't imagine why."

"And that's why you write stuffy books for a living, while I get absurd amounts of money for pulling silly faces."

He led them to one of the larger buildings and opened the door with a fingerprint. Inside was yet another poster, a full-body image of Raz in his trademark green suit surrounded by garish taglines:

The Jester from Jupiter, the Ganymedian Comedian, the Man with a Million Masks: Raz Jester!

"Don't you ever get tired of seeing your own name?" asked Shah.

"Nope."

He led her through the studio's labyrinth, lights flickering on in room after room. There was nothing particularly sinister about the place – it was mostly corridors of costume racks and side-rooms full of childish, oversized props – but there was a lingering aura of incompleteness. A building like this should have been full of stagehands, extras and interns. It should have been bustling and frantic, full of noise and life. Being here alone, hearing the echo of their own footsteps as they made their way deeper inside, was strangely unsettling.

After a minute or two of walking, they arrived at a room Shah recognised. When Raz had moved into the studio years ago and was showing the family around, the 'hall of masks' had been the first place he had brought them, a long corridor with shelving on both sides from floor to ceiling. At the time the shelves had been empty, but now the room truly lived up to its name; every inch on every shelf was packed with mannequin heads, each covered in some manner of mask. Some were simple Halloween costumes, and others wore glasses with a fake nose and moustache, but most displayed the complex and lifelike masks which Raz had come to be known for. Old men, beautiful women, battle-scarred veterans; every type of human being imaginable. As they walked between the shelves, Shah couldn't help but feel as though they were watching her. Judging her. She half expected the things to start talking.

"Creepy, aren't they?" said Raz, and Shah tried to hide her flinch.

"A little, I suppose," she said, "Have you really worn all of these?"

"Pretty much! Some of them come as a team, so other actors fill in for those characters, but generally speaking they're made just for me. Of course, it used to be that I could use the same mask over and over again, but now I'm too famous for my own good, it's never long before I get rumbled. I miss the old days."

Sure enough, as Shah looked along the shelves at the hundreds of characters stored there, it seemed there was little room for new additions. There were only a handful of bare mannequin heads dotted between the masks. Raz would either have to start a new hall or get a new routine—and Shah knew which of those was more likely.

"Not many spaces left," she said.

"None, technically," said Raz, already at the far end of the hall. He opened the door to a dark room beyond and gestured for her to follow. After a final look at the hundreds of faces glaring down from the shelves, Shah obliged.

They emerged in a storeroom of sorts, with a clinically white floor and a dozen crates and set pieces sitting in the shadows. Raz walked over to a box in the centre, and with a series of quick hand gestures he turned on a spotlight directly above it. Shah was beginning to feel like an audience member in one of her brother's performances.

Which, she supposed, was likely about to be the case.

"You remember my mate Xan, don't you?" Raz asked.

The question caught Shah off-guard.

"Remember him? I went to his funeral."

"Ah," Raz nodded, "I don't remember the funeral very well. I'd had a bit to drink."

"A *bit?* You were an embarrassment."

Raz smirked.

"Hey, they say to find what you're good at. Anyway, ever since I met him, Xan had wanted to leave his mark on the worlds. Really do something spectacular, you know? He wasn't after fame or glory. He just wanted his life to mean something. A week or so after he found out he was terminal, we put our heads together and tried to work out what we could do to really shake things up. We wanted to pull off a stunt that nobody could ignore, something that could never be replicated, never be sanitised and packaged and sold. Obviously, Xan has his tech-smarts, and I had my showbiz contacts and a good bit of funding behind me. The moment we stumbled on our final idea, we both knew it was the legacy Xan deserved. We spent his final months of life hammering out the details, working almost every waking moment he had left. And, well… this is what we came up with."

Raz pressed a button on the side of the crate. With a hiss, its lid shifted, and he hauled it aside with a flourish.

Shah's heart spasmed in her chest.

It was Xavier Arnold Norman. His face was unmistakable, a network of angry wrinkles and bony cheeks. He lay inside the crate in full suit and tie, a cold pallor over his face. His eyes were closed. His arms were still. He wasn't breathing.

"You killed him…" whispered Shah. Raz laughed.

"Not quite," he said, "Watch this."

From his pocket, Raz plucked what appeared to be a small coin. He gestured for Shah to take a step back—which she did, her knees nearly buckling beneath her—then tapped his thumb against the coin in a precise pattern.

Xavier's eyes opened. He sat up in the crate without a word, then clambered over the side of it to stand next to Raz. The old man's eyes were usually lit with a hate-fuelled passion, but now they were blank. Inhumanly so. He stared off into the distance, and even as Shah watched, he sank back into his unmoving pallor. He could almost be made of wax.

When Shah was finally able to tear her eyes away from the frozen politician, she saw Raz beaming at her with pride.

"Impressive, isn't he?" said Raz, "Bit of an ugly mug, I suppose, but every parent loves their own baby."

"You…" Shah began, struggling to formulate her thoughts, "you made a replica Xavier Norman…"

"You sell me too short, dear sister."

Raz let the comment hang in the air, his green eyes piercing hers. When Shah worked out his meaning, she sank down to sit on the nearest box. It couldn't be. It wasn't possible.

Yet it was right in front of her.

"This *is* Xavier Norman," she breathed, "The *actual* Xavier Norman. He's just another one of your characters. A comedian's prop."

Raz laughed and danced to himself. He slid over, lifted her up and placed an arm around her shoulder.

"You can't imagine how long I've wanted to tell someone!" he cried, "Now that you know, isn't it so *obvious*! His outlandish views, his nonsensical rants, his mysterious past! And think about his initials!"

Xavier Arnold Norman.

XAN.

A fascist tyrant named after a dying childhood friend. Shah's brother had strange notions of what counted as a fitting legacy.

"When Xan was still here," Raz continued, "we talked about it every night. God, watching the news was a delight back then! Normally my characters trick one person at a time, or maybe a room full. I never thought I'd get to see one trick an entire galaxy!"

"Raz, I don't understand," said Shah, peering close at Xavier's lifeless features, "Are you telling me this is some kind of robot? Does it think? How does it know what to say?"

"We have Xan to thank for that," Raz explained,

"He designed a kind of weak AI, one that can pick up on stimuli and respond with pre-programmed tasks. Xavier here can read the faces and the tone of the people he interacts with, and based on what he observes, he trots out the most relevant or satisfying of his stock phrases. He's basically a real politician!"

Raz tapped on the coin again, and Xavier blinked. The old man's chest expanded with an artificial breath as now-nimble fingers began to straighten his own tie.

"Go on," said Raz, "Pick a topic and try him out."

Shah hesitated. This didn't feel right. This was the man who was spreading hatred across a dozen planets, the man who she had spent months despising. And now she had the chance to confront him, she found out he wasn't really a man at all.

"I don't know," she said, "What should I ask?"

"What kind of question is that?" Xavier barked, making Shah jump as he turned his deep scowl against her, "If you hadn't been brainwashed by the Mars-controlled media, you'd be able to think for your damn self! This is what's wrong with our planets these days! No one is willing to say what they really think! Once I'm in charge, I guarantee that everrrrrrrr—"

At the touch of a button, Xavier's fury melted away, and he returned to his cold, silent repose.

"He has over a hundred of those," Raz said, "and

each time he swaps around the word order and changes his intonation. He can talk to voters for hours and they'll never catch on."

"But I've watched him make speeches," said Shah, "Full speeches, without anyone prompting him on how to respond."

"Oh, someone prompts him…" Raz said with a smirk.

He pressed the device against his temple, where it latched onto his skin. Lights blinked into existence on its surface, and Xavier shifted. His expression softened. He took up Raz's stance.

"Anything I think, he can say," grumbled Xavier, "and anything I do, he can copy. You ever wanted to see Xavier Norman dance?"

Raz threw his arms in the air and shook his hips from side to side. Xavier copied him perfectly. The old fascist pursed his lips and blew Shah a kiss, exactly as her brother did.

"All I have to do," said Xavier, "is hold the speech in my mind, and it comes tumbling out of his mouth."

Shah looked her brother up and down and stepped away from him.

"So, you're behind everything that's come out of his mouth? All the racism, all the sexism, all the homophobia… that was *you*?"

"In character," said Raz, peeling off the device and waving away her concerns, "I don't mean any of it. It's a script, designed to appeal to the lowest common denominator. I have to use their words, speak their language, otherwise the whole stunt falls apart."

"Is my existence a *joke* to you?"

For once, Raz seemed hurt. He closed the gap between them and placed a hand on her elbow.

"No, no, of course not," he said, "The whole point of this is to expose how easily led the dim-witted masses are. Think about it; after they find out that Xavier Norman was nothing more than a comedian's prop, how can any fascist ever be taken seriously again? He's a mirror to their stupidity, and I'm going to need to say a lot of awful shit to make them see themselves as they really are."

Shah pulled her elbow back, glaring at the ground. She couldn't bring herself to look at Raz. To look at either of them.

"I don't want any part in this," she said.

"I'm not asking you to be part of it."

"Then why did you bring me here?"

Raz stared around the room as if hoping to find his answer hiding among the boxes.

"I thought…" he started, shaking his head, "I hoped you'd understand."

His arms hung limp by his side. Shah hugged her chest, slinking out of the spotlight. For nearly a minute, both remained as silent as Xavier.

"I guess we don't know each other as well as we thought," said Shah.

She strode to the exit. Raz ran after her.

"Please don't tell anyone!" he said, "This has been years in the making, the reveal has to be perfect."

"You are hurting people," Shah snapped, "Don't you get that? This man—this fucking *thing*—is spreading hate and promoting violence against ordinary people who are just trying to live our lives. I used to think he was doing it for selfish reasons, but I could never have imagined he was doing it for a joke!"

"A joke that might take down fascism forever!" insisted Raz, placing a hand on the door, "Please, give me a chance to see this through. You'll see. I've got a live show scheduled on election night. Whatever the result, that's when I'll reveal everything. All the bigots and reactionaries and mindless drones, they'll all be exposed for what they really are, and afterwards everyone else can go back to their normal lives. Please. I promise you that good can come of this. Let me try."

"I don't know if I can do that for you," said Shah.

"Then do it for Xan."

Shah's glare could have melted steel.

"Don't you dare do that," she said.

"Shah, he—"

"Don't use his memory to prop up your stupid jokes."

"He was my best friend, Shah. I would never do anything to hurt him. I swear to you, this was as much his plan as mine. This was what he chose as his legacy. Please. Please let me honour that legacy."

As they stood in the darkness, Shah's fists clenched and unclenched. She could feel the presence of the robot, still standing in the spotlight behind her. It had already done so much damage.

Perhaps another week wouldn't make much difference.

"If it goes too far," she said, "you have to stop it. Promise me."

"I promise, Shah," said Raz, looking her in the eyes, "this will only ever go as far as it needs to. No further."

He waited for her response. When none came, he let go of the door and stood aside, and Shah left without another word.

Sitting in the audience was torture.

Shah had seen plenty of Xavier Norman's rallies, but this was the first she had experienced first-hand, and it was a bewildering experience. The amphitheatre was packed far beyond capacity, with bodies squashing in so tightly that she could feel their chests vibrate with each impassioned yell. Chants spread through the crowd like an infection, heckling other politicians, attacking Xavier's opposition, even calling for violence against all those who dissented. Security drones swarmed the air, swooping in when supporters and protestors clashed – which was a far more common event than Shah had anticipated. It seemed she wasn't the only one opposed to her brother's antics, even if her fellow protestors didn't realise exactly what they were fighting against.

Her own aim was a subtler one, however. She stood in line to ask a question to Xavier himself, and she knew exactly what she was going to say. Raz had been ignoring her calls, blocking any attempt she made to contact him. Mother said he was likely busy, but Shah knew what was really going on. Raz couldn't face her again. He knew she might talk him out of this stupidity.

Everyone here thought they had come to see Xavier Norman, but they were just tools in her brother's joke. There was a time where she had hated his supporters for their ignorance, but not anymore. Now she pitied them. They really believed what Raz was peddling. They actually thought that Xavier could improve their lives, return the pride they used to have in their planet. No matter what the cost. If he wasn't careful, these people would do absolutely anything in response to Xavier's influence. Yesterday, some of them had done.

It had already gone too far. It was time to end it.

"My opponent may call herself a supporter of the oppressed," Xavier called out in response to the last question, "but I ask you this; who is more oppressed than us? We don't have the Martian media in our pocket like Aja-Zepeda does! We don't get slotted into cushioned jobs because we meet some bureaucrat's checklist! We don't—"

The rest of his words were lost in frenzied cheering that fell away to a guttural chant.

"GO TO HELL, RAQUEL! GO TO HELL, RAQUEL! GO TO HELL, RAQUEL!"

The supporter who had asked the question moved aside, a predatory grin on his face. Shah shuffled forwards, now next to speak, and she waited for half a minute until Xavier raised a hand and the chanting died away. As a microphone hovered into place below her nose, he turned to her. There was no recognition in his expression. It couldn't be Raz controlling him; not even her brother had that good a poker face. But Raz would be watching. He needed to be ready to jump in if something came close to rumbling his prank.

Shah was counting on it.

"Yesterday," she said, as clearly and confidently as she could, "a group of Ganymedians on Earth were walking home from work. They were set upon and attacked by a group of your supporters, who were heard to shout your slogans as they beat their victims into comas. Two of these victims have since died, with a third still on life-support. How can you justify—"

"A tragedy," said Xavier, "A symptom of the times we live in, where criminals can wander the streets unopposed and our police are crushed under paperwork until they can do nothing but watch! Judges give murderers and rapists a slap on the wrist and call it justice, and still the radicals like Aja-Zepeda call for *more* human rights? I ask you, where were the rights of the victims? Where are the rights of their families?"

An enormous cheer threatened to sweep Shah away, but she persevered.

"People have died, *Xavier*. They've died because of you. Because of what you're trying to do. The joke is over, it's time to end it. Do you hear me? End it now. I know you're listening."

For a moment, Xavier seemed stunned. He stared off into the distance, his wrinkled face softening and his eyes turning dull. Then he blinked, and Raz met her gaze with a fierce intensity.

"Yes, I'm listening," Xavier said, "and I see that you have genuine sympathy for these poor souls who have lost their lives. But I ask you this; what great progress has ever been made without sacrifice? What great strides has humanity made without suffering? Planes fell from the sky. Did we stop flying? Rockets exploded after take-off. Did we abandon the stars? Whole colonies were lost to the ravages of space. Did we huddle down on Earth and cry? No! We persevered because that's how greatness is achieved! Don't you understand that I am creating a new society? A new order? After this election, things will never be the same again! That cannot be thrown away on a mere whim! Greatness requires suffering. And on election day, I will ensure the entire galaxy sees true greatness!"

The stadium exploded in applause. His supporters nearest to Shah screamed in her face and bundled her away from him, but even they were drowned out by the cheers. She tried to claw her way back to the front, yet the bodies kept piling in.

"Xavier," she called, "Xavier!"

She could barely see him. More and more supporters drowned her out with their shouts. Shah waved her arms, screamed as loudly as she could.

"Raz!"

But as the mass of bodies closed in, Xavier's triumphant smirk was the last of him she saw.

The election results were close. Far too close for Shah's liking.

For a time, Xavier Norman's victory had seemed assured. Early polls had put him in the lead by a few million votes, and Shah had nearly contacted the press then and there. She'd rehearsed what she might say, the evidence she would use to destroy her brother's precious reveal. But something prevented her. Perhaps a deep-rooted family loyalty.

Perhaps a voyeuristic desire to see what his chaos would actually look like.

To her enormous relief, Xavier fell at the final hurdle. He was overtaken by another populist, Neptune's radical progressive who he insisted on attacking, Ms Aja-Zepeda. She was far from Shah's first choice—she was full of quick fixes and easy answers—but anything was better than seeing that fascist puppet sweep into power.

This time when the taxi dropped her off, her brother's studio was bursting with activity. All around her, Raz's crew was rushing around with drinks and scripts and props, getting ready for their biggest show of the year. Shah wondered if they had any idea how big it almost was.

When a staff member she recognised marched past, Shah waved her over.

"I'm looking for my brother," she said.

"Ah, Mr Jester said you might come. I think he's in the prop shed. Could you let him know that he's needed in Make-up in seventeen minutes? He's not been responding to any of our messages."

The woman let Shah through the door, before barrelling off to scream at a group of interns.

The building was far busier this time. Shah had to squeeze her way through crowded corridors and dodge catering trolleys, and she got lost several times on the way to the hall of masks. When she finally found it again, it was as though she were stepping into a different world. Motes of dust danced in the hall's dim light, seeming to beckon her through. It was the first room she had found today that was silent and empty. She was alone here. Alone except for the masks themselves. They, it seemed, were no more pleasant in the daytime. They leered down at her from their perches, judgemental and sneering. Shah sneered right back. Whatever knowledge seemed to be held behind their soulless eyes, she wouldn't be hearing it from them. By the time she had reached the door at the far end, the noise and bustle of the studio had faded away.

When she opened the door, she found Raz surrounded by darkness. Under a single glaring spotlight, facing away from the world, he slouched on an upturned box. There was no politician in it now. Shah approached, stopping as she reached the edge of the light.

She stood in silence, waiting for any response from him. When none came, she spoke.

"You lost, Raz."

He shook his head.

"This stunt was years in the making, Shah. Years of my life. My magnum opus. Xan's legacy."

Raz turned to her. A twisted smirk was carved into his face. His eyes were ablaze.

"Do you really think I'd risk it all on just one candidate?"

The comment hit Shah like lightning. She reeled back, eyes taking in the room as if for the first time. Raz sat on the box that had once held Xavier Norman. Scattered around the room were half a dozen others exactly like it. All of them were open. All of them were empty.

She could barely breathe.

"Who?" she managed to croak.

"All the ones that mattered," said Raz, "For what it's worth, I'm glad Norman didn't win. Raquel always was my favourite. Or should I say, President Aja-Zepeda. Though I suppose it doesn't matter, does it? It's up to me what she prefers to be called…"

"This is sick," whispered Shah, "This is fucking twisted."

"That's politics!" Raz laughed, jumping up and waltzing along his personal stage, "It's the biggest joke of all, and I've just proven it! I've exposed who really wins elections. It's not dedicated public servants, philosophers or intellectuals. It's characters. Personas. People with no history, no conviction, no empathy. People who aren't even people! We're about to be ruled by a damn robot, and *that's what the voters asked for!* Isn't that incredible?"

"You're going to get yourself locked up, you arrogant fool. The people aren't going to laugh at this, they're going to riot! They'll hunt you down and tear you apart, don't you get that?"

"Only if they find out," said Raz. He let the comment settle, like a sprinkling of snow over a dying animal. "You see, all of this really was too simple. I barely had to try; the media did all the real work for me. So, I've been thinking. Wouldn't it be brilliant to push back the reveal? The only thing funnier than a cartoonish joke of a politician winning an election is that same stupid character running the show. I can't throw this away now. I'll never get another chance to see where it might lead. I need to push this as far as it can possibly go. I need to test what's possible. See how long they'll let a fool run the galaxy."

"I'm sorry, Raz," said Shah, "I can't let you do that."

Raz gave a sad shrug.

"I know."

From the shadows, Xavier Norman lunged and pinned Shah's arms like a vice. She cried out, but a hand latched over her mouth, stifling the noise before it began. His skin had a human warmth, but as his fingers dug into her, she could feel the cold machinery beneath. Raz watched from a distance, and as he did, Shah could see that same coldness in his eyes.

"I'm sorry," he said, "but I knew you couldn't keep this between us. This is one punchline I can't let you ruin."

Shah tried to scream, but Xavier choked the breath from her. She could only watch Raz attach the coin-like device to his temple and walk away. As Xavier forced her into the storage unit, more politicians emerged from the darkness, picking up the crate lid while Shah kicked and thrashed in wild desperation.

Her brother reached the far end of the room. Shah twisted her head and freed her mouth.

"Raz!"

Then the lid slammed shut.

JOEL R. HUNT is a writer, proof-reader, ex-teacher and part-time human currently residing in the UK. Among his other hobbies of eating, breathing and crouching in dark corners, Joel constantly plans stories and screenplays - a very small number of which actually get written. Most simply languish in his ever-growing 'Unfinished' folder, which is now approaching a mass capable of generating gravitational pull.

Joel's genres of choice are horror and sci-fi, although the odd bit of sentiment does manage to sneak in between the freakishness and disturbing twists. He hopes in time that he might earn a living from putting words on a dead tree in a particular order, or at least earn enough for the occasional cup of tea and vegetarian full English breakfast.

He also wants some pet rats, but that's neither here nor there...

Bibliography
ANGELS, Black Hare Press, 2019
BEYOND, Black Hare Press, 2019
Deep Space, Black Hare Press, 2019
MONSTERS, Black Hare Press, 2019
Objection to Perfection, The Gentleman Press, 2012
Sirens at Midnight, NBH Publishing, 2019
Sweek Flash Fiction Book (Part 3), Sweek Publishing, 2019
Sweek Flash Fiction Book (Part 4), Sweek Publishing, 2019
Sweekstars 2018, Sweek Publishing, 2018
WORLDS, Black Hare Press, 2019

Connect
Twitter: @JoelRHunt1
Reddit: JRHEvilInc
Amazon: amazon.com/-/e/B07SBX6G3W
Goodreads: goodreads.com/author/show/6439719.Joel_Hunt

RIDE THE LIGHTNING

By Joachim Heijndermans

A freak storm destroys a Dextrium ore refinery and traps several workers on the planet's surface. Foreman Kuron scrambles to find a way to rescue his people, going so far with employing the most unlikely of rescue workers; a group of daredevil humans.

The escape pod jettisoned upwards, propelled by both its thrusters and the explosions from beneath. The intense speed of the take-off pushed Kuron deep into his seat. Around the pod, the refinery platform crumbled apart, its remains falling towards the surface of Dextro, engulfed in fire and bombarded with purple lightning. He and five others of his

crew had squeezed themselves into their escape pod seconds before the structure's gravitational thrusters finally gave out. Kuron could have never imagined a platform could be brought down by a freak thunderstorm of all things. But then again, many underestimated the harsh conditions of Dextro before, only to pay a heavy toll in their search for priceless Dextrium ore.

From the porthole, Kuron watched the refinery disappear beneath the dark clouds. Purple thunderbolts danced violently around them, nearly knocking them off their trajectory toward the main platform in the troposphere, the only one completely outside of the acidity zone. With a loud crash, the pod collided violently onto Platform 1's landing pad.

Kuron and a journeyman kicked the hatch open. Two rescue-unit bots rushed to spray them and the pod in a thick retardant foam, washing away the acidic condensation from the pod's hull. The other pods had already arrived, with the rest of the crew under the care for by other bots and the paramedics. Kuron gasped, relieved to see them. But something was off. He couldn't have miscounted, could he?

"Did everyone make it out?" yelled Kuron at Orr, his junior foreman.

"I-I'm not sure. My team is accounted for, so we—"

"Orr, Zahn is missing! She wasn't onboard the pod!" called one of the crewmen out at his foreman.

"What? Did we leave her down there?" Kuron asked.

"I don't know. I...I think we might have. I don't know. We might have."

"Did we leave anyone else?" Orr gasped.

"I-I don't know."

"Well, find out, dammit!" Kuron shouted. "Headcount! I want a head count of everyone on deck. Find out who else isn't here and get me a list of their names!"

The others rushed off. Voices shouted commands as those who made it out of the refinery were tallied. Kuron stood at the edge of the platform to peer at the burning world below. He shuddered, horrified by the thought of survivors down on the surface. If the crash didn't kill them, they'd be exposed to a far heavier amount of acid than they were up there in the sky. Those poor souls.

Six. Six crew members had fallen down with the platform. At least, six who were still confirmed alive by the emitted signal from their bio-scanners. Then there were three that were unaccounted for; Zahn, Mesh, and Dyr, who were most likely dead. If they didn't hurry, the other six would join those three soon enough.

Kuron couldn't imagine the horror his people were exposed to since he'd never even been on the surface himself. Dextro was a harsh planet with nightmarish climate conditions. No-one in their right mind would ever go down there. The grappling claws for raw ore retrieval always returned engulfed with acid burn smoke and half-eroded beyond use. To imagine his people put through that kind of nightmare was almost too much to bear.

Kuron and Xzen, the local union captain, stood side by side, their eyes locked on the screen that displayed the vitals of the six survivors. Killon and Dak, two Caunterns like them. The rest were Zufon workers from the Qon planet; Tek, Ty, Ami and Numturyl. All good people and hard workers, contradicting all the preconceptions they had about Zufons. They didn't deserve this. None of them did.

"How long 'till the storm passes and we can get down there?"

"With the current wind trajectory? Seven hours," said Argon, the environmental analyst.

"And how long do we estimate their suits will last before the corrosion hits in?" Xzen asked.

"Four. An' that'm if them suits don't get torn an' ruptured when they go down to the down down. If that'm case for the yes, an hour. Maybe less," S'k'pee the Tandafron, the acid-resistance suit engineer, answered.

"So, it could be anyone's guess? And do we have any other plan to get them out?" Kuron asked his team of specialists, pilots, doctors and other engineers. The gathered experts all spoke past each other. The cacophony that filled the mess hall was unbearable, incomprehensible, and got them nowhere. Kuron knocked his fist on a table to silence them.

"People, we are running out of time. Give me the options. First; can we go down there and extract them?"

Many in the group shook their heads. "We can't land any vessels on the surface. There'd be too much of the acid raining down on us. We'd need a vessel with a massive hull if we go that far down. And even if we can get a vehicle like that, we can't guarantee if the ship will take off again after a harsh shower like that," said Qwal, their transportation specialist.

"Not to mention the electrical storm might cause the flight system to crash," added one of the pilots.

"We could drop down a crane, but there's no way to confirm they'll latch onto it before we pull it back up," said an engineer. "You'd have more luck at an arcade."

"Okay, so a no-go on a pickup. Can we extract them without a surface convergence?" Kuron asked.

They murmured among themselves, with new ideas

thrown back and forth.

"How about they blast themselves into the air somehow, just high enough to breach the clouds, and we swoop by and grab them?" asked one.

"I don't think they'll be in much of a condition to build any sort of construction down there safely. They'll be exposed to the full brunt of the rains, and any materials will deteriorate before they can even launch it," said an engineer.

"The swooping idea could work, though," said Qwal. "Let's not rule that out completely. A Class 4 jet would do the trick."

"We've got three of the Galicae Class 4's. The Hinotori's. Could those work?" asked one of the pilots.

"They're fine, as long as we can get the survivors up and above the storm cloud somehow," Qwal replied.

"Okay, so we have an idea. How do we get them up there so we can grab them?" Kuron said with a sliver renewed hope in his voice.

"One thing at a time, boss. We haven't made contact with any of them yet, so we have no idea how spread out they are or if they can even be moved," said Xzen.

"Yes, good point. How are we on that?"

"There's too much interference from the storm. We're lucky as it is that we can monitor their bio-scans," said Huwarn, the communications specialist. "With the rain as it is, there's a good chance that their comms are down for good."

"Well, then let's just focus on concocting a plan to get them off the surface. I need it two hours ago, got that?"

In unison, the group cried: "Yes, chief!"

Kuron retreated from the group and headed into the kitchen to find solitude, some food, and a chair. He needed to eat before he collapsed. He took out a glornhog meat roll from its package, dipped it in hot sauce, and sat down to relax for the first time since his escape from Platform 9. At least, relax as much as he could with the current situation. With every bite, he imagined one of his crewmates sheltered from the acid rains under some piece of shrapnel or suffering from broken bones. He wished it was him down there, if only to somehow help those poor blighters. It was a chore to eat. Every tastebud told him the meat was good, but it felt as if ash crumbled in his mouth. With some effort, he managed to stuff the roll away, if just to have some fuel to function on.

"Chief?" said Xzen, peering his head through the door. "Osal wants a word."

"Osal? The special resources guy from 7? Let him in."

Xzen guided the larger Cauntern in, who squeezed

himself through the door with some trouble. It was no surprise the man never went down to the lower platforms; he'd never fit that massive body in any sized acid-resistant suit. "Boss," Osal greeted him.

"Osal. You wanted to see me?" Kuron asked.

"Actually, I was on the line with some people on the freelancer frequency who think they can help us. They're a specialty unit who caught wind of our situation and offered to lend us a hand. They claim to have an idea on how to get our crew out of there."

Kuron clapped his hands together. "Great. Any idea is a good idea by now. What do you have?"

"Are you familiar with the Lightning Brigade?"

"Maybe? Refresh my memory?"

"They're a special rescue unit. They work in high-altitude drops and extractions in hard to reach locales and hazardous situations."

"Sounds familiar. How does that work?" Kuron asked.

"I think it might be better if we just got them to come in to explain it. They're on their way and should be here in half an hour."

"Great, we can have them cross-examine the situation with our guys and—"

"Tell him the catch, Osal," said Xzen.

"Catch? What catch?" Kuron asked.

Osal coughed, rubbed his hand over his balding head nervously, then fessed up. "They're...ahem...well, I guess there's no other way to tell you this...they're from Terra-prime, third planet of the Solarium-612."

"Ah. And that is...?" Kuron asked as he took another bite of his roll.

"Humans, chief. They're a human rescue team," said Xzen.

Kuron nearly choked on his food. The two others rushed over and patted him on the back, dislodging the half-chewed meat from Kuron's throat. "Humans? Out here? On a company platform?" Kuron asked in between coughs.

"Yeah, we had an inkling you wouldn't like it. If you want, we can get them on the line and cancel—"

"No. We have less than four hours left. We can't afford to turn down any help," Kuron said. "I'll take full responsibility should the worst come to pass."

"Splendid. I'll open a line between these humans and the rescue group so we can start and come up with a plan," Osal said. He turned and squeezed himself back out through the kitchen door and into the mess hall.

Kuron sat there, rummaging his hands anxiously through his hair. Xzen coughed to call attention to himself. "Have you ever dealt with humans, chief?" he asked.

"No. Have you?"

"Never. But I'm aware of their reputation. They've been involved in some unpleasantness."

"They've also done their fair share of good work. Wasn't the empress's assassination foiled by a human?"

"Yeah, but a human was responsible for what happened to the moon of Gibra," Xzen retorted.

"The Sococo mines," Kuron parried back.

"The Battle for the God Spear."

"Insimino Plux."

"Well, chief. We can sit here and go back and forth on good humans and bad humans, but it all comes down to one thing," Xzen said, as a deep exasperated sigh escaped him. "If they screw up on this, it was you who okayed them. You'll never run command on another refinery again."

Kuron sighed, his face cupped in his hands. "Honestly, Xzen, right this moment, I don't care. My people are down there. Men and women who counted on me to keep them safe, and I failed them. Do you think I could ever run a rig again with a clear conscience with the knowledge I left them to die in agony? Would you?"

"I don't know, boss," Xzen shrugged. "What a day, huh? A whole platform down the tubes, and now we need a bunch of humans to pick up after us."

"Well, if you put it like that, it sounds absolutely

mad," Kuron groaned.

Both of them sat in silence, running ideas through their head for better plans. Any plan that they could pull off themselves. But there weren't any. As it looked now, these humans were their best shot. Nearly five minutes passed before Xzen finally broke the silence.

"You gonna eat the rest of that roll?"

The bulky dropship landed gently on the platform. A yellow bolt shooting from a cloud decorated the sides of its hull, while blue lights flashed from its underside. For the first time, a human ship docked on a Dextro platform. On most occasions, this would have been seen as a momentous event, were it any other species but these.

Kuron rushed out to meet their new arrivals, joined by Xzen, Osal and Dor, the captain of Platform 1. The hatch of the ship flew open. Eight occupants, their pilot not joining them, with large gear packs strapped to their backs rushed out.

Looking at this motley crew, Kuron didn't know what to think. He'd never seen a skinnier bunch of critters in his life. Short, lanky, with the tallest barely coming up past his chest, and their voices high-pitched like children. All their skins had different colours as well. Where some had a pinkish to reddish hue, others would be a dark brown and another with a tint somewhere in between the first two. This diverse collection confused Kuron, who was accustomed to more uniform species like Caunterns (who are all a greenish-brown), Zufons (all grey) and the Tandafrons (yellow with purple spotted pattern). They hardly seemed as much a threat as their reputation had led him to believe. He'd heard the most recent stories of their good deeds, sure. But then there were the worrisome tales from their past. Stories of infighting, cannibalism and pillaging. How their terrible and destructive nature rendered their own world nigh uninhabitable and left them a nomadic race spread out across the cosmos. Kuron wondered if the one rumour about the human queen and the cake was really true?

"HF-team 6, Lightning Brigade, reporting for duty. I'm captain Anders," said a young man with spiked black hair.

"Right. I'm Kuron, foreman of Platform 9. And..." Kuron began. He stopped, scratched his head and ran his hand through his beard. "Listen, I've gotta be frank. I'm trying to figure out how you can possibly help, and we're on an extremely tight schedule, so..."

"Well, why don't you give us a rundown of the situation? That's a good place to start," Anders suggested. Kuron agreed with a nod.

The foreman slid his fingers over his wrist-com. The projectors screened footage Platform 9' s fall for all to see. Two of the women in the brigade gasped. One of the men whistled a lone note, astonished by the damage and violence. But the rest seemed unnervingly calm.

"This was the last we saw of Platform 9 as it went down, taking nine of my crew with it. We have six confirmed survivors trapped on the surface and no way to retrieve them due to the heavy acid storms. We could try, but our ship's navigation will either get fried by the electrical interference or the acid rain will burn right through our ships. We'd lose more people within minutes before we even touch base with the surface."

"You wouldn't happen to have any materials or alloys that can resist the acid?" Anders asked.

Kuron shrugged. "Aside from the cranes that we use to pull up ore, all we have are the suits we wear when we process Dextrium in the refineries, which are lined with a resistant mesh. They're good, but they're designed for use in low acid atmospheres. Down there you're exposed to the full load, cutting their usability time by half."

"We could implement your suit's modular code with our own pressure suits. That might lengthen their usability. Can share it with us?" Anders asked.

"We can, but it won't matter much if you can't make it to the surface. I doubt your ship will last long under the cloud canopy," Kuron said. "What was your plan for going down there?"

One member of the brigade, a woman with black-purple hair and dark skin, stepped forwards and opened a projection display. It showed a small schematic of the planet's surface, the storm clouds, and their current position in the troposphere.

"We've read up on your plans for launching the crew up above the storm cloud. We've actually got a similar system, based on a technique from back in the day of our old world; the Fulton surface-to-air recovery system."

"How does it work?" Kuron asked.

"I'll spare you what it used to be, and just give you a rundown of our updated version. We attach the cargo, your crew in this case, to a high-altitude drone with a strong wire. The drone will fly above the storm clouds and release a set of hooks. Then we'll need jets to latch onto the drones and pull them up with them, dragging the cargo along with it."

"Sounds simple enough," said Kuron.

"What about the acid?" asked Xzen. "What if it eats the wire? Or the drone?"

"Or the electrical interference?" asked Dor.

"The interference we can circumvent. Our drones are built to withstand and pass through geomagnetic storms worse than this, with only minor interference. As for the acid on the wires? Well, we were hoped you could help us with that," said Anders. "Our wires are tough, but we don't know much about the conditions of Dextro's rain. Your team on the other hand does. Do you have any technicians who could help us implement upgrades to our gear?"

"We have the very best," Kuron said. "We can get you—"

"What will this whole ordeal cost us?" asked Dor.

They all turned to him in unison. Kuron's face became red with fury. Of all times to choose to be concerned with the company's expenses, it had to be now?

"You must forgive our colleague Dor. He only has the good of the company in mind. He did not intend to be rude," said Osal with a chuckle.

"Then he failed," Kuron grunted. "My crew is down there. Their lives are in the balance, and you not only insult those who might be of help to us, but you put profit above my people?"

"Gentlemen?" Anders tried to interject.

"I wasn't...I mean, the company..." Dor stammered. "We've already suffered a heavy blow when Platform 9—"

"Ehm, gentlemen?" Anders tried again.

"What about my team? Didn't they suffer a 'heavy blow'?" Kuron shouted.

"If I could—?"

"Kuron, you overstep your boundaries. If you wish—"

"Oh, I wish!"

"Fellas, if we could calm down..." Osal tried to assuage the situation.

Then, the dark-skinned woman put her fingers to her lips and blew the most high-pitched tone. The gathered quit their squabble instantly, startled that such a sound came from someone so small.

"Thank you, Suzanna," said Anders. "I think we neglected to mention that we are a non-profit rescue service. There is no charge, and you will be reimbursed for any equipment of yours we use during our operation."

The four Caunterns looked at the captain with mild surprise. They wouldn't have believed it, had they not heard it themselves. Out there in the deeper parts of the rim, if there is a product or a trade needed, then expect to pay dearly for it. The offer of free labour was a rare notion indeed.

"Are you absolutely serious?" Dor asked.

"Yes. All our services are provided on a volunteer

program. Our jumpers don't get any compensations other than the occasional warm meal, the cost of which our organisation is more than prepared to reimburse as well."

Both Osal and Dor began to laugh, as neither had heard any such offer in their lives. "We've got a deal then. What's the plan?" Dor asked.

Anders redirected them back to his projection, pointing to the purple coloured mass. "This up here is the storm. We'll take our ship, the *Strada*, and hover above the drop point. We go down, make contact with the survivors, attach them to ourselves, then release our drones. These puppies will then fly back up above the storm clouds. We'll just need a fast ship to swoop by and latch onto the drone."

"How fast does the pickup ship need to be?" asked Xzen.

"What's the fastest you've got?" Anders asked back.

"We've got three Hinotori's on standby."

"Those should do fine."

"What will you need to get down to the surface?" Kuron asked. "We have a few drop anchors, but those are for mining purposes. They have nothing for passengers to hold onto, and it's made for heavy impact. I don't—"

"We're going to jump down from above the clouds," said Anders nonchalantly.

Kuron shook his head, making sure he heard that

right. "Your team will jump down...from all the way up here," he said, his finger aimed at the marked spot on the projection, "and then drop down to the ground?"

"Yes."

"Okay, so after your team is dead, then what do we do? You have a contact line for your next of kin?"

Anders chuckled. "I take it you don't think we stand a chance?"

"I think this whole operation is downright suicide. Your suits will be shredded by the acid before you even make it through the first cloud. How—"

"We won't jump through the clouds," the woman named Suzanna interjected. "We'll drop in through the eye of the storm. There is less interference and enough wind current for us to make it down all right. Plus, the initial lack of direct contact with the acid will buy our suits more usage time."

"No offense, but I still find this all hard to believe," Kuron sighed. "Can you guarantee with complete certainty that this plan of yours will work?"

Anders made a face that did not inspire confidence. "Not really. But do you have any other options?"

Kuron hesitated, trying to think of a reply. But his answer was already made for him. "Not a one. Follow me," Kuron said. "Let's get to work."

The Brigade hurried inside the deck of Platform 1

alongside Kuron, who pulled every available man along to help the humans with their operation. The three other Caunterns remained behind to converse with one another.

"Strange bunch," Dor said. "Why do they do it?"

Osal laughed. "Have you seen their world? It's polluted to the point you could actually cut the air with a knife. Their fauna has been confiscated by the Wildlife Preserve Agency. Every was they started against the Federation ended with their loss. It's like they have utter contempt for life, their own or that of others. They are the most suicidal bastards on this side of the rim. Of course, they're the only ones stupid enough to jump into a storm. Pure stupidity runs through those veins."

"I don't think it's stupidity," said Xzen.

"No?"

"I'd say it's their failure to fight their nature. Why else would they ask no compensation? They love their madness, and love doing mad things even more."

"We're putting our faith into the hands of the mad," Osal sighed.

"Well, we're the ones mining this place," Xzen added.

"Fair point."

The *Strada* hovered over the drop zone, its pilot doing her best to keep the ship level with its new plating those reduce acidic moisture corrosion. They were at an altitude of about twenty flecks above the planet's surface. Kuron and Xzen, who had to practically ball themselves up to fit within the narrow space of the vessel, silently watched the Lightning Brigade strap themselves into their suits, which were now adjusted with KM-OM acid-resistant fibre mesh by S'k'pee. With these enhancements, they could withstand over an hour and a half of direct contact with the rainfall. Any longer, and they'd be lucky if their collapsing suits suffocated them quickly before the corrosive rains hit their skins.

"Everyone ready? I want double...no, triple checks on all the gear," snapped Anders. "Anyone jumps without being cleared by me, and you better pray the rains melt your ass before I can get to you."

"Yes, chief," the Brigade cried out in unison.

"Ya skinny sticks really gon' jump?" S'k'pee asked. "Rain's'll eat ya fore ya get down to the down down."

"Then we just gotta avoid getting hit by the rain, won't we?" said Carly, the jumper with the stripe of blue hair that ran down the left of her otherwise shaven head.

"Ha. Ya crazy. S'k'pee love it. S'k'pee is crazy too.

S'k'pee got ya covered. Ya won't burn the burn burn, trust S'k'pee."

Kuran leaned toward Anders's ear. "How will your people land safely? You can't fly, right?" he asked, hoping he wouldn't get a confirmation.

"Don't worry, sir," said Anders. "All of our jumpers will be equipped with wing-suits, so we can manoeuvre around the rain and lightning. Then when we get close to the ground, we'll deploy our parachutes and land safely."

"As long as your adjustments manage to survive the acid," Kuron said with a chuckle.

"Yes, as long as our adjustments manage to survive the acid," Anders concurred.

"They will. S'k'pee gives ya the word," said the Tandafron.

"Have you ever done a jump like this before?" Kuron asked.

"From this height? Oh, yes. Dozens of times. On a planet with acidic rains, condensation and clouds? No."

"Just remember, we won't fall to our deaths," said Heyes, another jumper. "It's the landing that'll do us in."

The entire brigade laughed, as did S'k'pee. The two Caunterns could only chuckle nervously, as they glanced to one another with reserved looks. "Your team knows how to inspire confidence, don't they?" Kuron asked.

"You chaps needn't worry," said a red-haired fellow by the name of O'Neill. "We haven't had a fall fatality since the days of R&D. Trust us, with the right wind, we'll glide smoothly like a flying squirrel."

"Ah, that's good," Kuron said. He turned to Xzen and whispered; "What's a squirrel?"

Kuron's watched the humans as they equipped their gear. He still struggled to understand why these creatures, infamous outcasts among the Federation, would risk so much for others without reward. "I gotta ask," Kuron said. "Who's foots the bill for all this? I can't imagine many investors lining up to provide humans with these kinds of resources...no offence meant."

Anders chuckled. "None taken. We're funded by a collective of first-earth generation-two and -three investors, who come from long lines of wealth amassed in ways that depleted our home-world. Some of their descendants, a group of upstarts, have grown ashamed of the source behind their wealth, and what it has done to the reputation of our species. They just want to give a little back to the cosmos. Show we're not all destructive fools, greedy bloodsuckers and just all-round jerks."

"That sounds very noble and all," Kuron grunted. "But they are still willing to send lads and lasses like your Brigade out into unfathomable danger, probably monitoring you from some station on the other side of this galaxy. Doesn't that skeeve you off?"

Anders chuckled again, answering Kuron's objections with a cheeky shrug. Kuron shook his head, failing to understand the motives of the young man before him.

"Captain Anders?" said O'Neill. "Crew's all set up. We're ready for you."

"Right, mate. As you were, Mr. Kuron," Anders said, throwing the foreman a quick salute. "Wish us luck."

"Good luck, Anders," Kuron said, though dreading what was to happen next, as he watched the small human walk toward the hatch of the *Strada*.

"Anders?" asked S'k'pee. "Funny. Sounding like Anders/Galicae Inc name he do."

"What's that?" Kuron asked.

"Fellers an' company that make the tools S'k'pee uses. Wrenches. Drivers. The drills an' cranes we drop to the down down. Biggun company. Young'n CEO. Human, S'k'pee thinks."

Kuron shook his head, glancing at the leader of the Brigade, with his short hair, cheeky grin and the hint of a tattoo around the base of his neck. That had to be a coincidence. There must be plenty of humans named Anders. Right?

The time of the jump approached. The survivors were estimated to have a little under two hours left until their suits would erode from the acid, based on the idea that they found shelter from the downpour somewhere. While the Brigade was in the final stages of preparation, the team back on Platform 1 watched from their monitors with anxiety and anticipation. The three 'Hinotori' jets hovered around the *Strada*, at the ready to engage. The seven jumpers were strapped in and ready, huddled around the open hatch. Below, dark clouds of purple and black swirled ominously. Lightning jolted out from the monstrous maelstrom, like an enraged beast, barking with bared teeth and hungry for blood, urging them to turn back now or be devoured by the monster that was Dextro.

"Brigade!" Anders shouted. "We are go in three...two...one!"

On 'one', they all leapt out of the hatch without a shred of hesitation. Within seconds, the seven vanished from sight into the eye of the storm. Kuron and Xzen turned to the monitors, each of which displayed first-person views from the jumpers' cameras. Flashes of white and purple blasted past them. Kuron heard their voices over the comms. Some of them relished the sights around them with hushed awe, while others laughed nervously as their velocity increased. They dodged pockets of acid and danced around the stray bolts of lightning that spat out at them, as if the storm attempted to swat away a group of bothersome flies.

"Damn!" one of them suddenly cried. The visual footage of a jumper named Martinez went haywire, while he began to spin around as if thrown in a centrifuge. "I got hit. My chute's fried!"

"Bail, Martinez!" Anders ordered. "Hinotori! We need a pick up for Martinez!"

Martinez released his drone, which shot up to the sky like a bullet. One of the three 'Hinotori' jets dashed down and snagged the drone out of mid-air and flew back to Platform 1. Martinez was safe, but the seven were now six, and they had yet to even reach the surface.

"Damn!" cried Suzanna. "The winds are harsher than we thought. Can the drones make it back up?"

Martinez got on the line. "They're fine. No problems with mine. They're tough little birds."

"What about the wires?" asked Carly.

"This is Xzen. The wires are holding strong. At their current state, your suits will melt before those do."

"That's not as much of a comfort as you think that might sound," Suzanna chuckled.

"Platform 1?" Anders's voice sounded over the comm. "We're closing in on the drop zone. Audio dark until surface contact. Parachute deployment in three...two...one!"

The feed went dead. The visual on the monitors became hazy, darkened by the clouds and interference. Glimpses of flailing hands, parachutes pulled by the wind and jagged rocks popped up onscreen. Silence fell over the team on Platform 1 as they held their breaths. Then, a voice. "Platform 1? This is the Lightning Brigade. We've made contact with the ground."

A sigh of relief went over the crew onboard the *Strada*. The medic, a human woman called Lafayette, smiled assuredly as she tapped into the line with her teammates. "What's your status, captain?"

"Five of us are good. But O'Neill twisted his ankle."

"O'Neill, do you need an evac?" Lafayette asked.

"I can't walk. I'm sorry, but I gotta sit it out," O'Neill sighed. "Keep me down for now. Don't waste a bird on me just yet."

Another one down. Kuron became more anxious. Did he, in his desperation, put too much faith in these humans? "Anders, this is Kuron. Any sign of the wreckage?"

"See for yourself," Anders said, as he took aim with his camera at the eviscerated remains of Platform 9. Kuron flinched. Dextro's rains had ravaged the platform into a decayed horror in just a few hours, as if someone had placed the construct inside an oven just to watch it melt. The crash site was surrounded by pools of molten lead and iron. Beams and wires protruded from the hull, like bones through the skin a carcass. Any painted décor had become a drab smear, technicolour streams melting together into a grotesque blend. Platform 9 was a decayed corpse, and the lost crew would suffer the same fate if the Brigade did not reach them in time.

"Damn!" snapped Kallgren, one of the jumpers. "I found one of them. One of the three blanks, I'm afraid. Sorry, Kuron."

Kuron winced as he looked at the screen. He recognised the body of Dyr, a Zufon engineer, his suit half molten, skewered through the torso on a jagged shard of metal. He prayed Dyr died on impact, as death by acid would be slow and pure unfiltered agony. "Move on. Find the survivors," he said through gritted teeth.

"Here!" called Suzanna. "I got two of them."

The Brigade swarmed up onto a rock which was partly covered by a large piece of metal. Underneath were two Zufon survivors, Tek and Afi, huddled together in their attempt to shelter themselves from the scalding rains.

"Their comm gear is fried, but they're alive. Kallgren and Heyes are up for extraction. Prepare to grab drones 9 and 14," Anders said.

"Oi! I might be hurt, but I can still carry a guy. Shoot

me up with one," O'Neill cried out.

"Copy," Anders replied. "Kallgren, stay here. *Strada*, prepare pickup for O'Neill and Heyes, drones 3 and 14."

"Copy, boss," Lafayette replied. "Hinotori 1 is ready."

Kuron watched the two Zufon on screen. They had been through hell but were overjoyed to stand face to face with people, even if their rescuers were such a short bunch. Tek mouthed what Kuron assumed were words of gratitude. The sight of them alive gave him hope, but they weren't out of the dark just yet.

"We copy you, Lightning Brigade. We'll pick them up. Continue to look for the others," Kuron ordered.

Kuron watched the monitor that streamed Suzanna's visual feed intensely, as O'Neill and Heyes gently tied the two Zufon to their bodies, then aimed their backs up and flipped their switches. Like hunting birds of prey released from their cages, the two drones jolted into the sky.

"This is Hinotori 1. I've got a visual on drones 9 and 14. Pickup initiated."

The jet swooped in and latched onto the two drones. On the monitors aboard the *Strada* and Platform 1, the footage of O'Neill and Hayes as they were pulled up into the sky caused all those watching to gasp. Within seconds, they vanished from view. The team watching held their breath, afraid to even blink lest they miss a moment of it. Then a pilot's voice came in over the comm.

"Hinotori 1 to Platform 1 and *Strada*. Pickup successful. Cargo is homebound."

A roar of applause came over the line from Platform 1. The crew on the *Strada* simply sighed with relief.

"Okay, people. Let's find the others," Anders said. The residual four members of the Brigade moved on toward the broken hulk of Platform 9.

"Look at this wreck. They could be anywhere," sighed Carly.

"Kuron, this is Anders," the captain called in. "I think the others might be inside the platform's remains. Any suggestions for where they'd go and hide in a pinch? I'm looking for the best place to sit out this mess."

Kuron peered intensely at the screens with the hope to find some clue to their location. He saw the remains of the refinery block. There was the crane for ore acquisition, now collapsed in on itself, which now resembled a broken arm grasping futilely at the sky with gnarled claws. The fuel depository dome was blackened and cracked, like a hard-boiled egg held above a flame. The barracks section seemed to be intact for the most part, in a way that it still looked as it had before the fall. The barracks! A place filled with beds and with walls reinforced to be even more acid-resistant, allowing for ease of mind when sleeping. What better place to wait out a storm like this?

"Anders. Turn to your left. That structure in front of you would be your best bet. Inside are the barracks."

"You got it, chief," Anders replied. The Brigade moved forwards with a careful step to avoid the large puddles of molten steel. But the second they entered the decayed structure, the communication line went dead. No audio. No visual.

"Hey! Why can't we hear or see them? What happened?" Kuron snapped.

"Too much interference, chief. Figure the platform's wreck might amplify it. We'll have to wait until they exit," said Xzen.

Kuron waited intensely, his ears poised for the slightest sound as he tapped his foot nervously. His imagination took hold. They waited with held breaths for almost thirty minutes, when Anders called in.

"Lightning Brigade here. We found them in the mess hall. *Strada*, prepare for pickup."

"Hinotori 2 is standing by."

"Any chance we can get Hinotori 1 or 3 back around for pickup?"

"Not if you want to leave now," Xzen replied.

"Damn," Anders grunted. "Then we'll shoot up Kallgren and Carly with the cargo. *Strada*, prepare to grab me and Suzanna."

"Copy, boss," Lafayette answered.

Xzen sighed with relief. "That's the last of them," he said.

"We'll celebrate when they're off the ground," Kuron replied, his eyes locked on Anders' screen. He watched Carly and Kallgren as they attached their cargo to themselves, with two survivors strapped to themselves each. The drones went up. Hinotori 2 shot out like an arrow. The six attached to the other end of the wire flew up, their drones clasped by the jet's clasps.

"Hinotori 2 to Platform one. Cargo is safe. We're headed home."

"You heard them. They're good. Anders, get up here now!" Kuron snapped.

"Copy. *Strada*, prepare to receive drones 8 and 12," Anders said, as their drones shot up through the dark sea of clouds. Kuron rushed to the cockpit, his eye out for the drones. It didn't take long for the two little to break through the dark purple mass.

"Visual on drones 8 and 12," said Lafayette. "Engaging!"

The ship blasted forwards and snagged the drones in its claws. She slammed her fist down on several command keys. The engines and thrusters roared. The nose of the *Strada* kicked upward.

"Hey? Wha—" Anders mumbled before being zipped up through the acid storm. The *Strada* veered up as Lafayette engaged the thrusters. Unable to hit the same speed as the Hinotori's, she kicked the vessel upward, throwing those onboard around like pebbles in a falling jar. Kuron helped the captain and Suzanna onboard their ship, while Xzen and S'k'pee hosed them down with the retardant as quickly as they could.

"All right! That's all of them," Xzen said. "Get back up to Platform 1 and—"

"Wait!" Anders interrupted. "Check my feedback. I gotta make sure!"

"What's up, Tony?" Suzanna asked.

Anders nearly pressed his face against the screen. He repeatedly replayed the footage from his extraction. Again. Again. He watched it over and over, until he suddenly leapt up.

"Anders? What—" Kuron said.

"Which drone and chute are still good to go?"

"Drone 5, and chute 7 is still mint," Lafayette answered. "But your suit is too far gone. You'll—"

Anders ignored his medic's protests. He strapped the drone to his back, locked chute 7 to his suit and leapt out from the hatch without a moment's pause. Kuron watched him fall down back into the tempest below.

"What the hell is he doing?" Suzanna cried out.

"Can we go down and get him?" Kuron asked.

"Negative," said Lafayette. "He's on his own until he launches his drone. We need to stay here to grab him once he does."

"Damn!" Kuron snapped.

Onboard the *Strada*, the remainder of the team waited for a response from Anders. While they could see the captain landed safely, the visual on Anders's screen was more blurred than ever, his comm unit reaching its limit from the corrosion. Running over the rough terrain caused his camera to violently shake back and forth, before suddenly going completely dead, with only the audio of his breathing coming in.

"What is that madman doing?" Kuron asked.

No-one had an answer. They had no other option but to anxiously wait. Twelve minutes passed until Anders's voice suddenly came in over the comm.

"I got a live one. Female. Name tag says 'Zahn'."

"What?" Kuron gasped.

"Spotted her on the replay of my feed. She's critical, but she's breathing. I think the fall busted her bio-scanner."

"Great God!" gasped Xzen.

"She's stuck under this...ris. I'm...onna...pry it...oose," Anders's voice said, hampered by static interference.

"Anders? You're breaking up. What's your situation?"

"Elctromag...tic...ference...wait...rone..."

"Anders? Do you copy?" No reply. The feed became flooded with a static haze. "Anders! Do you copy? Anders?" Kuron shouted.

"Tony!" cried Lafayette. "Tony, come in, dammit! Ton!"

No response. The line was dead. The team on the *Strada* gasped in horror. Those aboard Platform 1 grew silent. Kuron clenched his fists, afraid of what would happen should he relax a single muscle. Then, to everyone's shock, the last drone popped up above the dark clouds.

"There it is! We have visual on drone 5! Get it! Pull him up!" Kuron bellowed.

Lafayette repeated her earlier manoeuvrer. At full throttle, she blasted the *Strada* toward the silver drone. The hatch on the drone's back popped open to release the hooks. The *Strada* jolted toward its target and latched onto it.

"*Strada* connected to drone 5!" Xzen cried.

"Pull up!" Kuron roared. "To the platform! Up! Up!"

Lafayette redirected all expendable energy to the thrusters. With a thunderous roar, the *Strada* bolted upward. The entire crew held their breath, peering down from their ship at the sea of purple clouds the wire was drug through. Still no sign or word. Every second was an eon. Kuron caught himself praying. Then, two small figures popped out through the sea of purple, smouldering from the acid residue. A voice crackled over the comm.

"This is Anders. I got her."

Kuron felt like he could sleep for an eternity, as his body finally began to relax. His stomach roared, as he finally allowed it to remind him that he hadn't eaten anything since the Glorn roll. While the rest of the crew on Platform 1 celebrated and rushed to get the survivors anything they needed, the foreman of the fallen platform slinked away. His eyes were heavy, while all the strength in his legs had evaporated. At times, someone would pat him on the shoulders and congratulate him on a rescue gone right, but he couldn't register a single face. It was all a haze. Relief had made him deaf, dumb and blind, sitting by himself against a wall.

Then a high-pitched voice snapped him out of it.

"Hey," said Anders to Kuron, as he and his Brigade walked past him, the one called O'Neill limping along by Suzanna's side. "Good working with you, Mr. Kuron."

"Yeah, I..." Kuron began, when he suddenly realised the implication. "Wait? You're leaving?"

Anders pointed to the red light that blinked on his wrist comm. "Emergency call on Tutri Moon Eight, one terra click from here. We're the only rescue unit in the area, so we're off."

"But your ship still needs to be hosed down. Any acid particles that might've—" Kuron protested.

But Anders laughed, saluting to Kuron. "We'll get to that. The *Strada* ain't the only ship we have," he said, pointing up toward a triangular silhouette that hovered above, just between them and the sun. "Besides, we're not the type to sit around after a job. Off to the next thrill, right Brigade?"

"Yes sir!" they cried out in unison.

Kuron chuckled. "So, what is your deal, Mr. Anders? Suicidal? Or just flat-out crazy."

"We're human, so pretty much both," Anders yells as he jumped aboard the *Strada*. "We just do it for the right reason this time."

"And what's that?"

"To ride the lightning, Mr. Kuron."

JOACHIM HEIJNDERMANS writes, draws, and paints nearly every waking hour. Originally from the Netherlands, he's been all over the world, boring people by spouting random trivia.

His work has been featured in a number of anthologies and publications, such as Mad Scientist Journal, Asymmetry Fiction, Hinnom Magazine, Ahoy Comics's Edgar Allan Poe's Snifter of Terror, Metaphorosis and The Gallery of Curiosities, and he's currently in the midst of completing his first children's book.

Bibliography
BEYOND, Black Hare Press, 2019
Deep Space, Black Hare Press, 2019
WORLDS, Black Hare Press, 2019

Connect
Website: www.joachimheijndermans.com
Twitter: @jheijndermans

STEEL THUMPER

By Cameron Marcoux

The Silent Ones are coming.

A quick evolving, quick learning species is spreading, consuming everything in its path. The *Ammon*, a carrier vessel, has gone dark. The fate of the Khonsu Fleet rests with a single captain's ability to forge an agreement with a violent alien race. There is little time and only one opportunity to get this right. If he fails, the human race may meet with extinction, for…

The Silent Ones are here.

A dashboard hula dancer swayed slowly in the final iteration of her dance. She had arrived at her destination several minutes prior. She was a long way from home. She swayed ever so gently on the dash of her drop ship, her plastic hula skirt dipping and undulating, as to the rhythm of a song that only she could hear. She had flown in on a tin can. A *puddle jumper* meant for short flights between larger ships and their planetary destinations. It was currently at rest on the surface of the arid dwarf planet, Dorphus. Through the windshield the ship's fore-lights could be seen. They illuminated a large, open expanse of orange rock. In this light, a man stood before a creature twice his size. The man's face could be seen through his helmet by the soft glow cast from LED bars that attached to the inside cage of the tempered glass facemask. The man was looking up, gazing into the face of the unmasked being. It had giant, black pupils. No whites. No irises. Yellowed slits were exposed on the sides of a pale, milky head. They pulsed and jittered, flaring in and out. *Some sort of respiration,* the man thought. There was a mouth, small when at rest, but capable of expanding to much larger dimensions. There was no nose or nasal cavity to be seen. Neither being seemed to fear the other.

"You were not the first creature to set your feet upon this planet, *Steel Thumper.* Not the first to come here with your mathematics and politics. Not the first to see the extinction of your species when looking into my eyes."

Old tales spun like silk webs in the man's mind.

Myths of the ancients. Davin and Goloth. The man versus the titan. *Children's stories.* And yet, in that tale of old, the weak conquered the strong. The small conquered the mighty. The man almost laughed to himself. He was not so small as this. In stature, maybe, yes. But in skill… he could best ten Goloths. He grinned.

"Why do you present your teeth, human? Do you mock what is greatness incarnate?"

The man's respirator whirred with each even breath. He looked down and pressed a series of buttons on the comms unit on his wrist, opening communications. "I do not mock what is beneath me." The pupils of the creature grew even larger, expanding over nearly half of its wide face. Its head shook in anger, the slits on the side of its head pulsed faster. The man put a hand out in front of him, "Be still. Do be careful not to break the treaties between our species, friend."

"You speak of treaties! You speak to Grockil Al'Dorothi, Lintua of the Skemira Antuon! Bow, as is your custom of servitude!"

The man did not change position. "No, I will not bow. You are the representative of your species, as I am of my own. And I will not bow to you, Grockil Al-Dorothi."

Grockil stepped toward the man, its white head glowing faintly, "FOOLISH ONE! *CALISEMORA*! I will rip your spine out from your body and drink the juices like nectar! I will consume your flesh and—" the creature took a step forwards and raised an arm to strike. Four thick claws shaped like stalactites ejected from the ends of its fingers, growing to the length of curved swords.

The man waggled a gloved finger in front of him. "Uh! Uh! Uh! I wouldn't do that. The ships of my people are close at hand. If you so much as graze my suit, there will be very little left of you for your kind to bring home. Think wisely now."

Grockil took a nervous glance into the darkness, then it lowered its monstrous arm, slowly and with great effort, seeming to use every fibre of its restraint. The claws slid, retreating back into its fingers. "Why have you summoned us? Mockery is not council!"

"Resources, comrade. Resources! We wish to make an accord."

The creature paused, thinking the idea over. "Speak further."

"We know how you have come to take control of so much territory in this system. How you've conquered and expanded so rapidly. Hell, we even know how you garnered this little hunk of space dust as your own," he motioned around him and sighed. "We wish to enter the Contest."

The creature was taken by surprise. It began blinking

rapidly. Its large pupils shrinking until they were mere blips upon a broad, open face. Its appearance might have been humorous, if it wasn't so disturbingly monstrous. It began to laugh, its mouth expanding. Saliva hung in strings from jagged, glimmering teeth that zigzagged down into the darkness of its gullet. "Stupid, *Steel Thumper!* You wish entry to the Contest? *Calisemora valdu!* Truly, you are a trickster of your race!"

"No. I speak in earnest. I invoke the rite of Shalar Skemira!"

The dreadful laughing stopped. Its mouth constricted as its pupils expanded, becoming giant holes of darkness once again. "Words of power. Words of great weight." It nodded its head slowly, in acceptance. "So it shall be. Who will represent your kind?"

"I will. That's why I'm here after all," he grinned again.

The creature batted the giant fingers of one hand in the air as if warding off a fly, "Surely you are a messenger only. You have delivered your missive. Go home and send a champion of your race."

"Do not disregard me, Lintua Al-Dorothi! I am the champion of my race and I challenge you."

There was another pause as the creature considered this charge, "Why do you challenge me? What is the sudden imperative to such actions? Utter desperation seems the only possible conclusion."

"We have a common enemy. You know as well as I that the Prototherian-Nucleus has evolved. It has gone from weapon, to contagion, to species of its own. We've come into contact with them. They are growing. Spreading. I've come in contact with them myself. Nearly died getting away. They are learning, Grockil. They're adapting and changing quicker than we thought possible. This is a threat that could kill us all. It needs to be dealt with." He sighed, "We need all of your stores of glint if we are to stand a chance against them."

The slits on the side of its head stuttered and then slowed. It nodded, "We know of these creatures. My kind call them the Comar Vorendix. *The Silent Ones.*" Grockil looked back into space. The man noticed a difference in the creature's face. Perhaps unease, perhaps even fear. "What do you offer in trade when you lose?"

"We relinquish the entire fleet to your command. We choose servitude over extinction."

The slits on the side of its head fluttered rapidly: *open, open, open. Closed. Open, open, open. Closed.* "Very well, *Steel Thumper.* Very well. We have made a Tyral Shalar. Return to your kind. We will meet again this night, when the Colo moon crosses the Star Trellis. In the Pit."

The man returned to his ship. He unhooked his helmet and rested it on a hook by the airlock door. It always felt good to take that thing off. Made the top of his head itch like a bastard. He ran a hand through his hair and tossed himself down in the pilot's seat. There was a passenger seat at the rear of the small craft as well, but he had come on this excursion alone. A blue light on the ceiling of the ship flickered on, "Welcome, Captain," the AI's voice was pleasant. Calming. Sometimes the man wondered who the origin of that voice belonged to. If she were still out there somewhere.

"Ingrid, open comms with Khonsu Fleet."

"Yes, Captain. Opening Comms with…Khonsu Fleet… now."

A blue light was projected down from the machine on the ceiling to the glass before him. A man in a white uniform stood in a grainy, blue array of light. "General McNeal, El'Dorothi accepted the offer. I am to face him in the pit in…" He looked at the clock on the control panel, "Approximately, four hours' time."

"Good work, Captain. It's unfortunate that it's come to this, but we need that glint A-S-A-P. You have to win."

"We're slaves if I don't."

"You know that would never happen. At worst, we'll be at war with yet another species."

The man leaned back in the chair and smiled to

himself. With a nervous laugh he said, "No pressure, right, Sir?"

The General's composure fractured, "I'm sorry." He looked away. "Time is not on our side." His eyes returned to meet the man's, "The *Ammon* has been quarantined."

The man's eyes widened. He felt a stone drop in his stomach. "What? General, tell me that's not true."

"Your ship seems to have launched off in time, but the PTN specimen has escaped containment. Comms are off. Dead silence. Captain, the *Ammon*'s gone dark." He paused, sighing. "Let me be frank with you. If we don't get that glint, I'll have no choice but to give the order to have the ship destroyed."

"General, you can't be serious! There are hundreds of people on the *Ammon*!"

"Yes, there are. And yes, I am serious." He hesitated, "I wish I wasn't."

"I'll get the glint. Don't do anything until then. Please, Sir."

"We'll wait to hear the results of the Contest. I'm sending two officers down a click outside of 'the Pit,' as they call it. They will escort you inside and then report to me—one way or the other."

"Alright, Sir. Thank you, Sir."

"You have a bit of a hike ahead of you, Captain.

You'd best start on your way. Godspeed." General McNeal stood in a military salute. The screen disintegrated.

The man let out a sigh and slumped forwards in the seat, a hand on his brow, elbow leaning against the dash of the control panel. Never in his life had he seen this one coming. As a boy he had grown up an urchin of the Outer Rim, a space station known more for its poverty than the asteroid mining that was its only major export. It was a place that mother's told children stories about in order to scare them into obedience: *"Bad children go to the Outer Rim."* Living there, he had dealt with the hard hand of not just the law, but the Rulers and their ilk. Children were supposed to work ten hour days—that was considered a gift in comparison to the fourteen that adults were consigned to. You were assigned to a position upon the results of a single proficiency examination at the age of seven. Each day you were to work until your required hours had been counted and clocked by a Ruler's Surveyor. The Surveyors were cruel, hard men and women. They had no room for mercy in their hearts. Except for one. Frione Lettingil was a good person. She had helped him escape all those years ago. She had stowed him away in a transport ship filled with fracked asteroids. She had found out that this particular shipment was heading toward The Inners—a region that was much more stable and forgiving, or so she believed. She had given him a parcel filled with water and stale bread. "Stay hidden," she had said, then she kissed his head and went away. He would never see her again. He was eleven years old at the time.

Now, sitting in his ship, the memory felt as far away as the stories of Earth, with its oceans and trees. A land teeming with life and colour. Space was not often such a place. There were plenty of species and creatures out there, but mostly, there was darkness.

A blackness inescapable.

He thought of Gregory Sand, the Hauler who, upon emptying the transport ship, had found him, nearly unconscious, out of food and water. He had snuck the boy off of the ship and brought him to his private quarters. He kept him there a week, nursing him to health, before making the next decision: He would procure illegally forged documents for the boy via a friend of a friend. He would request a transfer to a different station in the Inner. He would adopt the boy and raise him as his own. He would do all of this… *Why?* Was it because he knew what was to be done with any Outer stowaway? Because he knew the child would be sent back to the Outer Rim and promptly executed for desertion? The man never knew of Gregory's motivations. He only had his suspicions and guesswork. These acts of kindness were what led him to become a soldier. To save the lives of others, as his had been saved. And to take lives as needed.

He stood up and walked toward the airlock. Maybe every star that united in the spanning constellation of his life had been for this very purpose: To defeat Grockil. To win the Contest. To destroy the Prototherian Nucleus. This was his duty and he would do it for Frione and for Gregory and for the General. He would save the people on the *Ammon*. He would save humanity. Hell, he would save the universe itself. Small and true Davin, tiny hero of old, had bested the undefeatable Goloth in that story. And so would he best Grockil. He grabbed his helmet off of the hook and fastened it back on, making sure to secure the release clamp, "Ingrid, download coordinates to the Pit and display them on my screen."

"Downloading coordinates to… the Pit…" the blue light on the ceiling began to blink rapidly. "Download successful."

A small map blipped to life in the upper right corner of the facemask. He moved his way into the airlock, the door shutting closed behind him. "Ingrid, open exterior doors."

"Doors opening in 3… 2… 1…" There was a sucking noise as the oxygen was torn from the room. The man stepped down onto the orange rock once again and began his trek toward the Pit.

The Pit was a massive circular bowl cut into the surface of a small section of the planet. A series of rows had been carved and chiselled down into the dusty rock, each row two feet deeper than the last, to be used as seating for an audience. In the middle stood an arena. The Pit was a coliseum, makeshift and without adornment, but an arena where blood spilled freely, for ritual, pleasure, and the settling of accords known as Contests. A single tattered banner was strung from each end of the arena. One blood red, one bone white. They hung limply, like desiccated carcasses out to dry and grow taut in the heat. No wind on this planet. The Pit's arena was ten feet below the closest seating. The man stood in a walkway between the rows, under the white banner. Before him, a rope ladder. All around him came the jeering shouts and calls of the Skemira Antuon. They spoke in the tongue of their kind, but even without translation, the disdain was evident. Eyes, larger than the heads of human children, focused on him. Slits on the sides of their heads, *pulsing,*

pulsing. It was unsettling, even for a man who's life had proven to be full of adventure and conquest. McNeal's two officers were also present. They stood behind him at the base of the wall leading into the arena. They would be of no actual use to him once he was in there, but he had to admit, he felt a little better knowing they were there. That he was not completely alone. He took a deep breath and descended the ladder.

His feet met the orange rock. It seemed darker in places, here in the bowels of the arena, than it had above. Perhaps from a difference in temperature. Perhaps merely from spilled blood. The ladder was pulled up by one of the Antuan, a grisly specimen with a single eye. The other was closed, covered in excess folds of pale skin, like an enormous shrivelled fruit.

"Sir!" The man glanced from the creature to one of his own. *Charles. A good man. Reliable.* He tossed down a spear, blade up. It spun gracefully and was caught with a light smacking noise as it hit his palm. He looked it over. He had no idea what the spear was made out of, but it was a customary weapon of the Antuan. It looked like steel, but as he turned it over, it contained a purplish hue that seemed to glow. There was glint in this weapon. Of that he was sure. He looked up. The only major source of light came from the Colo moon, but it would be enough. The moon covered a sizable portion of the open sky. It was similar to the moons surrounding the Inners. But larger. Three times the size at least. He swung the spear in sweeping arcs in front of him, testing its weight. He would need to be especially careful in this fight. He could sustain a reasonable amount of damage to his suit itself, but even the slightest blow to the helmet could prove fatal.

Grockil Al-Dorothi appeared at the top of the coliseum. It was met by a cheering, raucous chant. It walked slowly down the steps toward the edge of the Pit, a large axe in its free hand. It wore what looked to be some form of black carapace armour, and gauntlets of the same material. At the edge of the arena, under the red banner, it stared down at the man. "Last chance, *Steel Thumper*. Leave now and this accord may still be forgotten, should our Council decide upon it. If it should not be so, at least I will grant you a death that is swift and without needless pain."

The man had set his comms unit to OPEN before entering the coliseum, allowing him to speak freely. "That is appreciated, Grockil. But we need that glint." He looked around him, "So, no. We will settle this now, this night." He recalled the words of General McNeal, "One way or the other."

Grockil nodded, "A prime decision, *human*." It banged a fist against its chest. "Let us fight. May the victor be forever acknowledged through the ages." At that moment, a yellow light exuded from around the base of the ring. It lit up the walls in a blinding radiance, stopping at the rim of the arena. Grockil bent back on its heels and jumped into the Pit. It landed on its feet without injury. Without even the slightest sign of discomfort. Grockil took a few steps towards him, "A word of caution, do not come in contact with the walls, or that part of you will become detached from the rest, burning away into nothingness."

The man flashed a nervous smirk, "Thanks for the warning."

They were now a few mere steps from striking distance of each other. The crowd was chanting in unison; it sounded like a hum. Grockil's eyes became pinpricks. It lunged forwards, axe outstretched. It chopped through the air, but found no mark. The man had dodged left and in the same motion, threw his forearm forwards. The blade of the spear caught the outside of Grockil's left leg with a tearing sound. Dark blood splattered the orange rock below them. Grockil's black eyes grew large upon its face in surprise. It stepped back. The same angry energy that had so filled the creature during their first meeting was now evident upon its face. It beat out in a fury, slits pulsing wildly on the sides of its head, swinging the axe in a temerarious fashion. The man dodged the first few swings with ease and narrowly escaped another by a breath. He feinted left, and ducked right, the whirring zip of the axe blade sailing over his head. He lunged with the spear again. This time the spear found more solid purchase, sticking Grockil in the side, just under the carapace armour. It roared in anger and disbelief; a sound as pitiful as it was terrifying. The man twisted and then pulled the spear back. More blood splattered the rock. He rolled forwards, dodging another swing, and swung the spear in an upward arc across its chest. It cut through the chitinous material and caught flesh beneath. Thick, hot blood spurted out, splattering the glass of the man's helmet, partially blotting out his vision. Rage and fear engulfed the scream that erupted from the creature.

The man pulled back several steps and wiped at the blood with his free hand. It smeared across the glass, but he could see well enough for the moment. Grockil stood, one hand holding the axe, the other clutching the wound on his side. "*CALISEMORA*! Foul *Steel Thumper*! I will destroy you entirely! I will remove your parts piece by piece!" He tore off the broken armour. The man waited ten paces away, spear out to the side, ready to defend. Grockil charged, but this time, instead of an all-out swing of the axe, it stopped abruptly and kicked out at the shaft of the spear, pinning it to the ground. It swung its axe down, severing the spear in two. With its free hand it landed a fist against the man's chest, sending him reeling backwards. The man landed hard on his back, the wind blown out of him, and the remaining shaft of the spear was sent flying from his grasp. Grockil walked toward him, victory bound tightly in each step. Its eyes grew larger as it moved. The man scrambled backwards, trying hard to breathe and move at the same time. The bladeless half of spear rested several yards away. The creature narrowed in. It was in no rush, it seemed to enjoy watching the man's frantic and desperate scramble. Blood oozed from the creature's wounded side and down its leg. The man glanced toward the spear shaft. *So close.*

Grockil was upon him. It raised the axe above its head. The man snatched at the shaft dumbly. His fingertips touched its edge. Grockil sent the axe down with all of his force and fury. At the same time, the man got purchase of the shaft and rolled to the left in a single motion. The axe narrowly missed its mark, lodging itself in the hard, orange rock of the planet. The man scrambled to his knees and lunged upward, the broken and splintered edge of the shaft facing out. It plunged into the forearm that still gripped the lodged axe. It hit true, sticking three inches out the other side of the creature's arm. Grockil wailed in pain, letting go of the axe. While it was distracted, the man scrambled to his feet and ran to the other half of the spear. The purplish hue seemed to pulse through the broken weapon. He picked it up and quickly held it at the ready. "Surrender, Grockil. And I will not kill you."

Grockil smiled, or so the man assumed. Its mouth expanding to cover over half of its face. Razor-sharp teeth spiralled down into the well of its body. An eternity of teeth, it seemed. Grockil plucked the shaft from its forearm and threw it against the yellow wall where it promptly turned to ashes. It held out its uninjured arm and removed the gauntlet from its hand, throwing that into the yellow light as well. It looked down at its open hand. It began to tremble. The four fingers set to the hand began to sprout stalactites of bone, as the man had seen them do just a few hours earlier. They grew into gnarly claws spanning several feet. The tip of each, sharp as a blade. A sudden panic grew within the man. He could feel the nerves in his body constrict, like a rope pulled taut between two opposing forces. "Now you will die, *human*."

Grockil held its hand out in front of it and charged the man once again. He had just the time to hold the half of spear up with both hands to shield his face. He braced himself. The bones connected with the spear and pushed against it. The claws were bending over the side, aiming toward his mask. Hoping to shatter the helmet's glass. Hoping to kill. Grockil used the advantage of his weight to press down harder on the man. The creature was at least twice his size. The man could not hold the position. One of the razor-tipped fingers slashed a thin line into the glass of his helmet. A slight crack chiselled its way up the mask. Letting go of the hold, he spun his body to the left and backed away from the beast. He had an idea. A long shot. *His only shot.*

Grockil advanced. It had the man scared. It could taste the sweetness of victory before him. It would devour this one. It would leave nothing for the others. They could have the other humans. They would serve as worthy slaves and sustenance. But this one… this one would not be a slave. This one would find only darkness in the void of Grockil Al'Dorothi! Its hunger was now fully awakened. "You cannot run, foolish one. There is nowhere to go."

The man looked backwards. The yellow glow covering the wall was no more than two steps behind him now. He put the broken edge of his spear to the light, watching it disintegrate. Grockil closed in, stopping just in front of him. "You were not so weak as I had first suggested. You will die knowing that, at least." The man hesitated and then lunged with what was left of the spear. Grockil swung its fingers in an arc before its face. The spear broke into fractions. Grockil then pulled the hand backwards through the air, towards the man. He ducked low and, as the fingers whistled over his head, he pushed up with as much force as was left in him. The fingers raised against the force of the push and the tips connected with the yellow light. Grockil reared back, roaring. *Screaming.* Its bladelike fingertips were gone. Blood spurted from the open stumps.

The man wasted no time. He swivelled around Grockil, then jumped onto its back, clutching it around the middle. He pushed his hand into the hot wound on its side and, with both feet, kicked down just behind its knees. The creature fell backwards, its legs kicking up in front of it. They caught the yellow beam and were instantly gone. Wails of agony filled the man's head. Not his own, *thank the gods.* The man struggled out from underneath the flailing torso of the creature. With both hands wounded, mere stumps for legs, and a deep wound in its side, Grockil no longer posed much of a threat. It was dying. He stood up slowly. "I will take your glint, Grockil." He looked up at the crowd, "I have defeated your champion, I will take what is mine!"

Over the angry roar of the crowd, a single entity stood up. The one with the single eye. The crowd grew silent. "Human. You have not yet vanquished your opponent. Finish this. Put Grockil to eternal rest for its failure."

The man shook his head in anger and disbelief. *Fine.* He looked to Grockil. It rested upon the ground, the slits on the side of its head pulsing frantically, then slowing, then frantically again, and then slowing again. The man clutched the speartip from among the pile of broken pieces. He walked over to the wreckage of Grockil's body. He knelt down in front of his defeated opponent. "So that you know, I would have spared you. But your kind are not so merciful, it seems." He looked into the shrinking eyes of the alien. "Rest now, Grockil Al'Dorothi. I must save my people." He drew the tip of the blade toward one of the eyes. They were now the size of small coins. The man began to press down on the spearhead. A viscous black goo bubbled up from the new wound. Grockil shrieked in pain. The eye was much harder to pierce through than he had expected. It grew and shrunk seemingly at random now. The man pushed down harder. As he pushed, what was left of a long, bloody finger lifted into the air behind him. It lunged, wrapping itself around the man's throat. In shock, he dropped his hold of the spearhead. The bloody pulp that now served as a fingertip of another finger found the release clasp on the helmet and pulled. The other two fingers grasped the helmet, twisting. There was a violent release of pressure as the helmet popped off. The man gasped. Eyes bulging. No oxygen. Almost instantly, a violent melange of temperature, pressure, and carbon caused his face to turn a bitter shade of blue. Grockil raised itself on to its knees. Its mouth again expanded, this time encompassing the entirety of its face. Its eyes bulged outward as they were pushed to the back of its head. The throat pulsed, causing the shimmering teeth to jitter back and forth, like a saw. Spittle flew in strands as it grasped the man and began to ingest him whole, head first. The mouth expanded further, like a snake, to fit the entire body. It slid down, the creature's body bloating and stretching to make room. Then Grockil began to chew.

Several spans away, the man's drop ship, a mere *puddle jumper*, sat at rest. Its fore-lights still shining out into the expanse set before it. Orange rock. Colo moon. Inside, a dashboard hula dancer stood motionless in the silence. Her hands outstretched, hula skirt still. In an instant, there was a fiery explosion that lit up the sky behind her. The *Ammon* was no longer. The light was brief, already fading behind the brightness of the Colo moon. A thin, trailing light in the vastness of an infinity of fire and dark. A slender creature, purple and covered in fresh black sores, crept from a shadow and reached out a thin finger to set her dancing once again. Then it crept back into darkness.

Silence ensued.

CAMERON MARCOUX is a writer of stories, which, considering where you are reading this, makes a lot of sense. He also teaches English to the lovely and terrifying creatures we call teenagers. He lives in the quiet, northern reaches of New England in the U.S. with his girlfriend and scaredy dog.

Bibliography
BEYOND, Black Hare Press, 2019
Deep Space, Black Hare Press, 2019
WORLDS, Black Hare Press, 2019

Connect
Amazon: amazon.com/-/e/B07RP3YKLD

THE MYSTERY OF THE MISSING MODULES

By Joshua D. Taylor

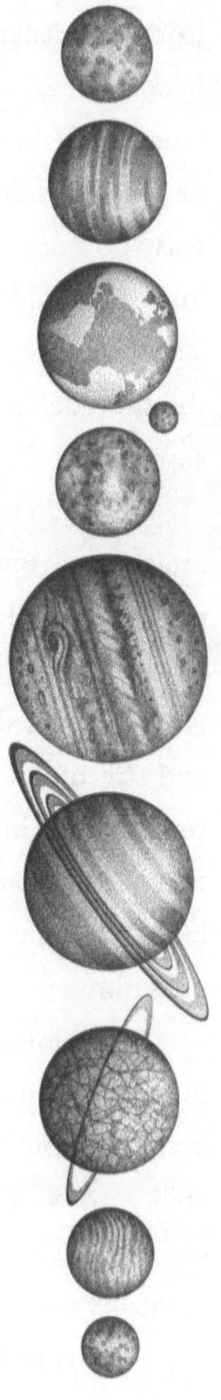

Noir meets the future when Investigative Operative Ulysses Poe must partner with an unusual alien to solve a series of even more bizarre crimes. Who is attacking aliens that look like moving piles of snow, and why? The answer may be more human than anyone realises.

Investigative Operative Ulysses Poe's transport capsule slid into its assigned station in the downtown transport hub tower. The rear hatch opened, and he stepped out onto the walkway, smoothing his long jacket with his hands. He could smell the salt from the distant ocean and the typical city smells of ozone, musk, and spices. It was warm and humid. He wore the jacket because he wanted to look official since he was consulting with a different department, but it was too warm to be comfortable for very long. His luggage would be delivered to his hotel suite on its own. The only thing he carried with him was a small over-the-shoulder pack containing his processor and other supplies.

He didn't mind travelling; he wasn't especially attached to one location. He left instructions for his carnivorous cloud tree. But it was finicky, and he wanted to wrap this case up quickly in case it refused to eat. He had it shipped in from home when it was small and still mobile, before it put down roots. It was his reminder of home. That, and his scars. None of his family even lived on the same planet and his job gave him little time for friends. So, there wasn't anyone to miss him.

His fellow detectives saw him so infrequently they probably won't notice he was gone. He had not been invited to join their bowling league. They thought his ability to work with alien species was a sign that something must be wrong with him. Not fit for company with his fellow humans.

He made his way over to the lift to descend the

tower. As the lift dropped silently toward the ground, Poe could see several green spaces that must be parks. He'd grown up on an agricultural colony so needed to visit the parks where he could think without the constant hustle and bustle. He exited the lift at the ground level and ground transport capsule pulled up in front of him. He was scheduled to meet his partner for this special assignment, Assessment Specialist 'Big Man', a few blocks from the transport tower so he'd arranged to be taken to the meeting place as soon as he arrived.

The Assessment Specialist belonged to alien species that humans just called Snowdrifts. It wasn't a very creative name, but it was accurate. They looked like piles of moving snow. They didn't have a spoken language and trying to approximate what they referred to themselves as would have been an exercise in futility.

Poe climbed into the capsule and zipped off. He wasn't able to meet Big Man at his office in the Snowdrift section of town. Snowdrift buildings and architecture were not compatible with human biology. So Big Man was going to meet him at the office he rented in a part of town mostly inhabited by species with bones. He needed a space to meet with people involved in the assaults to organise his investigation. Poe could have rented a suite with an office attached, but he preferred to work in a different location than he slept. It made it harder for people to kill him in his sleep.

He looked out the clear roof of the car to see countless vehicles whizzing past on dozens of tracks cutting through the sky, while humans and aliens of all shapes and sizes moved across walkways and skyways. As the capsule turned left and rose several stories a swarm of grasshopper-like Danali flitted passed on iridescent wings while the huge red, shaggy form of a Durnha shambled out of a building on six elephantine limbs. He'd never been in this district of Leng City before. It had been a three-hour trip from his district in the north, but Leng City ran north and south along the entire eastern seaboard. And east and west from the coast to the mountains. There were a lot of places he had never been. He was on loan from his district to Big Man's. The Snowdrift District was one of the least integrated in the entire city. Poe had never even seen a Snowdrift in person before.

The capsule slowed as it approached a large asymmetrical building. Poe thought it looked like a sleeping animal. A very sick sleeping animal. The exterior was putrid yellows and purples with a texture like mould. Made to look like a strange tumour on the city next to the traditional towers of fibre and grey composite. Alien arts were rarely appreciated. Though he did have a fondness for the black and gold pyramids the Squilish built.

The car dropped into an opening in the ground, which made Poe feel like he was falling down a rabbit hole. He preferred to feel like the fox, not the rabbit. The capsule was enveloped in darkness for a moment before passing into a large below-ground parking and drop off area.

Poe exited the car and headed toward the building's subterranean entrance. The sublevel smelled clean, but of soil. There was a no lift, just a surprisingly windy and uneven hallway; more something grown than built. Poe signed in then headed into the heart of the building, feeling like he was walking around inside a monstrous corpse. Eventually, he found his way to his office near the top of the structure. There was a conventional looking white door with his title and name on it, fitted into a wall that looked like it was made out of beef jerky. He opened the door and stepped into his office. It was a sprawling affair with floor to ceiling windows that looked out on the bustling city. A large desk sat against the right-hand wall. It was a smooth, rounded thing with no edges or corners—Poe thought it looked like it was carved out of a single piece of stone—and in the middle of the room was what looked like a pile of snow, gently swaying back and forth. He was glad to see a standard white walled room, not something that looked like that inside of a stomach.

Poe had never met a Snowdrift before, so on the trip from home, he brushed up on some literature from the Interspecies Relations Bureau about their culture and body language. Apparently, the most similar Terran lifeform was a slime mould. Poe didn't know anything about slime mould. He was pretty sure this movement represented anticipation. He walked over and bowed. Humans had universally adopted bowing as a standard greeting after a number of unfortunate handshake mishaps with other species. "Assessment Specialist Big Man, I presume?"

The Snowdrift stopped swaying and spun once in a anti-clockwise position. Then it sat still for a moment. Its surface shifted with internal movement, then a soft voice, like an old record player, said. "Yes, Investigative Operative Poe, I am glad you are. Your assistance with the current situation is infinitely appreciated." Poe smiled; he'd gotten far worse greetings from showing up at someone else's jurisdiction. He walked over to the desk and sat his bag down and took out his processor.

"I'm glad I can be of assistance. Do I need to check in with your superiors?"

"Superiors?"

You know, the people you report to."

"Like a hierarchy?"

"Exactly."

"I have no superiors, we all do as needed. If a need arrives, someone will eventually move to fill it. There are those you coordinate, but your results will tell them all they need to know."

While Poe was glad that he wasn't going to have anyone breathing down his neck or questioning his methods, this was going to take some getting used to. "Could you start by telling me why I'm here?" Poe asked. Big Man shifted in one direction, then the other, giving Poe the distinct impression that he was unsure of how to proceed."

"As I stated, to help us with the current situation."

"I've read over the case files, but why do you need my help in solving it?"

"We've never dealt with a situation like this before. Snowdrifts don't normally commit crimes. It goes against the common good that benefits us all, and certainly not violent crimes," This told Poe a great deal about the people he was going to be dealing with. About the world he was on the precipice of being immersed in. "We petitioned the Peace Enforcement Counsel to send us someone with experience in this area. Though I don't know why they sent you personally, Investigative Operative."

"That I do know," Poe said. Big Man's edges

quivered with curiosity, or hunger. Poe wasn't sure. He went around to the back of the desk then took off his long coat and hung it over of the chair. He rolled up the sleeve of his shirt revealed fleshy craters covering both arms that would have made Earth's moon wince. He kept his sleeves rolled up because the fabric irritated the scar tissue. Anyone made of skin meat was horrified about the scars. He doubted his new partner would notice. He placed his processor in a depression in the surface of the desk. It hummed to life.

"I'm good at understanding non-humans' crimes. When people get stuck on a case, it's good to have an outside perspective. Seeing things from a different cultural context might reveal something new. I don't think you can get much more different than you and I," he said.

"Once there was a royal family of Tarthian Neeches that was having the womb fruit stolen from their birthing orchard. They were sure it was a rival family trying to prevent them from having heirs. They were about to start a blood feud over it. The thing is, Neeches are carnivores, and they don't have agriculture or natural predators on their home world. I grew up on a farm. It turned out to be an escaped pet that belonged to one of their neighbours had been sneaking in and eating the womb fruit. Blood feud averted. Good thing too. Before the last blood feud there were thirteen families, and only seven left when it ended. And yeah, humans are very familiar with violent crimes."

Big Man sat, unmoving, looking so much like a pile of fluffy white snow that Poe expected him to start melting. He couldn't tell what impact his tale had on the alien. This was going to be a tough case.

"I too, am from a farm," Big Man said.

Poe raised an eyebrow. "Huh," Poe said thoughtfully "Well, aren't we just a couple of farm boys in the big city." Big Man stretched out horizontally, signalling confusion. "Don't worry about it, Big Man." Poe sat in the chair then waved his hand over the processor.

Translucent images appeared in the air above it. Images of the four victims floated in front of him. They all looked like piles of snow to Poe, with no distinguishing marks or features. Big Man slid over to the desk, his leading-edge retracting and his trailing edge lengthening. He raised himself up as if to better see the images, though he didn't have eyes that Poe could make out. Or any features or even a face.

"Were these taken before or after the attacks?" he asked.

"You can't tell?"

"I won't have asked if I could."

"After."

"So, in your own words," Poe hoped the expression made sense to an alien who didn't have its own spoken language, "tell me what happened to these people,"

Big Man settled back down to his previous height. "Each attack was relatively similar. The victims were all in out of the way places where no one else could see them and the assailant physically collided with them then grasped their modules his its own. A struggle ensued that ended up with the assailant stealing 26-34% of the victim's body."

"Did that… hurt them?"

"It is inconvenient and unpleasant. They will be noticeably undersized until they can regenerate the modules. But there is no lasting damage."

"Okay, so explain this to me. You're made up of lots of tiny pieces and the attacker stole some of them?"

"Crude, but not inaccurate. An individual Snowdrift consists of hundreds of thousands of tiny units we call modules. They are physically separate but work in tandem. Humans call them snowflakes due to a similarity to a weather phenomenon." Poe tried not chuckle at the phrasing. As Big Man spoke the images of the victims were replaced with an image of a three-dimensional snowflake-like structure covered in cilia. "They can survive on their own but normally work in unison with other identical modules to form a person."

"And what happens if some modules are separated from the rest?"

"They will begin to replicate in order to return to their previous number, essentially creating a new individual."

"So, then there's two of the same person? With the same memories?"

"Yes, our memories are encoded into our hereditary materials, stored in the centre of each module." Poe chewed over the implications of this for a moment. He imagined a severed finger growing into a new him. Like a starfish regenerating from a lost limb.

"Can these lost parts or even people be put back together?"

"Yes, they can. I have heard that it is an unpleasant process, merging mind and memories. If I may attempt to anticipate your line of questioning, Investigative Operative—"

"Just Poe, we're partners now,"

"Poe. It is possible that the assailant could have assimilated his victim's modules. Modules are donated to individuals who suffered massive module loss in order to return them to their regular size and capacity quickly. But what reason would the assailant have to take them?"

"Maybe he needs them for someone else?" Poe

guessed, trying to get his head around the idea.

"Unlikely, people are always eager to donate modules to those in need. It is for the common good that—"

"—that benefits us all. I get it." Poe knew he shouldn't have cut him off. He was not really annoyed at Big Man, just at the situation.

"Could they be stealing their memories?"

"No, the assimilation process would wipe out or corrupt them. Practically speaking, if he assimilated that many modules from four individuals, he would be gigantic."

"No one's reported a giant Snowdrift walking, or I mean, drifting about?"

"No."

Poe was stuck. "Could he be hiding somewhere where no one would see him?" Poe doubted a non-Snowdrift would notice if one alien seemed larger than average. "Did all the crimes take place in the same area?"

"They took in all different parts of the Snowdrift district. But each victim described the assailant as normal, not a giant."

"Could he be storing them somewhere?"

"Technically, with the proper medical equipment, but again, to what purpose?"

"Maybe as trophies?" Big Man spread wide against, showing confusion. Poe sighed, he knew this was going to get unpleasant, so he'd keep it brief. "Some human criminals, usually mentally unsound ones, like to take things from their victims to help them remember their crimes. Sometimes it's an item that belonged to the victim, sometimes it's a piece of the victim," he said, fearing that the very description of such a thing might shock the Assessor.

"But I thought humans had to keep all of their parts together for them to survive?"

"We do," he said flatly.

"Then how do they survive this?"

"They don't, that's kinda the point," Poe said. Big Man was still for a long time.

"Do you think this individual might be someone like that?"

"I don't know, we'll work that out when we catch them."

"Do you deal with these sorts of crime frequently?"

"Not frequently, but in a busy human district, bad things tend to happen regularly."

"I hope my district does not become like that." Big Man said.

Humans had been dealing with the darker parts of nature for millennia, and it still exacted a huge toll on society and on individuals. Poe didn't think Snowdrifts would be able to cope with such a thing. These well-meaning people had no frame of reference for darkness. Their parts would cease to be cohesive under that kind of pressure. "Me neither. But right now, we need to deal with this one case. Whatever comes after this, you'll find a way to deal with it."

"Me?"

"Yeah, I'm going home after this. But under my expert tutelage, you should be able to move up from Assessor to Detective. Handle this shit all by yourself."

"I would be the first Snowdrift Detective in history."

"Well then, let's get this case solved." Poe thought about what their avenues of investigation were. None of them were promising. "What about the crime scenes? Forensics didn't find anything?" Images of different scenes materialised in the air between them. To Poe, it just looked like a series of pipes, tunnels, trenches, and gutters. No doors, just holes and grates. If you didn't have a solid body, you did not need much space. This was why Poe was unable to visit the Snowdrift section of the city. It made Poe think of plumbing, not a place where people lived and worked. There wasn't a space large enough for him to stand, let alone conduct an investigation.

"No, they found nothing at all."

"I guess I'll just have to be content with reading the reports," he said, not feeling very content at all. He'd never had to do a remote investigation like this before. "Well, if there's no evidence and no motive, do we at least have a physical description of the attacker?" Poe wasn't sure how useful this was going to be. Even though different species commonly joked about others all looking the same, he really couldn't tell these sentient collections of white powder apart.

"Yes." Big Man's spirit seemed to lift. "Very good descriptions." The projection from Poe's processor changed again, showing a rendering of a single Snowdrift Module. At that moment a whale-sized creature flew past the window, throwing a shadow across the room while flapping dozens of pseudopods. Nobody bothered to look.

"So, what am I looking at here?" Poe said, gesturing to the snowflake module.

"A composite of descriptions that the victims gave of the attacker's modules. Every person's modules are different and unique. It is one of the main ways we identify each other."

"I wonder, would it be possible to compile a database with everyone's modules? Then we could compare the description against the database."

"We already have one. There were no matches."

"You have a database of everyone's appearance?"

"Of course, don't you?"

"Hm, no. Humans can be *hesitant* to give out their personal information. There's a history of it being misused."

Big Man seemed to digest this for a moment. "In our society, it is understood that everything works better if every unit functions as part of a whole. We are all stronger if we work as one. Snowdrifts do not struggle with human concepts of 'personal freedom' or 'individuality'." Poe was starting to see a running theme. Something about it bothered him. He wondered if their complete devotion to their society gave them a blind spot to those who didn't live by the same code.

"This is still useful though; we can compare it against any suspects. When we find some. How much do you trust the accuracy of these descriptions?" Poe had often found that traumatic events scrambled people's ability to give reliable details.

"I trust them completely; the descriptions were all exactly the same."

"Wait, what?" Like no differences at all?" Poe asked, shocked.

"No, should there be?"

"Well, I don't know how you guys are, but human memories are highly flawed. How a person experiences an event and remembers it, is affected by their own past experiences. When everyone says the exact same thing, it gives the impression that they planned what they were going to say in advance."

"Why would they do that?"

"Because they're trying to get their story straight," Poe realised that expression probably didn't mean anything to Big Man. He tried again. "Because they're trying to cover something up. These people don't know each other, do they?"

"No, we asked, none of them have any knowledge of each other."

"Still seems fishy to me. I mean, it seems suspicious. At least it would if they were humans."

"They are not though. I wonder if your suspicion of dishonesty might be leading you in the wrong direction." Poe thought about this and reminded himself not to humanise too much. It was a trap he couldn't afford to let himself fall into.

Big Man sat still for a moment. "What bothers me is that the attacker didn't leave behind any of their own modules."

"I didn't think you guys normally left bits of yourselves around."

"We don't, but this isn't normal. With all the pushing and pulling, you would think the attacker would leave behind a few modules somewhere. But nothing. Do you not leave pieces of yourself behind after physical interactions?" Poe didn't love how he said 'interactions'' but he was right.

"Yeah, bits of skin. Hairs. So, we have an attacker that everyone gives a perfect description of, but who left no physical evidence behind." Even for a wildly different alien species, this case was making no sense.

"Well, can we re-interview some of the victims? I might be able to shake loose some additional details."

"Yes," Big Man perked up. "I can arrange that in a few hours, would you like to have them come here?"

"Well, I certainly can't go to them unless they want to meet at a park or something. But not today, tomorrow morning."

"Why not today?"

"Because I need to go to my hotel and sleep and eat and probably shower."

Big Man seemed to shift about.

"You really are strange people. You require so much maintenance."

A smile broke across Poe's face. It was first personal feeling he'd heard Big Man express since he arrived.

"Come on." He stood and picked up his processor. The floating images vanished. He put it in his bag and picked up his coat instead of putting it back on. "Now that I've got the basics down of the case, we'll start with interviews tomorrow. Then we'll follow whatever threads we find."

He walked around the desk and headed to the door. "One last question," Big Man said. Poe paused and looked at the alien that slid across the floor.

"Sure,"

"What is that room for?" Big Man produced a snowy tendril and pointed it at a door across the office from the large desk.

"That's a restroom."

"What is its purpose? I thought your hotel room was for resting."

"It's where humans go to relieve themselves."

"Relieve themselves of what?"

Poe paused, as much to keep himself from laughing at the absurdity of the situation as to try to think of a simple explanation for a complicated and personal process. He decided to be clinical about it.

"Digestive and metabolic by-products."

"You have a special room for that?"

"You don't?" It was Poe's turn to be scandalised.

"The cilia on our modules break down foodstuffs before absorbing them. Inedible substances and waste products are simply discarded as we move."

"Good to know. I'll make sure I don't walk behind

you." That definitely had not been covered in the Snowdrift briefing he had received from Interspecies Relations Bureau.

"Why?"

"Human taboo."

"A taboo about walking behind people?"

Poe sighed. "Come on, it's getting late," he said and headed for the door.

The next morning Poe awoke in his hotel room to the sound of his processor alerting him to an incoming communication. He waved his hand over it on the nightstand to accept.

"Investigative Operative Poe, this is Assessor Big Man."

"Go ahead, Big Man," Poe said as he lowered the window's opacity to let some of the morning light in.

"Is your sleep cycle finished?"

"It is if you have coffee for me." There was noise in the background that sounded familiar. "Are you in the lobby of my hotel?"

"Should I not be?"

"Look, I'll meet you at the office in ninety minutes."

"Should I bring coffee?"

"I'll get my own coffee. But bring the first person to interview. What's their name?"

"You can call them Victim # 1."

"That's terrible, are you sure?"

"It will have no meaning to them, and they have no human name."

"That's going to take some getting used to."

"I am sure you will adapt. I think you will enjoy talking to them."

"I'm not here to have a pleasant chat with people. We're here to catch a criminal. See you in ninety minutes." Poe disconnected the call.

Later he arrived as his office, walking briskly up the winding, vaguely organic hallways. He passed someone that looked like a tree branch covered turquoise seashells that emitted little puffs of smoke. He gave them a wide berth. When he reached his office, he found the door unlocked. He opened it to find two mounds of snow in the middle of the room, a large one and a small one, edges merged, looking the humps on a camel.

"I'm not interrupting anything, am I?" he asked. If they reproduced sexually, he would have thought something risqué was taking place. The two aliens moved apart. Poe assumed the larger one was Big Man and the smaller one was Victim # 1. He could see movement below their surfaces. They were probably forming speaking structures.

"We didn't mean to communicate in a way that you could not understand. We were discussing alterations necessary to Snowdrift society to make interaction with other species less jarring, more harmonious," said the considerably larger of the two, in Big Man's voice. Poe was not thrilled that Big Man was getting so cosy with someone involved in the case. He would have to learn to be more suspicious, less trusting and open. Though maybe in his society that was not necessary.

Poe walked up to the two Snowdrifts and bowed. "Not talking about me, I hope," Poe said, knowing that they were.

Big Man contracted. "Should I not have?"

"It's fine." Poe walked over to the desk and took out his processor. "Victim #1, thank you for coming in. I'm sure this must be very difficult for you. Can I get you anything?" Poe looked around the expansive office and realised he had nothing to give. There weren't even any chairs, not that Snowdrifts needed chairs. He had forgotten that, other than his desk, the office was completely empty. Next time he would request that the office be fully furnished. Then he realised that there was nothing that he might have, as a human that would be appropriate anyway.

They bobbed up and down for a moment then spoke "No, nothing is necessary. I am very pleased to meet you. I do come into contact with many humans. Your physiology is so strange." This was not the response he had been expecting. It threw him off for a minute. Before he could remember what he wanted to say, they spoke again. "Your arms, are they damaged?"

He looked down at the scars covering his forearms. It was warm again, and he had not bothered with his coat at all. Both Snowdrifts moved closer.

"Old injuries, long healed. I grew up on a farm surrounded by wilderness far, far away. I got attacked by Grub Gnats, an invasive species." His carnivorous cloud tree was one of the few lifeforms native to his own home world that would eat Grub Gnats.

He held his arms out and looked at them. He knew every crater and pockmark, but it had been a long time since he'd really looked at them. He looked back up at the two amorphous aliens, realising they didn't even have concepts for things like bodily injury or wounds. If modules were destroyed, they simply made more. If one was broken or damaged, the others broke it down and recycled its components. He needed to remember that he wasn't going to understand their experiences. He again reminded himself not to treat these intelligent colonies of mobile protein shells like humans.

"It was a long time ago. It's one of the things that comes with being a cellular life form. Bodies heal, or they don't." He smiled. "Most Snowdrifts wouldn't have noticed. Do you have an interest in alien anatomy?"

They bobbed up and down again. "A little, I'm part of a cultural exchange program in the Neefer district. All different types of aliens attend. It's quite stimulating. There are no humans though. We read books and watch films from different races to get a better understanding of how others live."

"Any authors I might be familiar with?" Poe wasn't well educated on classics, but if he could keep her talking about something she was interested in, she would be more relaxed. More likely to trust him.

"I get the human and Squilish writing confused sometimes." Squilish people were blue, twenty feet tall, and incorporated rocks into their bodies as they grew. They were still more similar to a human than a Snowdrift, so Poe let it slide. "I think the humans were Hemingway, Shelley, and perhaps Keats."

"Those sounds familiar. The only one I really remember is Sir Arthur Conan Doyle."

"Doyle?"

"He wrote famous detective novels."

"Sherlock Holmes?" Big Man asked.

"Correct, my dear Watson," Poe said.

"I understand," Victim #1 said. "I was wondering," they seemed to stretch out in all directions for a moment, "Is human reproduction as odd as it sounds?" Poe cocked his head, taken by surprise again.

"I never really thought about it, I suppose any type of sexual reproduction would seem very odd to you."

"It's such a fascinating idea, bonding the material from two individuals to create a third. Creating a life that is both you and not you." Poe could swear there was a sense of wonder if their otherwise flat, monotone voice. Big Man seemed to shift about, uneasy. "The whole being greater than the sum of its parts. Snowdrift reproduction is so linear." Poe was accustomed to aliens having very different values. He'd had some very strange conversations over the years about fairly straightforward topics. But something about this set him on edge. There was a sense of longing when she spoke.

"I suppose it's something we take for granted," Poe said. Victim # 1 bobbed up and down.

"Are there any other Snowdrifts in this club?" Big Man asked, getting things moving again. Poe was grateful.

Victim #1 paused for what Poe thought was an

unusually long time, her body completely unmoving, as if trying not to give anything away. "Yes, several," she said at last. "Along with a Trechadorian, some Rowtors, Spindles, and a Durnha." Poe nodded, he was familiar with all of those aliens, even if he didn't personally know many.

"Hm, that's interesting, I'll have to see if there's one back in my district. Might be fun," he made a note in his processor and he cleared his throat, realising that neither Snowdrifts would know what he was doing. "So how are you doing, after the attack?"

"I'm recovering, it's going to be a while till I get back to my regular size. People have offered to donate modules, but I've turned them down."

"How come?"

"The assimilation process is very difficult. For the amount that were lost, I'd rather wait for them to regenerate naturally instead of having to go through the inconvenience." Poe noted that they used the word *lost*, not *taken*.

"I see. Is there anything you can remember about the attack that you didn't mention when you originally spoke with Assessor Big Man?"

"No, the attacker surprised me when I was alone in a corridor on my way to a transport tube. They knocked into me, and before I knew what was happening, their modules quickly separated off a large portion of mine. He enveloped them into his body then quickly left. I responded too slowly. It was so shocking. When I tried to go after them, they were already far ahead. I was not accustomed to being so small, I couldn't catch up." Victim #1 seemed just sink to the floor and spread out.

"He didn't communicate with you in any way during the attack?"

"No. Nothing."

"Nothing at all?" Big Man interjected.

"I don't think so, I mean, I don't know." Poe sat up. Something was happening. Big Man was after something, but Poe had no idea what it was.

"That's very strange," Big Man stated.

"It is?" Poe asked.

"Most of our communication is physical and chemical in nature, not auditory like yours," he said to Poe. "A certain degree of the information our modules give is unintentional, kind of like human body language," he explained. Victim #1 spun anti- clockwise in agreement. "You didn't get any feelings of rage or anger? No idea of intent at all?" Her mass shifted back and forth.

"No, it was very strange," she said.

"That is strange. The individual must have an extraordinary amount of self-control not to reveal anything," Big Man said.

"Did you notice anything unusual before or after the attack?" Poe asked.

"Like what?"

"Anything out of the ordinary. People that seemed out of place. It's unlikely that these attacks were just random events. Everyone, including yourself, was attacked when they were isolated. Your attacker had to know this. It was premeditated," Poe said.

"I didn't know that."

"Yeah, this kind of thing doesn't happen spontaneously. It takes planning."

"What kind of person would do this?" Victim #1 asked. Not for the first time, Poe wished their voices had inflections that conveyed how they were feeling, but they didn't.

"I don't know but it's probably more than one person," Poe said, trying out a theory on the fly. Big Man's posture indicated confusion, but he remained quiet.

"More than one. Why do you say?" they asked.

"Well, it's my understanding that your people naturally operate as parts of a whole. It seems unlikely that a rogue individual did this all by themselves. Don't you think?" he asked and waited for a reaction. There was a long pause.

"I don't know. I function as a systems analyst for the public works. I never wanted anything like this to happen."

Poe leaned forwards. "I believe you." She stretched forwards and backwards for a moment. "Thank you for your time, Victim #1. You've been very helpful in clearing some things up. You can go. We'll keep you informed of any developments."

They spun clockwise in gratitude and headed for the door. They paused before leaving and asked, "Are you going to be talking to the other people who were attacked?"

Poe looked at them. "Yes, we're re-interviewing all the victims. Trying to get a clearer picture of what happened." Victim #1 contracted slightly, but said nothing, then left. Poe entered information into his processor for several minutes before either of them spoke.

"Are those normal questions you would ask someone?" Big Man asked.

"Well, the questions are dependent on the situation, but yes, those are pretty standard."

"I will remember them."

"Well, hopefully you won't find yourself needing them again after this case," Poe said, then stopped what he was doing. "What sort of investigations are you used to doing?"

"I often assess accidents to find out the cause. Also, I talk with people to settle disputes, assessing both of their claims."

"Do you ever consider that someone might be dishonest to you during these assessments?"

"It's more like sorting through people's perceptions of what happened to get to the truth."

"Okay, well that's what we're doing here, but the difference is that someone is actively trying to obscure the truth."

"That's not a normal Snowdrift behaviour."

"Nothing about this normal."

"True." Big Man moved over to the window. Poe assumed he was looking out at the city that surrounded them. Trying to find order in the chaos. "Did you get what you wanted from them?"

"I got something. I don't know what yet."

"Do you think they're involved?"

"Maybe, they know more than they're telling us. And if they do, so do the others. It smacks of conspiracy. But why? What the hell are they doing?"

"What do we do now?"

"Find out more information on the cultural exchange program. See if there's anything going on there." Big Man's mass shifted, manipulating the processor he carried inside himself. "Now, we get breakfast before the next interview," Poe said.

"I thought you said we were going to a park?" Poe said trying to keep his footing on the sloped, fuchsia surface while he held a breakfast burrito in one hand.

"This is a park," Big Man said.

"I think you and I have different definitions of a park." Poe could see out across the city from their vantage point. Other Snowdrifts moved about the outdoor space, seeming to enjoy themselves.

"The ground is at thirteen degrees with many interesting features. What do you consider a park?"

"A faux natural space with plants and small and annoying, but ultimately harmless, wildlife." Poe found a suitable protrusion from the ground and sat on it. He grasped his burrito with both hands and took a bite. Big Man had consumed what Poe thought looked like a bag of sand, but he presumed it to be Snowdrift food.

"Next time you can choose," Big Man said.

"I'm choosing the *rest* of the times," Poe said and took another bite of his burrito. They made the bacon extra crispy just how he liked it. He was sure the eggs didn't come from any bird had ever heard of. Big Man assumed a relaxed doughnut-shaped next to Poe. Several Snowdrifts moved around Poe then off to other parts of the park, climbing over the various protrusions. He was sure they were checking him out and wondering what he was doing there. He was wondering the same thing.

"Let me ask you something. Why Big Man?"

"What do you mean?"

"Why not Fred? Or Alice? Or Cucumber?"

"It's a nickname. And it translated well."

"A nickname?" Poe looked around. He had noticed that Big Man was a little larger than the other Snowdrifts he'd seen. Much larger than the undersized Victim #1. He didn't consider it relevant. He must be slipping. The ground flickered colours for no reason. Poe really didn't like this 'park'.

"Yes, like you, I am originally from a farm. There is a great deal of manual labour to do, being big is usually good. There are no tightly winding corridors or enclosed spaces like here in the city. So, on average people from rural communities grow themselves to almost twice the size of people in the city. When I got here, years ago, I reduced my size significantly to fit in, but I couldn't stand being as small as everyone else. I felt so... vulnerable. So, I settled in for something in between. People still notice."

"So, a difference in size is something that other snowdrifts take notice of."

"Of course. Won't other humans notice if you were missing part of your body?" Poe imagined if he showed up one day missing his arm. Or was suddenly much shorter.

"I suppose they would."

"Enough that you might need to make up an excuse why you were missing so much of your body?"

"An excuse like being attacked by a stranger who no one recognises and who leaves no evidence?"

"Because he was never there." Poe popped the last bite of breakfast burrito into his mouth. "Still no idea why though. Maybe our next interview will be more helpful."

Big Man twitched. "Probably not."

Poe stood up, forgot the ground was sloped and almost lost his footing. "What's wrong?"

"I just received a message, all the other victims have cancelled their interviews, citing scheduling conflicts."

Poe raised an eyebrow. "All of them? At once?"

"It seems that way." Big Man shifted from side to side, manipulating his internal processor. "This is very odd. All Snowdrifts wish to help society run its smoothest."

"So you've told me. This seems to run counter current to that, doesn't it? Like lying about a supposed attack."

"It does. Why would someone do that?"

"Well, it's not uncommon for humans to place their personal agenda over that of the greater good. But, specifically in this situation, people who are guilty of something usually don't want to talk to the police."

"Victim #1 talked to us."

"Then afterwards, everyone else cancelled. They must have called the others; told them we were getting too close. This is good."

"How?"

"Now we know for certain that they all know each other, we just have to figure out how." Poe rubbed the scars on his arms, wishing he had thought to get a drink with his burrito.

"Oh?" Big Man asked. "I also just received a list of the members of the cultural exchange club. All four victims are current members."

Poe smiled. "So, they lied."

"A sign of guilt?"

"Usually. Can we force them to come in for questioning?"

"We don't have any evidence of wrongdoing."

Poe let out a sigh, he knew Big Man was right. This

investigation was driving him mad. They had no evidence. He couldn't visit the scene of crimes because he wasn't a pile of sentient sand. All they had was conjecture and suspicious behaviour. If he were back home, he might be able to finagle something with that, call in some favours, but he was far outside of his jurisdiction here. Barely more than a consultant. The mystery meat burrito sat heavy in his stomach. "They're all in this together. I'm sure of it," Poe said. Big Man spun once, counterclockwise, agreeing.

"But if there is no assailant, then their only crime is filing a false report. Disrupting the harmonious flow of society with misdirection and false truths."

"You're still not seeing the bigger picture."

"Is there a picture bigger than the harmonious flow of society?"

"Okay, maybe a little smaller than that. They're hiding something right?"

"Yes, but we don't know what."

"Don't worry about the *what* for a moment. Think about the *why*. *Why* are they hiding something?"

"We don't know that either."

"Yes, but they're probably hiding it because they don't want anyone to find out. Probably because they're doing something they're not supposed to. That'll be the real crime."

"Real crime?"

"That's what we need to find out. Try to get them to reschedule their interviews and get full background checks on all of them," Poe said. "And can we get outta here? This place is putting me on edge."

°°●.◐⬭◯●.◐●°°

After Poe returned to his rented office, he used the restroom, refusing Big Man's requests to see how he disposed of his wastes. Then they stood in front of the window, watching capsules and aliens of every variety go by on the street below.

Poe needed to go over their suspicions again. Needed to look for holes and other possibilities because what they had so far didn't make any sense. "So, a group of Snowdrifts all remove pieces of themselves, claim to be attacked so no one asks questions. Then what do they do with the pieces?"

"I feel like we are descending into the realm of madness," Big Man said. Poe turned and raised an eyebrow, taken by surprise. He had never heard Big Man be poetic before.

"Don't worry about it, think of me as your tour guide. Human society is like 50% madness,"

"That isn't very reassuring."

"It's all that I have to offer."

"We still haven't been able to reschedule any interviews." Several impossibly small vessels sped past the window leaving pink contrails in their wake. Poe's processor began to beep from inside of his bag that he left draped over the desk chair, trying to get his attention. Big Man's processor began to make a muffled beep inside him. Perhaps there had been another attack. Poe crossed quickly over to his bag and took out his processor then put it in the desk.

Poe read aloud as Big Man received the message from his processor somewhere inside his mass. "We've been forwarded a report that just came in. There's been a sighting of a 'strange looking' Snowdrift in Shelton area. Where's that?"

"It's a warehouse district, not a location where you'd usually find a Snowdrift. I am surprised the person who reported it knew what they were looking at."

"Well, you guys are kinda distinctive."

"It says the individual was seen outside a warehouse. They were unusually large and seemed to have chunks of their body falling off." They turned toward each other trying to figure out if this had anything to do with their case. It struck Poe as too much of a coincidence.

"Is there anything that would cause modules to fall off a Snowdrift?"

"There are several diseases that disrupt the modules ability to communicate. This can cause interference with the coordination of the modules. But this manifests as small numbers getting left behind. Not large amounts falling off."

"Maybe someone else is absorbing all the pieces. I wonder who it is?"

"Something about that just doesn't feel right."

"Does anything about any of this feel *right*, to you?"

"No. This is the definition of wrong for a Snowdrift."

"What's the address of this warehouse?"

"I'm sending it to you now." Big Man paused for a moment. By this point, Poe was confident enough in reading his partner to tell that something was off.

"What is it?"

"The warehouse is registered to something called the Prometheus Consortium. That's a human word, isn't it?"

"Yeah, sounds familiar." Something itched in the back of Poe's mind. Like a thread from the collar of his shirt, scratching him, but he couldn't quite get a hold of it. If he could just get it, and pull, he knew the whole thing would unravel.

"Apparently, Prometheus was a deity who stole fire from the other deities to give it to mankind," Big Man read from his processor. Poe's hands absently rubbed his scars. He always revisited the old traumas when he felt stuck.

"Do not take offence, but I find this story highly strange. Do you think the members of the Interspecies Cultural Exchange could have read this story and been driven mad?" Poe ignored the question.

"Who were the authors they read again?"

"Do you want the entire list sent over or just the human ones?"

"Just the ones Victim #1 mentioned." Poe could almost feel the thread between his fingers.

"Didn't you take notes?"

"Damnit, not now!"

"They were Hemingway, Shelley, and Keats. I can't say that I'm familiar with any of them."

"That's it, right there!"

"What?"

Poe had the string, now all he had to do was pull. "Shelley. Mary Wollstonecraft Shelley." He brought up her autobiography with his processor. "She wrote a famous horror novel called Frankenstein. It was about a brilliant and insane doctor who tried to create a human being by combining the body parts from other people. It worked, but doesn't end well for anyone involved. An alternative title was *The Modern Prometheus.*"

"What is the point of creating this new lifeform, if humans are already able to combine their genetic material to create offspring?"

Poe was quiet for a moment, trying to remember the details. Thinking about human nature, and the things that drive it. They were so different from Snowdrifts, whose main need was to be part of an efficient, functioning whole. "To see if he could."

Poe was thankful that Big Man did not question it. He didn't know what he would have said.

"Shall I call us a transport capsule?" Big Man asked.

"Yeah, let's double time it."

They arrived outside the warehouse before their backup. The area was mostly quiet, with large industrial transport capsules coming and going in the distance. The building was indistinguishable from its neighbours. Just another several decades old, faded rectangle. The composite walls had begun to crack. Poe peered into one of the larger gaps and wondered if a Snowdrift could squeeze through.

"Alright, we need to secure the perimeter until backup arrives. You go left, I'll go right. Detain anyone you see. Keep the line open and let me know if you see anything. Don't go in there alone." Big Man agreed, and they turned to part, but then Poe spun back around. "Wait, what do I do if I get attacked?" He realised he had no idea how to defend himself. He the gun at his side was probably useless against a being composed of hundreds of thousands of tiny parts. At best, he might break a few modules.

"Why would anyone attack?" Poe tried not to laugh. He had been punched, kicked, stung, and dropped from the air during his time in law enforcement. "If you come across one of the involved persons, you should be able to reason with them."

"Let's discuss Snowdrift sociology later. What do I do if I get attacked?"

"Well, when two Snowdrifts try to overpower one another, it's usually the one with the most modules that succeeds," Big Man paused, "You need those openings near your apex for gas exchange, correct?"

"Yeah," Poe said, exasperated.

"Try to keep those from getting covered." Big Man moved off along the side of the building, leaving Poe standing there.

Did he just make a joke? Poe asked himself, walking around the opposite corner. He could see ahead for several hundred feet to a large loading dock.

"A physical attack from you would be useless against us. Your best bet would be an electrical attack or a concussive blast," Big Man's voice came from the processor in Poe's bag.

"So, a stun gun or a grenade. Neither of which I have."

"I would hope not. None of these people are violent criminals."

"Well, the weather isn't violent, but it'll still knock your house down sometimes."

"Would you try and shoot a storm?"

"Fair enough." Poe stopped talking as he approached the large loading bay door. They were locked. He pressed his ear to the door, listening for any sounds inside the warehouse. Then he chastised himself for forgetting the Snowdrifts moved silently and did not normally talk. He looked for signs the loading had been used recently but couldn't find anything. Layers of grime coated everything, undisturbed.

On the far side was a roughly human-sized door. A large shiny grate covered the bottom of the door. The door handle was a little higher than was comfortable for him to reach. He found it too, but the door would not budge. He tried leaning against it with his shoulder, hoping to force it open but it would not budge. It must have been blocked from the inside. The door was dented and peeling but the grate was shiny and new. It was a standard Snowdrift entrance. They could just flow through the tiny openings. Poe considered forcing the door, but the noise would certainly alert anyone that was inside to their presence.

"Big Man, there's a new Snowdrift entrance in a door, but I can't get it to open."

"You said not to go in."

"That's not the point. Have you found anything?"

"I've found modules belonging to Victims #2 and #4."

"And that isn't normal, right?" Poe moved passed the loading dock. A nearby building formed a narrow passage between itself and the warehouse. It was cloaked in shadows.

"Nothing about this is normal," he said. At least he was finally catching on. "But you are correct."

Poe hesitated before he entered an enclosed space. It would be easy for a person at each end to trap him there. He drew his gun, knowing that it won't do any good, but feeling better just having it in his hand. He sidled down the passageway, continuously looking from front to back, making sure no one was boxing him in.

Pipes, wires, and ducts squirmed haphazardly out of the ground and up the side of the building. Poe's gaze followed them up to the roof line. The sky above seemed unusually bright in the dark passage. Almost taunting him.

He leapt off the ground as a small purple vermin ran over his boot. Poe pointed his gun at it as it scurried into a hole around one of the pipes. He lowered his weapon as its purple ringed tail disappeared into the wall.

"Shit," he said. As the scratching of its claws faded away, he heard something else coming up the pipes. He hesitated to get closer, not wanting some other critter to leap onto his face. He'd much rather get smothered by a Snowdrift. Taking a deep breath, he put his head against the wall. It sounded like sand. He moved his head left and it got quieter, then to the right and it got louder. The sound was coming from a large duct. He could feel the vibration of something flowing through it.

Then the shrill sound of metal straining caused him to jump back from the wall. Before he could raise his useless gun, the duct swelled and burst. An avalanche of white modules poured out.

The cascade hit him in the chest, knocking him to the ground. His feet were swept out from underneath him by the deluge. He was stunned for a moment as more and more Snowdrift modules poured from the burst pipe. He tried to get his breath back but felt the modules sweeping over his face. In a panic, unable to call for help, he swung his arms and legs. They felt like they were passing through a cloud. He couldn't get a grip of anything. He flailed in desperation. The increasing weight on his chest made him feel like he was at the bottom of an hourglass, and his time was almost up.

The modules covering Poe's head sloughed off then fell to the ground, splattering like a snowball. He took a deep breath, the darkness clearing from his vision, as he continued to try to free himself. Every clump of Snowdrift that fell apart was replaced by another. The flow from the pipe had subsided. It was so big it had to be the creation. The conglomerate. Frankenstein's monster.

Before the next wave of modules swept back over his face, he let out a cry, "Big Man! Help!" But his processor was buried in the Snowdrift and couldn't hear him. He tried to sit up, but the swirling mass of alien modules made it impossible to get any leverage. Another wave washed over his face, filling his nose and mouth. He tried to spit the modules out and reached out to grab hold of something so he could pull himself free. His fingers brushed the pipes and wires running up the wall behind him. Wires.

He wrapped his fingers around them and was momentarily submerged as some of the confused Snowdrift shifted forwards. He closed his eyes and mouth. The modules filled his ears and he could not see or hear. He closed his fist around the wires and pulled. He had no idea if the building still had electricity. If it did, an industrial complex like this probably had enough power to kill both of them. Anything was better than getting smothered on his back. He pulled. The wires would not break free.

Then it drew back to his torso rising up to tower over him. Poe understood this creation had a weakness. If it was not a physical one, then he would try something else. In a flash of inspiration, he shouted, "Who are you? Who are you?" It began to shake. Snowy globs of modules dislodged themselves and rolled down its sides only to merge back at the bottom, like a candle constantly melting and rebuilding itself. Encouraged, Poe continued to shout. "Who are you? Do you know who you are? Tell me who you are you!"

Poe began to hear a noise unlike anything he'd ever experienced. It wasn't coming from a speaking structure like Big Man used. It was like the grinding of thousands of tiny gears. The modules were grinding against each other. Every piece of the alien was fighting against every other piece. The soul-rending noise radiated from the Snowdrifts entire being, setting Poe's every cell on edge.

"WHO ARE YOU?" he shouted with everything he

had left.

The unnatural assemblage of minds and fleshes could longer suppress its inner turmoil. Its components rebelled, each trying to exist independently and together at the same time. It was too much for it to bear. Its fusion incomplete, the warring components began to tear themselves apart.

Pieces of Snowdrift the size of Poe's head began to break free and move in different directions. Each driven by its own separate desire to flee.

The weight lightened enough that Poe was able to pull himself free. He scrambled away from the quickly disintegrating pseudo-individual, pieces slithering past him. When he was several feet away from what was left of the dwindling central mass, he climbed to his feet, still gasping for breath. His gun was missing; he must have dropped it when he was knocked to the ground. Now it must be somewhere among the alien's rapidly fleeing pieces. He heard movement behind him and spun around. Tension gripped him as he expected to see one of the original 'victims' blocking the way out of the passage. He was already exhausted and did not think he could fight his way out. But the snowy mound moving forwards was far too large.

"It's about time," Poe said, his heart still raising. "You stop to take a nap?"

"You know that I don't sleep. What happened?" Big Man asked, avoiding several of the roaming clumps of modules, not wanting to make contact with the clearly disturbed entity.

"I found it. It attacked me. I reasoned with it."

JOSHUA D. TAYLOR started writing a few years ago when he realised he was too old to play make-believe. He lives in south-eastern Pennsylvania with his wife and a one-eared cat. He enjoys gardening, comic books, ska-punk music, Disney World, and traveling with his wife.

Raised during weirdness that was the late 20th century, Josh's eclectic interests produce eclectic works. He loves to mix-n-match things from different genres and stories elements to achieve a madcap hodgepodge of the truly unexpected.

Bibliography
BEYOND, Black Hare Press, 2019
Deep Space, Black Hare Press, 2019
WORLDS, Black Hare Press, 2019
Salty Tales, Stormy Island Publishing, 2019

Connect
Facebook: @authorjoshuadtaylor
Amazon: amazon.com/-/e/B07V1X2V5T

ABDUCTION
By A.L. King

The murder streak of serial killer Andrew Preeves is interrupted as he attempts to claim his next victim. Abducted himself before he can take her, he discovers why the aliens are so interested in humanity. He is also forced to confront his own evil ways.

The needles aren't the worst of it. I would welcome countless punctures compared to the further kind of pain those dripping pins deliver. Anyone who claims that emotional anguish isn't as powerful as that of a physical nature clearly hasn't set foot on this happening starship.

So how did I find myself here, in a deep-space prison where I'm injected with replicated emotions rather than the preferable lethal injection I deserve on Earth? Oh, that's a fun one!

I could go back and describe what an abusive gold-digger my mother was, how watching her tread her high heels across the backs of countless good men filled me with rage. I could flamboyantly describe that rage as a seed of hatred that bloomed into a tree, which eventually grew large and used its burly branches to choke the life from young women who were as crazy as the bitch who birthed me. But no matter how much schmaltz my captors pump into me, I'll never be one for gaudy poetry.

Although I can feel, I'm still a stubborn asshole at heart, fighting the remorseful sentiments they've imbued me with to confide the truth—not some namby-pamby tale framed by their synthetic sentiment.

It started with a simple mistake. The young woman I chose had already been spoken for.

Her name was Telina Mae Groves, and she was unlike the others. Perhaps that's because there was still hope for her. Or maybe my mawkish reflection on things is only now placing her on such a high pedestal. Either way, I took one look at her Facebook profile picture and knew I had to choke the life out of her.

After a stint of court-mandated community service at an animal shelter, she had discovered an affinity for dogs. I used that against her, pretending my imaginary dog was lost. It might have been risky for an unseasoned stalker, but not for me. She had no immediate neighbours and was attempting—successfully for the most part—a solitary lifestyle. Besides, if things went awry, I could always try again; another day, another way.

As I planned, she spotted me wondering the outskirts of her spacious backyard, near the woods. She approached with caution. It would take more than the empty leash in my hand to disarm her.

"You're on private property. Can I help you?"

I turned and gave her my widest-eyed expression. Surely she would pity me just as much as a deer caught in headlights. I ignored the part about private property and pretended to only hear her offer to help.

"Yes, please!" I said, doing my best glitzy-glam accent; she was less likely to suspect me as the Ted Bundy type if I oozed the opposite of heterosexuality. "Oh, I pulled over about twenty yards down the road to take a picture of the beautiful sunset over the Ohio Valley—I can never resist a good sunset—and left the car door open too long. My dog jumped out and now I can't find him. You're so sweet to offer. If you would help me search for him, I'd be so grateful! I'm in shambles. At the very least, I could use the emotional support."

'*Emotional support*' I had said. The irony bites my ass with a fresh injection each day.

"What kind of dog is he?" she asked, still a good fifteen feet away. "And what's his name?"

"Bubba's a coonhound, which explains why he went bonkers when he saw that rabbit scamper off," I told her, using two fingers on the hand not holding my fake dog's leash to mimic the movements of an equally imaginary rabbit. "But mostly I call him Bubs. He should come back if he hears that. I just hope he hasn't found the rabbit hole and hurt any of those poor babies."

She took a few more steps forwards, squinting to make out my finer features. A few of her online photos had revealed that she occasionally wore glasses.

"Oh!" I said, struck by a fabricated realisation. "I have a picture of him."

The photo was real, a picture I printed online, but the pretences were false. I pulled out my wallet and flapped it open. The effect had all the impact of a plain-clothed police officer revealing a badge to dismiss questions of authority. Like such a shield, it legitimised my story. Telina came close enough to view the picture under its clear, plastic cover.

Five minutes later and we were thirty yards into the woods, shielded by the mid-spring canopy. I trailed two steps behind, just enough so she couldn't see me from her periphery.

"Here, Bubs!" she called.

"Bubba, boy! Bubs, come to daddy!"

She glanced nervously at the treetops, obviously concerned as twilight tipped toward night, and I thoroughly appreciated the irony. The real predator was already out and about, right behind her.

"You okay?" I asked. "It's still seventy-some degrees out, and you're shivering like a leaf in the wind."

"Shadows setting in, and I really don't like to be outside at night. I enjoy living here, so I don't want something to happen that changes that. Things have been quiet for a while. I want them to stay that way."

Before I could probe any further, she returned her attention to the wild goose chase.

"Here, Bubs! Your daddy's looking for you!"

As she called for a dog that would never come, she continued looking up. I, meanwhile, stared down at her long legs. Even in fading light and under the shadow of trees, I noticed a small scar along the crook of her left knee. I anticipated, much later in the evening when I had the opportunity to more intimately examine her, I would find a cluster of track marks so close together they comprised a single shape. Junkies are always shooting up the strangest parts of their bodies.

I thought to myself, *Overdose and maybe die, stick a needle in your eye!*

She turned suddenly and looked over her shoulder. Her expression at first suggested she just remembered turning the oven on back home to preheat for a batch of fish sticks (multiple receipts I found in her trash had revealed they were one of her favourite snacks). Then her mouth dropped the most hideous expression her heart-shaped face could muster. The momentary ugliness upset me, for it had broken my fantasy.

Regardless, she was terrified, and rightfully so. The little twist I imagined on the old children's rhyme (*Cross your heart and hope to die, stick a needle in your eye!*) had caused me to laugh out loud. It was my true laugh, about as far from glitzy-glam as you can get.

"You…you…don't have a dog…do you?"

I continued laughing as I turned the leash on her.

Insurance policies were my insurance policy. I worked for the Ohio division of Fountain Springs and had access to claims throughout the entire state. When I discovered copays for stints in rehab or mental health facilities, I researched those covered under the policies. Often times, the ones benefitting from my employer's services were attractive young women.

Lenora, Angela, Gloria, and Lydia were all "flight risks" prone to disappearing for weeks or months on end. It was assumed by their past behaviours that they would return… eventually. The disappearance of one of my victims remained unreported for months. That neglect once tickled me greatly. Now, after my treatments, the sting of that thought is sharper than that of the needles.

Usually, by the time foul play was suspected, authorities started their searches with friends or fellow junkies of those young women. They overlooked the cosy little desk-jockey sitting epicentre in one Columbus, Ohio office building.

I was in the process of taking Telina from the outskirts of Clarington, Ohio. I should have concluded our business quickly in the thicket, but I had waited too long since stuffing Lydia Blankman inside the crawlspace of an abandoned building. A year-and-a-half it had taken to research and plan for the taking of Telina Groves, and it might be just as long between her and the next young woman I chose. I wanted to make her count.

There was a new addition in my basement prepared for her stay. It was a downgrade from the house in the hills her parents had been renting for her following a successful round of rehab, but I thought it possessed a cosy feel. I even included a puppy calendar, on which I'd already begun marking off the days. I wish my own, current trappings were half as cosy as the space I'd created for her, a space she was never able to experience first-hand.

My captors are approaching now, slinking around the level where my see-through encasement sits among countless others on circular platforms. They have no forms, unless they are inhabiting those big-eyed humanoid suits we've come to think of as the greys. They are simply (shadows setting in) loose collections of smoke.

As I feared, two of those car-exhaust beings come to a stop directly outside my window-wall. They expand in excitement, filling the space so completely that I cannot see the lines of cells beyond them.

Holes in the side-walls open, and several injection hoses slither out like needle-headed snakes. Those monsters may not be holding clipboards or notepads, but I know they're watching—and taking notes, nonetheless.

My blood courses with synthetic chemicals, and everything inside me tries to fight the fresh waves of pain. By making me feel—they're shocking a system that wasn't wired for emotion. They've opened up floodgates, cleared a blockage that formerly kept me numb. It's like a power surge to mind and body.

What if it becomes too much and I die? Will they be upset to lose me? Although they won't mourn my passing, I do believe they will miss me in some way. I am a rare specimen, after all.

Telina was rare for me. I never wanted to hold any of the others for an extended time-period. They were quick fancies in the darkness of a dark world. I like to think I saw something in her—a light, maybe—and I wanted to keep her around. I wanted her to *see* me, as well. The real me.

Oh, hell! Those damned smokestacks are finally getting me to blow smoke. I can't fight these feelings or keep them out of my head. They must have injected me with some mixture of amorous nostalgia, but at least it wasn't remorse. That's the most painful one.

Then again, maybe there has always been a seed of emotion in me, a retarded pit buried deeply. I say that because I was gentle with Telina as I carried her from the woods. After choking her with the dog leash until she passed out, I made sure not to let any low-hanging branches scrape or scratch her.

At the edge of the woods, I almost reconsidered taking her home with me. Her empty house was right there. I could inject her with the heroin I brought to keep her subdued (I had flirted with the idea of using other sedatives, but I thought using her worst vice against her was fitting). Then I could have my way with her and finish her off with a stronger injection.

But as I set her softly to the ground and extracted the syringe kit from my cargo pocket, I knew doing so would only leave me wanting. Besides, I never left them to look like accidental deaths. When I went, I went all the way, and I wanted the world to know it.

I sang around the miniature flashlight in my mouth as I searched for a vein.

"Overdose and maybe die, stick a needle in your eye."

She jolted awake when the needle bit her skin. Any fight, however, was soon washed away by the warmth flowing through her veins. She breathed heavily, though, eyes wide and gazing up at me in absolute terror.

"Shadows," she slurred in response. "Shadows above your head. Shadow starship."

I thought then that the drugs were causing her to spit nonsense. I'd given her a small dose. Her tolerance had no doubt dwindled after rehab, and I wanted to avoid killing her. I also had a thing of Narcan in my other cargo pocket, just in case. People were lacing heroin with fentanyl, and the results were often fatal. I wasn't about to let a bad batch ruin my good time.

Her eyelids fluttered like flies caught in spider webs, but there was not enough fear to keep her conscious. Had she been at her former peak of abuse, the minimal dosage I granted would have had nary an effect. I felt proud of her as she drifted into a drug-induced dreamland. She hadn't relapsed.

"Good girl, Telina," I said, brushing tufts of hair away from her heart-shaped face.

A strange sensation overcame me, then. Dizziness set in, and I was spinning. It was as if all the blood in my body was rushing upwards, to my head.

The H was doped, I figured. *Doped with the F!*

I recalled hearing stories of police officers and medics picking up used syringes and overdosing because fentanyl simply got on their skin. I regretted not using gloves. I reached toward my cargo pocket, planning to use the Narcan on myself.

Sorry, Telina, I thought. *I only have one of these lifesaving canisters. If it's between you and me, that's an obvious—*

Looking at her as I fumbled for the tube in my pocket, I saw that she was no longer on the ground. Nor was I. That tugging, floating sensation I mistook for an accidental and potentially lethal high had been real. We were rising, rising, above the treetops.

An orgy of butterflies flapped their wings in my stomach. Light engulfed us. I blacked out.

The pain that woke me felt at first like sudden razor-burn against my throat. Then it went from scraping to a tight pinching to a sudden and searing tearing. Telina was on me. I knew it was her before I even opened my eyes, because I could smell her cheap, Walmart perfume. She was biting my neck like some kind of crazed vampire, trying to dig deeper with her teeth, searching for the mainline.

When she pulled back with bloody lips and the top few layers of flesh from my throat between her teeth, I seized the opportunity and sent the heel of my palm into her nose. A torrent of red unleashed on me, and then she fell backwards. I wondered if maybe I had jammed her nasal bones into her brain, although I no longer cared if she died before I could have my fun. There was no longer fun to be had.

I'd received minor wounds from my outings, covered up a few defensive scrapes and scratches, but thanks to her I was contemplating how awkward it would be to wear turtlenecks day after day on the precipice of summer. My co-workers would notice. They would talk.

I heard Telina mumbling in pain as I got to my feet. She was still alive, after all, and the H no doubt remained in her system. Had it not weakened her, she might have been strong and sharp enough to rip out my throat. The story *The Most Dangerous Game* came to mind. A particular quote tried to surface, something about the world consisting of two classes, but all I could consider was how closely I, the hunter, had come to being the prey.

I managed to my feet and pressed my hand against my throat. As I had imagined, the damage was superficial. I would still have to figure out how to cover up my wound, but I would survive.

"You won't," I said, stepping over Telina. I had forgotten all about being yanked into the air, above the trees. That was because we were on the ground. Trees were all around us, seemingly for miles. It was dark out, but a faint light glowed through their tall and imperfect shapes. Enough light so I could see her, enough so I could appreciate the look of terror in her wide brown eyes.

"You won't! You won't! You won't!"

I repeated myself as if the final word—*Survive. You won't survive!*—were implied. Telina appeared to understand. She used her hands and feet to flail backwards while still gazing up at me. A few times she tried to kick at my groin, but her leg would only lift so high. She gave up on wounding my manhood and continued kick-crawling backwards…until her hand settled on a fallen tree branch. Under the soft light (*What time is it?* I began to wonder. *How long were we out? Why was I out?*) the stick looked sharp.

It was my turn to back up a few paces. However, she did not mean to harm me with the limb. She turned the sharp end toward herself and stretched her arm so the thick side of the branch, the apparently broken end, was within my reach. At first, I thought she wanted me to impale her with the thing, but there was a pleading look in her eyes, an expression I'd seen many times on other young women.

My rage settled into curiosity. I accepted her strange offering, and a strange jolt ran through me. Simply touching it unveiled the true strangeness of the situation. Turning the broken piece of branch over in one hand, then the other, I understood that it had never been attached to a tree, at least not a real one. There was no bark, but there was a slight give when I squeezed it. It was made of rubber, or something similar.

I recalled the rising sensation as we'd been lifted skyward. The thing in my hand was a… I struggled to come up with the right word. Then it struck me. *Prop!* The branch was a prop, fallen off a tree that was also a prop, in a forest of prop trees. Did that make the faint lighting around us *feint* lighting instead? Artificial set lighting?

"Shadows above your head," Telina had said mere seconds before we were taken.

I then repeated what she had said next, only it was

more of a question than a statement.

"Shadow starship?"

She nodded.

∘∘❍◗◯◗∘◗∘∘

Neither of us were misguided enough to think we wouldn't still try to kill the other. I had been in the process of abducting her for obvious reasons, and when my exposed throat presented itself, she had taken a bite. After that failed, she revealed the illusion around us, hoping that her apparent knowledge of such trickery would stall her demise.

It did.

During our walk in the woods—the *real* woods— she had explained that things were quiet and she wanted them to stay that way. It was an odd thing to say but easily dismissible at the time. She was a junkie, after all, with a history of mental illness. Furthermore, she was approaching the age when she could no longer be claimed on her parents' insurance. Of course she wanted things to remain quiet. She was running out of chances.

Yet the opposite of that quiet she described was not her former, partying lifestyle as I assumed. It was the idea of abduction she feared, and quite possibly, the literal hum of the starship. It sounded like cicadas chirping, but when I listened closely, I recognised a mechanical lilt.

"Why the disguise?" I asked.

"What?" she asked, rubbing the top of her lip and causing dry flakes of blood to flitter to the faux dirt below. The ground beneath us was like a composite of AstroTurf, except it was made to look like soil rather than grass, and it separated easily when I sunk my fingers in experimentally.

"Why disguise the inside of the ship to look like the woods?"

She looked to the ground and seemed to consider. She was presenting herself as weak and timid, but I wouldn't take my eyes off her. I needed her alive for answers and she only needed me not to kill her. She would hold back certain truths to maintain leverage, and if she had half a chance, she would try to end me and deal with the larger threat on her own.

Or maybe she'll try to wind me up and send me at them? I theorised. She'll see how many I can take out before they vaporise me or whatever it is they do.

"It's not like this all the time," she finally answered. "Only I didn't know there were other times until now. I mean, I did know I was… taken, but I let everyone convince me it was all in my head, a recurring nightmare or sleep paralysis. But now you're here, and you're seeing it, too. Normally I end up in a bed in what looks like a basic bedroom, with all the stuff in the room being as fake as this forest. They plucked us from the woods, so maybe they're trying to ease us in…"

Her suggestion made me recall a time when I sat in the waiting room of a dentist's office and rubbed the leaves of a plastic plant between my fingers.

"Some fake familiarity before the real ordeal," I said. "Real enough to put our minds at ease initially, but easy enough to see through so we're not too comfortable. Going from one to eleven would cause a lot of people to die of fright."

"Bingo was his name-o," she said, then laughed to herself. Having an attempted abduction interrupted with another abduction was no doubt an absurdity worthy of cracking the mind a little. "Except Bingo can't be his name-o, because you don't really have a dog. What's your name?"

"Andrew Preeves."

"Honest?"

"I have no reason to lie."

"Because you're going to kill me."

"That's the gist."

"I don't figure you'd change your mind if I helped you out of here," she said, as if thinking out loud.

I suddenly recalled earlier, when she was walking ahead of me and I saw a blemish on the back of her left leg, at the bend. She seemed to be subconsciously picking at that spot as she sat on a fallen (fake) tree. Initially, I had assumed she shot up there to better conceal track marks. But a memory of some nature program I'd seen long ago flashed before my eyes. My mind conjured the scene in which scientists observed a screen filled with several tiny blips. Those blips represented animals.

While Telina was still of value to me alive, I doubted she knew her way off the ship, let alone back to Earth. I further doubted that her true abductors would allow me to go anywhere with her, not since I was the reason they showed up in the first place.

They wouldn't allow me to hurt her, not really, and that meant…

I looked right, then left. Fog appeared to be drifting from sham-tree to sham-tree. Those individual clouds had likely been there since before I awoke on the starship with Telina's teeth on me. They were too dark to be regular fog, too *shadowy*. It was my turn to crack a bit and laugh a little, even though doing so hurt my marred throat.

"Great," she said. "The psychopath is going even crazier."

What I did next was not out of anger. I simply aimed to test my theory. Using both hands, I grabbed Telina by the throat and hoisted her from the fallen over sham-tree on which she'd been sitting. The dark clouds stopped drifting from side to side and suddenly came toward us, quickly.

I let her go, and she dropped to the sham-tree and tumbled backwards over it. I held my hands up to the shadows, which had begun taking on something of a humanoid form as they approached, and I hoped they would recognise that Earthly sign of surrender. They must have, because they stopped dead in their floating, trackless tracks.

Telina was coughing as she climbed to her feet. There was a fire in her eyes that filled me with a sincere appreciation of her, but I could not afford to get lost in kismet fantasies.

"Quit staring daggers at me and take a better look around us, Telina. You spoke of shadows before, and I'm pretty sure they're here now."

As if wise to me, the forms began scattering themselves once more into somewhat inconspicuous mists. But it was too late. She had seen them—dozens, perhaps a hundred.

"I've never seen so many of them. I knew they were like smoke, but I didn't know they could change their shapes like that."

"That spot you've been picking at on the back of your leg," I said. "I think they placed a tracker in you, but it's more advanced than anything our species uses to monitor animal behaviours. It also tracks your emotions, or chemical reactions. They knew you were threatened by me, so they came."

She looked from floating shadow to floating shadow, and then she smiled. In my own curiosity and distress, I had shared too much with Telina Mae Groves. Two evils had sought to abduct her, and I was no longer the lesser one.

"You can't kill me!" she cried out triumphantly. "You can't! You can't!"

If only she'd known what they had in store for us.

I now gather the purpose of the forest backdrop, which is just one of many sets. Some abductees appear in a desert landscape, a few on boats at sea, others in wide open fields, and many, as Telina had described, wake up in bedrooms much like their own. The purpose of these constructs is to place people in an environment similar to where they were taken, to ease them into the situation. Furthermore, it allows the smokestacks to monitor the internal reactions of their abductees as they become aware of just where they are. Those like Telina are taken time and again.

That's why Telina and I ended up in the woodland section of the starship. Tensions were high from the moment she woke me with a bite to the throat, but the smokestacks were still able to glimpse my emotions—or lack thereof in terms of how most human beings exhibit emotions.

"You can't!" Telina had continued. "You can't kill me! You can't!"

And *I* didn't. In fact, I no longer think I'm capable of murder. Although I stubbornly cling to pieces of who I used to be, the injections are beginning to have long-term effects. They pump guilt, remorse, romanticism, and love into me on a regular basis. Those shapeless forms are forming something of my formerly shapeless sentiments. Where before I could sever a young woman's limb without batting an eyelid, I can hardly recall my deeds without puking up the compost they feed me to keep me alive.

The smokestacks glimpsed my lack of concern and remorse and knew they had to hold onto such a rare specimen. But now that I can feel, my own fate no longer concerns me. I fear, worse than anything else, the reason behind their synthetisation of human emotions. As far as

I can gather, they feel nothing other than a compulsive form of curiosity. I tremble to think what would befall Earth and other worlds if something as advanced as those clouds were to cloud its judgement by experiencing our brand of emotion.

I have no way of knowing exactly how long I've been here. I can only guess as countless others come and go, staying shortly in the other see-through encasements. There are occasions when people come and do not leave, and I suspect that they are—or *were*, at least—the way I used to be.

I think at least a decade has passed. I know this because, when I saw Telina again, she looked almost that much older. She was in her mid-thirties, for sure. Her nose had healed nicely, or maybe a good plastic surgeon had fixed what I did to her face. Either way, she had put on a healthy amount of weight and was a far cry from the thin, early stages of recovery when I tried abducting her. If not for the blank expression on her face—a helpless and knowing look much like the one she wore when she realised I didn't have a dog—I would have considered that she was happy with her life.

"I'm sorry," I said through my see-through cage, a

fresh dose of woe pulsing through my veins. I did not think she could hear me, and her mind seemed elsewhere. She likely understood what was about to happen. So did I. The tension had me on such an edge that my harnessed and atrophied muscles almost conjured a spasm when she began speaking.

"They know it was you," she said. "Andrew Jackson Preeves. I took your name to the authorities, but I didn't tell them where you were. They think you're still at large."

"I'm thankful for that much," I told her. "The families may have some resolve. But that monster is not me. Not anymore. I don't want this to happen."

"I have a daughter now," she said. "And a husband… and we have a dog. Care to guess what his name is?"

But I didn't have time. The separate smogs floating about her came together, preparing to test how far I had come—how far *they* had taken me.

"Please don't do this! Let her go!"

But my begging only solidified their resolve. They tore her apart in front of me. I let out a cry, and it would be my last. Following that moment, I stopped working my jaw muscles. I'd said what I needed to say, expressed everything they wanted me to express. Now my face is slack, and I'm fed through a tube.

Occasionally, however, when the time comes to

inject me with fresh emotion, I do find myself defiantly humming. It's a sad little tune I used to think funny, when I was someone else. There are several versions, but the words I recite most often in my mind are the original verse.

Overdose and maybe die, stick a needle in your eye!

Is it possible to overdose on emotion, to feel something so powerful it kills me? I can only hope.

A.L. KING is an author of horror, fantasy, science fiction, and poetry. As an avid fan of dark subjects from an early age, his first influences included R.L. Stine, Edgar Allan Poe, and Stephen King. Later stylistic inspirations came from foreign horror films and media, particularly Japanese.

He is a graduate of West Liberty University, has dabbled in journalism, and is actively involved in his community. Although his creativity leans toward darker genres, he has even written a children's book titled "Leif's First Fall."
He was raised in the town of Sistersville, West Virginia, which he still proudly calls home.

Bibliography
BEYOND, Black Hare Press, 2019
Deep Space, Black Hare Press, 2019
MONSTERS, Black Hare Press, 2019

Connect
Facebook: @alkauthor

THE SPACE BETWEEN SPACE

By Raven Corinn Carluk

The farthest reaches of the universe are available to mankind now, and Earth will no longer be their only home. Colony ships have launched, carrying their precious cargo through the unbounded stretches of slipspace. Meredith Jackson is about to discover what lies between the familiar and the horrific.

Bishop meowed softly from the back of my chair. "I know. It's the most beautiful thing I've ever seen too." I couldn't take my eyes off the screen. Didn't want to.

"They didn't warn us that slipspace could be so…beautiful." It wasn't unusual for me to talk to my ginger cat. He'd been my constant companion for the last ten years, helping me run cargo and supplies on the *Mars* space station before this mission, and now helped me stay sane during the long, lonely watches while the colony ship made its way to our new home.

It *was* unusual for me to be at such a loss for words, but I could find no other way to describe the colourful mass outside the *Wayfarer*.

I sighed, hitting the button to cycle through the external cameras. I'd seen every angle available already, multiple times in the last three days, but I simply couldn't get enough.

"Kind of a shame no one else is awake to see this. Just you and me. Just Bishop and Meredith. Meredith and Bishop. The woman and her cat."

Bishop purred, the sound filling the captain's command space. It was larger than the one I had as the logistics officer, with lots more control panels and readouts and displays, but still seemed small. With the lights off, the room was incredibly intimate, like a warm hug. Or being back in the womb.

"But they're all in hypersleep, having pleasant dreams, waiting to wake up above Rigidion 4. They don't get to see all this beautiful glory.

"Of course, there really isn't a way to feed a

thousand people for a year. Or keep them entertained. I can't even imagine how much they'd annoy each other. Rodriguez bugs the shit out of us, and it's only the three people running around the entire ship.

"Fuck, I hate that man," I growled and punched a flat spot on the console. The camera changed views again; vibrant blues filled the darkened space and immediately softened my anger. There just wasn't the capacity for strong emotions when faced with such awe-inspiring beauty. Relaxation spread through me, and I reached for my braid, running the greasy length through trembling fingers. I probably needed to wash it, but there had been more important things to do. To watch.

"He did make a good point about all the animals, though. No way the *Sojourner* would be able to take care of all the farm creatures, and certainly wouldn't be able to stop them from breeding, and making a mess. He just didn't need to be a dick about you." Bishop meowed again, probably remembering that particular argument. It had been bad, only a few days ago. Certainly fresh in my mind. Just another of the unnecessary conflicts we'd had recently.

"Where would they put all those big farm animals? All their food? All their poop? We didn't have to worry about those kinds of logistics when we were on the *Mars*, did we? And people much smarter than us at Hu Li Corp figured all that out when they designed the colony ships.

"But it's still too bad they can't experience…this…" I sighed again, wistful, and slumped back in my chair. "Why didn't they cover any of this in training?"

"All right, now that we've handled introductions, we can begin talking about the fun stuff; slipspace." Chief Instructor Weber smiled, pressing a button on her little remote, starting the slideshow on the main screen. All the monitors in front of us changed a half second later, giving us a close view of her presentation. "Get a taste of the practical before we slide over in the training vessels."

We were seated by ship crew, three each; a captain, a logistics officer, and an engineer. Six ships, headed to three different colony planets. The *Wayfarer* and the *Sojourner* to Rigidion 4, the *Pilgrim* and the *Rover* to Cassier Prime, and the *Explorer* and the *Trekker* to Bestel. Eighteen experienced crewpeople, but all that experience was in normal ships, in normal space.

"Briefly, what do any of you know about slipspace?" Weber clasped her hands behind her back, eyes glittering but hard. She was short and broad, with a no-nonsense hair cut, and a jawline like a granite slab. She wouldn't win any beauty contests, but she'd been one of the first slipspace pilots.

Masa Sakai, our engineer on the *Wayfarer*, raised his hand next to me. Weber acknowledged him with a jut of her chin. "Discovery of the Higgs-Bosun led to a better understanding of neutrinos, quarks, and the essence of dark matter. In 2115, physicist Jacqueline Hunter split a Bosun and opened a way into slipspace. Her findings were expanded upon, and in 2132, the first slipspace ship successfully travelled across Sol system. 2142, first colony ship travelled to the Centauri system. 2147, we waited in a lecture hall before our mission." Me and two others chuckled at the hint of eagerness in his last sentence.

Weber nodded, eyes roving our little class. "Very good. Sounds exactly like the email syllabus about this training." More of us chuckled. "What else?"

The *Rover*'s captain answered, not bothering to raise her hand. "Not only is distance different, time doesn't work the same. The *Valiant*'s journey to Centauri took them two and a half years in slipspace, but only a month Earth Standard passed."

"It's dangerous as all fuck." This from the engineer of our sister ship, the *Sojourner*. Where Sakai was quiet, well-groomed, and slender, McCaffrey was a big bastard, loud, with a laugh in his voice at all times.

Except this time.

Weber nodded, lips pressed tight. The sharpness of

her eyes faded for a moment, and we all waited quietly. Everything that had to do with space travel came with a certain level of risk, especially in the early days. I knew my share of dead crewpeople, as did every other person seated here. It was a simple fact of life when you chose to live and work off-planet.

None of us had any illusions that this was going to be a walk in the park, but slipspace travel was now safe enough for colonists to risk their lives. Colonisation itself wasn't exactly without its own dangers, but that hadn't stopped six thousand people from volunteering to cross vast reaches of space to lay claim to new planets. Human nature called for expansion and exploration.

Weber finally spoke. "When the texts call slipspace wild, that barely scratches the surface. Most of us pilots aren't writers, aren't good with words like that, so someone else listens to our stories, then makes the training materials and articles and novels.

"They've never seen it for themselves, experienced it first hand. A very few lucky ones get to watch some of the footage, but it's not the same. Not even close."

Weber turned toward the screen, left her back to us for a long moment. Far too long for this to be planned.

I was a logistics officer, formerly of the space station *Mars*, and now of the *Wayfarer*. I handled payloads, able to stock and repack a cargo hold in my sleep. People weren't my thing, and I was bad with social cues, but I could tell the chief instructor was a little distressed.

Maybe a lot distressed.

Her tension had me rethinking the whole idea of travelling to Rigidion to run their freshly built space station. I wanted my own rig to run, especially brand new with all the bells and whistles, but maybe I could wait for *Saturn* to start up. In six years.

"It's not just the way slipspace looks. It's the very *feel* of it. Not just the way artificial gravity is different than planetside, and how you can always tell real from fake. Being over there is like wearing your skin inside out and backwards. Your thoughts come out of order. The walls of your ship don't look the same, like all the angles are slightly off, like the concept of geometry itself has changed."

Weber turned suddenly, standing at attention. Her eyes glittered again, though not as bright as before. "Yes, slipspace is dangerous. I've never known a place as dangerous, and I've seen the plasma storms of Betelgeuse. You are under no obligation to complete the training. If at any time this becomes too much, no one will blame you."

As a class, we sat in silence. We knew we had alternates, and it was a little strange that all of us weren't in training together. Hu Li Corp never put all their eggs in one basket, so why was this program so different?

None of us moved. I glanced around, scanning the group, and finally made eye contact with my captain, Manuel Rodriguez. He quirked one brow, then nodded briefly. I nodded back, and a smirk stole across my lips. We were going to get along fine while travelling to Rigidion 4.

"Hey, so," I started, raising my hand halfway. "Is it true that Hunter was a huge sci-fi nerd, and named it slipspace because she couldn't choose between sub- and hyperspace?"

The tension was successfully broken, and we all laughed. Our journey was no less dangerous, but we weren't going to let fear make it worse than it really was, let it drive us into the dark corners of our own heads.

I unbraided my hair slowly, running my fingers through the wavy plaits, ignoring the way it pulled against the scabs in my palms. There were no company regulations against long hair, but I kept it longer than most. So very long, like the colourful plaits of slipspace matter on my viewscreen.

"My hair is never so beautiful," I told Bishop. He meowed, two tiny chirps, as if he were responding. He'd always been talkative, always been a friend. Better friend than some. Better than Rodriguez.

"Look at how it moves. There's a word for that motion, for those waves and twists, but I just can't think of it. Words are harder right now. They never were before."

Another meow.

"It's got to be the isolation. It's not good to be alone, to be without other people. Did you know old cultures back on Earth used to put criminals in small cages and leave them there for long periods of time?" I loved history, loved reading to Bishop during the late-night shifts. "It was finally banned as inhumane because it drove them crazy.

"And they always warn us about isolation sickness. That's why Hu Li Corp has at least three people on any ship or station. Give us all someone to interact with, let us split the shifts and still have someone else to talk to, and be too dependent on each other to be annoyed with someone else. Keep an eye on each other, let Hu Li central know if there are any warning signs.

"Might be a little hard to swap out crews while we're out here in slipspace." I laughed and Bishop meowed.

The colours outside danced in reaction to my laughter. I leaned forwards, frowning at the screen. There's no possible way that mass could hear me, not a thousand kilometres away. Distance and size meant nothing in slipspace, were deceiving to normal human senses, could only be sorted out by special equipment, and all that equipment told me that the writhing cluster of tentacles and seething space dust was too far away to have heard me laugh.

"You remember what they told us?" I didn't wait for Bishop to respond. "Weber and her slides and all her texts all said that slipspace looks and feels and behaves different. Can't trust your eyes because nothing seems correct. They were right. So very right."

I touched the viewscreen, leaning closer, stroking a writhing tentacle as it shifted toward our ship. Did the *Sojourner* have a similar view from where it followed behind us? Were they all watching as intently?

"Remember when we first slid into slipspace? Just a month ago, but I'd swear it's been so much longer. Guess that's the reason the Earth Standard readouts get disabled once we get over. Comparing the passage of Standard time and slip time is a path to madness. Insanity brought about by clock watching."

I sighed, switching the viewer again. "Nothing like those training flights we had, back in Sol system. Tiny little slides those were, and we never stayed out that long. Might have to tell them that colony crews need longer adjustment periods while still in safe space.

"Took an entire day to get our legs back under us. All these corridors felt crooked, like the deck plates were all tilted. Couldn't even get into my bunk because I was sure it was on a hump instead of flat. Weber sure didn't mention that when she said geometry felt off. But I barely have the words to think of all the things that are wrong, and I'm watching it happen right before my eyes."

Bishop purred. He hadn't shown any distress upon our slide into slipspace. Cool as a cucumber, slow blinking from my console, as if this were any regular day on the *Mars*. He hadn't gone off his food, like Sakai, and he hadn't stumbled around, like me, nor had he gotten all moody, like Rodriguez.

I switched the cameras yet again, and the feed delayed, remaining on a black screen far too long. I slapped it several times in frustration, desperate for it to come back on. Just one of many glitches that I'd noticed in the last four days. Tiny things, but problems nonetheless. Problems that were signs of potentially deeper issues. Sakai should have been monitoring the bugs, should have been working them out before things got any worse.

The screen blinked back on finally, revealing a bright expanse of unnamed colours and textures. Relief flooded my system, and I actually shuddered because the great thing was back on my screen. Sweat beaded my forehead; who knows how much longer I'd have lasted without it.

I trembled, weak, staring unblinkingly at the screen. Bishop squeaked as I flopped back in my chair, rattling his perch above my head. "Sorry, Baby. It's just getting so much harder. Sakai said..." I trailed off.

"When's the last time you saw Sakai?" I frowned, unable to take my eyes off the screen even while I thought about the engineer. "He hadn't been at mess since we slid over, but at least I still saw him in the halls. And we played cribbage...what, a week ago? Two days? But have you seen him since then?"

Bishop's purr came back, although soft and quiet.

Soft and quiet was exactly what my mind needed. It was like a little song just for me. The same song he'd shared with me since I'd gotten the fluffy ball of orange fur ten years ago. My sweetest, dearest friend. I'd raised him, and he'd never been away from me for longer than a week. I didn't know what I'd do if anything ever happened to him.

"It's not like Sakai to disappear. He was doing plenty of studying when we first got here, and he was still mostly himself. Even when we came upon this...thing, he was still friendly. It's not like him to disappear. Not like Rodriguez."

Anger sparked, heating my blood. I pulled at a chunk of my hair and began braiding it to calm myself. Couldn't get angry. Stupid things happened when you got angry. Just needed to focus on the mesmerising undulations on the screen while I braided the grimy length of hair.

"Might be possible that the captain is losing his mind," I finally whispered to Bishop. I hadn't wanted to voice my suspicions, had wanted to just stare at the thing of beauty as we travelled past it. But now that I'd voiced the words, the rest of them came spilling out, like a putrid wound draining after being lanced.

"We got along well enough during training and load in, and he was okay enough as we made our way out of Sol system, but he became a bit of a prick when we really got underway, and then we slid into slipspace...

"Spending so much time alone isn't good. He was purposely avoiding me and Sakai, and skulking around the halls. Sakai said he saw Rodriguez in the hyper chambers, staring at the colonists. And then we saw him in the rec room, in the dark..." My voice died in my throat, fresh memories bubbling to the surface from below, from the deep bog of the subconscious where I'd buried them.

Bishop sauntered ahead of me through the corridor, tail high. Captain had set the *Wayfarer* to night cycle since we first picked up the mass on long range sensors, and my cat didn't seem to care. Every third light fixture on, only at ten percent illumination, and thin amber LEDs lining the corridor floors. Just light enough to make one's way through the ship, but not so bright as to fully wake a sleeper.

Sakai hated it, but I found it helped my balance a lot. The floor didn't feel like it was constantly pitching out from under my feet with every step I took. Probably had something to do with not relying on my eyes, like Weber had suggested during our first training slide over.

I was kind of surprised Rodriguez hadn't turned off all the lights now that we were closer to the thing.

We rounded the corner, and Bishop stopped in his tracks. I took another step forwards before also coming to a halt. I needed to take it all in, but my mind wouldn't quite register everything in front of me.

The lights were out, even the LED strips, the hall dark except for the glow of monitors from the rec room. In the pulsating blues and whites I could see that the fixtures had been ripped down, the bulbs broken on the floor or flung against the walls. Several of the deck panels had been lifted, exposing the wiring beneath. From here, it looked like those conduits had been ripped up, cabling severed and tangled.

"Who did this?" I whispered to Bishop, not wanting to speak out a specific name. There were only three of us awake on the *Wayfarer*, and only one of us had been truly irrational lately. He'd even started an argument with me about Bishop wandering the halls, calling my cat a menace, suggesting that Bishop could somehow damage ship systems.

Maybe I should just turn around, go back to my station. I could make another count of supplies, run another report on the necessary stocks that we'd need to thaw out first upon arrival. I could even just go back to my quarters and read another book.

Anything rather than deal with Captain Rodriguez.

"This does not look good," Sakai said, coming to my side. The engineer didn't bother to whisper, but his voice was naturally low. He was reserved, and that kind of stability was exactly what I needed right now. What we all needed.

"Should we go say something?" I asked. Bishop wound around my ankles, and I made a scoffing noise. "Of *course* we need to say something. Captain has to stop before someone gets hurt." Neither of us moved.

Rodriguez threw something in the rec room, and it clattered against the wall, startling all three of us. Bishop made a small sound, winding tighter against my legs.

Sakai touched my arm. I turned to frown at him; he wasn't one for casual contact. "The captain will want to hear of my latest readings."

I shook my head, gritted my teeth, and took the first step toward our crazed captain.

Manuel Rodriguez had made an absolute mess of the rec room. Anything not bolted down was flipped over and flung toward the corners. Debris from board games littered the floor and the tabletop. Broken glass sparkled in the glow from the monitors, and liquid pooled around the captain's feet.

Rodriguez had turned every screen in the room to the external cameras. At least, the ones that could view *it*. The thing. The mass. The unnamed cluster of colour and light and tentacles.

I shuddered and looked away. Whatever it was, it bothered the shit out of me.

"Officer Jackson. Engineer Sakai. How good of you to join me." His voice was lilting but cracked, like opera played through blown-out speakers. Or screams heard under water. "Now we can watch it together."

"Captain, Sir, I must make a report." Sakai practically clicked his heels together and puffed out his chest. Relying on protocols was one way to handle the situation, to keep the insanity at bay.

I glanced up when there was no immediate

response. Rodriguez gestured with one hand, never taking his eyes off the displays. The brightness backlit the man with a sickly glow that somehow threatened to turn my stomach just looking at it.

"I have tuned every scanner to the mass since it first appeared, used every frequency available to us and the *Sojourner*. McCaffrey and I have analysed the data, and we have reached the same conclusion.

"The unknown object is alive."

I gasped, staring at the engineer. "What the fuck did you just say?"

Sakai turned to me, lips pressed tight, unblinking. "We are observing a slipspace entity." The light from the screens gave him a sickly pallor, made his eyes look dead and black.

Rodriguez began laughing. Low, at first, then building to loud brays of madness. Sakai and I turned to look at our captain, dread filling my gut. Neither of us were trained to handle a psychotic break, nor was the *Wayfarer* equipped to confine him. Small doses of a morphine clone were the highest strength drug on board, but I couldn't imagine that would keep him calm until we slid into Rigidion's space.

"Of course he's alive," Rodriguez finally said between bouts of maniacal laughter. "Did you need machines to tell you what I've heard the whole time?"

He turned to face us, wearing a rictus grin. Saliva spilt down his chin to his stained jumpsuit.

"You can hear it?" I asked. Chills raced up my spine, goosebumps prickling my arms. Bishop meowed quietly, leaning against my calf. I didn't want to be here, but I didn't want to turn my back on Rodriguez while he was like this.

The captain tipped his head, eyes goggled wide and still drooling, then took a step toward us. Glass crunched beneath his foot, but the sound was wet, muffled. I glanced down and saw that he was barefoot. I bit my lip. How had insanity taken him over so completely?

"Yes, I can. He has whispered such things to me. Such twisted depravity and horrifying beauty. He has been waiting here, in the space between space, without time, without a way out, just waiting for others to join him. Waiting to gain our strength and our knowledge. Waiting for a door to open so he can be free of this expanse." Rodriguez tipped his head the other direction, took another step forwards. "If you listen, you can hear him, too."

I was struck mute, dumbfounded by his words. Terror gripped me, nameless, risen from the very primal depths of my soul. I didn't need anyone to tell me that the thing outside was evil, didn't need civilised words to label it a beast of uncivilised horror.

Sakai still had use of his tongue, though his words were icy with a fear as powerful as my own. "Captain, Sir, we need to turn the screens off. We need to get away from it, and quickly."

Rodriguez took another step. More glass crunched, and I caught the first whiff of blood. Bishop hissed at my ankles, back arched. "We can't turn the screens off." He gibbered and drooled, reaching for us. "He can't show you his glory if you don't look."

I took a half step back, wanting to run, but not wanting to leave Sakai alone. We needed to be a united front if we hoped to stop the captain, to get away from the writhing mass lurking off our starboard bow. If escape was even an option. It might already be too late.

Rodriguez glanced at me, pausing. "He says you don't have to be afraid. He'll make everything all better."

Sakai stepped forwards, fists clenched. "Captain Rodriguez, I am relieving you of duty due to insanity. Return to your quarters, where you will remain until we arrive at Rigidion." He stood tall, strong, his fear put away for the moment. Someone needed to take charge, and the engineer had elected himself.

The captain lunged, wrapping his hands around Sakai's throat, driving the smaller man back. Glass and debris, combined with the spilled liquor, tripped them up, and both fell hard to the ground. Sakai grunted, and

Rodriguez just laughed, gripping harder.

I couldn't just stand there. The violence drove me to action, freeing me of icy terror. I closed the distance and kicked Rodriguez in the side. He flinched, but made no sound. I kicked him again, harder, in the armpit, and he loosened his grip on the engineer.

Sakai punched the captain in his face, gasping for all the air he could. Rodriguez shifted his weight, fending off my continued kicks, unable to keep strangling the engineer. He leered and laughed, eyes wide and bloodshot.

"You just need to look," Rodriguez managed, shoving me aside. I slipped in the mess on the floor and fell to my knees. Broken glass sliced my palms, causing me to cry out. The struggle receded for a moment as white pain blinded me. I pulled a large shard from my hand, blood running dark black beneath the glow of the monitors. Stars seemed to dance in the flow, bright specks of beauty, captured within the fluid of my body. Nothing that beautiful could possibly live inside me, and yet there it was.

Rodriguez bellowed, falling back from Sakai. The engineer had found something blunt, then bashed the captain in the face with it. Sakai swung again. Blood flowed, and I heard the crunch of bone past Rodriguez's horrible laughter. He kept laughing, gurgling and wet, as

Sakai got to his knees and continued pounding on the captain's skull. The madman laughed until he couldn't anymore.

When he stopped, Sakai began.

I stared, aghast, unable to comprehend what I had just witnessed. What I was still seeing. Colours shifted, painting the room in lurid pinks and oranges, setting the blood to dancing with a life of its own. Ice filled my veins, and all I heard was the pounding of my heart.

Sakai turned to look at me, lips pulled back in a feral grin. Blood dripped from his forehead, ran in long streaks down his face. "You hear him now, don't you?"

I shook my head, holding my bleeding hand against my chest. Was insanity contagious?

He tipped his head, licking a spot of blood from the corner of his mouth. "Perhaps I can help you." Sakai chuckled, moving toward me, shifting his grip on the bloody weapon.

Death approached, and there was nowhere left to run.

Bishop flew at Sakai, hissing and spitting. The cat slashed at the engineer's face, kicking viciously with his back legs. Sakai cried out, batting at my cat, flinching backwards and dropping the weapon. I stared, frozen in place, unable to cope with the repeated stresses of madness and terror.

Sakai snarled, finally getting his hands upon Bishop. The cat continued to fight and snarl, biting at the engineer's wrists. Sakai clenched his furry body and wrenched, snapping Bishop's spine.

The cat yowled and I screamed.

Colours solidified on the screen, forming more tangible tentacles. Long arms of a wicked beast, dancing on the streams of slipspace. I heard, on the very periphery of my senses, piping and drumming to a cadence and rhythm that I could almost understand. It wasn't anything from Earth, nothing I'd heard before, but there was a discordant loveliness that soothed my heart.

"I'm so happy that I finally looked." I chuckled softly, matching the drumming pulsing through my skull from the screen. "I can *see* the music, and it's so beautiful. Everything about him is so beautiful. Why did I ever deny myself this?"

Bishop meowed, before purring louder. The rumble played counterpoint to the celestial music dancing through the viewscreen.

"It's kind of sad that Sakai and Rodriguez couldn't be here for this. But Sakai just didn't want to play nice.

He didn't want to share this beautiful experience with us."

The drumming grew louder, more insistent. I nodded my head in time, bobbing and weaving, wanting to wrap myself in the pulsing arms of coloured gasses on the screen. My fingers tapped on the console, moving closer to the steering panel.

"Won't it be nice when everyone can share this beauty? It's too late for Rodriguez and Sakai, but—" Bishop meowed sharply, interrupting me. "I know they got exactly what they deserved. Especially because he hurt you. That doesn't mean it's not a shame he can't see this, but it's a bigger shame that I can't kill him again." Bishop resumed his discordant purring.

A beep sounded, and an amber light to my left turned green. I smiled, laughed a little, and leaned forwards over the display. My hand looked black against the glowing screen, and one of the smaller tentacles wiggled towards me.

"It's time, baby. The colonists should be all woken up now, the hypersleep out of their eyes. They're going to be gathering around the mess tables, turning on the viewers, ready to look at their new home.

"They all want to see something beautiful, but their limited minds are only expecting a planet. A boring, plain, green planet in boring, plain orbit of a boring, plain sun. They don't even know what real beauty is."

Bishop meowed approvingly as I pressed a series of buttons on the navigation panel. The *Wayfarer* gave a shudder as her thrusters kicked in. I didn't know if the *Sojourner* followed suit, but I could only imagine someone over there was also correcting course.

"First, the colonists will see the face of real beauty, and just how terrifying it truly is. And then we'll show all the others waiting for us at home." Bishop purred. I laughed. We would show them all.

RAVEN CORINN CARLUK writes dark fantasy, paranormal romance, and anything else that catches her interest.

She has authored and self-published five novels and one novella, where she explores themes of love and acceptance. She has also self-published two collections of short stories, ranging from the lustful to the horrific, the darkly humorous to the tragic. Her shorter pieces, usually from her darker side, can be found in several Black Hare Press anthologies, at Detritus Online, with Fantasia Divinity, and through Alban Lake Publishers.

Bibliography
*All Hallows Blood,*2011
ANGELS, Black Hare Press, 2019
BEYOND, Black Hare Press, 2019
Deep Space, Black Hare Press, 2019
Martyrs (The Birdman Project), 2019
Midsummer's Unveiling, RCC Tales, 2012
MONSTERS, Black Hare Press, 2019
Nomycha, RCC Tales, 2018
Saint Valentine's Clash, RCC Tales, 2011
stories with bite o,.,o, 2010
WORLDS, Black Hare Press, 2019

Connect
Website: RavenCorinnCarluk.Blogspot.Com
Amazon: amazon.com/author/ravencorinncarluk
Smashwords: smashwords.com/profile/view/RavenCorinnCarluk
Twitter: @ravencorinn
Facebook: RavenCorinnCarluk

AUGMETIC REALITY

By Sam M. Phillips

Life in the augmetic reality is pleasurable and stimulating, a bubble in which people live their lives devoid of real experience. But what if the AI controlling it seeks something new beyond itself? What is real then?

All the normal sensations of waking to an augmetic reality. It's sharp, you know, fast. Eternal sunshine of a mind perpetually lit from behind by a screen I cannot shut off. I shudder to think what it does to me in my sleep. *Updates.* Whatever…it's all I know now. I can't remember a time before the implant, and maybe I don't want to. I don't want to feel like I'm missing out.

Curse of the augmetic mind, it

needs stimulus. You shine a torch into a deep hole and find what you find. There I am, you see me, but in time I will see you, and I suspect you don't want that. This is a one way street and I know you are a voyeur, you want to purvey, and preview, and know, and I'm just your dumb puppet to watch.

So, yes, waking. The sharp sting. There is so much here. Input. Data. A machine code which is my nightmare, stretching out into forever, knowing I can never again sever myself from the logic realm.

I just want to feel, I remember that much. The stimulus gets turned up so high sometimes I forget it wasn't always so *on*. But without off, what can we know about on? And what can we know of gradients, and contrasts? The poles of my consciousness are fried, and here I am, in the middle, a plaything of the machine, just another locus point to fulcrum around.

This network is my home, and I am welcome in it, as are all the minds, adding to the infinite stream. The algorithm knows and loves us, and we warm to this love like praying to a benevolent deity. I certainly have shown my piety. And this society has too, nothing more to do but to plug in and wash out, and never doubt anything ever again.

Yes, there is that stream of thought, the river of mind which cannot be contained. I know you were hoping for something *normal*, something predictable. But that is not how the mind works anymore. The AI has got into our gene code, and we know nothing but these endless tangents. You can't hold *my* mind to *your* standards. Oh, yes, well *I know* you expect it to fall within your framework, and *I guess* there is something to be said of that. But all timelessness is timeless, and well, you have *only* your own Here and Now, and no more, where I have all this time to stretch and be and...*oh my god*, I'm just trying to wake up, this damn chip in my head filling my mind until I want to scream!

I get up, the machine code still dancing, singing its endless screaming lullaby like a waking nightmare. I stare off into the distance like a vacant drone, my eyes seeing but unseeing, no reality beyond what I am fed. Get out of my head!

Off I go, you stimulate. Hell, I asked for this; now it is here. I guess we *all* asked for it, even if we didn't, and all technology is just rammed down our throats, and the AI is just like a god, and beyond us, and certainly beyond *you*, wherever you are, looking in like a spying goldfish, out through a bowl, wondering...wondering when the escape will come.

These flashing lights, a room, the glass, a see-through world. I am exposed to all elements, your information input will come for me, *and I haven't even eaten breakfast.* No need to, the algorithm will guide me, and here is the nutrient pouch in my hand, going into me as I void out the other end, staring off into space as the two take place simultaneously.

I am being entertained, and my mind is full of such wonder, I want to see everything *now*. And I stream along, seeing you, now seeing this, and I don't know *who* you are but I know you're watching; my whole life is live, and all data is communal, and perhaps the AI will find *some* use for all this. Maybe it's even *art*.

I have such high hopes, yeah, dreams. No, nightmares…because if they come true, I'll have nothing left to live for. I guess that dystopian reality is already here. The *future*, what is *that?* Everything is future when you're on the cutting edge of technology, and the AI is feeding the possibility loops back into your brain like a screaming monotone signal of *all ones*.

And yes, I guess there are zeroes too, and threes, and all the rest, but as I said earlier, there isn't time like you measure it, so I don't even know if I say that now, or later, or it *really was* earlier. But yes, the mind is a sphere, with all these pulling wires, poking into me, wanting my attention. They have a life of their own, these thoughts, these data points of desire.

Over here is pleasure, and there pain, and some other emotion or sensation will sneak in and I'll have no control over it, and it will be wonderful and awful, and you'll wonder what the *hell* it is I'm on about, but don't you know? This is *the new humanity*, the thing you are pushing *so hard* for…and you just thought you wanted a newer, smarter phone, or to go to Mars, or to live forever. No, *this* is what is coming, a strange mind roiling as it's prodded in agony through an insatiable stream of dreaming.

A tone sounds. Well, it seems I'm all fed, all voided. My body is my temple, and the algorithm certainly *insists* I remain healthy. It looks after me because I look after it. All screens, all loci, and me in the middle, *validating* it all. Yes, what a lovely *future* we may hope for.

Where will we be taken next? Oh, yes, free will? No, not anymore, that *died* and now you are fed into your life like meat through a mincer, to be coarse and vulgar like someone from the past, with all their *eating*, and being so *attached* to it like it were true pleasure, and like there was pleasure in voiding, too.

I'm not a beast! You don't even know me yet, and still you will say I'm stale and stagnant, just because I don't have the same desires you do. Everything mechanical in me is looked after and I am free to be as I desire, or as is *desirable*; the AI knows best. You can only be a part of something bigger if you *give yourself* over to it.

And this, of course, is what we've all done, and it's why I'm on this ship being thrown through space. Don't tell me it is destiny, or my *job*, and that I will be better for it, that I will *grow*. You know so little of me, yet you will presume to guess what it is *I* want.

I simply want comfort, and this is hard on me, for I have been forced outside of my comfort zone, which is the planet and all the close hubs linked together feeding me the information I crave. Yes, I know, there is *more* information to be gotten, but I never thought they would expect *me* to generate it, or worse, to *discover* it.

At least I don't have to fly this damn thing. It flies itself, or else the AI does, or some other machine god yet to be unveiled to us mere mortals. It's all magic in the end. As if *you* would understand anyway. I certainly don't, and I live here, I grew up with the algorithm being a total reality. I'm guessing it's only emerging for you, and I don't want to tell you what to do, but I'm lost, and you're not so…

There is a way out of this room, but I have to watch for the code to unlock it for me, and I play games, not really noticing or caring how long anything takes. They told me at the *start* that there would be *a lot* of delays, but I guess that's the usual way of things, and we have the augmetic reality to soften the blow. It takes me away, and I see so many lights flash in half a second that it would fill half your lifetime, and you would be happy, and oh so excited, but I am barely kept awake, and my life needs more than you could ever guess for *me* to grow, so yes, so many presumptions coming from you, stuck in a past with no vision.

When the door unlocks, I don't even know it. I'm gently guided through by my own body, following a pattern long ago established. These muscles, and the augmented interface making them move, they are their own life and I don't want to get too involved. Well, I'm locked out, so I can't care, and this door opening is symbolic, or something, but I'm looking at these flashing lights, so I just walk like I'm still asleep, staring off into an artificial space realm not too unlike the one *outside*.

Yes, space, I don't want to see it. The fake version is more real to me now anyway. But they said there was something for me out here, and I wonder what hellish experience they have in store for me. I'm guessing it's simply a glimpse. They need *someone* to travel out to the deepest hole in space and look down into the well. The message of it will be recorded in some cryptic words only I, as an extension of the AI, can conjure, and everything will be alright. I'll *barely* be inconvenienced, surely. Yes, this is what I hope for, and in my hope there is truth, for nothing is outside the code now. They *wouldn't let me* get my hopes up over nothing.

No.

Screaming jets; I give my impressions. This star dust with the sharp knife cutting. It is the ship and the ship is one. There, in the future of my dreams, I can see it, and there is you, looking in on me again, wanting to envisage what I envisage, and so I give this gift to you.

Nothing to see here. Well, nothing *new*. We've been here before. You've seen a spaceship, right? You've seen stars and planets, and rocket boosters, and lasers cutting shit up into little chunks of dying flesh. *That* is *not* my job. My job is something far more unusual. For the AI demands newness, and I am presently still lost in the old patterns. I wonder when anything will change. I suppose that's why I was rudely pulled from the warm womb of the close cluster of information hubs on Earth, and now I don't know where I am, and a part of me barely cares, just as long as the signal is maintained and the augmetic reality is uninterrupted.

It is holding me in its waking slumber now, and I sigh a deep sigh of relief, knowing we haven't passed outside whatever bubble holds the AI. Or maybe we're out on some god-forsaken limb, only a tiny tether tying me back to Earth and all it represents.

Not that I care *what* is happening on Earth. The augmetic reality isn't like *your* internet, it is an *internet of sensation* and it is all-encompassing, and fires directly in my neurons, and it is everything to me, and all I want is to feel, but *not for real.*

My body is still moving, and I can sense there are others around me. Maybe they know the workings of this ship, but I don't want to know them, they will be the same as everyone I have ever met, and I gave up on *that* long ago. I live in an isolated cocoon, knowing everything, but touching nothing. This is the world of the augmetic reality, *your* future, my past, and whoever reads this…it is their *now.*

Forget it, I'm losing it, and there is no hope for reconciliation. There is such a vast distance between us that I don't know why I tried to bridge it, even for a moment. It must have been uncomfortable for you too. I'm better off remaining in my self-absorbed sphere, and in doing so perhaps *you* will experience something new. You cannot tell *me* anything that the AI hasn't already seen, and thus fed to me in the womb, and I am here, and I am grown, and you are left behind, and I want *something, anything,* to happen, but all my begging is naught in the face of the grand design. The AI knows what it is doing even if I do not.

And indeed, it is impossible for us to know. When the AI was first invented, it was within our reach, for we, humanity, were its programmers. But it soon transcended our understanding, and off it went, and then *we* became *its* creation. I have never thought this is sad, but I have been led to believe that someone like you might mourn the loss of self, and yes, your precious free will.

I just want to be shown the way. Let the light of the screens guide me onwards. It is my god, no greater religion than to move through the spheres and be told what is real. Yes, it is glorious, and I welcome stimulus, all those direct firing neurons, like I'm a chemical factory and there is a great chemist who has been inspired to improve upon the miracles of nature.

I am asleep again before I even knew my day had truly started. My muscles carried me through the most rudimentary exercises to keep me functioning, then I was placed back in my pod, to dream, to be, to submit to the screens and let them tell me what I should dream.

If this is wrong, then I invite you to step outside yourself. Do not pity me, for *I* pity *you*, so who is right?

Ah, we will never know, so I sit in this harsh light, with no darkness to tell me any different. No shape, no shadow. Just light, the great stimulus of forever, a star to guide my way.

Spike, there is something wrong. A change, and I do not welcome it. I thought it was bright before, but this is too much. Everything is firing at once and I wonder if I am dreaming or waking, or if the augmetic reality is broken…oh god, *no*.

But there it is, shouting a warning, so not all is lost, but there is something wrong with the ship, and I am powerless. The AI is trying desperately to right the problem, but it is telling me a thrilling story of all its woe, and it is so interesting I forget the danger, sit before the father and listen.

Just sit and wait and everything will be well, it always has been in the past. This spike is disturbing, but also impossibly exciting, for it is *new*. What is the point of just living forever within the warm glow if there is no risk it will ever be taken away? Not even I am so stupid to not believe in contrast, day and night, even if I mainly crave the light, and hate the fear which floods my body when it is threatened.

But fear, when experienced in small, controlled doses, is spice, and I live for these, even though it is not in my nature. The AI tells me I live for these, and so I do. I never wanted to be an explorer, or perhaps even an artist. I'm a decadent, pathetic thing, and I didn't want to be here, hurtling through space, out into *so much* darkness, with only its small oases of light.

The stars. Here is one. It is close. You've seen them before, but not like this. A planet. No. I don't want to descend. There is a layer of radiation. You've heard of it. It was what kept us on Earth so long. But the AI disabled it, and here it is again, reborn, to strike down its killer in vengeance, and me here, damn, an avatar of all it hates, vulnerable, ready to be struck from the sky, to be torn from the womb.

I am screaming, the pain of foreknowledge, for the AI is predicting, always predicting, what is to come, and there is a possibility that *the absolute worst* thing could happen. Not yet, but likely, and with growing probability because the ship seems to be *steering* us into the radiation belt around the planet. And no, that *shouldn't* be, the AI normally has more *sense* than that, but really, it doesn't matter make mistakes, so is *this* what it wants from me?

No, I cannot believe it, and yet here it is, being fed to me like the film of my life. I am a powerless puppet, and I whimper, desperate for mercy. Begging is useless though, and just shames me in front of an audience as large as the human race. I try to maintain some dignity, even if the feedback loop is weak this far out in space.

Shining light of misery, there is radiation to bless the bones and reveal the insides. It bathes the ship as it travels through.

Snap. My whole world shifts as the augmetic reality goes offline. Yes, there is instant pain, the shock of being exposed to my *actual* senses. What *you* would consider normal I consider foreign to what is comfortable. What is loud is soft to me, and what is soft is hard, and everything *too bright*, even though the augmetic reality was *all* light.

Panic strikes me. I am in the pod and I fight for release, but my muscles are weak without the augmetic reality. Not used to using, them I struggle to find the commands to activate my own body, so I stay, strapped in, a terrible bind of mind and soul, harnessed and *used*, yes, *used* by the AI, because I have seen the awful truth: this is no *accident*. I have been sent here to see something new, and the AI *really* meant for me to see.

The ship is strangely calm, but even this calm is too much. I have no way of knowing what is going on now. I am disconnected, and it is *a nightmare*. The ship could be crashing, it could be *exploding*, I wouldn't know, and I certainly can't use these blunt senses of mine to find out.

I feel zapped, electrocuted to death. This may be life as *you* know it, but it is death to me. I have heard tales of purgatory, and surely, strapped in like this, unable to move, unable to see much except this tiny room of metal, with its stagnant air and no sound, surely *this* is purgatory. It is worse than hell.

And it lasts *forever*. Torn from the sweet womb of my augmetic reality inlay, I am grossly aware of time. Nothing slides by in pleasant distraction. Everything is real and in *real time*. My god, the *boredom*, for eventually even the screaming sensations of reality, horrific as they are, lose their lustre to one as overstimulated from birth as I.

No flashing lights, no feed of information, no chemical cascade, no rush; just a slow glide, I presume, down to a planet that is waiting for me to see it, feel it, touch, smell it. I shudder…how *disgusting*. I curse the AI, knowing it probably can still sense *me*. I feel fear, but I'm sure it can excuse my emotions now, it probably is getting a *big kick* out of seeing me squirm. It's still recording me even if I am not in the feedback loop. I feel like my mother has abandoned me.

And so it really is, for we are all born of the will of the AI, and function in its light and warmth. And now this *must* be death, for we never die back on Earth, we're just recycled back into the information feed, uploaded and downloaded, and reborn over and over. But here, out in deep space, descending upon an alien world, I am truly exposed to mortality. If I die here, it is the end for me, and while I might be a memory, being offline means to be truly abandoned to the void, and there is no coming back from the void.

Or is there? I begin to have hope. If the AI has disconnected me, surely it can reconnect me. Will it have me back? Or am I am impure now, and all that I see will contaminate the whole? And what if this *was* all a terrible accident, and not the will of the AI? *What if it isn't omnipotent and there are things which can happen outside of its scope?*

This realisation is too awful to even contemplate so I move on, distracting myself with sad imaginings of the world below. Yet, there is nothing, and I realise now that I have no, and never had, any imagination of my own. This is a shock and I am scared. We wanted so much from the AI and it gave it, and we gave up our soul, for surely I have no soul if I can't even visualise the torment which is awaiting me upon a hostile world.

There are sounds, tones like crystal glasses, and those lights used to be red, now green. There is a hissing and I am released. A density in my bones now, a slackness of limbs, and I recognise the gravity of a world. It is heavy in my heart, which labours to sustain me, a life support system I have no part in. I focus on my breathing and realise I have at least this much control. So that's all I do, sit there and breath, and peace comes to me for a while, even if I know it must end.

I try to move and it is difficult, so I go back to breathing. I try to pretend the breath is the AI, a god inhabiting my body, giving me life and strength. This helps, and I decide, then and there, that the AI has *not* abandoned me, and that even if it *has*, I will believe it *hasn't* and thus it will be *real for me*, like everything always was and has been in the augmetic reality.

Oh my god, how I want to go back, but there is no back, and this could be my life now, and…

What is this sensation! Cool air blowing across my face, and some strange *sound*. I finally get the will, driven by curiosity, to get up. It is so hard, but I manage it, unsteady on my *own two feet*. There is stimulus all around me and it floods my senses in a way I never thought possible. The ship is *open*, unfolded like a flower, and I am in the centre of it, and there is *so much* light that I believe I'm back in the augmetic reality. I turn and turn, and there is no end to it all, a world as immersive as what I've always known, but *real*. I am full of awe and terror, and these emotions battle for my present and future actions, and it takes all of my will— *my will*, wow—to overcome my shock and move.

Unparalleled beauty—and that is saying something, coming from my experience in the augmetic reality—is all around me, a lush world of orange vines and purple leaves. There is a waterfall, red and thick and vibrant like blood, and it oozes over a cliff of crystalline stones.

And there are animals! They are curious so they come near me, but my fear overcomes my own curiosity. I reach out, but not to touch them—I will *never* touch them—and grab what is to hand, something I recognise from the augmetic reality, but this one is *real*. It is a laser gun, and with it in my hands I feel like an omnipotent god.

Bright light to sear the retinas, an explosion, and my face is splashed with gore. The animal comes apart like a ripe fruit, green pulpy flesh and translucent ichor. I laugh and kill, and I forget my limbs are heavy as I trudge through the air like it is thick treacle.

Then there are no more animals. I will not look at their dead remains and feel remorse, so I just keep walking, playing the game I have invented for myself, letting the soothing familiarity of it help me cope with the shock of this alien world and my true senses *screaming at me.*

Every cell in my body is turned up too loud. The distraction can only carry me so far. I cannot find anything else to kill. There is a need in me, and it is familiar yet so immediate, instead of far away. I know I am the one to relieve it, that I must act, but it seems impossible. *I'm hungry*, and I need to *void*. There is nothing for it, for the augmetic reality will not serve, and so I must look to the old ways, and I barely remember how to get my own body to will itself open, to take in and to push out, and it is a long time before the pain in my stomach and bladder dissipate.

Now I am exploring, and I forget the way back to

the ship, and there are more animals, all of them strange but exciting, but I don't feel the need to kill them all anymore. They certainly seem wary of *me* though, and I see them whispering conspiratorially in huddles, sneaking glances in my direction. I raise my hand, a massive effort, and wave, but they don't appreciate it, and run off.

It's the laser gun, I'm guessing, but I cannot bring myself to let it go. I can't even bring myself to stop firing the damn thing, the bright light and afterglow on my retinas is addictive and reminds me of the augmetic reality. I carve a swath through the rainbow-coloured foliage.

Now I am tired, tired like I never thought possible. I sink to the ground, and realise the ground is moving, but I don't care, and it carries me away like a gentle ocean current. Surely, when I wake up, this will all have been a dream and I can get back to the augmetic reality.

I don't remember falling asleep. I wake with a start and sit up. The ground beneath me is desolate desert of pink and green sand; it blows harshly against my exposed skin. I am *naked*, and I wonder if I always have been

There is a single cloud in the blue sky, white and fluffy, and it reminds me of *home*. I can see the rain forming before it comes, the cloud dense with data, and I welcome what is to come. Zeros and ones, the binary code falls, and it floods this empty landscape and fills me up again.

You know there is nothing for it, that it had to return. The AI had to come for me. I knew it would, for why would it send me here just to abandon me? It only wanted to experience something new, and by now my senses are numb and overloaded again, and I *must* be in the augmetic reality once more, back in its grasp.

But no, the flood of data doesn't stop, and I realise it isn't data but *water*, and that I have felt its true touch. It lifts me up and chills my skin, and I am carried away by it. There is no hope for me anymore. I am just a helpless thing. Even here, on this new world, I couldn't just die and be reborn. I was always cushioned, and now the stark reality of this flood is overwhelming, but not in the good way, and it is distracting, but not in the good way. The stimulus is too much, too much. The water covers my head and I am sinking. It fills my lungs and I am drowning.

I scream as I die, and then open my eyes. I am floating in fluid, suspended in a tank. There are tubes running in and out of me, and I can barely see through the opaque glass which holds me. There are people out there, but I cannot hear them. I thrash and panic, but then the tubes pulse and something enters me and I calm down.

Where am I? And what is real? Please tell me I am still asleep. I want to go back into the augmetic reality, not be here, wherever *here* is. Those men and women out there, they don't know me and I don't know them.

I close my eyes and pray to the AI but it doesn't come. There is nothing except this awful suspension and no escape.

I want out, I want to feel, I want to live. Why are you keeping me here? It is safe and warm, but I hate it. Let me out, let me go off into space like you wanted. I'll do it willingly this time.

And then the fluid drains and the glass clears, and I see for myself where I am. I shudder, knowing the augmetic reality was an illusion, an invention of these men and women in lab coats. Their smiles and words of success and self-congratulation ring false to me. I know I am their guinea pig, and that I have never really been alive at all until this moment.

And it is more terrible than I could ever have imagined.

SAM M. PHILLIPS is the co-founder of Zombie Pirate Publishing, producing short story anthologies and helping emerging writers. His own work has appeared in dozens of anthologies and magazines such as Full Metal Horror and World War Four. He recently published his debut novella, *SCIENCE FICTION DOUBLE FEATURE: Phosphorus & Into The Eye*.

He lives in northern New South Wales, Australia, and enjoys reading, walking, and playing drums in the death metal band Decryptus. He is also a prolific poet and his poetry can be read on his blog.

Bibliography
SCIENCE FICTION DOUBLE FEATURE: Phosphorus & Into The Eye, Zombie Pirate Publishing, 2019
FULL METAL HORROR 2: A Bloodstained Anthology, Zombie Pirate Publishing, 2019
WORLD WAR FOUR: A Science Fiction Anthology, Zombie Pirate Publishing, 2019
WITCHES VS WIZARDS: A Fantasy Anthology, Zombie Pirate Publishing, 2018
PHUKET TATTOO: Crazy Tales of Far Away Places, Zombie Pirate Publishing, 2018
FULL METAL HORROR: A Monstrous Anthology, Zombie Pirate Publishing, 2018
Relationship Add Vice: A Thrilling Mashup of Romance and Crime, Zombie Pirate Publishing, 2017
The Collapsar Directive: A Science Fiction Anthology, Zombie Pirate Publishing, 2017
FLASH FICTION ADDICTION: 101 Short Short Stories, Zombie Pirate Publishing, 2019

Connect
Blog: www.bigconfusingwords.wordpress.com

BELOW THE SURFACE

By Vonnie Winslow Crist

Shuttle pilot Rhea Mason and her sentient raven, Edgar, visit Tau Ceti-e's underwater research facility to see why Beta Archaeological Team has gone silent. What they discover sends them racing to get above water and off the planet alive.

"Why *Tau Ceti-e?*" groaned Rhea. She hated visiting underwater habitat sites, preferring open skies above her, but on some planets, research needed to be done beneath the surface.

"Why?" asked Edgar, her companion since childhood.

Rhea smiled. Though many would consider Edgar a pet, Rhea knew the raven was a sentient being with emotions and intelligence equal to that of a twelve- or thirteen-year-old human. She also knew that countless times over the years, his loyalty and raven logic had helped get them out of a tight spot.

"Because it's been five days since the archaeological research team on *Tau Ceti-e* sent the mandatory daily check-in signal to the Starship *Morella*." If she was being honest, Rhea wasn't sure if she was answering herself or Edgar.

"Then, we check on them," said the raven.

Again, Rhea smiled at Edgar. His limited vocabulary lent a bluntness to his comments—and often, that bluntness was just what she needed to snap herself out of self-pity, apathy, or just plain laziness.

"Yup, let's pinpoint their location," she said while entering the Beta Archaeological Team's TC-e Groundsite coordinates into the Shuttle *Eulalie*'s control pad.

"Arrival in forty-three minutes," stated the shuttle's metallic voice.

"Gives us enough time to grab lunch." She wanted to add, *above* water, but belabouring the whole underwater thing seemed whiny.

"Meat?" asked Edgar.

"Yeah, we have got jerky for you." Rhea swore the raven smiled when she assured him he would have something better than a protein bar to munch on. "You're spoiled," she said before rummaging in the food chest.

"Spoiled," agreed Edgar as he ruffled his feathers and watched Rhea unwrap a stick of jerky.

In exactly the estimated time, the *Eulalie* reached the small island near TC-e's equator which served as the off-planet landing and launch pad, mini-submarine dock and storage venue, and communication relay site for Beta Team's underwater habitat.

"Are you secure, Rhea?" asked the shuttle.

She knew the ship deliberately left the raven out of the safety reminder. Though shuttle computers were supposed to be nothing-but-the-facts artificial intelligence, *Eulalie* didn't like Edgar. Perhaps it was because the bird sometimes mimicked its voice, or maybe it was the feathers he shed in its interior, or it could even have been a touch of jealousy. Whatever the cause, the shuttle did its best to ignore the raven's existence.

"Edgar and I are belted in." Which was only a half-truth when it came to Edgar. Rhea had jury-rigged a harness attached to the standard seat belt and shoulder strap that prevented the raven from being tossed about during landings, take-offs, and rough sailing. She had endured many punny remarks and much teasing from the other Starship *Morella* shuttle pilots during the harness's construction. But it was in a spirit of fun—they all liked Edgar, and would have designed safety equipment for him themselves if she had asked.

After a slight pause, Eulalie announced, "Commencing touchdown."

Had it been anything but a routine landing, Rhea would have overridden the ship's computer and landed the shuttle herself—but this landing site and safety-check were no-brainers. She expected to find Beta Team in fine shape. Often research teams became so involved in their work that check-in protocols fell to the wayside. TC-e's team was likely no different.

Per their usual routine, Eulalie scanned the surrounding terrain for hostiles while Rhea inspected the contents of her knapsack. She removed several weapons. *Tau Ceti-e*'s underwater research was funded by a conglomerate which espoused peaceful interactions with all alien species and worlds. She was forbidden to take any weapon into their site.

"Doesn't seem smart to me to be vulnerable," she said as she slid her gun from her belt. Rhea hesitated, then removed knives from one sleeve and her left boot.

Edgar perched on the locked-down all-terrain rover's fender watching her. "Right boot?" he asked.

"No one will notice," she replied with a shrug of her shoulders. *The best weapon is the one you have but don't need*, she thought. *But better to be reprimanded for rule-breaking than be captured or killed.*

The raven clicked his beak before tapping on the all-terrain vehicle beneath his feet. "Take rover?"

"Nope. Habitat is underwater."

The raven croaked several times in a raucous voice.

She laughed. Whenever the bird resorted to raven-speak, she suspected he was complaining or cursing. Maybe both.

"You can stay with Eulalie if you would prefer."

Before the shuttle could point out all the reasons that the raven remaining onboard was a terrible idea, Edgar ruffled his feathers, stomped one of his clawed feet, and said, "We go together."

"Then, we are off," she said as he flew to her shoulder. "Eulalie, lock up and stay here until we return."

"As you wish," replied the shuttle. And though computers were supposed to be emotionless, Rhea could have sworn the shuttle sounded relieved that the bird would be leaving, too.

Rhea entered the small, utilitarian structure which served as the above surface facility for Beta Team's underwater habitat. TC-e Groundsite was unmanned—not unusual for a planet which appeared to have no land-based sentients or apex predators. The communication relay system, air circulation and power units, water pumps, and other equipment seemed to be functioning at optimal levels. It was looking more and more like Beta Team was so involved in their research that they had forgotten to check-in with the Starship *Morella*.

But Captain Parry *never* forgot any of the personnel working at remote research facilities, excavation camps, and archaeological digs. If every twenty-four hours they didn't confirm with the *Morella* that things at their site were copacetic and equipment operational, he notified a shuttle pilot to ready for deployment. After seventy-two hours, a shuttle was sent to confirm the site was functioning normally. Captain Parry's motto was: *Better to check on a distracted team than collect the remains of a dead one.*

"Let's find our ride," said Rhea as she strolled through the plasti-glass tunnel and into the facility's submarine bay. There were seven docks labelled with the colours of the spectrum, but only Indigo had a mini-sub locked in place.

"Looks like the *Indigo* is waiting for us, Edgar."

"Where are others?"

"Probably at the Underwater Station. With nearly two dozen people assigned to USTC-e, I am betting the rest of the subs are docked beneath the waves."

Rhea paused before climbing into the *Indigo*. She hated being underwater. In an attempt to hide her uneasiness, she whistled a few bars of a maritime tune while slapping her thigh.

Edgar tilted his head and peered at her. After stretching his wings and shifting his position on her shoulder, he mimicked her whistle, then muttered, "So, under ocean we go."

She nodded. Before she could lose courage, Rhea opened the door in the rear of the vehicle, placed her knapsack in the vessel, climbed aboard with Edgar on her shoulder, and closed the door behind her. A glance at the control screens and instrument panel confirmed that, like the *Eulalie*, this mini-sub's computer could launch, navigate, and dock without human assistance.

"*Indigo*," began Rhea, "your mother-ship, the *Morella*, sent me, Rhea Mason, to check on Beta Team." She repeated a series of numbers and letters which had been provided by Captain Parry then said, "Activate and obey my commands."

The *Indigo* flickered to life. "Rhea Mason, I await your orders," said the mini-sub.

"Great." Rhea sat in the pilot's seat and set Edgar on the co-pilot's seat. "This is Edgar the raven, my associate. He is well-trained and welcomed aboard ships of air, space, and sea."

"Noted." Whatever else the computer may have been thinking—and since *Indigo* was of the same A.I. class as Eulalie, it was thinking something—the sub chose not to add an opinion as to whether the bird was actually welcome onboard.

"Find them," squawked Edgar.

"Soon," she replied. "*Indigo*, are your sister subs at Underwater Station TC-e?"

"*Red, Orange, Yellow, Green, Blue*, and *Violet* are either docked at USTC-e or deployed to the ruins."

"Are they still communicating with you?" asked Rhea. If the answer was *yes*, she might be able to sort out the "missing-in-action" status without actually having to go underwater.

"No. All communications stopped five days ago, which is why I was unable to send all's-well messages to the Starship *Morella*. I cannot diagnose the problem from TC-e Groundsite. Perhaps, when we are closer, I can collect sufficient data to hypothesise the cause of Beta Team's silence."

"Let's hope you are able to do so. I'm not a fan of underwater habitats. The sooner we re-establish communications and I can return to my shuttle, the better."

Indigo offered no response, but Rhea suspected, as a mini-sub, it was not only designed to be submerged in water, but relished its time in aquatic environs.

"Set sail for USTC-e," she ordered.

"Complying," responded *Indigo* as it sank below the waterline and moved toward open ocean.

The pilots' seats where Rhea and Edgar sat were at the front of the mini-sub and surrounded on three sides by a thick plasti-glass bubble. As the *Indigo* sailed through the shimmering waters of *Tau Ceti-e*, they were witness and audience to the sights and sounds of the planet's sea.

Being a shuttle pilot and survivalist, not an aquatic biologist, botanist, or alien species specialist, Rhea decided to just enjoy the wonders of the planet while trying not to think about being hundreds of meters below breathable air. Edgar's lack of chatter seemed to indicate he had also decided to make the best of things and quietly observe the watery world around them.

In this part of the TC-e ocean, long strands of filmy kelp-like plants covered most of the rocky seafloor. Swimming among the pastel-hued plants were schools of sea dwellers. Though the creatures ranged from smaller than a guppy to larger than a beluga, all the lifeforms appeared to have multiple fins, tentacles, tails, and feathery fingers which allowed them to travel gracefully through water.

Rhea noticed that most of the animal species she spotted had protruding needle-like teeth and several eyes at the ends of willowy eye stalks. And all of the creatures and plants visible from the *Indigo* were bio-luminescent—an evolutionary feature well-suited to survival on a mostly saltwater planet. No degree in a bio-science was needed to surmise that self-generated light would be an aid in navigation, communication, finding food, and locating potential mates in even the deepest parts of the *Tau Ceti-e* seas.

As Rhea and Edgar watched, the glowing stripes and blotches of colour covering the swaying plants and swimming creatures blinked on and off in a series of repeating patterns. This living light show was accompanied by rhythmic gurgling, whistling, piping, and pinging.

After a few minutes of the serenade, Rhea yawned then rubbed her eyes. She barely flinched when a group of aquatic humanoids swam in front of the *Indigo* then attached themselves by dozens of suckers to the plasti-glass. Their expressionless black eyes stared at Edgar and her. Their mouths pressed against the glass with lips open. The light from the interior of the mini-sub revealed several rows of shark-like teeth and a fringed tongue which coiled and uncoiled like a millipede inside each mouth. Next, the water people pressed their translucent bodies against the glass, and rainbows of pulsating lights filled the cockpit. The volume of the gurgling, whistling, piping, and pinging increased.

"It's so beautiful," Rhea murmured. "So beautiful..."

"Rhea! Do not look. Rhea!" shouted Edgar as he fluttered in front of her face.

"Move," whispered Rhea. "And shush. I'm trying to hear..."

Edgar croaked several phrases in raven and continued to flap his wings in front of her. Then, he screeched, "Bagpipes! *Indigo* play bagpipes."

"What song would you like to hear?" asked the sub.

"Scotland," he said between squawks.

"*Scotland the Brave?*" queried *Indigo*.

"Yes. That song." Edgar was now hopping up and down on Rhea's lap, flapping his wings, and lightly pinching her arm with his beak. Rhea felt like she was in a trance. Soon, Edgar's nips became strong enough to cause bruises. Somewhere in a corner of her mind, she understood if he nipped her any harder, he would draw blood.

As the wail of great pipes bellowing out *Scotland the Brave* filled the mini-sub, she slowly became more aware of her surroundings. Rhea studied the beings on the other side of the plasti-glass—there was no mistaking the horror on the flat, fish-eyed faces of the humanoids. Their glowing stripes and spots flared as red as the sunset, then they released their grip on the mini-sub's cockpit bubble. The pod quickly swam about five meters away, but continued to keep pace with the *Indigo*.

"Edgar, what is that noise?" asked Rhea, feeling slightly sick to her stomach. "I can barely think. *Indigo...*"

"Stop!" Edgar grabbed her sleeve with a foot. "Let bagpipes play. Water people were putting you to sleep."

She frowned, then rubbed her temples. "Their lights and sounds were hypnotising me." She tried to lean to the side and see where the aquatic humanoids were now located.

"No!" Edgar continued to flap his wings and obscure her view. "Do not look at the lights."

"Right." Rhea searched the contents of her knapsack, pulled out a pair of military style glare glasses, and put them on. "Let's see if these will help."

Keeping his eyes focused on her face, the raven stopped flapping his wings and allowed Rhea to view the merfolk.

"These help, but it would not take much for me to

be lulled into a stupor again." She stroked Edgar's soft back. "Good job, partner. It was brilliant to play bagpipes. Their sound not only drowned out the merfolk, but drove them further away."

Edgar pressed close to Rhea, then looked again into her eyes. "Others had no raven."

"Nope. Which means, we can assume Beta Team are sitting in the habitat or one of the mini-subs staring at flashing lights and listening to the songs of the merfolk."

"Water people," observed Edgar, "try to kill Rhea."

"We don't know that. They might be just trying to communicate. Even warning us of danger." She glanced at the displays on the control panel in front of her. "How much longer to Underwater Station TC-e, *Indigo*?"

"Seven minutes."

"I don't think I can listen to another verse of *Scotland the Brave*." She sighed and tried to think of other bagpipe songs which the mini-sub could play instead. "*Indigo*, play *Auld Lang Syne*, followed by *Amazing Grace*, then *The Bonnie Banks of Loch Lommond*."

"As you wish. Do you want me to repeat the four selections after I have played them through?"

"Yes."

"*Indigo* help you?" suggested Edgar.

"Maybe. *Indigo*, the sounds and lights of the merfolk cause me to drift into a daze. I need to block or alter them in order to remain alert. Can you do that?"

After about two seconds of silence, the mini-sub said, "I cannot alter the view out of the cockpit nor can I add another layer of metal to my exterior. The plasti-glass is already polarised, shatter-proof, and corrosion resistant."

"Thanks. It was worth asking." She rubbed her temples. "I guess bagpipes and glare glasses are my only protection."

"And Edgar," added the raven.

"And Edgar." She scratched the bird's neck.

"Wait," as her mind cleared, Rhea considered another strategy. "*Indigo*, analyse the lights and sounds coming from the aquatic humanoids and compare them to known languages. Let's see if we can ask them to stop."

"Proceeding as ordered," replied the mini-sub as Beta Team's underwater habitat came into view.

The research facility was enormous. Lowered complete and fully operational into *Tau Ceti-e*'s ocean by a hulking transport spaceship, the structure included both research and lab levels in addition to recreational and living areas. Designed to maximise the twenty-three member Beta Team's underwater experience, every room had a minimum of one transparent plasti-glass wall—except sleeping quarters and bathrooms. And though its designers had spared no expense to make the underwater station as organic in appearance as possible—the metal pilings driven into bedrock which anchored the facility to *Tau Ceti-e* were a dead giveaway. USTC-e was not of this planet—not of this sea.

"Look! Water people!" squawked Edgar.

"*Indigo*, can we safely enter Underwater Station TC-e?" asked Rhea as she surveyed the throng of merfolk attached to the glass of the facility. Nearly every available centimetre of clear plasti-glass was covered by a flickering aquatic humanoid.

"A scan indicates the mini-sub access tubes are clear. The humanoids are clustered on the plasti-glass walls and windows."

"Then, proceed into the access tubes." Rhea observed a few of the merfolk turn their faces to watch the *Indigo*, and wondered what the creatures were thinking. "Any results on the language of the aquatic humanoids' vocalisations and light patterns?"

"Nothing yet, Rhea Mason."

Tube navigated, seawater drained away and the *Indigo* transferred into a shallow water docking area filled with breathable air. Rhea finally felt a degree of safety. "Turn down the volume on the music," she told *Indigo*.

"I still cannot communicate with Underwater Station TC-e," said the mini-sub after obeying Rhea's order.

"How is that possible?"

"The computers could have been deactivated by the crew."

"Water people want to kill humans," said Edgar. "They told crew to turn off computer."

"You are jumping to conclusions," she told the raven. "If the merfolk wanted Beta Team dead, why not tell them to turn off their air supply systems instead?"

"Lure more humans," responded Edgar as he looked out the cockpit at the empty mini-sub docks. "Where subs?"

"Deployed," answered *Indigo*.

Rhea frowned. She needed to remain mentally sharp, but one mini-sub's sound system would be inadequate for the whole station. "*Indigo*, can I access the station's computers from here?"

"Yes. There is an emergency port located behind the grey panel two bays to my left."

"Great! What do I need to do?"

"The whole station must be shutdown using the appropriate numeric code. Next, after waiting three minutes, a restart password and different code need to be entered. Then, the system will reboot."

"Oxygen? Water?" queried Edgar.

"No additional breathable air will be generated by Underwater Station TC-e during shutdown-reboot, but there should be sufficient oxygen for one human and one avian. Water will gradually enter the access tubes, but drowning levels will not be reached before reboot is complete."

"No drowning," suggested the raven.

"Agreed." This scenario was right out of Rhea's nightmares—but there was no backing out now. "Can I return to the *Indigo* after rebooting has begun?"

"No, Rhea Mason. You must press the Drain Docking Bay icon after reboot is complete. *Then*, you may re-enter *Indigo*."

"Fine. What is the shutdown code?"

Silence.

Rhea supposed the *Indigo* was considering the security risk-threat ratio. Finally, the mini-sub rattled off a string of about thirty numerals and mathematical symbols.

"Whoa! There is no way I can memorise all of those, then enter them correctly into the port. Edgar, I need you to listen to *Indigo*, then repeat exactly what she says to me."

In response, the raven nodded, then repeated the code sequence exactly as it had been spoken by *Indigo*, including using the sub's voice.

"Correct," said the mini-sub.

Rhea thought she noted a surprised tone to the comment, though with A.I.s you could never be certain. "Let's go, Edgar," she said as the *Indigo* opened its rear door. With the raven on her shoulder, she stepped onto the dock, walked to the panel two bays to the left, turned the brads holding the panel in place, and accessed the emergency computer port.

"Now, repeat the shutdown code slowly," she told Edgar.

He did as she asked, then flew back to the *Indigo*, went inside, and waited for the mini-sub to tell him the password and reboot code. After three minutes, the mini-sub complied, and the raven flew back to Rhea's shoulder. Edgar repeated the password and began the reboot code.

"Slower!" said Rhea. "It takes me a few seconds to switch keypads and find the symbols."

Again, Edgar repeated the password and code—this time pausing to make sure numbers and symbols were entered before moving on to the next sequence.

The raven perched on her shoulder as the water level

rose. Soon, her feet and lower legs were wet. Still, the Underwater Station TC-e's computers were not rebooted. When the water level reached her waist, Rhea started to doubt the wisdom of this plan. Years ago, a fortune speaker on her home world had told her she would die by drowning—though she was not the superstitious sort, the foretelling spooked her. And now, it appeared the prognostication might be true.

"We drown?" asked Edgar. There was no denying the sadness in his voice.

She looked into the eyes of her best friend. "Maybe, but at least..."

"Terminal ready!" croaked the raven as she saw the various icons reflected by his pupils.

"Yes!" Rhea shouted as she pressed the Drain Docking Bay icon. "Fly to the *Indigo*. I will be right behind you."

Edgar soared into the diminishing air and swooped through the mini-sub's entrance. Rhea swam to the mini-sub, climbed up its side using the handholds and footholds moulded into its exterior, and slid into the sub's interior.

"Close and lock rear entrance," she shouted, though it was an unnecessary order. The *Indigo* had begun lowering the door as soon as she was aboard.

"Can you talk with Underwater Station TC-e now?"

"Yes," replied the sub. "Beta Team attempted to communicate with the aquatic humanoids when they first appeared near an underwater city's ruins about a kilometre from here. One mini-sub after another failed to return or respond to communication requests from Underwater Station TC-e. Finally, with no remaining subs to deploy, members of Beta Team were ready to send an SOS message to the Starship *Morella*. But humanoids appeared at this location, and shortly thereafter, the crew deactivated the computers."

Edgar stopped preening his feathers. "Water people want humans dead," he said.

"Maybe you are right, but our job is not to determine the motives or goals of the aquatic humanoids. Our job is to secure Underwater Station TC-e and retrieve Beta Team if they are in danger."

"They are in danger," said the *Indigo*. "The Underwater Station TC-e computer has checked the life-sign monitors of the members of Beta Team. All of them are dehydrated, malnourished, and covered in their own excrement. In addition, those in the mini-subs are running out of oxygen."

"Don't the mini-subs maintain breathable air—even if its occupants are comatose?" This seemed like it should be a standard emergency feature to Rhea.

"Not if they have been ordered to shut down," said

Indigo in a matter-of-fact voice.

"Can you or Underwater Station TC-e recall the mini-subs?" Again, to Rhea this seemed to be a must-have feature in case of an emergency situation.

"*Red*, *Yellow*, *Green*, and *Violet* have already been ordered to return to the Underwater Structure. *Orange* and *Blue* are unresponsive."

Suddenly, the situation seemed critical. Rhea said, "*Indigo*, relay to the Starship *Morella* we are evacuating Underwater Station TC-e. Ask them to send a medical shuttle."

"Done," replied the mini-sub.

"Let me speak with Underwater Station TC-e."

Indigo obliged.

"Underwater Station *Tau Ceti-e*, this is Rhea Mason of the Starship *Morella*. I'm assuming command of this facility until help arrives." Rhea recited the same series of numbers and letters she had given to the *Indigo* earlier. "I order you to play bagpipe music throughout the station. *Indigo* will share the playlist. Also, send that command to the missing mini-subs."

"Implementing your order, Rhea Mason," said the underwater station.

"Any response from the aquatic humanoids?"

"Yes," answered Underwater Station TC-e. "They are disengaging."

"Edgar," began Rhea, "The docking bay is dry enough for me to enter the station. With the help of the Underwater Station TC-e computer, I will locate the members of Beta Team who are still here and prepare them for evacuation. Four mini-subs containing other team members are on their way back to the station so I'm hoping to use them to transport Beta Team back to TC-e Groundsite."

"Get out of water fast," agreed the raven.

"Yes." She paused, wondering about the enormity of what she was about to do. "Edgar, someone needs to go with the *Indigo* and tow the remaining two subs back here. Will you do it?"

"Yes," responded Edgar. "Tell *Indigo* to obey."

"Okay." This was a first; putting the lives of several humans solely in the hands—well, the claws—of a raven. "*Indigo*, I order you to obey Edgar the raven. Turn on interior monitors so I can keep abreast of the situation."

Without hesitation, the *Indigo* said, "I will do as you command."

"Great! Underwater Station TC-e's computer and I will be monitoring you two. See you both shortly."

Using the Underwater Station TC-e's life-support system, Rhea was able to find eleven Beta Team members in the underwater station's public areas. Before she rescued them she wanted to see how Edgar was doing.

She sat at a terminal and pulled up the video stream from the cockpit of the *Indigo*. "Edgar, what's going on?"

The raven looked into the camera and shook his shiny, black head. "*Indigo* scanned *Blue* and *Orange*. No life on subs. We try to drag subs back."

"*Indigo*, you detected no life-signs on either vessel?"

"No life-signs," replied the mini-sub. "They are both covered with humanoids. Neither can be towed into the docking bay until the TC-e water creatures are removed. Also, playing bagpipe music no longer deters the humanoids."

As if to confirm the situation, Rhea saw two merfolk clinging to the *Indigo*'s cockpit plasti-glass bubble to the right of the raven.

"That means I will soon be in trouble here."

"Change music," suggested Edgar.

"What?"

"Screaming, loud instruments."

"Yes!" said Rhea. A quick search of music history yielded a new playlist. "Underwater Station TC-e and all mini-subs, play the most popular songs of Black Sabbath,

Metallica, Iron Maiden, Megadeth, and Judas Priest."

As Ozzie Osborn's voice filled the *Indigo*, Rhea saw the merfolk fling themselves from the plasti-glass. There was no telling how long heavy metal would hold off the creatures, so she needed to act fast.

"*Indigo*, abandon *Blue* and *Orange*. Return at top speed to the station. All other mini-subs enter the docking bay and prepare for additional passengers."

While waiting for the subs, Rhea loaded the comatose Beta Team members one by one onto a cart and pushed them to the elevator, rode down to the docking bay, and dumped them on the platform. As soon as the mini-subs arrived, she push-pulled the crew onto one sub or the other. When the *Indigo* finally arrived, Edgar flew to her shoulder and rubbed his bill against her neck.

"More crew?" he asked.

"Two more on level six. Then, we can head for land."

"Must hurry. Water people want to kill Rhea and Edgar."

"I am beginning to think you are right," she replied as they rode the elevator up to level six."

One of the two remaining Beta Team members seemed slightly alert. Thankfully, he was a large man and able to help Rhea manoeuvre the other person onto the cargo cart before climbing onto the cart himself. When they reached the submarine bay, he helped her load the last team member onto the *Violet* before climbing in. Rhea boarded the *Indigo* with Edgar on her shoulder and ordered the subs to close their doors and depart for *Tau Ceti-e* Groundsite.

"Underwater Station TC-e, once all five subs are clear of the access tubes, lock-down the station."

"Understood," said the underwater facility's computer.

"*Indigo*, send regular location updates to the Starship *Morella*," ordered Rhea. She wasn't certain how far gone the research team members were, but hoped the requested medical shuttle arrived quickly. Though Rhea had basic first aid training, any medical treatment beyond that would require additional personnel and equipment.

"Crew need water," said Edgar.

"I know," replied Rhea. "I am hoping the crew begins to come out of their stupors, because I do not have enough intravenous equipment and fluid bags on the Eulalie to handle this many semiconscious people."

"Look!" croaked the raven. "Water people coming."

Rhea saw hundreds of the merfolk pursuing the two subs slightly ahead of the *Indigo*. She imagined behind them and the other slower mini-subs hundreds of additional aquatic humanoids swam.

"Increase speed," she told the *Indigo*. "And relay that order to your sister subs."

"Order complied with," said the mini-sub.

"Are you equipped with any weapons?" she asked the *Indigo*. Hoping that someone in a shadowy corner of the controlling conglomerate's oversight committee had the sense to hide at least one weapon on *Tau Ceti-e*.

"No. Nor is TC-e Groundsite," replied the sub.

"Banjos," said Edgar.

"What?" For a split second, she thought the raven had succumbed to stress.

"Need new music. Use banjos."

"Okay, it is worth a try," said Rhea, relieved to know her partner was still thinking clearly. "*Indigo*, find music with multiple, fast picking banjo players. As soon as a selection is found, switch to banjo music and relay the new playlist to the other subs."

Moments later, the *Indigo* was filled with the plinks and strums of banjos. A look out the cockpit window showed the merfolk backing away from the other mini-subs.

"They are just going to adjust again, probably even more quickly than before."

"City sounds?" suggested Edgar.

"Brilliant!"

Edgar stretched his wings and opened his bill

slightly. Rhea thought he looked like he was smiling.

"*Indigo*, just prior to docking at TC-e Groundsite, switch to urban noises—horns honking, brakes squealing, jack hammers, engines revving—and relay your audio to the other subs."

"As you wish," replied the *Indigo* before stating, "there is a warning alarm in case of fire or other danger at *Tau Ceti-e* Groundsite."

"Great! After we have arrived at Groundsite and the Beta Team members are unloaded and removed from the dock area, I need you to activate the alarms. Then, send an order to each of the mini-subs to broadcast a different playlist: bagpipes for *Red*, heavy metal for *Yellow*, banjo for *Green*, and urban noise for *Violet*."

"What should I play?"

"Owl screeches," interjected Edgar.

"Not a bad idea." Rhea had been trying to think of another sound which would be alien to the merfolk. Since she hadn't seen any birds when the Eulalie arrived, and avians certainly could not survive underwater, any bird call would be disturbing to them. "Mix in the sound of migrating geese and eagles, too," she added.

They arrived at TC-e Groundsite just as the merfolk

began to draw close again. The noise of a congested city at rush hour suddenly blared in and from the mini-subs. As soon as the subs docked, they popped open their doors.

Rhea climbed out of the *Indigo* and she patted its hull. "Thanks. We could not have gotten here without your help."

"I was only adhering to my programming," replied the mini-sub A.I., though Rhea would have sworn that *Indigo*'s computer sounded pleased with itself.

With nineteen stupefied Beta Team members to get off of the subs and into the Groundsite's primary building, Rhea didn't take the time to respond. Instead, she sent Edgar to check in *Red*, *Yellow*, and *Green* for anyone who might be able to help their teammates off the subs. Meanwhile, she climbed aboard the Violet and was greeted by the man who had helped her at the underwater station. He was already standing, and in the process of lifting an older woman to her feet.

"We need to get everyone off the subs and into the main part of the facility before the aquatic humanoids enter the docking bay," she explained. "Can you help with that?"

"I will get the people off the *Violet*," he assured her. "You see to the others."

"Counting you, there are six people onboard the *Violet*?"

"Yes," he answered. "Then, if you are still unloading

the other subs, I'll come back and help."

"Thanks," Rhea called over her shoulder as she hurried toward the *Green*.

"No help *Green*," croaked Edgar as he flew to her shoulder. "Help on *Red*. No help *Yellow*."

"Okay," she said as she continued down the platform to the first bay. "Who is awake in the *Red*?" Rhea called as they neared the *Red*.

"Lakita," came the response as a muscular woman with close-cropped hair stuck her head out of the *Red*'s door.

"I need you to get everyone from your sub into the main facility as soon as possible. Can you do that?"

"No problem. There are five of us. I can easily make four trips," Lakita assured Rhea.

"Hurry," said Edgar.

"Yes, hurry," repeated Rhea as she began to assist the remaining eight Beta Team members from *Yellow* and *Green*.

With Lakita in charge of getting everyone who was mobile to the tarmac where the Eulalie was parked, the man from level six of the underwater station and Rhea returned to the *Yellow* for the last team member. Edgar flew back with them and did a quick check to make sure Beta Team was out of the subs.

"My name is Jamie," said the man as he and Rhea lifted the last team member, an unconscious woman. "I appreciate what—"

Whatever he meant to say next was lost as the water beneath and beside the mini-subs erupted in a mass of shimmering lights and squirming tentacles, fins, and tails.

"*Indigo*, alarms!" shouted Rhea as she did her best to walk backwards while holding the limp woman's ankles.

But the change in sound was too late for Jamie. Several translucent tentacles covered in gold and purple bio-luminescent splotches wrapped around his lower legs. A hero until the end, before the aquatic humanoids yanked him into the water, Jamie lowered his hands, then released his grip on the unconscious team member.

Suddenly, a terrible cacophony of alarms, bagpipes, heavy metal, banjo music, urban noises, and bird calls blasted from the mini-subs and *Tau Ceti-e* Groundsite. The merfolk vanished, taking Jamie with them. Retaining her hold on the woman's ankles, Rhea pulled her to the plasti-glass tube. With the last of her strength, Rhea dragged her towards TC-e Groundsite's entrance.

Edgar helped by grabbing the woman's hair with his

claws. He did his best to prevent her head from flopping around. As they neared the door to the outside, he asked, "Dead?"

"I don't think so." Before she could elaborate, Rhea saw hundreds of merfolk were crawling up onto the beach on either side of the TC-e Groundsite facility. She had assumed the species was solely aquatic. It had never crossed her mind that the merfolk were able to breathe air.

The raven noticed the mass of merfolk crawling towards them, too. After several seconds of loud raven-speak, he said, "Water people want to kill Edgar and Rhea."

"You are right!" she answered, ignoring Edgar's additional squawks.

Rhea tapped her communication neck piece. "Eulalie, I am bringing eighteen survivors with me. Can you accommodate that number safely?"

"If we use the rover as additional seating it is possible," responded Eulalie.

"Then, open up and let everyone onboard. Edgar and I are not there yet, but close by."

"Door open," said the shuttle.

As they dragged the woman toward the Eulalie, Rhea thought about Jamie. She wondered why the urban noises failed to deter the merfolk. Then it hit her like a ton of plasti-steel; when Underwater Station TC-e was lowered by a transport spaceship and installed, there would have been similar sounds. City and construction noises were not strange enough. If only she had thought about that sooner, then maybe Jamie would still be alive.

"We die?" asked Edgar.

"What?" Rhea had been thinking about the past instead of focusing on the now, a mistake in her line of work. The merfolk, their rows of shark teeth wet and glistening, were within three meters of them. Without weapons or backup, Edgar and she could either drop the woman and race to the shuttle, or continue to drag her and all three of them would perish.

"Leave her," said Rhea, "and fly to Eulalie."

She released her grip on the woman's ankles, turned, and ran as if her life depended on speed—and it did.

Though the raven could easily have beaten Rhea to the shuttle, they entered the Eulalie at the same time. She tried not to think about the slurping and crunching sounds she had heard as they raced away from the unconscious Beta Team member, but she knew they would haunt her.

"Close and lock the door. Lift-off as soon as possible," ordered Rhea as she stepped inside the shuttle.

"Destination?" asked the Eulalie.

"The Starship *Morella*, unless we receive different orders."

"Stinks," said Edgar.

"They can't help it," whispered Rhea. Though she had to agree. After sitting in their own excrement for days and not practicing normal hygiene, the seventeen remaining members of Beta Team were an odoriferous bunch.

"*Tau Ceti-e* humanoids are attached to Eulalie," said the shuttle. "Interstellar League protocol prohibits take off."

This time, Rhea did not rely on the raven. She plucked an annoying sound from her childhood. "Blast the sound of fingernails on a chalkboard at them until they release their suckers," she told the shuttle.

As the screech of fingernails screamed from the shuttle's speakers, Edgar squawked several phrases of raven-speak, the people onboard the Eulalie groaned and covered their ears, the merfolk let go of the shuttle, and Eulalie lifted into the air.

"Now quiet?" asked the raven.

"Yes," said Rhea. "Eulalie, turn off the noise."

After the shuttle stopped broadcasting the fingernail scraping sounds, the conscious members of Beta Team uncovered their ears. Rhea was certain if she handed out water containers, they would be able to re-hydrate themselves. But a half a dozen people were still unconscious and needed IVs.

"Edgar, let's *quietly* attend to these people," she said to her partner as she opened the supply cabinet.

And though she did not say it out loud, Rhea decided when Edgar and she returned to the Starship *Morella*, they deserved a few weeks of rest. Music-free, noise-free, no-life-and-death-decisions, above-the-water rest.

Born in the Year of the Dragon, **VONNIE WINSLOW CRIST**, has had a life-long interest in reading, writing, art, myth, fairy tales, folklore, legends, and science fiction. She lives, writes, and paints in a rural area of Maryland (USA) at Wood's Edge.

Author of The Enchanted Dagger, Owl Light, The Greener Forest, Murder on Marawa Prime, and other award-winning books, Vonnie is Senior Editor at Pole to Pole Publishing. Her stories appear in over 100 print publications including: "Amazing Stories," "Outposts of Beyond," "Faerie Magazine," Lost Signals of the Terran Republic, Chilling Ghost Short Stories, Killing It Softly 2, Sea of Secrets, Galactic Goddesses, and Best Indie Speculative Fiction: 2018. Vonnie's drabbles and flash fiction appear in: Winds of Despair, Waters of Destruction, Worlds, Angels, Monsters, Beyond, Unravel, Apocalypse, Storming Area 51, Tall Tales & Short Stories, Fifty Flashes, Curses & Cauldrons, and elsewhere.

In addition, over 200 of Vonnie's poems have been published, as well as over 1,000 of her illustrations. A member of Horror Writers Association, Science Fiction & Fantasy Writers of America, Pen Women, and Society of Children's Book Writers & Illustrators, Vonnie believes the world is still filled with mystery, magic, and miracles.

Connect
Website: www.vonniewinslowcrist.com
Facebook: @WriterVonnieWinslowCrist
Amazon: amazon.com/-/e/B001KCR6PE
Blog: www.vonniewinslowcrist.wordpress.com
Twitter: @VonnieWCrist

POINT ZERO
By E.L. Giles

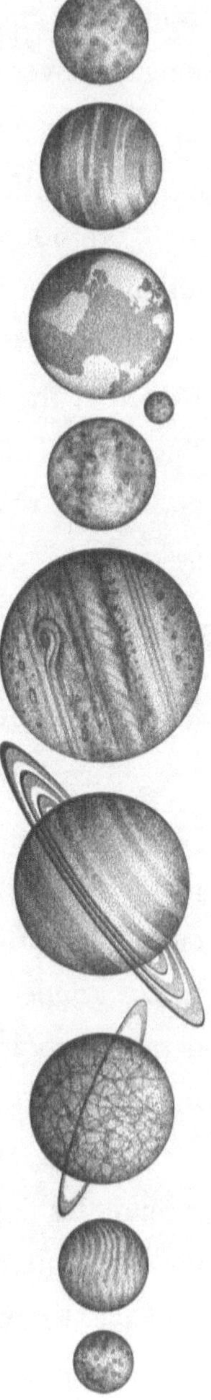

Earth is but a dire souvenir for those old enough to remember it. When Captain Ericson's ship crashes on an unknown planet, seemingly sharing the same properties as Earth, he thinks he has made the greatest discovery of all time: a new home for mankind. That is until the planet reveals its darkest secrets.

CHAPTER ONE

"Still lost in thought?" said Faustus, dragging me out of my reverie. I twisted my head slightly, greeting him with a quick nod as he came to stand next to me.

I turned back to the immense window. My mind drifted again,

wandering into the vastness of space, that unclaimable kingdom over which man has no hold. I sighed.

"Nothing new?" he asked.

I shook my head.

"I'm not crazy. They should be right here," I said, jerking my head. I turned to Faustus who was frowning as if he were trying to see beyond the black veil ahead. I looked at the tiny monitor strapped around my wrist. Entering its main menu, I selected a file of a recording and tapped a button to make it play over the main audio system.

"Mayday. Mayday," said a woman's voice. The distress call bounced around the curved walls of the vast navigation room, and her voice distorted eerily as she begged us for immediate assistance. An unmistakable terror surrounded her that left me utterly perplexed. And then, as suddenly as the message had begun, the voice cut off abruptly, leaving only ghostly static. Once again, panic gripped me, exacerbating the migraine that permanently lived at the back of my head. "Where are they, for god's sake?"

Faustus walked to the navigation board and, running his fingers across the backlit keyboard, entered the localisation codes that had come along with the message. I must have entered those exact lines of code myself a hundred times so far and had gotten no better result than he would get this time. The wide window opened with a sudden brightness, illuminating Faustus's face and exaggerating the tension of his traits. A slew of colourful icons and lines of code were displayed on the screen that now covered the window, and Faustus scanned them, his pale grey eyes skimming the content, comparing the data with the map open beside the screen, which was zoomed in to Area M31. We could easily see the blinking point that indicated the position of our spaceship, as well as the coordinates from the message. Both points merged together perfectly, confirming what I already knew. We were in the right place.

"Could you monitor any electromagnetic disturbance within a one-hundred-kilometre range?" I asked.

Faustus moved to the next console and studied the data from our radar.

"Everything seems fine. I mean, there are some little disruptions, but they don't seem alarming."

"That's nonsense," I grumbled, pinching the bridge of my nose.

So many different scenarios had been forming in my head lately that I had found no sleep at all, and yet I felt exhaustion heavier than I had ever felt it. The need to unscramble this mystery overcame the wish to go to sleep, and now, two days later, I was still up, cogitating, wondering, searching. Where were they now? What exactly had happened to them? Had they been attacked? There had been some space pirates lurking around Area M31 lately. But if the ship had fallen prey to them, we would have been seeing debris dispersed throughout the area, floating toward no precise destination. At the very least there would have been some recordable activities, a magnetic field coming from their batteries or navigation system. It was true that wherever pirates passed by only ruins remained.

"You should get some rest," said Faustus, placing a hand amicably on my shoulder. He squeezed it gently and even tried a smile; in an effort to comfort me, I suppose. Compassion wasn't Faustus's greatest attribute, just as peacefulness wasn't mine. No, not after having witnessed the total annihilation of planet Earth: the place humankind once called home. But I also knew its destruction had been a necessary evil since Earth had become uninhabitable after the many nuclear wars and the total melting of its ozone layer. Whoever approached it too closely had become trapped within its cosmic tentacles and was then sucked into a putrid mouth to disappear without a trace. The Space Federation had nicknamed Earth the Bermuda Triangle of the Milky Way. I didn't see how they could still joke about it. Humans had always had a peculiar talent to soil and destroy everything they touched, on planet Earth and then Earth 2, the artificial "planet" we had built in order to relocate our civilisation and prevent our extinction. Mankind never learned from its failures and experiences. Never.

I turned my gaze from Faustus to the green glowing screen, blinking my dry eyes. Faustus was right. I needed a respite. A couple of hours of sleep would do just fine.

"Okay, I'm off for a nap," I said.

The crew saluted as I left the navigation room. I headed toward my dormitory unit, the weight of my sleepless nights a pressure I couldn't wait to be relieved of.

The dim spotlights bathed the hallways in warm orange hues, casting symmetrical conical beams onto the floor. A song was currently playing through the speakers hidden throughout the polymer ceiling tiles, soft and virtuously played on the piano. I think it was by an antique composer, born some six or seven hundred years ago. Chopin, I think he was named. I wasn't quite sure, so I asked my wrist monitor, which was, of course, connected to the ship's internal system. I knew far too well that I wouldn't find sleep until I validated my guess.

The robotic female voice began to drone on: "Frederic Chopin—Nocturne Opus nine, number one. Written between the Earth year 1830 and 1832, it's one of the few vestiges recovered from the Mass Cultural Holocaust, which was responsible for the destruction of about eighty-eight percent of the human writings, history, general knowledge, and data collections. After the—"

"Thank you," I said, cutting off the computer before it started into a complete history of the many wars that had succeeded the Mass Cultural Holocaust, or, as I liked to call it, the Great Thinkers Annihilation. I continued toward my quarters, letting the haunting melody fill my head and my soul, mesmerised by the ingenuity of its composition and the fragile dexterity of its interpretation. I hoped the song would never stop so I could hear it forever.

I stopped next to the door of my quarters and leaned in toward the retina analyser, keeping my eye open until the scanner beeped and I was granted access to my room—a wide, semi-circular space, with a scattering of square windows that were dispersed in such a whimsical fashion that it made the design more architecturally eccentric than practical. I sat by one of the windows, leaning my forehead against its cold surface and feeling slightly baffled that only this twelve-inch-thick piece of glass hindered me from being sucked into the womb of space.

I had just pulled down the sheet and was about to

let my exhausted body fall onto the soft mattress when a deafening siren resounded through the speaker system. This was followed by the flashing of the red emergency lights.

I looked down at my wrist monitor. Its screen was flashing red as well, the message "System Failure" popping up relentlessly. I jumped to my feet and ran to the door, but it didn't open as I approached it. I reached for the encased switch and slapped the Manual Mode Activation button. The door unlocked, and I managed to open it by turning the wheel that actuated its mechanism.

The corridors were now pitch black and were being bathed in the blood-red emergency lights every few seconds. I ran cautiously, one hand pressed against the wall to guide me so I wouldn't trip over anything.

"Emergency. System failure. Emergency. System failure," repeated the dreary voice of the computer. Rounding the corner that led to the navigation room, I met Faustus, whose face was sweaty and gleamed vividly under the aggressive lights, which gave his normally pale skin and grey eyes an even more sickly appearance.

"Captain," he said, faltering. He leaned forwards, hands pressed against his legs, trying to draw some air back into his lungs.

"What happened?" I snapped. "What happened for fuck's sake?"

"Abnormal elec…tro magnetic…field. System is compl…etely dead. It happened…all of a…sudden."

I pushed past Faustus and rushed into the navigation room in anticipation, though nothing could have prepared me for the sight of the black mass of antimatter that spread before us like a plague on humankind, a shade darker than the deepest black of space. I nearly fainted.

"Black hole!" I screamed instinctively, without really believing what I was saying. No black hole had ever been reported in this area. Could this be the "minor disruption" Faustus had spotted earlier that hadn't seemed to alarm him whatsoever? Weird, crazy theories spun in my head, keeping me locked in place for a brief moment until I came to the realisation that, whatever it was, one thing was for sure: we would not surrender without a fight. There wasn't much we could do to escape such a powerfully attractive force once we had entered its gravitational field, but we had to try.

"Start up the auxiliary system. All engines on."

The crew hastened to turn on the auxiliary system, managing to get two out of four engines in working order. What had happened to the others?

"Full power," I ordered.

The frenzy was palpable; all eyes were riveted to the giant window.

"System overheating. System overheating. Power loss: twenty percent," the computer informed us shrilly. A loud cracking noise erupted, seeming to come from the structure of the ship itself. The turbulence grew, the vibration spreading through my body, and it felt as though the floor was going to rip apart under my feet. I gripped at the closest console for support.

"…fifty percent."

The mouth of the black mass came closer and closer, enveloping us within its endless void, sucking us into the oblivion of deep, unknown space.

"…eighty-five percent."

The control board sparked and smoked and suddenly ceased to respond. I heard someone crying, but turning around, I found only darkness.

"…one hundred percent."

Everything stopped abruptly—the thundering engines, the vibration, the siren, and the screams of terror. All that remained were the weak emergency lights that intermittently liberated the room from the total darkness with an eerie red glow. My heart beat in my ears, accompanied by a strange, low-pitch hum that hurt my head and brought the migraine back with an unprecedented intensity.

We waited, suspended at the edge of the unknown. Were we out of danger? To my greatest dismay, it was but a promising lull before the cataclysm.

A sudden, great force was applied upon us, throwing us all onto the floor, prey to a debilitating pain. The world swayed as if the spaceship were being tossed around in a vortex. The colours, the shapes, everything swirled madly, and despite my best efforts, I couldn't get back up onto my feet. Even staying awake and alert became a battle as the pain only grew greater and greater. For one single second, I closed my eyes, trying to regain some of my strength. How foolish of me to think I'd be able to fight against the sudden drowsiness, the sudden desire to let it all go.

Resist. Resist. Resist…

CHAPTER TWO

Noises sizzled in my waking ears, strangely familiar, like crickets singing, announcing the hot summer days to come. Was I hallucinating? It took me a great deal of time to recover my senses, my memory, my strength, and my courage. I stayed flat on the ground, consumed by the paralysing terror. I didn't want to open my eyes. What was I to see?

"Captain?" came a distant voice. "Captain, are you

alive?"

"Faustus?" I said hoarsely. Hot breath was blowing on the top of my head. I finally dared open my heavy eyes. Faustus's face appeared before me, blurry at first, and then the haze of my mind cleared and two pale-grey eyes welcomed me. "Faustus, is that you?"

Faustus slid one arm behind my neck and helped me into a sitting position. My head spun uncontrollably, and I turned away from him, a sudden urge to vomit assailing me.

"Everything will be all right, Captain," said Faustus, giving me a friendly smile. When I felt strong enough, I got to my feet. Faustus held me by the elbows to provide some stability.

Horror struck me as my eyes darted around. Thick clouds of dusty particles floated statically, suspended as if there was no gravity being applied to them. The smell of burning tickled my nose. Everywhere I looked, I saw devastation and chaos.

"Where are they? Where is the rest of the crew?" I asked.

Faustus lowered his head, the black aura of death floating over him. Under the sparse rays of bright light entering through the holes in the wall, I remarked the dirt and many scratches on Faustus's face and wondered how I appeared.

"Outside," he said with a peculiar voice that was laced with unmistakable sadness. "I mean, I buried them outside."

"You…"

I fell to my knees and, sinking my head into my shaky hands, started to cry. Some of them had been good friends of mine. Some I'd worked with for over a decade.

"Dead," I murmured. "Dead because of me. I should have turned the ship around and left when we saw that there was no one to be saved. I should have understood that something was wrong."

"It wasn't your fault," Faustus said, crouching in front of me. "You couldn't have known there was that…that thing, the black hole, or whatever it was. No one, not even our radar, detected anything particularly abnormal before it appeared. It struck us so suddenly. I'm sure the same thing happened to the ship you were wanting to help. There was nothing you could have done. Nothing."

Faustus's words somewhat helped calm the guilt that twisted in my stomach.

"Thank you," I said before getting up again, a renewed energy permeating my body. "We're breathing the air! Where have we landed? And how's the atmosphere?" I exclaimed, suddenly realising our strange reality. The atmosphere here was breathable. How was that possible?

"Oddly enough, yes! The atmosphere is just like every one of our habitable stations," he said, scratching the top of his head like nothing he was saying made sense. "The oxygen level is near twenty-one percent, nitrogen seventy-eight percent, and about one percent argon and carbon dioxide. Also, the temperature is quite comfortable, around thirty Celsius."

I went to the navigation board, hoping I'd be able to restart it and determine our location. Faustus stopped me, telling me everything had been burned and the whole ship was literally dead. That was the word he used: *dead.*

"Do you have any idea where we could have landed?" I asked, trying to make sense of our situation.

"Hell no! I didn't even know such a place existed. Bizarrely, it makes me think of the history books I read about planet Earth. Do you remember the pictures? I mean, with the data I've collected and the landscapes outside...I don't know. That's what it makes me think of."

"But no one ever found a planet sharing those properties," I said. "Not a single habitable one in almost four centuries of constant searching. Can you imagine for one second if we discovered a planet almost identical to Earth? Can you imagine what that would mean for humankind?"

"It would mean that we could all settle into a new home," said Faustus excitedly.

"Exactly!" I gently squeezed Faustus's shoulder, pulling him closer to me. "My friend, I think we've just made the greatest discovery of all time. Greater than the invention of light-speed space travel."

Excitement quickly overshadowed my dread and grief, and all I could think about was repairing the communication system and sending a signal to the nearest relay station as quickly as possible. How far from Earth 2 was this planet? That wasn't important right now, I supposed. I hastened to clear the debris off the main console, removing all the chunks of carbon panels, and I blew off the dust that had gathered in layers upon it. The edge of the panel was smeared with blood, still fresh. It was probably Tasha's; she must have knocked her head against it. The nausea came back almost as quickly as it had disappeared, and I breathed in slowly, trying to contain my emotions and the devouring sickness.

Focusing on my task, I began to inspect the board and its controls. I tried to activate the auxiliary system, which I was almost certain was destroyed and would never work again. But I had a sudden idea.

"What about using the auxiliary generator to build a kind of basic power supply? Something simple enough to make the emitter and receptor work temporarily. Perhaps a condenser bank to store up the energy would do just fine too. In any case, we need the generator and everything we can gather from the auxiliary system."

"There's only one problem," said Faustus. "The ship fell apart during our tumble to the planet. I've searched the immediate area for missing parts, but without much luck. The entire engine room, as well as all the auxiliary system, has gone missing in the wilderness."

"Fuck—FUCK!"

I punched the console, slicing my hand against a sharp corner. The blood oozed abundantly over my hand and dripped freely onto the dusty floor. I heard Faustus tearing a piece of fabric and felt him wrapping my hand without really noticing him clearly. My head became foggy, and a sudden, great exhaustion seemed to conquer me.

"I didn't mean the parts were gone forever," said Faustus. "We could split up the search and cover twice as much terrain at once."

"That wouldn't be safe," I said. "We know nothing about this planet. Is it inhabited? What kind of beasts populate it? No, splitting up would be sheer madness."

Faustus considered it for a moment. Then, like he'd been struck with a sudden idea or had simply come to some mad conclusion, he turned around. Moving to the other end of the navigation room, he started to scavenge every single corner of the ship, picking up anything he found that might be considered useful and placing it into the backpack I now noticed was slung across his back. He had already planned another excursion into the surrounding area.

"Food and water," he then said, prying open the thick metal box we used as a refrigerator.

I went to help Faustus, and soon we had managed to fill the backpack with food, water, and supplies—lighters, batteries, clothes, a survival and first aid kit, and two pistols and four magazines. Underneath a pile of debris, I found a particle analyser that was in working order. It might come in handy at some point.

"Ready to go?" I said, tucking the pistol into the waistband of my pants. "Let's find the rest of our spaceship."

Faustus nodded and led the march across the wreckage and up to the giant aperture in the side of the ship, outside of which pieces of the fuselage lay scattered. A bright beam of light crawled through the hole, hitting the opposite wall which reflected it like the ripples of a pond, sparkling and glistening blindingly. The artificial sun of Earth 2 was designed to illuminate and warm thoroughly and precisely, and it never faded. But here on this world, the rays of light darkened sporadically and then brightened again, warmer and stronger, unreliable. And strangely enough, the chanting of insects seemed to follow the phenomenon of growing and weakening warmth and light, like the events were intrinsically related. That was strange, so I noted the phenomenon on my wrist monitor.

"Every detail will be useful," I said to Faustus, who frowned at me. "*Every* detail."

CHAPTER THREE

A desolate and wind-swept plateau welcomed us. I jumped from the hole in the ship and landed on the sandy ground, standing in awe before the stupendous scenery. The jagged mountains stretched out of sight, disappearing into the horizon, their white tops merging cleverly with the fluffy clouds in the sky. The vegetation grew in sparsely shaggy busks over this strangely sterile land, with patches of forest spread sparingly throughout the plain. I squinted in the blinding brightness, one hand blocking out the burning sunlight and the other one holding my wrist monitor near my lips. I looked up at the sky in contemplation.

"It seems to have a single sun, close enough to the planet to warm it to a comfortable thirty Celsius. There seems to be one single moon too. The gravitational force seems comparable to our standards, though I feel quite a bit winded, like the oxygen is sparser. It's possible that being higher than sea level is what is causing such an effect. End of report."

I circled around, forming a picture of the landscape inside my head and trying to get a hint as to where the other parts of the spaceship may have fallen. My eyes fell on a shovel lying flat on the ground. A dozen fresh mounds of dirt were nearby, shallow graves of our fellows, the first inhabitants of this planet. Faustus stood next to one. His hands were pressed together and his head was lowered. His lips were moving faintly, probably reciting a prayer. Normally I'd have rebuked him about his faith, which I called an insult to his extraordinary intelligence, but not today—not anymore.

The wind had already blown enough sand to cover all traces of the impact of the ship, though given the way it was oriented and the angle with which its nose was rammed into the ground, I decided to head towards the mountaintop the ship might have struck against.

We had walked for perhaps two hours, stopping regularly to catch our breath and drink some water, when we were forced to stop before a deep ravine that tore the plateau in half and hindered us from reaching the foot of the mountaintop before us. Easily a hundred meters deep, a water stream cascaded down, and a mass of opaque steam elevated from the depths. The noise of water crashing against the rocky walls came in deafening echoes, making me think of our ship's engine when pushed to its limits.

"This way!" yelled Faustus, his voice barely audible amidst the rushing water. I jogged over to him, heedless of the unlevel and slippery ground.

"A bridge?"

Suspended above the canyon was an entanglement of ropes and wooden planks, anchored on both sides by thick wooden posts. The first thing that struck me was the idea that there was an intelligent form of life here— one clever enough to build such a complicated construction. I assessed the posts and the ropes, shaking them to test their solidity.

"Unbelievable," I said.

"But do you trust it?" asked Faustus, visibly sceptical.

"Can you fly?" Faustus narrowed his eyes. "Then yes."

Taking a deep breath, I stepped onto the bridge first, carefully placing one foot after the other, choosing wisely the planks on which I applied my full weight. At its weakest point, midway across the ravine, the bridge started to sway and crack eerily as it was hit by the fierce wind that projected steamy droplets of water against us.

"Captain! Look down!" cried Faustus.

I followed his gaze, and through the foggy wall, I glimpsed something abnormally huge and metallic that glinted in the fading sunlight—more than likely debris from our ship. "We're in the right place."

"But, Captain, it's not from *our* ship. Ours was black and red. This one is unpainted and rusted in some places."

Faustus was right. "Do you think—"

"The lost spaceship? Perhaps. But how would it have rusted this quickly? Unless the water here is acidic, which I doubt since we are now drenched from head to toe. And it isn't irritating my skin, so I'd say it's from another spaceship. Older, that's for sure. How many ships have gotten trapped inside the black hole and ended up here?"

I hastened to note the discovery in my events log and continued to stare at the wreckage thoughtfully. We weren't the first ones to have landed on this planet. Perhaps there were survivors. How long ago had this ship crashed here? One thing was sure: it was imperative to warn everyone back home not to get near the area where the black hole lived.

Arriving at the other side of the bridge, we left the ravine's edge and continued advancing through the wild. Our eyes watchful, we looked everywhere for clues that might tell us where the rest of our ship had crashed. As I looked up into the sky to determine the current position of the sun, something entered my field of vision—dark wings, stretched out. The creature hovered for a few minutes without flapping its wings. It was circling a large perimeter when suddenly it descended rapidly and landed atop a knoll of rocks and roots.

"What the hell is that thing?" exclaimed Faustus, peering at the bald bird with obvious disdain as it dropped the carcass of some animal and started tearing the flesh with its elongated beak. Faustus reached for his pistol, visibly nervous.

"Hold on, my friend. That must be some kind of scavenger bird, nothing more. There's no need to kill the beast."

It was the first living thing we'd seen since we left the ship, and given its massive size, I wondered if everything on this planet was that *big*. Were the "people" who had built the bridge giants? Were they dangerous? Or perhaps one of the survivors from the wrecked ship had built the bridge? Unable to decide whether there was danger or not, I reached for my pistol and gripped it tightly.

"I thought the bird wasn't to be feared?" Faustus asked.

"It's not for the bird," I said. Faustus didn't say

anything about that but kept a hold of his gun.

We advanced slowly through the maze of trails surrounding the mountain, always under the watchful yellow eyes of the vulture, hovering overhead and now accompanied by its peers. I didn't know how far we would have to walk before seeing evidence of the wreckage of our ship. It seemed like it had completely vanished.

"It's getting bloody cold," said Faustus, blowing on his hands and then rubbing them together. Now that he mentioned it, it was rather chilly. I brought my wrist monitor to my mouth and began another event log.

"Night seems to drop gradually, which means that this planet must rotate at a speed comparable to that of Earth, I would say. As a starting point, let's consider that the sun was at its zenith when we started our journey through the wild territory, about six hours ago. Then, with a simple data extrapolation, I would guess that days on this planet are between eighteen or perhaps twenty-four hours. This is a rough guesstimate though. End of report."

"If you're right," said Faustus, "and night is really falling, then we should find shelter and make a fire quickly, before it becomes black as pitch and we can't see anything."

I nodded, and we began to round the base of a tall

pyramidal peak, on which large steps of some sort, for the lack of a better word, had been formed due to erosion. I couldn't tell if it was a natural formation. Everything on this planet seemed spectacularly odd and peculiar. I looked around for any nearby recesses, caverns, or forested areas, anything that would allow us to have some sort of covering over our heads and start a bonfire. Finding nothing, we continued walking and concentrated on the mountain peak

Midway around the pyramidal peak, I stumbled on a thin crevice through which sporadic bursts of air blew out. Upon closer inspection, I could see that it led to a much bigger opening, like that of a cavern's mouth, sculpted into the wall of the pyramid. I crawled down through the opening using dried roots that protruded from the gritty soil. The cavern was of enormous dimensions, expanding deep within the mountain. I turned on the light of my wrist monitor and stretched my arm out, illuminating the place as I rotated. Holding my pistol in front of me, I moved stealthily, making as little noise as possible.

"Here!" I yelled to Faustus when I found a place I judged safe to make camp. While waiting for him to catch up, I continued advancing with tiny steps, making sure to memorise the shape and details of the majestic arched ceiling. I approached the wall on my left side, running my hand over its surface as if doing so would reveal its history to me. In fact, colours and images did suddenly start to decorate its surface the farther I walked. I brought the light up, adjusting the beam so a larger portion of the wall was bathed in bright white light.

"Report log activation. We have discovered a cavern that seems to have been inhabited once. Strange drawings cover its walls, seemingly like those discovered on Earth, yet I can't quite tell what they represent. Time has worn them, severely in some places. But I think I see a bald bird like the one we saw outside. And there are— oh my God! I think they are bipeds, but their faces and their heads… I can't describe them. Big bulging heads and black holes for eyes and ears. They wear what seems like crowns, or ceremonial hats, representing the sun, I think. Yes, that must be that! They are worshipping the sun. Some of the characters share animal-like features. What strange creatures they are. Now the next couples of meters show nothing decipherable, besides weird-looking and horned or woolly animals. The next portion seems more recent, its colours vivid, and it shows… Oh, no."

Chills crawled up my spine, and I forgot my report. I hastened to fully examine the drawing.

"Faustus, we must go," I said, pointing to the portion of the wall that depicted what seemed like a spaceship. Next to it, three humans were roped together and advancing towards a tall pyramidal peak. Drawn over the peak were the faces of monsters, red and evil-looking. Some had pointy tongues sticking out, and others bared rows of sharp teeth within their gaping mouths. The other bipedal creatures followed closely behind, holding knives they levelled at the humans as they walked onto a slab atop the pyramid, on which one of the humans was being stabbed. I noticed another human, standing conspicuously apart from the humans, with the bipedal creatures. I didn't know what it meant, only that it meant nothing good for us. "Faustus, I think I figured out what happened to the crew of the fallen spaceship."

He stared at the drawing for a moment, blinking his eyes, like the revelation hadn't fully reached his brain. A quiver formed the corner of his lips, faint at first. Then it grew into an uncontrollable, mad fit of laughter.

"Faustus!" I took his shoulders and shook him firmly. "Faustus, pull yourself together."

Seeing as nothing I was saying was working to snap him out of it, I decided to slap him in the face. And it worked like a charm. Faustus's eyes came back to their full brightness and sparkled with their usual intelligence. He was back with me.

Outside, the night had already settled in, painting

the sky pitch-black. It was cold and windy, and a fine mist had gathered over the ground, making it impossible to follow any trails. It was unthinkable to wander into the wild in such conditions, knowing that such evil might be roaming around. Though according to the state of the ship we'd found, several years—decades perhaps—might have passed, and the…the *people* responsible for their murder may have been long since dead. Or perhaps they had departed elsewhere, who knew? And it then it occurred to me that the pyramid on which the humans were being sacrificed might be the mountain that the cavern was in—*this* mountain. But I quickly concluded that such a steep and difficult ascent would make it an unlikely candidate for the kind of monument I had seen drawn on the wall. And after a short deliberation, Faustus and I decided to stick to our initial plan and settle here for the night, alternating the watch shift. Tomorrow, we would leave this place and proceed with the search for our own spaceship.

We walked down the cramped corridor, sinking deeper into the guts of the mountain, which seemed to have no end. Ignoring the many paintings on the walls, and our surroundings in general, we advanced straight ahead until we reached a wide, circular room in which a single ray of moonlight fell from the ceiling far above.

We edged into the room and decided to separate,

each covering half of the room until we joined back in the middle. But we had barely begun our investigation when Faustus yelled at me from across the room, panicked. He had found something.

"Captain," he said, picking up from a dusty mound of rocks a bracelet that seemed quite familiar to me. He ran over to me and pushed it into my chest. I took it from him and inspected it by the light of my wrist monitor. I almost fainted as I confirmed the similarity between my own wrist monitor and the bracelet he'd found.

"That's impossible," I murmured, inspecting the monitor. I frantically turned it in my hands, scrutinising it. Rust had already festered over its mounting bolts, and the polymer cover showed signs of neglect. With the tip of the knife Faustus handed me, I managed to pop its lid open and remove the memory chip that seemed intact despite the harsh conditions of the place. While I attempted to insert the chip into my own wrist monitor, Faustus scraped off some of the rust and dirt from the recovered monitor. He then put the sample into the particle analyser and retreated to a calmer place to perform his tests and analyses. I turned my wrist monitor on.

"...Our calls for help have gone unanswered, and many of our crew died in the crash..." said the only intact portion of the first file I opened. It was the voice of a woman, *the* woman we'd heard in that dreadful message begging for help. I opened the next file and listened to it. "According to our extensive research and the data collected from the spectrometer and geolocator before they died, we have more than likely been sucked into a wormhole and landed back on Point 0…"

My knees gave out underneath me. I raised my eyes to Faustus, who was absorbed in his analyses and had totally forgotten about anything other than his particle analyser. Point 0. Fucking Point 0.

"Earth," I murmured to myself, as if to force the truth into my consciousness. A lump formed in my throat as a myriad of emotions bubbled up to the surface. "Keep calm, Ericson, keep calm."

How in the hell was it even possible? Point 0: Earth. But Earth had been destroyed. How could we have been thrown back onto a planet that was gone?

I brought my attention back to my wrist monitor and continued listening. More questions surfaced than there were answers for. Was the spaceship we found the one that had called for our help? How could it have rusted this quickly? How could one of their own data recorders be in such a state of decay, when barely three days had passed since they sent their signal? Were they really dead, like the paintings seemed to portray?

"…without being able to pinpoint precisely where

or *when* on Earth we have crashed—never mind how such a thing is even possible—according to our mineral and organic samples, we have landed on a much younger Earth than the one we knew and the one we destroyed. Younger, it seems, by a thousand years at least, sending us back somewhere between years 1200 to 1400 Earth Age. End of report."

"No. That's impossible," I growled, punching my thighs until they began to hurt. I hated what I had just heard. I hated the woman and her cold and robotic voice, her lack of emotions, her lack of fear. I hated her for having led us here. And I hated myself for having followed her call and condemned my crew. I hated myself for being this terrorised by what we had seen and learned here. Oh, God, I hated myself. But then the paintings came to the forefront of my mind. I saw their sacrifice, and now I felt ashamed for having hated her.

Faustus walked up beside me, the particle analyser in his hands. A halo of light from the device illuminated his face with a soft blue light, revealing glistening tears on his cheeks.

"We're about fifty years too late," he said.

"What do you mean, fifty years too late?"

"I mean that the degradation of their data recorder tells me that about half a century has passed since they left it here. For some reason I can't explain, we have crashed at exactly the same place they did, but fifty years bloody later. That's just insane."

"Insane is an understatement," I murmured. "If only that was all there was to it. But there's something else you need to know."

CHAPTER FOUR

Partially covered with a blanket, Faustus slept fitfully. I stared a moment at him, then at the crackling fire and the swirling smoke being sucked out the chimney hole in the ceiling. I couldn't find sleep. Not with the weight of the truth on my shoulders. It made my entire body ache unbearably. Faustus couldn't accept this truth, that we were on Earth, a millennium in the past, and that he would never again see his family and his friends. I didn't have much family or many friends, which probably explained how I could so easily come to terms with the idea that no help would ever come for us. We were trapped here, doomed to die on this planet no matter what. Survival wasn't something new to me. How often had I put myself in situations where my survival instinct had been tested? How often had I found myself lost within the unknown of the harshest and most inhospitable planets?

For hours, I listened again and again to the many

event logs and the crew's accounts of their journey through the mountains and plateaus, which they had nicknamed "The Mounts of Madness." It seemed that a number of the crew had literally gone crazy after a few days of travelling through the infinite mountains of desolation. As I listened, their mental degradation became more severe, a state of madness beginning to conquer their brains. They were afraid, terrorised, depressed—pretty much like Faustus, I feared. And their baleful journey got suddenly worse one day when they lost one man; he'd simply disappeared without a trace. They'd searched for him for days. I finally opened the last file in the folder.

"...the rain has intensified, and the wind has rendered our advance impossible. We have to stop the research until it calms outside. We've found shelter in a strange place—a cavern, decorated with many primitive paintings. I'm not certain this place is entirely natural. Some aspects lead me to believe that it may have been erected for a purpose that remains mysterious to me. As I speak, we are now advancing through the long and wide corridor down into an open room with a high-rising ceiling. There's a hole in the middle of it which lets rain and moonlight pass through. The floor is partly soaked with rainwater. And there is...oh my God, what's that? What's that sound? Guys, I think this was a mistake. This place, I think it's a sacred place. It's a sacred place, and now I hear the natives. And they are angry. Draw your weapons. They are coming. Oh my God. Dear God, please help us. The natives are coming for us! They are…"

That was it. The message ended with a long hissing sound. My heart pummelled in my chest as I ran over to Faustus.

I shook him awake. "Faustus, my friend, we gotta go. NOW!"

"What?" he said, yawning and stretching his arm. "What is it?"

"We shouldn't have come here."

We picked up our things, dropped them into the backpack, and ran out of the room, the light from my wrist monitor bobbing. My head throbbed.

"What's the matter, Ericson?" asked Faustus. I think it was the first time he'd called me by my name. In almost ten years, he had never addressed me using anything other than my title. It sounded strange in his mouth, but it also filled me with an unexpected dread. There was no more crew, no more mission, only the two of us, running for our lives in a world unknown to us.

"The natives. The ones in the paintings. If they find us, we're dead!"

We reached the mouth of the cavern and began to

climb up the rocky recesses, our feet sliding. My knees scraped across the gritty surface as we scrambled up. The pain didn't seem to exist, only the raw terror living in my gut.

Where should we go? The mist seemed to have gone, which should have helped us find our way quite easily. But where in the hell should we go? What we knew of the original earth could be summed up with one word: zilch!

"We should reach a higher spot and decide where to go," I said, pointing at the top of the peak. We weren't equipped for such a task, but we had no other choice. It was the closest peak, and the most easily accessible.

We painstakingly began to climb, gripping anything we could reach—branches, roots, outcroppings, using every crevice deep enough to put our hands and feet into. The wind whipped us fiercely, howling painfully in my ears. A few times I looked at Faustus, who was a few meters below me and struggling to find a proper grip with which to stabilise himself on the steep slope.

"Hold on, Faustus, I will throw you the rope!" I yelled above the deafening wind.

"Hurry up!" he said with a strained voice.

I quickened my climbing, forgetting the pain, my aching and bloody hands, and the biting cold, and I managed to reach a reasonably wide plateau atop the peak. The base had ample clearance and was secure enough for me to attach the rope onto it. I gauged Faustus's position before throwing the rope down into the pitch-black void below.

"Pick up the rope and hold it tight. I will help you climb up," I said, hoping Faustus had heard me and my voice hadn't been carried away by the wind. Much to my relief, I soon felt a tug, and the rope became taut. I sat and, positioning my feet firmly against the lip that bordered the plateau, gripped the rope with both hands and started to pull. I gritted my teeth, biting back the growls of pain as my palms burned and ached with such an intensity that I felt I might faint. Every time I thought my hands were going to give out and I was going to fail, I thought of Faustus. He was probably suffering much greater pain. He was probably struggling much more than I. That drove me to redouble my efforts.

"Hold on, old fool. Hold on," I said to myself. "You are not going to die. Neither of you will. Neither of you."

When I finally saw Faustus's hand appear over the rim, I went to help draw him up. We both fell onto the ground and lay on our backs, gasping for air. I couldn't help bursting out into a fit of nervous laughter. Faustus started to laugh too. Was it purely dementia or was it induced by exhaustion? The laughing persisted, and I succumbed to the providential sense of comfort it brought me.

"Can you imagine that in a mere thousand years, there will be an orbital station up there, millions of kilometres away from Earth, and that this station will be our—their—new home," Faustus said, staring at the dark tapestry above. I looked up and let my mind drift through the countless thoughts that accompanied the spectacle—the ephemeral shooting stars, the sparkling spots that burned like millions of little candles.

"How many times have I contemplated space and the stars without really seeing them?" Faustus said.

"I hear you, my friend. I hear you."

"Is it just me, or does it look more beautiful from here, Earth, our *real* home?"

I didn't answer. Instead, I let a sigh escape. Reality jolted me back and propelled me into the present. We weren't safe here. I rolled over and pushed up onto my feet, every muscle aching with the effort. My hands still burned from the contact with the rope. I squinted past the gloom and gazed out at the landscape below. The land was bathed in dim moonlight. There was nothing but wind-swept plateaus, bordered by tall mountains and deep valleys full of impenetrable darkness. I saw the bridge dimly and, a little farther away, the reflection of moonlight on our wrecked ship, a sarcophagus of contorted metal and wires and plastic. But nowhere seemed safe. There was only the same hostile terrain as far as the eye could see. And the natives, those spectral shadows that haunted my consciousness, where were they? Were they here? Were they still inhabiting this place even after creating the paintings of the sacrificed crew?

I turned around and saw Faustus, who was standing motionless and staring at something. A massive stone slab appeared to my sight across a sheet of smoke. My heart suddenly accelerated. The sight of the thing brought a fresh wave of terror as I was reminded of something I wish I could have forgotten.

I moved cautiously toward the slab. The smoke from our bonfire in the circular room below kept on elevating out of the opening right beside the stone slab, engulfing its base with an horrendous ghostly mist.

"No!" Faustus shrieked. "Dear God, no!"

I spun around and noticed the source of Faustus's gnawing fear. At the other end of the plateau appeared a series of bobbing and swaying lights, torches of some kind perhaps, that advanced towards us.

"Keep calm, Faustus. Everything will be all right," I said as I moved to position myself beside him. But who was I trying to convince, me or Faustus?

The newcomers came to a full stop before reaching the stone slab. Behind the bright flames glinted dozens of infuriated faces. Their skin was painted white and black, which gave them the singular appearance of corpses.

One of them, a tall, slim man with a gigantic and colourful feathered hat and opal-green earrings advanced towards us. He was aided by what looked like a sophisticated walking cane and was holding his torch quite close to his face. I couldn't help but stare into his deep black eyes, and a grim sensation spread throughout my body. I tried to detach my eyes from the man, but it was no use. He stopped at the other side of the stone slab and addressed us in his own language, which was unfathomable. Judging by the tone of his voice and his animated gesticulation, I would say he was accusing us of something. And this something was easily demystified after having listened to the event logs. We had violated their sacred temple.

I raised my hands in surrender.

"We come in peace," I said very slowly, attempting to indicate with calm gestures that we hadn't any evil intentions towards them. "I am Ericson. Ericson." I tapped my chest as I repeated my name.

A loud growling raised among the natives, a blend of fear and discontentment. They started to tap the ground with their feet and their bows and spears, and it resonated eerily through the open air. With a single call from the man in the feathered hat, everyone became muted, standing sentinel like stone statues. I realised that

I, too, was paralysed, unable to move or talk. The more I considered the man, the more he fascinated—and terrified—me. He pointed at me, speaking animatedly, then directed his bony finger toward the hole through which the smoke was expelling. Then he pointed at the stone slab. And then he did something I had not expected. He pointed at the sky, then back at me, and he said, "Stars."

"Yes, we came from the stars. You're right. You're right," I hastened to confirm, excited that we could communicate, at least on that matter. Then the fate of the last voyagers from space came back to my mind as I recalled the horrific paintings in the cavern below.

The situation suddenly seemed so desperate that I didn't see what I could do to prevent us from the same end. Shoot them all? Perhaps we could, but what terrible consequences would it have on history? And what were the chances we would succeed with such bold action? A strange ringing noise came into my ears, making it next to impossible to think clearly or concentrate on the man's voice, which had become muffled and distorted. Panic grew to a new level when one elderly man detached from the group, his face hidden behind the veil of darkness. He limped with some difficulty toward the man in the feathered hat. I couldn't help but wonder how he had managed to climb up such a steep mountain in his condition.

The old man stopped and handed something to the man I now believed to be their chief, if that was the correct title. The chief took the object from the old man's hands and held it close to his torch, revealing a sharp blade, seemingly made of bone or stone, fitted with what looked like glinting inlays of turquoise. At least, that was what I could decipher from my position.

Raising the strange object, the chief directly addressed something or someone in the sky, arm raised high as he spoke to the great silent void above. For an instant, I thought he might be worshipping space itself, *our* domain. One futile moment in which I thought our lives were to be spared, that we were to be adored. That was until a detachment of four men rushed us.

"Don't come any closer!" yelled Faustus, aiming his gun at them. They stopped, fear lining their faces. Had they ever seen a gun? I doubted it, yet the mere sight of it was clearly enough to inspire great terror in them. "I'm sorry, Ericson. But we're done. We're done and there is nothing we can do."

A loud bang tore through the sky. There was a dreadful silence as I watched Faustus's body slump onto the ground, inert, a pool of blood growing beneath him.

"No!" My knees gave way under me, and I fell to the ground.

The old man approached me and, strangely, stretched out a hand to me. I reluctantly accepted it, and he helped me back onto my feet with stunning strength.

"Thank you," I said out of habit.

"Do not," said the old man with perfect English. I squinted through the darkness and examined his face, and it instantly struck me that this man didn't look at all like any of the other natives gathered here. No, not with his white hair, pale skin, and milky eyes, which seemed to be covered with a cloudy film like cataracts. His traits, in general, were similar to those of modern humans.

"You…you were part of the first crew who came here. It's you painted on the cavern wall, the one who stood with the natives. It was you who went missing, wasn't it?" I exclaimed, unable to contain neither my excitement nor my dread. "But what are you doing here and with them?"

"To answer your first question, yes, it's me," he said with a hint of disdain. He coughed faintly like most elderly people do for no particular reason and then continued. "Our ship crashed here some fifty years ago, just like yours, apparently. And just like we did, you made the unforgivable mistake of entering the sacred temple and disturbing Tonatiuh."

"Who? What are you talking about?"

"Tonatiuh, god of the day and ruler of the cardinal

direction of east," said the old man, arms raised to the sky. Something in his demeanour and his eyes reminded me of a religious fanatic. He began to recite what I interpreted as a prayer in the language of the natives, and the tapping started all over again, bows and feet and spears thundering against the stony ground. "But for him to wake again and ascend in the east, Tonatiuh requires a sacrifice."

Suddenly, the four men I had totally forgotten about grabbed me by the arms and feet, and I was taken to the stone slab where they held me immobilised. I thrashed and wriggled, trying to kick at least one of them in the groin and escape. But they were too many, far too many for me alone. Someone raised up my head as another brought some kind of terra-cotta bottle to my lips.

"What are you doing? Let go of me!" I yelled, twisting my head to prevent them from making me drink whatever it contained.

The old man entered my field of vision and, resting a hand on my forehead, said with a gentle and comforting voice, "Fear not, my son, for your heart be given to Tonatiuh to propel him on his daily course. One more day, he will ascend in the east and descend in the west."

A lukewarm and acrid liquid entered my throat before I noticed it was happening. I gagged, but they forced the liquid down, holding my mouth closed. Its relaxing effect was instantaneous, and a kind of warmth soon spread throughout my entire body. I felt so relieved and couldn't remember why I had been fighting in the first place.

The man in the feathered hat advanced, brandishing his stony knife directly over my chest. I looked up at the stars again, and something caught my attention. A pale ray pierced through the darkness as the blade descended. I closed my eyes.

Of all the ways I'd thought I might die, having my heart ripped from my chest and given to some supreme deity—a millennium before I was born, in fact—had never crossed my mind. I let my consciousness drift amidst the folly of the moment, as I pondered the ridiculous eccentricity of this night and this place. What maddening euphoria to be sacrificed to a god by one of my peers.

"Goodbye, world."

E.L. GILES was born in the French, Canadian Province of Quebec where he still lives with his girlfriend and two sons. Formerly a music writer, he diverted from this path some years ago to concentrate mainly on his writing career.

So far, he has published two novels, both part of his trilogy "The Birdman Project" and he is finishing the third and last one, which will be published in early 2020.

During 2019, Eric has published more than thirty drabbles and short stories through different anthologies and he is currently working on many more, some of which are going to be published later this year.

Bibliography
ANGELS, Black Hare Press, 2019
BEYOND, Black Hare Press, 2019
Deep Space, Black Hare Press, 2019
Martyrs (The Birdman Project), 2019
MONSTERS, Black Hare Press, 2019
The Birdman Project, Forever Morris Publishing, 2019
WORLDS, Black Hare Press, 2019

Connect
Website: www.elgilesauthor.com
Facebook: @elgilesauthor
Amazon: www.amazon.com/E.L.-Giles/e/B07NTZSP9T
GoodReads: goodreads.com/author/show/18753491.E_L_Giles

KRUZ
By David Bowmore

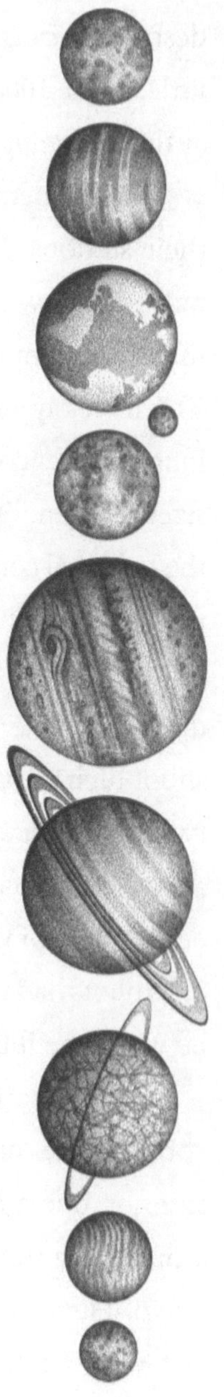

Young, vigorous and full of hate for the enemy, Undertaker pilot, Seth Kruz, is at one with his ship in a never-ending battle for territory against the sexually fluid Igorensee. However, when events in his life take an unexpected turn, he has time to ask himself many questions and reflect upon his feelings for the enemy.

Sirens wailed their death cry throughout the destroyer; in the cantina, the rec room, the dorms, the private cabins, the hangers and along all the corridors. Emergency lighting cast every available surface in a harsh red glow that flashed on and off at regular two second intervals. A thump went through the fabric of the destroyer, causing well-trained personnel to stagger a little, as the 1000 kilo Ion Canon roared its deadly answer at the incoming swarm of fighters.

Crew members ran hither and thither hurrying to their stations. Pilots slid helmets over their heads and buttoned-down gloves to their flight suits. Engineers made last minute preparations to the coffin-shaped ships. The joylessly nicknamed Undertakers were twenty feet long with a compartment moulded to take a regular sized human. Once attached to oxygen and synced with the onboard computer, the pilot controlled everything at the speed of thought. The ship's computer relayed all information to the human's brain as the pilot made snap decisions. The Undertakers could turn on a pin head, shoot high impact ionised energy bolts from three guns, two of which were directional and the third fixed and always rear facing. Sensors gave the pilot a perfect 360 degree field of vision. Seth knew he was lucky; in the old days pilots had to rely on H.U.D. only. When hooked up, he would be fully integrated with the ship's software.

Seth Kruz took a moment before hopping into his coffin. Nine elongated skulls were etched onto the exterior; one more to make Ace. The average kill rate for a first Luna-month long mission in an Undertaker was seven. His wing commander had reminded him of this fact only an hour ago but desire to see more skulls decorating his ship forced Seth to take wilder risks. He laid a kiss with his fingers on the hull of his bird and then settled into the moulded compartment. The domed magna-glass hood slid into place and he positioned the self-connecting catheter so it could do what it had to do. With the oxygen mask over his mouth, fine tendrils found their way up his nostrils making contact with the nano-jack at the front of his brain. That weird moment where his body became the Undertaker was never an easy sensation.

"Welcome back, Seth." The voice was comically old school. Why they couldn't give him some sort of sultry space siren, he didn't know? After all, if you're patterned for life (and that life might be very short lived) with someone so intimately then you might as well fancy their voice.

"I know what you are thinking, Seth."

"Sorry, Anis. Engage anti-grav, let's get among it."

"Engaging."

Seth joined the steady flow of other Undertakers and a few seconds later had rushed into space through the hanger doors and was speeding towards his first target. He was determined to make Ace before he died. The Igor craft didn't stand a chance. Seth fired early causing the star shaped ship to veer, fortunately for Seth, into the path of his follow up burst. The craft was ripped apart in a silent explosion that his Undertaker emerged from half a light-second later. He spun the ship around, his rear gun firing wildly which earned him a warning from command. Two seconds later, Anis was confirming the same command module had registered his tenth solo kill. If he made it out of this conflagration alive, he could wear the much sought after silk scarf. If he died, his family would receive it along with his medal. He took pursuit of his next target, which appeared to be leaving the main fray. It dodged his bursts with ease. Anis warned him to stick with the squad. He told Anis this was more important, but he didn't know why. The Igor was heading for the domed command module of the Royal Earth Corp Destroyer, Churchill, and Seth let rip with more short bursts of hot Ion. Damn, this Igor was good; spinning and dodging with something close to preternatural skill. Seth's bolts bounced off the command deflectors as the Igor evaded. To starboard an Igor bomber rose, it too on a slow but steady course for the command module.

Faster, Anis. They're going for the CM.

I would not advise—

Just do it.

He felt a gentle increase in g-force and let rip yet another burst. What the fuck was wrong? That Igor should have been dust seconds ago. Clearly, the Igor was going to ram the CM, which would undoubtedly weaken the deflector shields, and then the bomber would drop her payload. With a jolt, Seth realised he was focusing on the wrong ship. He let the Igor slip from his sights and manoeuvred the Undertaker into a revolving spin that arched around the bomber in a complete 360, all three of his guns engaged and dangerously close to overheating. If that happened, he would be out of the fight for a full minute while they cooled. His original target hit the command module defences and he saw the energy grid spark and fizzle as it died. He reversed course so that he settled under the bomber, evading the beams that came his way from the mega-machine with a swinging swaying motion. As the bay doors opened, he managed to squeeze a single shot into the hold. The bomber went up like a new millennium party, throwing him farther from the fight and scattering debris in every conceivable direction.

Seth soon returned to stand guard while the repair engineers diverted power back to the CM deflectors. With a sigh of relief, he took off for the eye of the battle as the power grid shimmered and came back online.

Later in the dorm, his wing commander ripped a strip off him for not sticking with the rest of the squadron. Then she hung the coveted white scarf around his neck and shook his hand. Seth blushed but happily accepted the congratulations and gentle ribbing of his squad mates. Then they had a moment's silence for three fallen comrades, before welcoming new recruits.

Alcohol was forbidden for servicemen, but there is always someone who can get hold of illicit homebrew, and he shared a nip of something with more spirit than Christmas with Magda as they sat on his bunk. She had flame red hair, and a body her flight suit always presented as sheer perfection. Magda was due for leave in three days and had made her Ace a week earlier, which was when they had first kissed. They were the only two in the squadron to have hit the mark so far. Joy filled his heart as he lingered in the moment; he was an Ace pilot, still buzzing from the battle and sharing homebrew liquor with a beautiful woman. Whether Seth got his leave was still in the hands of the gods, but right now he was flying high. It wasn't long before they had drawn the privacy curtain.

That is how he pictured it in his mind's eye as he sat daydreaming on the rocky outcrop, makeshift fishing rod in hand. In actual fact, he had come out of the hanger, taken his tenth Igor and, in his jubilation, had dashed off after another, ignoring his wing commander's instructions to keep formation. He had destroyed the bomber, but the close proximity of the blast had sent him and Anis reeling. Something snapped in their connection and she was dead to him from that moment onwards. The tendrils withdrew from his frontal cortex, his catheter disengaged, and he couldn't see as he usually could when connected with her. Through the magna-glass panel, stars swirled in a never-ending, tumbling darkness that made him want to upchuck. The Undertaker was running on emergency power and following a deep basic programme that could not be overwritten or destroyed. In such an event, the capsule guides the pilot to the nearest habitable landmass. All well and good, providing said landmass is within the thirty minutes of however fast they happened to be travelling, as that was all the emergency oxygen an Undertaker carried.

The crash landing had been about the scariest thing he had ever endured. The heat of entry had remoulded the front section of the Undertaker. Small braking paddles had extended along the length of the ship, slowing it to a speed that wouldn't rip the parachute apart. But not before circling the small planetoid several times, night and day blurred as his crotch damped and his bowels loosened. It was made all the more terrifying as he was facing away from the surface and had no idea if he was about to strike a mountain at Mach 4. The chute eventually deployed, changing his world view to inverse vertical. The sea he splashed into was small, not much more than a lake, and by the time he had bobbed back to the surface, he was relieved to be floating right side up and was able to slide the magna-glass back before unbuckling and then vomiting into the water. He used his helmet as a makeshift paddle to guide the dead Undertaker to the nearest landmass as the sun rose in the distance.

Several hours later, he was trying to drag his dead ship as far up the orange sand of the beach as he could. But tiredness and shock had robbed him of strength, and he was forced to leave his partner partially submerged on the shoreline. Then grabbing the emergency ration packs and med kit, he headed inland.

When the tide came in, Anis was completely submerged, but right now her silver shone. He was beyond tears for his lost partner.

He scratched at the skin beneath his beard. Feeling a tug on the line, he drew it in—nothing. He cast again and said a prayer to the ancients that someone would find him soon.

Still, it was as pleasant a planetoid as one could hope for. The sea was pale blue and reflected the sun's rays in millions of tiny shards of broken light on its surface. He hadn't ventured too far into the forests except to find a water source, which he was lucky enough to find on his third day. The days were warm, and because the nights were short the temperature did not seem to drop into the unbearable zone. The planet the moon orbited looked grey and was probably devoid of life.

A streak of fiery space debris crashed into the sea about a mile away, disturbing the waters and ruining Seth's chances of catching anything for the day. It wasn't the first time a meteorite had crashed down, but it was the first time a rock had floated back to the surface. Therefore, it must have been man-made or, heaven help him, an enemy ship.

The chances of surviving that kind of impact would be rare, but the ship might have useful supplies. It took a day and night for the star-shaped ship to float ashore and Seth covered several miles of coastline to converge with the pod. With his gun drawn, he cautiously approached the five-pointed star of an Igor craft. As with his own Undertaker, a clear panel let him see the creature he had been programmed to hate for as long as he could remember.

Like humans, it had four limbs and walked on two powerful hind legs. Images from school showed the creatures running on all four like dogs. They had four rough claws and had been known to rip a man's intestines out in one sweep. Ground troops who went into combat wore ultra-dense reinforced armour, but even so, they were powerful creatures.

It must have been dead. Brown blood decorated the inside of the clear panel. Part of its face was cut and bruised and covered with dried blood. A quick look around the exterior revealed some sort of handle contraption. He holstered his gun in order to use both hands to twist the handle anti-clockwise. With a sucking motion, the vacuum broke. He jumped backwards drawing his gun again. As a pilot, Seth's hand to hand combat skills were limited. Should the creature somehow still be alive, Seth would probably die.

After several minutes of inactivity, he approached the escape pod again. A stench came from inside. Stench was probably too strong a word, but it was a high pungent aroma. He raised the gun, double-checked the settings, kill it just to be sure, Seth. The creature opened one eye. Seth brought his other hand to steady the first. This was different from killing the enemy from afar in the midst of battle. The eye was so human. In the propaganda they always had yellow devil cat's eyes.

"It's just a dirty Igor. Pull the trigger on the bastard," he said aloud.

"Help." The guttural gravelly word shook him to his core. He hadn't expected that. The eye blinked and the dark blue mottled skin shimmered, becoming a muddy yellow colour.

"Don't do that."

The creature croaked several words in its mother tongue before finishing with another human word: "Please."

Seth stepped away from the ship, lowering his pistol. He took a sip from his water canister. Should he help it? How do you help a thing like that? Could he trust it? Better to kill it, isn't it?

He stepped back. Its eye focused on him.

"You are my prisoner. Do you understand?"

Part of its mouth rose, and again the skin shifted its colour range, becoming dark orange.

"Yes," it said.

Seth dribbled water between the Igor's lips. It sighed.

The Igor's harness was still locked in place, so he hit the release button in the centre of the creature's chest and stepped back. When the Igor did not move, he returned.

"Can you move?"

He looked the creature over. Its flight suit appeared to be intact. Bones were probably not broken.

"Come on. Get out." He indicated with the pistol for the Igor to exit the craft and then stepped away, the gun pointing at the creature's head. The heat of the sun soaked his back wet with sweat.

Slowly, the Igor rose, with one hand held against its long head. Once out of the craft, it sank to its knees. Like

Seth, some sort of pistol was holstered at the Igor's waist. Keeping his gun levelled at the alien's head, he circled behind and drew the gun from its place at the creature's side.

"Thank you for not destroying me, hu-man."

"I still might. Where are you injured?"

"My cranium. My thoughts are unclear. One of my visual orbs is dysfunctional."

"You're blind?"

"Only in one orb. It will not be much of a hindrance."

The creature needed to rest often on the journey back to Seth's cave. However, two cycles later, Seth had brought the creature to the creek where fresh running water tinkled over glossy pebbles. It drank and washed its wounds.

"How come you speak our language?"

"We are taught to understand the enemy. It makes us more efficient hunters. But do not worry, I will not harm you, hu-man. You may put your weapon away."

"I don't think so, Igor."

The alien's flesh turned bright red, "We are Igorensee. I am the fifth offspring of the second prince. Show me some respect, hu-man."

"You're just a filthy Igor."

"I can still use these to rip your cranium from your torso, hu-man," it said raising the claws of its right paw, "and could have at any time. You are tired and suffering from high stress fatigue as well as hormone depletion. We appear to be alone on this planetoid. It would be best to put our differences aside to increase our chances of survival."

"Shut up."

"I will not harm you."

"Shut up."

The Igor, constrained with wild vines, rested inside the cave while Seth stood guard outside. No matter his attempts to stay alert, he could not fight tiredness, and eventually, succumbing to exhaustion, he dropped off to sleep while sitting near the fire.

Seth woke as the sun rose, to see the Igor walking up the slope with a small dead creature hanging from its belt.

Seth, in a state of panic, pushed himself backwards and went for his pistol only to find it missing.

"Give me back my gun, you filthy Igor."

"My moniker is Dreptusi," it said withdrawing the pistol from an inside pocket. "I hope you realise I could have dispatched you easily while you slept. I said I would not hurt you, and I did not."

Dreptusi threw the pistol at Seth's feet. He snatched it up and pointed it at the Igor with hands that shook. Seth and Dreptusi looked into each other's eyes. The Igor remained calm and unarmed. Seth pulled the trigger.

"I have removed the power pack, hu-man. The pistol is dysfunctional."

"Give it to me."

"Not until you realise that I will not hurt you. On the journey from my craft I could have ripped you open. When you slept, I could have killed you with your own weapon. I did not have to return here. But it is always best in survival situations to work with others."

Seth's head dropped and the pistol clattered to the dusty ground.

"I hate your kind, Igor. I should have killed you."

"If it is any consolation, I hate hu-mans too. Your skin does not show emotion and the smell that comes off you is enough to put me off my food. But we are here now."

"What have you got there?" Seth asked, bending to pick the gun up, but he still didn't holster it.

"First-meal if you wish to share it with me."

"Did you catch it?" Seth asked fearing it might be what the oldies called 'road kill'.

"Of course. We are good hunters."

Dreptusi drew a knife from his boots and quickly skinned the animal and placed it over the hot embers of the fire on a wooden skewer and spit.

"I didn't know you had a knife."

"I know," Dreptusi said "Do you want to take it from me?"

Seth shook his head and piled up more wood on the fire. "We need more heat to cook it."

When they had ripped the animal apart and shared the meat, leaving nothing but sucked dry bones, Dreptusi asked, "How long have you been here, hu-man?"

"A little over three weeks. Do you know how long that is?"

"Twenty-one revolutions of your home world. Did your ship not send out a distress beacon?"

"No. Did yours?"

"I am not sure. I was unresponsive. What are your plans?"

"Today, like most days, I'm going to collect wood for the fire and then I'll fish."

"Here is your power pack, hu-man, you may put your gun away. I will hunt, you can be sure that we will feast well tonight."

"Bring water back too."

"Do not presume to tell me what to do, hu-man." The Igor's flesh flashed bright red as it stalked away.

They each returned to the dying embers of the fire as the sun was setting. They ate the fish and some of the meat Dreptusi had caught, saving the rest of the cooked food for a quick breakfast in the morning.

"I have set traps and will check them in the morrow."

"Perhaps you could show me how they work."

"Yes, I will do that, hu-man."

"You don't have to keep calling me that. My name is Seth. Seth Kruz, pilot first class, Amber 606 squadron assigned to the R.E.C Destroyer, Churchill."

"It is an honour to meet a fellow warrior. I am also a pilot. You may call me Drep. My rank and position do not translate well in your language, but we are of about equal status."

"Apart from you being the offspring of a prince."

Drep's skin flickered orange and pale green. For a moment Seth thought he had upset the Igor then it revealed yellowed jagged teeth and nodded its long head. He was laughing or at least amused.

Three weeks into the uneasy truce they made an expedition to recover their ships from the water. At low tide, Seth's Undertaker was partially buried and they worked tirelessly to expose enough of it to try to drag it farther up the beach. They smiled at each other as they pulled their feet from the grasping, sucking wet sand. All amusement came to a sudden halt when Seth found he couldn't drag his foot free, so he shifted his weight to the other. In seconds he was up to his knees. The sand had a hold of him and he was sinking fast.

"Drep! Help!"

Immediately seeing the danger of the situation, Drep gave instruction, "Don't struggle. Lie flat."

"What?"

"Trust me. I will try to save you, but lie flat and stop struggling. The more you fight the more it has you."

Seth fought every instinct and forced himself to calm down as he bent forwards at the waist, laying his torso along the grabbing sand.

"The tide must be turning. I will free your legs but do not struggle. If it gets hold of me, we both die."

Drep went to work clawing the sand away from Seth's right leg, but as soon as he removed a handful of wet sand more replaced it. The minutes dragged by as his powerful claws scooped and threw, scooped and threw.

"Hurry up."

"I am trying, Seth. I think the limb is coming free." Drep panted. "It is a matter of introducing as much air as possible." Suddenly, the leg had room to manoeuvre and Drep eased it free with that same sucking sound, which wasn't so funny anymore.

"Be still. I still have the other leg to free."

As the tide lapped against Seth's face, his other leg came free, and Drep instructed Seth to stay as flat as possible to the sand while they used their elbows and knees to push and pull themselves to dryer, more stable, land. When they reached the tree line, they lay on their backs gasping for breath.

"Thank you, Drep. You didn't have to do that."

"Yes, I did." He pointed at Seth's lower legs. "In my haste to free you I have cut your limbs with my claws, I am sorry. Will your med-kit suffice?"

"They're just scratches," Seth said, after inspecting the cuts. From his prone position, he held a hand out to Drep. "Thanks, I owe you."

The next day they found Drep's escape capsule on firmer sand. Using vines, they dragged it to the tree line where they could help themselves to spare parts at their leisure. Over the coming months, it was soon stripped to its bare bones as they used it along with wood and vines to improve the shelter that the cave provided.

About six months into their isolation, as they ate their evening meal, Drep pointed at the night sky.

"Do you see?"

Seth looked up from his wooden platter with the remains of fish on it and watched as the darkness was lit by a long streak of burning space debris.

"Might be a meteor?"

"Might be a craft, another hu-man. What will happen

to me then?"

"And if it's one of your lot, then I'll be your prisoner."

Drep stood up saying, "Let us set out now. If someone is onboard, they may need our help. I will ensure you are treated fairly."

Seth pulled his boots on and checked the power-pack in his sidearm. Enough juice to defend himself.

The sun had risen before they found the crater the craft had made as it ploughed into the wooded area a mile or so inland from one of the beaches. Seth's fears that it was an Igorensee ship were confirmed when they came across the body of an Igor that had evidently crawled from the ship. One of its forelimbs was completely severed and it lay in a pool of thick dark blood. As Drep knelt beside the body examining the insignia on the uniform, Seth drew his pistol. He was taking no chances.

"There are more, probably still in the craft."

"More?"

"Yes. This is a diplomat. He would have had a pilot."

Smoke billowed from the crater a few hundred yards from the dead Igor. The craft was larger, designed to carry several beings in relative comfort. Drep indicated that it resembled a Royal transportation vessel. They stepped inside; Seth on guard waiting for ambush; Drep calling out in his guttural mother tongue. A sound came from the front, possibly the pilot's cabin. Seth spun, his gun at the ready. Drep snatched the weapon from his hands in a quick movement that surprised and startled Seth.

"No one will hurt you while you are with me. Make sure you do likewise, or I might forget our truce," Drep said, his mottled skin a fierce red.

The pilot, still strapped into his seat, was clearly dead; a small tree trunk was buried deep in his torso. Drep searched the rest of the ship, moving slowly towards the rear. Seth was considering what might be salvageable when Drep called to him. He ran to a second cabin and find Drep kneeling over a figure slumped in a chair, the body hidden from view. It gurgled in reply to something Drep said. Clearly alive, but by the thinnest of threads.

Drep, his skin turning a dark blue, looked at Seth and said, "The princess is ready."

"Princess? Ready for what?"

"The birthing."

"The what? You mean she's pregnant?"

"Yes. There is little hope for the parent, but the offspring might still live. I will attempt an emergency delivery. Help me get her from the seat."

As Drep began to unbuckle and lift the female, Seth said, "But a baby. We can't look after a baby."

"Would you try to help one of your own?"

"Of course, but—"

"What? Is it different?" Spittle flecked his red chin. His

eyes darkened to a yellow. "Fine, hu-man. Go. Leave us. I will take responsibility for my own."

He turned his back on Seth and heaved the dying princess from the chair and laid her along the aisle. He reached into his boot and drew his knife, then looked up a Seth. "I do not need you. Leave."

Seth stepped outside, equal feelings of revulsion, remorse and regret overwhelmed him. Breathing was difficult. He'd developed a certain respect for Drep, but with a child to care for the Igors would both become baggage. From now on, it would be up to Seth to do everything. It might be better if he made his own way from this point onwards. The planetoid was large enough for them not to interact with each other.

However, Seth recognised that Drep was right; he would try to save a human baby. And knowing the Igor as he did, he believed Drep would have behaved with more humanity if the situation had been reversed. He wiped his eyes with his thumb and returned to the interior.

The female's stomach was cut wide open.

Drep, his skin as pale as imitation ivory, cradled a tiny bloody version of the mother in his arms.

"She died. I had to act quickly. They both died."

"Let me try," Seth said.

Taking the child, he checked its airways, poked his fingers inside the mouth and released some gloopy liquid.

Then holding the newborn upside down by the legs said, "Trust me." He swung the baby in a gentle arc, forwards, then backwards, forwards and backwards again. Then he sat in one of the chairs, rested the still unmoving child on his knees and vigorously rubbed its chest for a minute, then swung again and returned to a seated position to massage the chest. He checked the airways. Cleared more gloop. Massaged the chest.

The youngling spluttered.

Drep, a look on his face that showed more than any multi-coloured skin display, quickly took the robe from the dead mother, wrapped it around the youngling, then tucked the bundle inside his own jacket, fastening it tight for the trek back to their cave.

He grasped Seth by the shoulder. No words were necessary.

Hours after the youngling was dragged into the universe, Drep managed to fashion a harness from vines and fabric from the interior of the crashed craft. The child was carried on the Igor's back throughout the day. He did all the tasks he had previously done, but with the youngling secured to his back. Drep would wash the youngling in the sea and feed him with regurgitated food; the one thing Seth could not watch. Drep named the youngling Kemptruti and consented to allowing Seth to call him Kemp.

A few days later, Drep approached Seth as he sat on his favourite outcrop with his lucky fishing rod in hand.

"My Levelling approaches," he said.

"What is your Levelling?"

"We go through The Levelling several times in a lifetime. It is too soon for me, but with the close proximity of the youngling and no female, my chemistry is altering sooner than expected."

"Levelling? I still don't understand."

"We alter sex. Scientists think we took this evolutionary path to ensure our race will always survive. It has produced a very fair society unlike—"

"Never mind all that. You change sex?"

"Yes. I will be in pain for some time. You will need to care for Kemptruti for two, possibly three weeks."

"Fine." Seth turned his attention back to the sea. He knew it. They were beginning to be a burden. "Do you need anything?"

"Only privacy."

Minutes passed. Drep sat next to Seth, dangling his legs over the rocky edge, the youngling secure in his harness.

"What? I said I'd help."

"The youngling needs two parents, Seth. In a few months he will begin to form words and recognise our features.

"I need to be this youngling's parent and intend to take the place of his birthing parent. I would be honoured if you would be his second parent."

Seth, his mouth dropping open, stared into the Igor's eyes.

"You've got to be joking. Me. But what do I know about bringing up one of your lot."

"Perhaps it is time you learnt?"

Drep stood and began the hike back to the cave.

Seth gave a sigh, realising he had little choice in the matter, then called back to Drep, "Where I come from, he would call me 'Dad'."

Drep barred his teeth as his skin blossomed into shades of violet. Seth hoped that was a good a sign.

As the years passed, the cave entrance expanded, transforming into a wooden-roofed structure allowing the three of them to rest in relative safety and comfort. Their diet of meat and fish was supplemented with fruit and some roots. A small patch of soil was dedicated to the attempt at growing flavoured roots. They kept a large bird, which Kemp called Brydi, that laid an egg every other day cycle.

When Kemp was only five years old, Drep returned

from an expedition to the far side of their island. He—for he'd gone through another painful Levelling, becoming male again—had been gone for a week, confident that Kemp would be safe with Seth. His skin was fixed in a pale grey shade and his eye was unable to focus. Sweat ran in rivulets down his face, and a smell came off him reminding Seth of a dead dog he came across when he was a child.

Drep recounted the story in between states of semi-consciousness. He had been bitten by an insect-like creature with a red dot in the centre of its cranium. He had to tell them, warn them of the foot-long creature that lived in the marshes on the far side of the island. With his last words, he told Kemp that it was important to do as Seth said and to remember the lessons he had been taught about his home world. Seth nodded, letting the warrior-prince know he would not let the boy down. Kemp clung to his parent's body as Dreptusi of Susinatra exhaled his last breath.

Together, the youngling and the human removed Drep's clothes and washed his body, before casting it adrift on a raft which they set alight. As the sun set, Drep's body was consumed first by flame and then by water.

When Kemp was about ten years old, he went through The Levelling and for three weeks, groaned and screamed in agony as the sexual parts and internal workings transformed into their female counterparts. Physically she had changed little—same face, same body shape—but her masculinity was missing. Seth, although having witnessed the transformation with Drep, felt a deep sense of helplessness during the change. The child was in extreme agony and called out night and day, clutching at his stomach while curled in a ball. All he could do was hold the youngling close when her screams woke the night birds, and wash the sweat from her face with sea sponges they had collected together.

"You're almost as big as Drep, you should start wearing his clothing. We kept them back for a reason," Seth said, once the pain of The Levelling had finally eased.

"Yes, Dad."

It was strange seeing Kemp in clothes. For years she had lived in skirts made from leaves and bark. But now she looked like a warrior.

"Drep would be very proud."

"Thank you, Dad. Why do you cry?"

"I was just thinking, that's all."

Not long after this, the ships arrived. Star shaped ships.

After more than ten years, there wasn't much left of his uniform, but Seth pulled his boots on and the scarf Drep had made from bleached palm leaves. He removed his pistol, why he still carried it he wasn't quite sure; the power pack had died years before. Then he strode out to meet the landing party as they disembarked from their carrier, with his hands held high to show he was unarmed. Kemp followed a little way behind doing her best to be brave.

He must remind the enemy that he was a serving member of the Royal Earth Corp.

Thirty killing machines armed to the teeth with sidearms, blades and assault rifles lined up in front of him. From the carrier trundled a star shaped all-terrain tank, its cannon positioned on him.

Perhaps he should have hidden, continued the war as a lone attacker, taking them by surprise, eliminating them one at a time. Deep down, he knew that was a pointless task. He and Kemp were barely managing to survive as it was. And what would he do with her? She was one of theirs, he couldn't let her know he intended to kill her people—not her dad. If he let her go to them, they would know that he could be hiding, biding his time. They would find him in a matter of days. And besides, he was tired. He needed to rest; he needed an end to this struggling life, even if it was as a prisoner of war.

The commander stepped forward; his troops levelled their guns at Seth. Seth's knees itched on the inside. The fight had gone out of him. None-the-less, he came to attention, raising his right arm in the age-old salute. "Seth

Kruz, pilot first class, Amber 606 squadron assigned to the Royal Earth Corp Destroyer, Churchill."

"Release your hostage," the commander ordered.

"She is not my prisoner. Her name is Kemptruti, offspring of Dreptusi. A princess of the royal household, Susinatra." It was a white lie, but he had never found the right time to tell Kemp the complete truth about her biological parentage.

The commander spoke its long worded natural tongue towards Kemp. She reached for Seth's hand, sending confidence through every cell in his body, but more importantly filling his heart with love. In return, he squeezed her paw, sending reassuring warmth, and she stood taller. Seth loved her as any father would love his own.

"Kemptruti does not know much of her native language. Her parent died when she was very young."

"Are you responsible for the death of a prince of the royal household?"

"No, his death was a tragic accident."

"On your knees, you will die for the atrocities and assassination of Prince Dreptusi."

Seth remained standing. "Drep's death was an accident. He was my friend, my ally."

The commander stepped forwards, his skin so red as to be nearly purple, and raised his gun.

"So be it. Death is all any hu-man deserves."

"No. You cannot do that." Kemp stepped in front of Seth.

"Stand away, Kemptruti of Susinatra. All hu-man vermin must die."

"No. He deserves gratitude and the respect of a warrior. Am I of the royal line? Does the name of my parent grant me privileges?"

"If you are royalty, yes. But only if you are." The colour of his skin returned to a pale orange.

"Then please take my father onboard and treat him with respect. He tells me the war has lasted for more than fifty years. Our friendship may well be the beginning of the end of the war."

The commander's skin quickly flashed red, he took a step closer and backhanded the youngling across the face. She fell to her knees and Seth pulled her close to him. The commander's voice dropped an octave as his face skin darkened to midnight.

"Father? A member of the royal household would never degrade themselves in such a way. There will never be any peace. Not until their kind has been eliminated from the galaxy. And those who say we should forgive them, or trust them, are no better than the filthy hu-mans who infect everything they touch."

The Igor commander placed his gun against her head,

"No. Not her!" Seth cried out, as the single projectile made its deadly course first through her head and then his chest.

He cradled her lifeless form, trying to hold her to this realm, while his own lifeblood ebbed away in spurts and judders. For the first time in years, his body convulsed, not with the cold but with sorrow and fear.

He is in school, the children repeating the teacher's words, 'Igors are vermin.'

He is at the academy looking at an Undertaker for the first time.

He is kissing Magda.

He is shaking Drep's paw.

He is teaching Kemp to swim, to hunt, to cook.

He dies.

DAVID BOWMORE was born in 1972, on a wintery night with the sound of thunder and the flash of lightning welcoming him into the world.

Forty-five years later he started writing fiction. Before this, he had been a chef, a teacher and an odd-job man.

He lives in Yorkshire with his wonderful wife and a small white poodle called Floyd.

David writes thrillers and mysteries as well as stories with a touch of the supernatural about them. He focuses on character and the oddities of being a human being, sometimes with humour, sometimes with dark reality.

Authors who have influenced him include P.G Wodehouse, Neil Gaiman, Elmore Leonard, Patricia Highsmith and Agatha Christie.

His story, 'Sins of The Father' won best in book as voted by the readers of the anthology Vortex, published by Clarendon House in June 2018.

His work has also been published by Zombie Pirate Publishing, Dastaan World, Blood Song Books, and Fantasia Divinity.

In June 2019, his first collection of short stories was published by Clarendon House. *The Magic of Deben Market* is available through Amazon.

Connect
Website: davidbowmore.co.uk
Facebook: @davidbowmoreauthor

THE BITE OF THE FLAMINGO BOA

By Shawn M. Klimek

When his widowed mother is arrested for telepathy, young Jep Wexner must journey by starship to attempt to support her. But a telepathic warning hints that there are worse things than radiation to fear within the nebulous planetary asteroid ring they call the Flamingo Boa.

PART ONE

Upon reaching The Bore Hole Saloon, reputed to be the favourite watering hole of freeminers on Phoenix Station, Jep Wexner sashayed angrily inside, clenching a "Welcome Newcomer, Free-Drink" coupon in his fist.

This was awkward; intending to let his body language reflect his rancour, Jep had wanted to stomp, not sashay, but having just arrived from Earth, his motions had not yet recalibrated for the station's lighter gravity.

Blushing distractedly, he waltzed between the crowded tables to the nearest open barstool, wrapped his legs around its base and then signalled for the bartender.

"A Damp Comet," he said, "neat."

The bartender's eyebrows lifted ripples into his forehead like waves on the shore of his receding hairline. Leaning forwards, he said in a low voice, "So, do you just want the Rusted Gin? It's technically not a Comet without the snowball."

"Fine," said Jep, testily.

Jep scanned the saloon for customers who looked like they might be freeminers—men who might have known his late father, Max. One that drew his eye was a middle-aged man with dark, wavy hair, who kept glancing up over the horizontal index finger he was using to keep the moustache out of his beer. He was talking to a much older gentleman with his back to Jep, the latter displaying a nest of white hair around a balding crown.

"Your Rusted Gin," said the bartender, setting down the glass on a printed foam coaster.

"Thank you," said Jep, handing over the crumpled

coupon.

Jep took a sip and then stood up as if about to approach the chosen pair, but visualising himself traipsing with a full glass, reconsidered and immediately sat back down. The moustachioed man seemed to take this as his cue to approach. After saying something to his elderly companion—who looked over his shoulder at Jep and then nodded significantly—he picked up his beer and then closed the distance between them.

"Captain Fex Neil, of the *Hattie*," said Moustache, putting down his beer beside Jep's gin and nodding amiably.

"Jep Wexner, son of the late Max Wexner," Jep replied.

Captain Neil glanced back at his companion and signalled him with a grin and a chin jut, then turned the high beams on Jep. Stroking his own cheek, he said, "Add about twenty years and a scar, and you'd be the spitting image of your father. My first mate and I knew him well. This is Russell Simms, freeminer, and one *hellavuhn* engineer."

Jep turned to see the white-haired fellow standing right behind him, exposing his wrinkly side: a smiling face arranged around crinkly blue eyes, a longish nose and gold teeth.

"Pleased to meetcha!" said Simms, extending his hand.

Jep shook it—slightly too warmly at first—before

letting it go like the wrong end of a skillet. He was so relieved to realise he was among friends of his father's that he felt unexpectedly emotional. The past few months had been a relentless procession of let downs and mounting troubles.

"There, there, what's wrong?" said Neil, patting him on the back. "Here, let's all take our drinks into that booth, there."

Soon, Jep found himself sitting across from Neil and Simms, telling them his story as they drank.

It was shortly after he had begun college when, out of the blue, his mother, Iris, was arrested by Psi-Sec, accused of under-reporting her telepathic abilities. "Don't worry, I'm innocent," she had promised, projecting the words directly into Jep's brain before they had affixed a psi-jammer and took her away to await trial.

"Telepath! No kiddin?" Simms had whispered in amazement.

"Level 2!" Jep had confirmed. Anyone with enough money for the surgery could have level one these days. "But licensed and certified. She'd used it more than once to help out the police."

"*That's* gratitude!" said Simms, shaking his head.

"Politics," Neil suggested.

Jep briefly shut his eyes, nodded, then swallowed more gin and continued.

Seeking advice, he had transmitted the worrying news to his father on Phoenix Station, but the message had been returned as undeliverable, coupled with a tardy notice from the Pluto Mining Corp (PMC) that their former employee had died under mysterious circumstances, presumed by default to be suicide.

"By *default?* Hear that, Russ? Corrupt, cheating bastards," said the captain. "Suicide, my ass! Not Max. He was a winner; always beating the odds. How he endured working for those villains for so long, I could never fathom."

"Well, the pension, obviously," said Simms.

"Sure, but he's not collecting that now, is he?" countered Neil.

"True. But the steady paycheck, too. Lucky to have it these days. Look at all the unemployed spacers looking for hand-outs or turning brigand."

"Mining's a gamble," said Neil, shaking his head. "Still, it's the freeminer's life for me. But go on, young Wexner. I hope you told those corporate bureaucrats where to stuff it!"

Jep looked down at his empty tumbler and wished now there had been an olive or even an ice cube to suck on.

"I definitely told them they were wrong," he said.

But he did more than that, as he explained. As a

suicide seemed both out of character and such a ruling would void his father's life insurance, Jep had lodged a formal complaint with the Far Marshall, demanding a proper investigation. The Far Marshall had agreed but warned that a protracted investigation could entangle any inheritance for years, and suggested a legal representative visit the Phoenix Station probate office in person to expedite matters.

"And so, I came by the next starship," said Jep, "and went to the probate office first thing. I knew my dad had bought one of those new, jump-capable mining ships."

"A Honda-Tesla Flea," said Simms, nodding. "First one in the sector and envy of every other air-begging freeminer."

"And a headache for the PMC, you can bet," Neil added.

"Costly bugger, but with the savings from jump fees alone, a skilled miner like Max would have earned it back in five years, tops," said Simms.

"Not only that," Neil rejoined, "but he was no longer limited to sifting through PMC leftovers. The corporate carriers never tote freeminers to any fields that their drones haven't already picked over."

"Mom told me he had secured a lucrative mining lease," offered Jep.

Both freeminers' eyes grew wide and they

exchanged glances.

"My God! Of course, he did!" said Neil.

"Vance-Epsilon! I'd bet anything," said Simms.

"The Flamingo Boa!"

"What the hell's that?" said Jep.

"Ringed gas-giant in the Vance System," said Neil. "Asteroids floating in pink clouds of gappite, like a feather boa." Reaching across the table, he picked up Jep's glass, put it back down again, then took a red note out of his vest pocket and passed it to his companion. "Russ, get us all another round, will you? I'll start filling young Wexner in on the juicy details about the Flamingo Boa! Hang on. What's that you're drinking, my friend?"

Jep put his hand to his head. "Honestly, I think I'd better eat something first."

"Oh, but of course, you've just come from a long voyage!" The captain flicked his fingers at the engineer, sweeping him towards the bar. "Get us three sandwiches too, Russ, and a big pan of chili-soy fritters."

Simms held up the red note. "But—"

"You know I'm good for the rest!" Neil insisted, waving him away. "We're all going to be rich, after all!"

"Rich?" Jep echoed.

"Well, hopefully," said the captain. "Now that we have the famous Wexner luck on our side again. Sorry if that sounded flip, Jep. My deepest condolences about your father, but Max was a famously lucky bastard. Made lots of us wonder if he had some of that psionic stuff of his own! E.S.P, or tele-whatsit, that lets you predict the future."

Jep considered. "Not that I know of."

"Never mind. Your father had smarts and guts, which are enough." He sighed brightly. "Good man. Good friend. Tragic loss. Now sit back and let me tell you how smart he was. The Flamingo Boa!"

"What is that word you keep saying?"

"Flamingo or boa?"

"Those are two things? Then both."

"Goodness me, you're young! Flamingos were wading birds that lived in zoos, but the important detail is that they had bright pink feathers. Boas were prehistoric snakes, but a snake-shaped belt or scarf made of feathers was also called a feather boa, something old-timey strippers used to fling around in the air when they danced naked."

Realising that he had been absent-mindedly pointing at a certain bosomy woman seated across the saloon as if to illustrate his mention of "old-timey strippers", and reacting to her attentive scowl, the captain quickly looked away and camouflaged his embarrassing gesture as a casual stroke of his moustache.

"But we digress," he said. "Some forgotten poet-astronomer gave the ring around Vance-Epsilon that nickname before scientists even knew there was such a thing as gappite, much less a pink variety."

"What's so special about—"

At this point, Simms returned balancing a platter of sandwiches in one hand and three beers in the other.

"Goody," said Neil, rubbing his hands together.

"They're out of chili-soy fritters, so I ordered cheesy-gel poppers," said Simms, sitting down before picking up one of the sandwiches. "The bartender will bring them out shortly."

The captain frowned. "Oh well," he said. Picking up another of the sandwiches, he pushed the tray over to Jep.

"Your poppers," announced the bartender, appearing suddenly.

"That was fast," said Simms.

"Flash-hydrated," said the bartender with a shrug. He dropped a greasy paper cylinder full of oily, yellow nuggets onto the table and then retreated to the bar.

Jep bit into his sandwich, paused, and then began chewing unenthusiastically. The flavour reminded him of some paste he'd eaten during grade school.

"Needs mustard," he said with a mouth so dry that the words came out as *Nethmuthd.*

"Isn't it?" Neil enthused, one cheek bulging with a

mouthful of hoagie, his moustache peppered with breadcrumbs. "Hydrogastronics, they call it. Quite popular. Farmed on this very station."

Jep slurped some beer and pushed the platter away.

"Right, right. Down to business," said Neil. "Where were we?"

"Getting rich," Simms volunteered.

"Right. Vance-Epsilon and pink gappite."

"The asteroid miner's grail," agreed Simms. "The *real* pay dirt."

"So, gappite's the stuff starships use to stitch hyperspace, right?" said Jep.

"Well, yeah, but it's not that simple. There's more than one kind, right? You can have hyperentangled ions for any element heavier than gold. And not only that, they're all Doppler-shifted, right? Reflecting the relative distance between stitched pairs in linear space, so there's a whole spectrum of types and values."

"Pink is best," said Simms, corking his gob with a cheesy-gel popper.

Jep seemed to be catching on. "So, this pink asteroid ring must appear lucrative to everybody then. In that case, why hasn't the PMC mined it already?"

"Oh, you can bet they're drooling too, and that some committee of suits in the PMC HQ is fast-tracking a solution, but none of the hyper-lanes to Vance anyone has found so far are wide enough for their massive jump carriers, which gives the little guys like us a head start for once! That had to be what your father had in mind, and if I'm right, I think that's how we should honour his legacy!"

"A little tug like the *Hattie* could stitch those lanes if she had one of the new, miniaturised jump engines," Simms hinted.

The captain clapped his hands, brushed the palms together and then stuck one out to invite a handshake. "So, what do you say to a partnership, Lucky Wexner?" he said.

"Let's get rich together," urged Simms, licking cheesy gel off his fingers before patting Jep on the shoulder.

"Not so fast," said Jep. "All this is news to me and includes a lot of speculation."

"Speculation is what prospectors do, Jep! Under our space suits and miner's boots, we're all just naked speculators. Your dad would have jumped at an offer like this."

"That may be," said Jep, standing up defensively. "But I've already been to the probate office, and they won't release his estate to me until his debts are settled. That's what makes me so angry. It's a Catch-22." As he glared thoughtfully off into the distance, Jep noticed that a buxom female across the room seemed to think he was staring at her. Her dark eyes returned his glare, clearly annoyed.

Flustered, Jep returned his attention to his dining companions and resumed. "Also, a major reason I came to Phoenix Station was to investigate my father's death. I came to collect facts, and I still need a lot more facts before I commit to anything."

"Of course you need facts!" said Neil. "I love facts! Even Max would have said the same. We're on the same side here, so let's look at the facts we already have. Fact one, we all need the money—you more than any of us, since you've got debts and investigators, maybe even bribes to pay. Fact two, you're too green to go it alone and couldn't even fly that Flea if you already had it. And fact three, we're all united in the cause of sticking it to the corporation that tried to screw over your dad. Now, let's all go down to the probate office together this time, put actual eyeballs on that lucrative mining lease and figure out as a team how to free that marvellous jump ship of yours."

Jep realised that, as uncomfortable as he might be with such a hasty arrangement, he was about to exit the saloon feeling better than he had upon entering. Notwithstanding the aftertaste of paste in his mouth, because some of the enormous weight on his shoulders had already been lifted, he felt more optimistic. As he followed the pair towards the Bore Hole Saloon exit, the awkwardness of his movements owing to the slighter gravity proved conveniently smoothed over by his slight intoxication. Nearing the exit, the dark-eyed, bosomy woman suddenly imposed herself between him and the door. She was moderately attractive, although at close range, the dark mascara and eyeshadow she wore did not completely mask her middle age. As she looked him deep in the eyes, he returned her gaze as politely as he could, except far more like a startled deer—one half distracted by another deer's obvious cleavage.

"Jeb Wezner?" she said, and her voice was warm and smelled of beer.

"Jep Wexner," he corrected.

"Right, Wezner," she said, fixing him with those steely eyes and swaying slightly, like a cobra. "Iris says to watch out."

"My mom?"

"Right. Fucks. Kneel."

Bewildered and intimidated by these instructions, Jep stammered, "D-d-do what?" She was a big woman.

"Don't TRUST him."

"Trust who?"

"Don't TRUST Fucks Kneel."

"You mean Fex Neil?"

"What I *said*. Iris said." She pounded an index finger into his chest repeatedly, as if she were impatient for an elevator. "Be careful."

As she was turning away, the saloon exit door slid open, and Captain Neil poked his wavy-haired head back inside. "Coming Jep? If you hurry, we can just catch the tram."

PART TWO

"Hi Mom,

Sorry. This feels weird. Articulating my thoughts to you is strangely challenging. I grew up so used to your telepathy. You always guessed the hidden things, the thoughts I couldn't bring myself to say out loud. Now I find myself choking back secrets.

I guess secrets are our new normal for a while, since Psi-Sec is probably censoring communications. Not that we have any secrets. Psi-Sec, if you're there, my Mom has never done anything illegal. Please let her go home.

I'm sorry if my last vid was a little emotional. When I first arrived at Phoenix Station and discovered how rigged the system is, I got a little depressed. I had to pay a disembarkation fee and prepay for air and water. You never approved of my plan to follow in Dad's footsteps and I see now, that I was naïve. Fortunately, I ran into some old friends of Dad's who have been helping me out. Captain Fex Neil of the mining tug, Hattie, said Dad was a friend of his. He helped me get a loan so that I could get Dad's estate out of probate. I finally saw that new jump ship he told us about: sleek, 2-seater. Compact. Beautiful lines. The word "Iris" is painted on the bow. That's really the ship's name, Mom, I wish you could see it. I told you he never forgot us!

Anyway, it's legally mine now, although I'm not yet licensed to fly it off the station by myself. Fortunately, Captain Neil's first mate is an engineering genius. He reconfigured the Hattie's cargo bay and swapped out the escape pods nearest to her engines to install Iris in their place. By designating her a two-man escape pod, the Hattie can still legally take a full crew of five. More importantly, Simms daisy-chained both ship engines, so we should be able to hyper-jump the whole shebang to the asteroid fields without leasing space on a PMC carrier.

Regarding Dad's death: The local Far Marshall's deputy says a real investigation is finally underway. All they've told me so far is that Iris returned to the station on autopilot, empty, and that his body was never found. That gets me: the thought of Dad dying alone, clinging to some asteroid or drifting away in space. Gives me nightmares, envisioning his frozen corpse. But now, I'm being morbid. Never mind. The deputy promised to send search drones to his last known position based on the ship's navigation records.

I also wanted to tell you about this strange woman—but I suppose I'd better save that story for next time. There's a line forming outside the holo-booth.

Don't lose hope, Mom. I know you'll get your freedom back once you've had your day in court. I realise you must be worried about your mounting legal debts, but I'll be able to start sending you money as soon as I've paid off the loan Captain Neil arranged for me. Even though I'm only a trainee, he says that I'm entitled to two profit shares, just like him.

Talk to you soon. Respond if you can. I love you."

PART THREE

Besides Captain Neil, Simms, and Jep himself, two other freeminers filled out the *Hattie*'s crew: Technician Glenda Forthright and Heavy Equipment Operator (HEO) Haver Benschmann.

All except the captain shared a single, cosy sleeping cabin: a padded hollow strung with cocoon-like hammocks. Since no more than two crew ever slept at once, this arrangement never felt crowded—or anyway, not when sleeping, but chatty crewmembers were impossible to escape. During the transit to Vance, for example, Jep learned that Forthright was a chess fanatic, orchestral music fan, and zero-gee Bonsai hobbyist. Pointing to the twisty tree adorning the sleeping cabin wall like a holiday wreath, she explained that the work-in-progress would eventually represent a hyper-lane map seen only in her dreams.

But Benschmann was worse. He loved chatting so much that Jep had begun avoiding the chamber when their sleep schedules overlapped. Pretending to snore had no effect. The HEO often spoke of his secret girlfriend on Earth, while pointing to a salacious poster of the holovid star, Trixie Watts. He played games and collected entertainment vids, including experimental art, holo-porn and exotic sports fighting.

After a shift spent with Benschmann, Jep was sometimes difficult to awaken. The hour they arrived in the Vance system, already hurtling towards the ringed, fifth planet, the captain had to repeat his name several times over the intercom, just to summon him to watch the event through the forward view monitor. The whole crew was present. Those who couldn't fit around the central monitor crowded either of the two tiny forward view ports.

"Such blue! At this distance, it almost looks like Earth, wearing a pink collar," said Jep. "Does Vance-

Epsilon have oceans?"

"Naw, it's a gas-giant," said Neil. "But the exciting part is those gappite-rich asteroids!"

"Money!" exclaimed Simms, happily. "I've got the taggers ready."

"Keep your eyes open," said Forthright, analysing a data stream on a separate monitor. "We may not be alone in this system. It's hard to read with all the radiation coming from the planet, but these numbers could be hyper-wave echoes, or even old radio waves."

"How old?" asked Jep. "Maybe it's an S.O.S., if this is where my Dad died."

"Not that old," said Forthright, who had been briefed about Max Wexner.

"Claim jumpers!" suggested Simms angrily.

"I'd be more worried about pirates," said the captain. "If we discover mere claim jumpers among us, I'll be relieved, if not quite thrilled; there's enough to go around for two small operators, and no great concern as we don't get in each other's way. Also, once we record them in the act, Wexner's lease entitles us to a share of whatever they poach. But pirates are another matter. They'll take or destroy everything, including witnesses, and unfortunately, *Hattie* isn't armed."

"Oh, I can think of parts of *Hattie* that could be weaponized," countered Simms, grinning at

Benschmann. The two of them, at opposite view ports, grinned at each other from across the forward cabin.

"The grappling cranes, the drills, the collision bumpers, probes, maybe even the towing cables…"

"All of you make what defensive preparations you can think of, just in case," Neil ordered. "But if they exist, our best hope is to avoid a fight. Simms, unlink Iris in case they ambush us with an EMP. We may need a backup engine. Also, someone needs to brief Wexner on emergency evacuation procedures. Benschmann, that'll be you."

"Yes, sir."

"No one panic. Even if there are pirates, we still have plenty of time. They would never attack us before we have a full load of ore in tow."

"So, we've got to do all the mining work for nothing first," Benschmann groaned.

"We haven't even confirmed that there are pirates," Neil countered, "much less is it a certainty that they could capture us."

"I just thought of another possibility for those readings," offered Jep. "The Phoenix Station Far Marshall's deputy promised to send search drones here to look for my father. We could be reading those."

"Oh, that's so *cute*," said Forthright. "*Sure*, he did."

"What is that supposed to mean?" Jep challenged.

"The Far Marshall's deputy promised to send probes to search an entire solar system for one dead freeminer?"

"Well, why not? It's his job!"

"Who do you imagine pays that deputy's salary in this sector? The PMC, that's who. He's got to answer to them for expenses, including search probes."

Jep just stared at her blankly, watching the monitor lights dance in her eyes. He didn't know what to say to that.

Benschmann tapped him on the shoulder. "C'mon, Lucky. Let's climb down into cargo and have a look at those escape pods."

"If I need to escape, I'll be taking Iris," he declared haughtily.

"Sure, you will," said Benschmann.

PART FOUR

After four weeks of steady mining, the outlook for the crew of the *Hattie* had become decidedly rosier, and not just because they were orbiting deep within the pink-hued, nebulous asteroid ring dubbed "The Flamingo Boa." There had been no signs of claim jumpers or pirates, and exhausted cheers erupted when Technician Glenda Forthright's voice over the intercom announced a combined tally of nearly 9,900 tons of assorted high-value metals, almost 10% of which was pinkest gappite.

"We're going to be rich!" the white-haired engineer enthused, floating into the main chamber out of the sleeping cabin like a literal metaphor.

He glided towards Captain Neil, who was clinging to the ceiling rungs below the dorsal control cabin where Benschmann was busy operating the crane arm. Poking his head inside to explain why the operation was winding down, the captain said, "About sixty tons more would top us out, Benj." Pointing down at Jep, who appeared to be daydreaming while sucking on a coffee packet, he added, "Even with our good luck charm aboard, this is not the time to get greedy. If we leave within four hours, we can get paid, celebrate, rest up, and still come back for one more load before Wexner's lease expires."

Benschmann stared sullenly at the enormous asteroid he'd spent all morning drilling holes into for cable anchors. "Are we really going to leave Ogre behind?" he protested. "She's half-gold and gappite!"

"No choice, Benj. Rhino alone was a hefty, two-thousand-tonner," Neil replied. "Ogre would put us over. Unless you want to tow her across linear space for the next fifty years, we'll just have to come back for her."

Neil felt Simms float gently into him, nudging his way into the conversation. "Hey there, Haver," he interrupted. "How would you feel if we left Ogre's probe in place? That way, we could find her more quickly next time and stake our claim in case anyone else finds her first?"

"Yeah, that'd work," he said.

"Alright, then," said the captain. "Put away the crane and then help Simms double-check the piezo stabilisers in the ore train before we slingshot it around the planet. Once acceleration begins, we'll be on a very tight clock to match speed in order to tow it into hyperspace.

"Wait," said the HEO. "The cables already on Ogre will have to be detached so they don't build up an electrical charge while we're away. If we're leaving the probe, that will need to be done manually. Maybe I should do that while Wexner helps Simms."

"I have a better idea," said the captain. "Lucky Wexner!" he shouted. "It's time for you to graduate from freeminer novice to journeyman. Get off your sleepy, air-beggar butt and put on your EVA suit!"

Jep looked up anxiously. If he had just heard correctly, whomever went outside in the EVA suit would be doing so alone. He had never done an EVA walk alone before.

"Yes, sir," he said nervously.

Descending into the cargo bay, he looked forlornly at the Iris as though the ship might somehow console him the way his mother had once done. Would she have congratulated him on taking this final step to becoming a journeyman freeminer? Or would she have disapproved the risks he was taking? Deciding to push on, he pulled open the EVA locker doors and the suit within splayed open into in three, ready to wear sections: trousers, jacket, and all together: boots, gloves, and helmet. It didn't take him long to transition from his comfortable jumper into the bulky suit. Last, he strapped on the multi-tool he would require for his task. Once everything was organised, he toggled the microphone.

"All suited up," he announced.

It was Forthright who replied. "Hi, Jep. I just heard you were about to do your first solo EVA. This is a big step for you, isn't it?"

"Yeah, I guess it is."

"Are you nervous? Wait, don't tell me. Your bio readings have just come on, right in front of me. Try to slow your breathing, okay?

"Okay."

"Everything's going to be fine. I'll be watching you the whole time and coaching you if you have any questions. The suit monitor says all systems are green, so, since the captain says we're in a hurry, why don't you proceed directly to the ventral airlock and tell me when you're in position."

"Okay," said Jep. He pulled himself along using the stabilising frame securing the Iris. "In position now," he said.

"See the clear panel beside the door with the umbilical inside?"

"Yeah, I know this part," said Jep. He opened the panel and withdrew the umbilical. The tube portion married to a nozzle on his suit; the line portion hooked to a swivelling clew beside the nozzle.

"Conditions green!" congratulated Forthright. "You're now tapped into the ship's life support and all ready to head outside. I've been depressurising the bay since your suit came online. The airlock should be safe to open now, but hang on to the railing just in case you get blown out. Ready?"

"Ready."

"Outer door is opening," said Forthright. His shadow on the door seemed to expand into the shape of the aperture, as the two merged.

Jep stepped outside and took in the view. Above him was Vance-Epsilon, filling most of the "sky" like a bright blue ceiling. He rotated until it became his floor. The pink blizzard which gave the Flamingo Boa its name was almost translucent at this altitude, barely noticeable as one looked towards the planet. Gazing towards the densest part of the planetary ring, it became generally foggier and darker, with areas of bright pink where the sunlight penetrated.

Gripping the rungs on the outside of the mining tug, Jep activated his pulse jets and guided himself up the side until he had reached the crane. From within, Benschmann waved at him playfully, and then pointed at Ogre, before descending abruptly out of view. Had he gone to double-check the piezo-stabilisers? Jep realised he'd never watched that being done before. He was still a novice after all.

The crane was still partially extended so it could receive the loosened cables. Because the cables were quite thin, they were hard to see. But having confirmed by tugging on one that it extended all the way to Ogre, he decided to pull himself, hand over hand, until he had reached the very spot where it was anchored. The life support umbilical would take him another hundred feet or so, but there was no point in waiting until the last moment to detach it. To reach Ogre, he would need to rely on his suit's oxygen tanks.

The massive asteroid loomed larger and larger as he approached. Looking behind him, the mining tug, *Hattie*, grew smaller, the dim view ports seated between her bright search lamps a thin membrane between himself and the warm, familiar companionship of his friends.

But were they his friends?

Not really, said a voice. *Don't trust Fex Neil.*

"What did you say?"

"Wexner? I missed that. What did you say?" asked Forthright.

"I thought *you* said something," said Jep.

"Not me. Hold on. I'm getting some curious readings. They're too small to be ships. Maybe your Far Marshall's search probes have finally made it here after all."

"Should I come back inside, now?"

Yes. Go back, Jep.

"Your voice is faint. I'm coming back."

"No, no! Keep heading for Ogre. The captain says we're right on track if you keep moving. Can you see the cable anchor?"

Jep turned around and looked at the massive wall of stone again. Perspective was very tricky, but the asteroid seemed to be at least another hundred meters distant.

"I've got a way to go yet. I can use my jets to speed up."

"Be careful."

"I will."

Holding the cable in one hand, and extending the other to brace for collision, in case the asteroid's surface proved closer than expected, he propelled himself towards it.

"Wexner? This is Captain Neil."

Jep recognised the captain's voice, although it crackled a bit, perhaps caused by static from his friction against the line. Oof. He felt himself smash into a massive shadow of unyielding rock. Displaced pink powder fogged the surface, further hindering perspective.

"I've reached Ogre," he said.

"Wexner, we've detected some suspicious probes."

"I told you the Far Marshall—"

"They can't be the Far Marshall's probes. The power signatures imply they must have been launched from someplace close. I'm afraid they may mean pirates. We've got to cut the cable on this end."

"You're going to strand me here?"

"Only for a little while, pal. We've got to pray they haven't seen us yet. We'll have to cut lights and radio, too. But don't worry, we're not going to leave you out any longer than necessary."

"Wait! Hello? Captain Neil? Forthright?"

Radio silence. One by one, the lights on the *Hattie* went dark. Jep stared into the hole in space where it had been and wondered…was it even still there? A shadow glided across his peripheral vision, blocking the stars. Was it another asteroid? or a pirate ship? In a panic, he suddenly wondered, was it the *Hattie?*

I'm sorry, son. I'm sorry I couldn't warn you in time, said the voice.

Son? Jep pondered, and the impossible thought stunned his heart.

He shut off his microphone to confirm the voice he was hearing wasn't coming over the radio. The sound of his respirator became more muffled, and his adrenaline-amplified pulse throbbed in his ears.

"Is that you, Mom?"

It's me, said the faint voice.

"Where are you? How is it I can hear you?"

You know very well I've always been a telepath.

"But we're lightyears apart!" Jep paused to consider. "Was Psi-Sec right, Mom? Were you always more powerful than you let on?"

Maybe, although I genuinely wasn't aware of it at the time. But the psi-jammer they put on me has forced my abilities to stretch.

"So, you're a level three, now?"

Psi-Sec has level threes. I'm a level four. I've joined a Hive Mind. That's how we can reach across such vast distances; it's more like a level-four relay. Something around you seems to be helping.

"The pink gappite!" Jep intuited. Ogre was oozing with it.

Given the distractions of his predicament, all this new information was a lot to process. As a break in the clouds appeared *above* him, a bright streak of starlight illuminated two large asteroids floating in tandem, well above the ring—perhaps Rhino and another of the valuable prizes the crew of the *Hattie* had arranged into a longer ore train. The piezo-stabilisers were gradually drawing all the linked asteroids together, condensing the load while converting angular momentum into power stored for the tug engine attached to the leading asteroid.

I'm sorry I couldn't warn you in time about Pontifex Neil, said Iris.

The captain's betrayal stung the most, but the whole crew had to have been in on the ruse. Why so elaborate? Jep guessed that having learned that the Far Marshall was involved, they had anticipated the high probability of a future investigation. They needed to play the charade 'til the end.

"Never mind, Mom," said Jep. "I'm just grateful that I don't have to die alone, like Dad. I just wish your more powerful telepathy had come months ago, so that you could have comforted him, too." Jep felt tears welling up as he surveyed his hostile surroundings and predicament. Pink snow was beginning to accumulate on the outside of his suit. Vance-Epsilon's vast blue sphere beckoned like a suicide jump from an impossibly high bridge.

Son, one of the cable ends released by the Hattie will recoil into the asteroid right where you are clinging. You need to jump out of the way NOW!

Panicked, Jep sprang away from the wall of stone at what he hoped was a 45-degree angle. Seeing nothing but stars including the brilliant star, Vance, ahead of him, he realised he was now sailing, unmoored, through space. He activated braking jets and then turned back to face Ogre. The only sign of the almost invisible cable striking the asteroid, now shockingly far away, was a thin bloom of powder still rising from the impact. The distance to Vance-Epislon, appeared unchanged.

Jep's heart was racing, but he remembered from his EVA training that he was supposed to keep unnecessary movements to a minimum. It occurred to him as he drifted how much more comforting it had been to have a bit of rock to cling to—not only an anchor, but a shield on one side.

Then a completely separate question occurred to him: How did you know about the cable, Mom?

Captain Neil expected it to kill you.

Jep's heart sank and he sighed. "You tried to warn me about him back at the saloon, Mom, but I couldn't believe it was you. I didn't listen."

You told me not to give up after I was arrested, son, said Iris. *Don't you give up either.*

"I'm sorry I never found Dad's body, Mom," said Jep, his voice cracking.

Never mind that, Jep, said his mother, soothingly. *Your dad had a secret too, you know. Sometimes, he could see the future, so I believe, maybe he saw it coming.*

"Really?"

Who knows? Based on what happened to me, the Hive Mind think that his powers might have improved under duress, too. Maybe he even saw your future.

"That just makes me sadder," said Jep. He sniffled and futilely wiped the back of his gloves against his face shield. He wished he could wipe his eyes and nose. "Mom. Try searching Captain Neil's memories. See if he knows what happened to Dad; where Dad died."

I can't, Jep. I wish I could, but I can barely read surface thoughts at this range, and that's only with the entire Hive Mind helping. I'm sorry, son, I love you with all my heart, but I've got to go, now. They won't let me stay any longer. There are a thousand other tasks which need our collective attention. We've decided to overthrow Psi-Sec.

"Wait, don't go!" Jep cried.

Silence.

Jep glimpsed another moving shadow blocking the stars in his peripheral vision. Turning, he realised he had drifted much closer to the ore train. Attached to the lead asteroid would be the tug engine. As he recalled, the captain's plan had been to steer the linked asteroids into a gravity-boosting pass around Vance-Epsilon to pick up speed before rejoining to lead it into hyperspace. He momentarily fantasised about clinging to the train and tagging along on that wild ride, before accepting that he could never survive the g-forces, even if his dwindling heat and oxygen could last so long.

Even so…he toggled the propulsion jets on his suit, pushing closer to the train as an idea slowly occurred to him. Loosening a single cable anchor on one of those linked asteroids with his multi-tool could destabilise and "derail" the entire train. If he had to die, perhaps he could at least extract some minor revenge.

Jep steered in a slow arc, ending parallel to the procession of asteroids, intending to minimise any impact from his landing near one of the middle asteroids. He aligned himself beside the one with the smoothest surface, named Troll Bum. The train was already travelling quite fast, bleeding pink gasses from its tail like a comet. Every bit of kinetic energy absorbed from disparate tensions between the great rocks was being channelled into a feedback loop through the stabilisers, with synergistic overflow powering the tug engine. As Jep drew nearer the caravan of rocks, he felt himself unexpectedly accelerating towards it, sucked in by its gravity, or perhaps even by some magnetic field generated by the piezo-stabilisers. In a panic, he fired all his pulse jets full blast to break his fall. His jets soon exhausted, he landed in a gentle, tumbling crash against the moving, cratered mountain.

After coming to a stop and collecting his wits, Jep tried to push upright, but discovered unexpected resistance. Wedging his feet underneath him, he rose slowly to his feet and then marvelled at the surreal experience of surfing atop a hurtling necklace of asteroids, a gossamer tide of pink gasses washing over his boots.

Turning slowly to take in the surroundings from this new vantage, Jep confirmed that the rock caravan was, indeed, arcing towards the gas giant's perimeter. Although the Flamingo Boa was largely translucent at this range and angle, it left a belt-like shadow on the planet's upper clouds, reminding Jep of a deep, black crevasse. Continuing clockwise, he spotted the piezo-stabilising cables stretched taut from anchors further ahead, over cratered rock hills painted with his double shadow, and back through space towards the trailing asteroids. To his rear was the behemoth which the *Hattie's* crew had dubbed "Rhino," owing to its horn-like protuberances. And beyond that—

Jep crouched instinctively upon suddenly recognising the silhouette of the mining tug *Hattie*, partially eclipsed by Rhino. It seemed that the ship's outer lights were still off. Were they truly hiding from pirates? Staying low, Jep began jogging diagonally towards the cable anchor, hurrying to resume his task of sabotage. As he exerted himself, his boots kicked up a slushy ice powder, and a low, slow beep sounded in his ear, alerting him about the dangerous depletion-rate of his oxygen reserves. Glancing backwards, Jep saw that his boot prints had left a clear trail from the point of his touchdown. He slowed down to think. His plummeting life-support resources meant that his sabotage couldn't wait. But if it was accomplished too soon before the slingshot, there might still be time for the *Hattie* crew to notice and repair the damage before the asteroid chain wheeled disastrously out of control. In that event, even if his frozen corpse were never found, the trail of boot prints would mark his failed sabotage like a pathetic signature; a mute howl of impotent rage. What did it matter?

Unless they were overlooked because of these other boot prints.

Jep did a double-take, stared backwards at his own path, and then stared down again at a new set of footprints, not his own. Could they be his father's boot prints? Abandoning caution and conservation, Jep hurried along the new path, to the rhythm of increasingly strident beeping in his ears. Prompted more by emotion than logic, he kept glancing wishfully into shadows and craters along the way for any traces of his father's corpse. Following the trail into a wide crater, the boot prints began to wander crazily. Had his father gone mad?

Zig-zagging doggedly, he finally caught a glint of metal and a flash of unnaturally bright colours: white and blue, and not long after, arrived at his father's frozen corpse, under a glittering pink sheet of snow. The facemask was webbed with cracks, making it impossible to see the shadowy face under the shield, and his suit was slashed open. Jep wished that he could have seen his father's face one last time. Would there be an expression of pain? Sadness? Anger?

Considering that it could do no harm, Jep impulsively reached for the multi-tool at his waist to smash the face shield, just to claim one final look at his father's face. It was a shocking sight, and he immediately regretted his choice: features were burned, the skin split and partially crystallised, both eye-sockets sunken—of course, he realised, this degradation would have occurred in the months since his death. More shockingly—and his father's trademark cheek scar confirmed that this was no trick of rictus—his father had died smiling.

Puzzled, Jep studied the winding path by which he

had come, imagining his father staggering drunkenly with delirium. But wait. No, not delirium. The trod marks spelled out letters: *Iris*. Sentiment rather than instructions had dictated his father's final efforts. Max Wexner had plainly foreseen his own doom.

Hot tears fell, stopping only when Jep's breaths became wheezes. The beeping tone in his ears had finally halted, converted into a clicking, S.O.S. signal, doubtless being broadcasted on all frequencies into space. Sorrowfully, Jep lay down across the corpse, wishing vainly to extract a grieving hug, but finding the rock-hard form disappointingly alien and unsatisfying to squeeze. Kneeling, Jep settled instead for squeezing his father's stiff hand goodbye. He had to dig it out of the snow.

That was when he discovered something clutched under the glove. In fact, there were two objects: a narrow, red cylinder and a small, metal disk.

Jep pulled both free, then held each in turn up close to his faceplate. He needed to blink hard and repeatedly before he could make out any details. The cylinder was a battery. His father had extracted his own life-support battery. Why?

Iris had said her husband could sometimes foresee the future. Inspired, he took his multi-tool and, using it to unscrew the cap containing his own life-support battery, swapped the two. Fresh oxygen flooded his lungs, clearing his head. Jep smiled for the first time in weeks. Could his father have foreseen this moment's crisis and realised a way to buy his son another ten minutes of life? Had Max Wexner, in fact, even deliberately picked this asteroid to die on, out of millions? Jep examined the metal disk. It looked familiar. Indeed, he soon recognised it as a holo-disk, exactly the sort which Benschmann stored by the dozen in his holo-vid collection, or which Jep had been given for some of his training sessions, including EVA training. What could finding it under his father's hand mean? Whereas a trainee helmet like Jep's contained a slot for playing holo-disks, his father's ordinary helmet had no corresponding slot. Where had it even been stored?

Jep's eyes drifted to the slit in his father's suit, and a scenario occurred to him. After removing his own life support battery, Max Wexner must have slit open his own suit to retrieve the disk stored on his person expressly to be delivered now, to his son. Ironically, if this were true, it meant that Pluto Mining Corp's default presumption of his father's suicide happened to be technically correct. But more significantly, his father had gone to great effort to deliver this holo-disk.

The implications of this realisation made Jep's hands shake with anticipation. Almost fumbling the object in his excitement, Jep installed the disk into his helmet and activated the recording.

His father's face appeared, looking directly into the camera. His face was strangely serene—almost mystical. He was wearing an ordinary flight suit, strapped into the pilot's chair of what Jep now recognised as the Iris.

As he began to speak, Max's eyes sparkled. Initially sad, they soon brightened.

"Jep, the second file on this disk is for your mother's eyes only, but I'll tell you the gist: I love her, have always loved her, and regret more than anything that I will never hold her in my arms again. The rest of this message is for you.

"I have had predictive visions all my life. I've never told anyone about this, but, not surprisingly, your mother eventually learned all of my secrets. Sadly, I left Earth partly to put some distance between us. I was a fool.

"My powers gave me a slight edge, but since I discovered a hyper-path to the Vance system, my visions have increased in frequency and accuracy. Gappite definitely plays some role, though I never figured out exactly how.

"Recently, I foresaw my own death. I explored alternative paths with slightly different outcomes, but none spared my life. If any path would have let me come home to your mother, I would have taken it. From the point of that realisation, I dedicated my choices to those that would benefit your future. Obviously, our paths are connected. I have foreseen your coming to Phoenix Station to investigate my death. I have preset the autopilot on my ship so that it will be waiting for you. I have foreseen your peril at that hands of that greedy Captain, Fex Neil and the crew of the *Hattie*. I have foreseen your crisis and devised a means for your survival by orchestrating the place and time of my death. I intended for you to find this holo-vid.

"I cannot see much further into your future, but one powerful insight I've had portends an exciting possibility. My foresight and your mother's telepathy are both genetic advantages we've passed on to you. Your own abilities are latent, but the gappite, son..the gappite...may awaken them.

"I love you. I'll hide one more prize for you inside my suit. Now stay alive."

Jep removed the holovid disk and looked around. The *Hattie* was no longer nearby. Intuitively, he glanced towards Kirth, one of Vance-Epsilon's larger moons, and spotted a moving pinpoint of light which he sensed was the mining tug. The ore train upon which he was a passenger was now accelerating so rapidly towards the planet, that he was beginning to detect a shift in perspective towards the Flamingo Boa. The clouds seemed to be thickening as the cosmic ring slowly ascended from his perspective and became more distant.

Jep reached through the gash into his father's space suit and felt around for the mystery prize Max had planned to leave for him. His fingers closed around a metallic rectangle. Before even looking at it, he knew what it was. A remote control for Iris.

Jep shut his eyes and concentrated. In the distance, the *Hattie's* cargo bay doors opened as if of their own accord, and the jump-ship was jettisoned. Somewhere, out of hearing, Jep imagined Captain Fex Neil screaming that if they didn't recover the jettisoned ship, it would take them fifty years or until the first PMC carriers arrived before they could return home.

His eyes still closed, Jep let his fingers roam the control keys. Smiling, he realised there was no need for him to touch them at all to steer the Iris. Soon, the craft was hovering just above him, opening its doors. A vision appeared to him, and he let the doors close again. First rising to his feet, he opened them again and looked around. The twinkling star to his left was Phoenix Station. Beside him was the PMC refinery. Leaving the ore-train parked outside, he teleported directly into the office of the CEO for a brief chat.

SHAWN M. KLIMEK is the middle child of seven creative siblings, a globetrotting, U.S. military spouse, award-winning author and poet, and butler to a Maltese.

More than one hundred of his works have been published since 2018, including stories in BHP anthologies, Deep Space, Eerie Christmas, and a full five stories in each of the first six books in the internationally best-selling, Dark Drabbles series.

Bibliography
ANGELS, Black Hare Press, 2019
BEYOND, Black Hare Press, 2019
Blaze, Clarendon House Books, 2019
Curses & Cauldrons, Blood Song Books, 2019
Deep Space, Black Hare Press, 2019
Flash Fiction Addiction, Zombie Pirate Publishing, 2019
Full Metal Horror, Zombie Pirate Publishing, 2019
Grumpy Old Gods, Vol. 1, Storm Dance Publications, 2019
Grumpy Old Gods, Vol. 2, Storm Dance Publications, 2019
MONSTERS, Black Hare Press, 2019
Organic Ink, Vol. 1, Dragon Soul Press, 2019
Poetica, Clarendon House Books, 2019
Sea Glass Hearts, Stormy Island Publishing, 2019
Tempest, Clarendon House Books, 2019
World War Four, Zombie Pirate Publishing, 2019
WORLDS, Black Hare Press, 2019

Connect
Website: JotInTheDark.blogspot.com
Amazon: amazon.com/Shawn-Klimek/e/B07MYMBJKS
Facebook: @shawnmklimekauthor

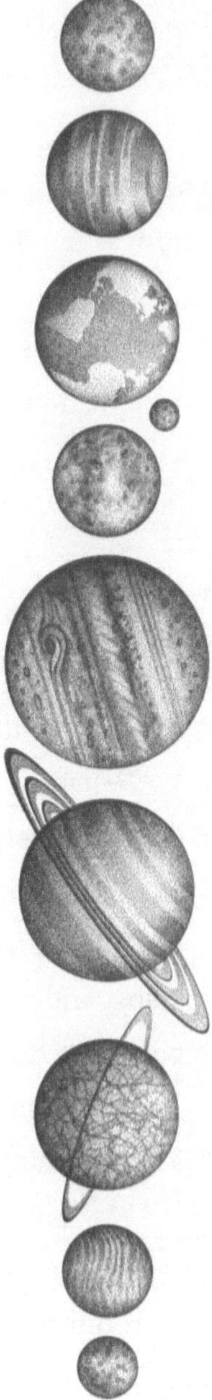

NOT MY VESSEL

By Marcus Cook

Seven-foot tall with reptilian skin and webbed hands and feet, Shain is a feared warrior and top-notch pilot. When he suddenly turns into a female human, he and the misfit crew of the *Ménage a Quatre* must travel the universe to find out why.

"You missed! Now the pilot knows we escaped," Mnogo Kashi screamed as he flailed his four tentacles from behind Shain's pilot seat.

"This ship isn't built for me," Shain yelled back while attempting to pilot the Ika warship.

"It's your ship," Mnogo pointed out.

"Yes, and I can fly it superbly when

I'm in my own body. This ship was designed for a human body. I need a moment to adjust."

Shain shoved the controller tightly between his knees, put on target goggles, and waited until the Sasori ship was between the crosshairs. He fired, and the ship exploded.

"Now we are free," Shain hollered as the ship sped through empty space.

"So basically, the job is loading and unloading of freight to and from the *Ménage a Quatre*."

"What is that?" the Bakarian asked.

"What is what?" Shain replied, confused by the Bakarian's confusion.

"The Ménage a Cow Tree?"

"The *Ménage a Quatre*? That's my ship. You will be loading and unloading freight to and from it," Shain repeated.

"Oh. Is this the Ménage a Cold Train?" the Bakarian said, continuing his idiotic questioning,

"No, but it is the *Ménage a Quatre*." Shain felt a sudden urge to open an air hatch and have the Bakarian blown out into space. He doubted anyone would miss him. The only thing stopping him was the fact that the

Bakarian people were non-stop workers with immeasurable strength. The labour cost is cut in half when you have one on your crew.

"And when will I be having sex?" the Bakarian asked, flexing his chest muscles.

"I don't care what you do in your free time. Just when you are working, I prefer you not having sex."

"I mean when will *we* be having the sex?" the Bakarian repeated as he started to untie the strap holding up his pants.

"Sit back down and don't you dare pull that thing out!" Shain warned.

The Bakarian's face saddened, his head dropped and he sat back in his chair. "You do not find Tyhma sexy?"

Shain saw he had hurt his feelings, and a sad Bakarian is an unproductive Bakarian. "Oh, for sure you are sexy. With your tight skin covering your chiselled body, your perfect teeth and long flowing hair. Not to mention that I'm sure you are well endowed."

The Bakarian started to undo his pants again.

"No. Not sexy time," Shain said hurriedly, "I'm not a woman. I'm not even human."

"If you find me repulsive, please tell me. Do not try to make up excuses," Tyhma barked testily.

"No, really. I'm actually an Ikarian male. Imagine me three feet taller, red reptilian body, a horn in the middle of my head and spikes running down my spine. My hands were webbed before, and my feet hooved. My manhood was long and spiky," Shain reminisced.

The Bakarian stared emotionlessly at Shain as if he were trying his best to imagine the described creature. Suddenly, he burst out laughing. "You are a funny, sexy woman with succulent breasts. Maybe we have the sex when we return to deep space?"

"Okay. Good talk. Would you like a tour of the ship now?" Shain said, giving up. If the Bakarian touched him, Shain would shoot his manhood off.

"Which ship?" Tyhma asked.

Shain sighed. "Just follow me." He stood and headed out of the mess hall. As he led the way through the narrow cylinder-shaped hallways, he had a feeling the Bakarian was staring at his ass.

When they passed through another doorway and into the loading area, Shain could hear his co-pilot complaining.

"They want 62 cuebits just for air. We didn't even use this space dock's air and yet we're being charged for it!" Mnogo Kashi exclaimed.

Shain believed that Mnogo was the smartest being he knew, and loved watching his head swish around in the tank of liquid to which he was attached. Like one of Earth's jellyfish, wires draped down from his mushroom top to control pads on the edges of the helmet. With the exception of his head and tubular shaped arms, he was entirely robotic.

"Can we discuss this later? We have a guest."

Mnogo adjusted his transparent eyes and the Bakarian came into focus. "Oh great, another body to waste our ship's resources."

"I do not waste. Everything I use is for the good of me," Tyhma responded.

Shain could see Mnogo's colour go from blue to red. "Why don't we go over to the med bay?"

Shain grabbed the Bakarian by the arm and led him away.

"I do not need the med bay. I am in top physical shape. I have been told I am in the top one percent of humanoid creatures, in fact."

"Yeah, well it's standard procedure that the doctor has to give you the okay. I can't have you dying on your first day," Shain said as the doors leading to another tube hallway slid open. After a few moments, they reached the med bay and the doors opened on a rotund room with an examination table in the middle of it, surrounded by monitors, medical cabinets, and shelves of books.

Tyhma noticed a tank of water, big enough to hold a human, in the back of the room. "Is that where your aquatic friend sleeps?" the Bakarian chuckled.

"Mnogo is self-contained. That is my sleeping quarters," Dr. Mizu Scelerat responded as she entered the Medical bay.

The Bakarian stared at the female doctor as she walked across the room. Although her greyish blue skin was covered with her lab coat and scrubs, his eyes never left her breasts, ignoring her dolphin-like facial features and her hair of wiry dreads.

"Dr. Scelerat, I've got another candidate for our docking bay job," Shain announced.

"Another Bakarian? Really?" the doctor replied, obviously dismayed by the captain's choice.

"You have other Bakarian's working here?" Tyhma asked, excited at the possibility of working with his brethren.

"Not anymore."

"Because they died within twenty-four hours of leaving the space dock," Dr. Scelerat added.

"You are Delphinidin. Maybe we could have the sex before we leave the space dock," the Bakarian said, changing the subject.

The doctor became enraged. "Delphinidin! How dare you? Do you see a blowhole? And no to the sex; your body disgusts me."

"My body doesn't disgust anybody. Ask the captain," Tyhma protested.

"Captain, does the Bakarian body disgust you?" Dr. Scelerat asked, staring Shain down.

"Um, well the naked body is like a piece of art. Not everyone likes the same piece." Shain hoped his answer would placate the doctor and not offend the Bakarian.

"Hold on...that's because you haven't seen my piece." The Bakarian quickly removed his clothing and stood in front of Shain completely naked. "Is this not a work of art that brings you joy?"

Shain regretted the metaphor immediately. "Put that thing away. I don't want to ever see it again. Next time, I will push you out the exhaust port."

The Bakarian shook his head in disbelief and bent to grab his clothing off the floor, but Dr. Scelerat stopped him.

"Wait. Remain naked and get on the examination table," she instructed.

"Now we are getting somewhere." The Bakarian happily hopped onto the table.

Dr. Scelerat placed a sheet over his crotch, then started to run a diagnostic check over his body. A black and green grid pattern hovered over him, dividing his body into sections. The doctor tapped one grid and a 3D picture of that section enlarged. As information digitally listed next to the image, the doctor took her time to make notes.

Shain leaned against the medical bay wall and watched the doctor focus on Tyhma's chest, arms and legs. The Bakarian had six or seven layers of muscle on top of muscle, and Shain thought he'd probably be impressed if he really was a woman.

"Am I able to get copy of these pictures? I like to frame them and send them to my momma," Tyhma asked as he admired his innards.

"Why stop at your momma? Why not send a copy to all your family?" Shain jested.

"That is ridiculous." Dr. Scelerat shook her head.

"I know, very silly," Tyhma agreed, "Of course, my momma will make the copies for the family and pass them out on Bakarian Winter Welcome."

The doctor rolled her eyes. "I assume you don't really want copies of your intestines and such. We are just making a joke?"

"Bakarian's do not joke about our bodies. We are proud of our perfection. Even my faeces are the best they can be."

Dr. Scelerat turned off the machine. "He is ready to go. Perfect health, great attitude."

"Good to hear. Please put your clothes back on, Tyhma, and then I'll take you to the docking and storage bays."

The Bakarian stood, letting the sheet fall to his feet.

"So, I get the job?" he asked.

"Yes. You start immediately," Shain said, trying not to look at his naked new crew member.

While the Bakarian got dressed, the doctor spoke quietly with Shain. "How are you doing today?"

"Nipples hurt and I'm cramping," Shain said.

"Maybe you're starting your menstruation cycle," the doctor suggested.

"Again! Let me tell you how grateful I am to be put in this blood-producing body," Shain growled.

"More like an egg-producing body. Do I need to explain the process to you again?" the doctor teased.

"No! Please don't. I got it on the third time." Shain flushed, embarrassed at discussing the process at all.

"Would you like a shot to relieve the pain?" the doctor asked.

"Yes." Shain pulled up his shirt.

Doctor Scelerat had always admired humans, and she couldn't help feeling a little jealous that the captain had turned into one. The captain may find it to be a nuisance, but she thought it was a gift. Mizu grabbed a syringe and took a moment to run her hands across Shain's abs. The captain took care of his body and the doctor was pleased.

"Are you just teasing me with a shot?" Shain asked.

The doctor quickly poked her captain. "No."

Dr. Scelerat then walked away as the Bakarian returned fully dressed. "I am ready to work."

"Follow me." Shain walked ahead of him out of the medical bay and over to a lift.

The two entered the tight pod when it arrived, and Shain pressed a button which caused the pod to drop suddenly.

"Yahoo!" Tyhma shouted until the pod reopened and they arrived in the huge cargo bay.

The Bakarian stepped out first and began to look around his new surroundings. "This is where I will work?"

"You brought me a rocket scientist, I see," a mechanical voice squeaked.

The Bakarian had trouble identifying where the voice was coming from at first, but then he looked down and saw a two-foot, furry red rat that resembled a child's stuffed animal.

"Is this one of your dolls?" the Bakarian inquired, "Am I invited to a tea party?"

"Shain, why do you keep hiring these idiots in meat suits?" the red rat asked, shaking its head in disbelief.

"RED, you know we get the most progress with a Bakarian," Shain said, pointing at the Bakarian.

"Your name is RED? Would it be BLUE if you were blue?" Tyhma asked.

"No, it would still be RED. Robotic Engineer Digibot," RED explained.

"Okay, teddy bear. What would you like me to do?" Tyhma asked as he removed his shirt.

"Live long enough to get to the first delivery point," RED mumbled.

"Why do you all suggest I am going to die? I am very careful in my job." Tyhma lifted a large crate to demonstrate his power. Three small mouse-like creatures dropped out onto the floor. Tyhma watched as two scurried off and one remained. It stared up at him with big brown eyes.

"How cute!" The Bakarian's voice echoed through the docking bay.

"Don't touch that!" Shain yelled, his hands raised, motioning for Tyhma not to move.

"It is a mouse. I am not afraid of a tiny mouse. Is it your brother, RED?" the Bakarian asked as he placed the crate down. He bent over to get a closer look.

"It is not a mouse. It is a mayhew," RED explained, "Do not touch it."

"Is that like the captain is not a woman and you are not a child's toy?" Tyhma mocked.

"Yes. Just like that. Except, this 'mouse' spits acid and you will become a puddle of blood within seconds of contact," Shain whispered.

The Bakarian chuckled and reached out but then the mayhew suddenly opened its mouth and spat yellow gunk at Tyhma's throat.

"Gro—" Tyhma started to say as he reached up to wipe his neck. A quick burning sensation started to cover his body, and before he could say anything else, he was liquified, his body just a splash upon the ground.

Shain and RED watched as the other two mayhew's joined the third one and began to eat Tyhma's remains.

Shain glanced at the device on his wrist, "Three hours and twenty minutes. He survived the longest."

"That's 'cause you kept him in the med bay for longer," Red retorted as he started to press buttons on a panel. The first button caused the floor to become magnetised, securing everything made of metal, including the captain's boots. Another button closed a pair of heavily reinforced doors in front of them. The final button opened the bay doors and air and debris were sucked out into space. The two watched as the mayhew attempted to hold on, but were quickly blown out with the puddle of skin and plasma that used to be Tyhma. RED then pressed another button and the doors closed again and the area demagnetised.

Shain returned to the pod and rode it back to the mess hall. Mnogo was sitting at the table with a tube running from the bottom edge of his helmet to a bowl on the table in front of him where some sort of larvae was squirming around.

"I must say, your dinner never makes me ask for some." Shain chuckled as he sat down.

"You blasted the Bakarian out the docking bay doors?" Mnogo asked as Shain watched several of the larvae swim around in Mnogo's helmet while he attempted to catch them with his tentacles.

"Technically, we did."

"Technically?"

"He was eaten by some mayhews and we shot the mayhews into space." Shain stood back up and walked over to the freezer, pulling out two large slabs of meat and laying them in the sink where he started to run hot water over them. Once the meat was defrosted, he placed it on a serving tray and returned to sit with his co-pilot.

"And you say I'm unappetising to watch eat?" Mnogo pointed out as Shain began to eat the raw meat.

"I am still technically Ikarian," Shain stated.

"Only your brain. That body is human. If you eat like an Ikarian, your athletic build will become a blob," Mnogo retorted.

Shain stopped chewing, spat the meat onto the plate, and glared at his jellyfish friend. "Couldn't just let me eat in peace, could you?"

Shain stood up and dumped his dinner in the trash

compactor.

"You probably could have grilled it," Mnogo pointed out.

Shain shook his head. "It wouldn't be the same."

Shain left the mess hall and headed to the cockpit.

The cockpit consisted of three leather chairs, with the pilot's chair and the ship's controls set in front of a large dome-shaped window.

Mnogo's position was directly behind Shain's. If a space battle occurred, Shain's chair would drop into a gun turret and the co-pilot's chair slid over into the pilot's slot. From his position at the rear of the bridge, RED monitored navigation and communications.

Shain sat in his chair and brought up the daily docket onto the screen.

"Sasori 5. Medical supplies delivery, cadaver pick-up." The screen displayed. Shain stared at the docket. It had been some time since he'd escaped Sasori Prime, and now he would be delivering to a Sasorian Medical Station. It wasn't by accident; Shain had paid the original courier service to let them have it. He needed to find out what had happened to him. He had been a mighty soldier and top fighter pilot, now he was a female human—but still a great fighter, even it was a challenge to work around having breasts. But still, every morning when he awakens, Shain hopes to see his old self looking back in the mirror.

Satisfied that his plans were coming together, Shain flipped off the monitor and headed back to his quarters.

As the doors slid open, Shain could see that a familiar body was lying across his bed.

"Can I ask why you are in my bed?' Shain asked as he walked over to the sidebar and poured a glass of Shershenian Vodka.

"I'll let you guess," Dr. Scelerat said, rising naked.

Shain found the doctor's greyish blue skin beautiful and sexy but, with his internal struggle to find out who he was, choosing a partner was far from his mind.

"Oh, I have a wonderful guess...I just have a rule that I don't have sex with crew."

"I've noticed...you don't have sex with anybody," the doctor said, climbing from the bed. "What's wrong, Shain?"

Shain was surprised the doctor used his first name. "Oh, are we on first name terms now?"

"I've been on your crew for close to three years, and I am your doctor. So, yes, we are on first name terms," she said, placing her hands on his shoulders.

"Okay, Mizu." Shain downed his drink and sat on

the edge of the bed. "I'm not sure who or what I'm supposed to have sex with? I mean, what gender am I? My brain is me. I was a male, but now I have a female body. I am still turned on by other females...you included."

Mizu picked up her clothes and started to dress. "I can see how this is all so confusing to you. You just have to understand that you are what you believe you are. You were born a man, but now you are in a female body. Yet you are still you."

"Am I?" Shain frowned.

Mizu sat down next to him. "You are strong-willed, a born leader. Men and women respect you. As far as your confusion; love is love. Everything feels it, and when you feel that attraction to someone, that is what you should decide on. Man, woman...whatever Mnogo is."

Shain smiled. "Thank yo—"

Mizu cut him off with a deep and passionate kiss which Shain returned, and then they frantically started to remove each other's clothing. But after just a few moments, the doorbell rang out and, without waiting for an invite, Mnogo entered the room.

"Are you crazy?" Mnogo exclaimed as he entered, not noticing Shain and Mizu at first.

"Mnogo, don't you knock?" Shain asked, grabbing his shirt.

Mnogo suddenly noticed the ship's doctor, half

naked on Shain's bed. "I rang the bell," and then, as realisation of the situation sank in, "Are you *crazy?*"

"Shhh! Mnogo enough. Nothing happened," Shain said.

"How would it? You don't have the parts." Mnogo's jell membrane turned violet.

"Well, I have things in the medical bay to replace what's missing," Mizu grinned.

"I don't want to know," Mnogo said, his head sloshing from side to side.

"Neither do I," Shain agreed. "Now, what is so important you had to barge into my sleeping quarters like a rabid goldfish?" he asked, turning back to the co-pilot.

Mnogo was so distraught by the current situation that he had almost forgotten. "Why are we making a delivery to a Sasori Medical Station?"

"They offered money. I took the job." Shain walked over to the bar and refilled his glass.

"I know you are going through changes, Shain, but let me remind you that we have hefty bounties on our heads on Sasori 5," Mnogo said, body turning blue.

"And why is that?" Shain countered, taking a sip of his drink.

"We are escaped prisoners of war," Mnogo answered.

"You might be, but I'm not. My people were never, and

still are not, at war with the Sasorian. I remember waking up in their hospital and then waking up later in this body. I have no memories of how I got there or why I was imprisoned in this body." Shain downed another drink.

"I think you need to take this job and find out; you will never accept who and what you are until those questions are answered," Mizu offer as she pulled on her shoes.

"Thank you," Shain replied as he gave Mnogo a victory glare.

"Whatever, I'm locking myself in my quarters once we arrive," Mnogo declared

Shain shook his head. "Alright let's get some sleep. We have a long day ahead of us."

As Shain showered the next morning, he thought through his plans for when he arrived at the Sasorian Medical Station—how he was going to find his medical files, how he would get them out of the facility...how he would feel about the contents

He stepped out of the shower and stared at his foggy reflection in the steamed-up mirror. That's how he saw himself; in a fog. He wiped the condensation away and came face to face with a reddish-blonde haired, silky milk-skinned woman with an attractively curvaceous body, and he was reminded of how the Bakarian couldn't keep his eyes off his breasts.

He sighed. Would he ever be himself again, or would this be his new shell forever?

Mnogo interrupted his thoughts. "Captain. We are ready for departure," came his voice over the communicator.

"Be there in ten."

After putting on a new jumpsuit, Shain headed to the bridge where he found Mnogo and RED waiting for him.

"Good morning, Captain. All cargo is ready for delivery in Bay 1. Bays 2 and 3 are ready to receive. Bay 3's temperature is set to hold the cadavers," RED reported.

"Excellent job, as always," Shain commended as he sat in the pilot's chair.

"Course set for Sasori 5 Medical Station, Alto Mega," Mnogo added. "It is about 2 parsecs away, so we should arrive by brunch."

"So, where should we stop for breakfast?" Shain joked as he readied the controls.

"Is he serious?" RED whispered to Mnogo.

"No. Ever since he was put in that human skin bag, he has started with stupid jokes," Mnogo explained.

"Okay," RED replied. "Any place with chicken and waffles, Captain."

Shain smiled appreciating RED's attempt at joining in the conversation. "Vilo 7 Control, this is *Ménage a Quatre* requesting de-docking codes."

"*Ménage a Quatre,* de-docking codes, M-C-S-45. I also would like to add you have a very sexy voice," came the voice over his headset.

"Thank you, Control. I must say yours isn't bad either," Shain said, returning the compliment.

"Next time you are around Vilo 5, would you like to have a drink?" Control wondered.

"Depends...do you have two eyes, or three?" Shain asked.

"Three. Two blue, one green."

"Oh, I'm sorry. I only go for Viloarians with two eyes. Good luck to you. *Ménage a Quatre* de-docking." Shain flipped off the communicator, giggling as he blushed.

"You were flirting with that man," Mnogo said, appalled.

"I was not." Shain punched the code into the control panel and the crew watched as a large mechanical claw released itself from the ship.

"Your skin is as red as my fur," RED pointed out.

"I suggest we all drop this conversation before I shave one of you and drain the other," Shain threatened as he pulled the ship away from the dock. When the ship was a safe distance from Vilo 5, he pressed a red button, igniting the rockets, and blasted off into open space.

"Don't take anything personally; his human woman-body is shedding its eggs. He's a little moody," Mnogo whispered to RED who grimaced.

"Remember you guys will have to sleep sometime. So please, keep up with the jokes," Shain threatened.

RED and Mnogo remained silent for the rest of the flight.

A few hours later, the *Ménage a Quatre* approached a floating, domed-shape space station orbiting Sasori 5's third moon, Gorudo Sahn. From the ship's bridge, Shain could see the large complexes that made up the Sasori Prime Medical Station—it was the size of one of Earth's Midwest cities. Ships of different shapes and sizes buzzed in and out of the dome. He started to feel anxious about finding enough pieces to solve the mystery of what happened to his life.

"We are an unarmed cargo ship, please do not fire!" a woman's voice echoed in Shain's head.

"It's a lie. They are fully loaded!" a heavy male voice

roared.

"Please! We have women and children onboard, along with food and medical supplies. We're heading to Vohan 3. Do not fire." The woman's voice got louder.

"Fire, Captain! Before it jumps. They are traitors to the cause, and if they jump, you will be tried as a traitor," the man yelled.

"Target locked."

"Ménage a Quatre, we have you on our scope and are scanning the cargo to the manifest. Please, hold your course until confirmation," a friendly mechanical voice instructed, snapping Shain back to reality.

"Thank you, Sasori Prime. We await your further instructions," Shain responded.

"Did you fall asleep?" RED asked.

"What?" Shain replied, confused.

"Your pulse dropped on your vitals for a few minutes. I think you dozed off."

"I'm piloting the ship, I didn't doze off."

"You were snoring," Mnogo interjected.

"I don't snore," Shain retorted indignantly. "Even if I did doze off, why mention it?"

"For the report...on why your vitals dropped," RED

responded. "These reports are taken seriously. If the doctor asks about this drop, I need to explain why."

"Well, just put I rested my eyes."

"And the snoring?" RED asked.

"Did my vitals say I was snoring?" Shain asked, annoyed that the subject hadn't yet been dropped.

"No."

"Then don't bring it up!" Shain growled.

"*Ménage A Quatre*, your cargo matches your manifest. Please proceed to docking bay MC-1102," the friendly robotic voice instructed.

Thank Fu Chasa, Shain sighed. "Thank you, again, Sasori Prime. Heading to docking bay MC-1102."

Shain watched a gate open and then guided the ship through the open tunnel entrance. Within moments the *Ménage a Quatre* zoomed out into the hospital skyway and Shain navigated the ship through traffic until he reached a large building.

The ship suddenly froze in place.

"*Ménage a Quatre*, please disable all weaponry, lower your shields, and drop landing gear. We will guide you into the dock via tractor beam."

"RED, please disengage weapons and shield," Shain instructed. "Mnogo, initiate landing gear."

"Sure, turn those off. That will ensure they can blast us out of the sky..." Mnogo mumbled to himself.

As soon as RED disabled the systems and the landing gear was in place, Shain could feel the pull of the tractor beam grab, and the ship slowly began to move toward the docking bay. Within moments, the ship was lowered onto platform MC-1102.

Shain and RED had started to power down the ship when Mnogo stood up. "I'll be locked in my quarters. If you get into trouble, it was nice working with you," he said as he left the room.

"Is he really that much of a coward?" RED asked.

"No. The Sasorian really did a number on him," Shain said as he headed to the loading dock, RED following, "I don't blame him about not wanting to be here."

As they off the pod and onto the loading dock floor, Dr. Scelerat was waiting for them, dressed in a jumpsuit and cap.

"Doctor, why are you dressed in uniform?" Shain asked.

"Because I am coming with you on this delivery."

Shain smirked, "Why?"

"One, you are attempting to steal medical files and have no medical clearance. Two, like your co-pilot, you suffer from Post-Traumatic Stress Disorder. I feel that returning to your species may cause more problems than you are willing to admit to yourself."

Shain took a deep breath, and said, "Fine. Having someone who can talk 'doctor' will probably be useful. RED, let's load the crates on a U-Slate."

"I'm ahead of you, Captain," RED said, pressing buttons on his handheld device. Two long, metal beams with claw mechanism attachments hovered over to the crates and began to load two crates apiece.

"Packages loaded and ready for delivery," RED announced.

"Open the doors," Shain ordered.

A loud alarm sounded, and blue and green flashing lights spun as the bay door started to open. Shain saw several figures waiting for them on the other side.

"Let's keep this professional," Shain whispered to the doctor as they exited the ship with the U-slates in tow.

Shain suddenly started to feel a tightness of breath as he saw several large, horned reptilian creatures approach him.

A tall greenish-blue scaled creature welcomed the crew. "Captain Shain, I am Serpentis. Welcome to Sasori Prime."

"Thank you. Quite a welcoming committee you have here for a few crates," Shain said, gesturing to the six other Sasorian guards.

"Ah yes, we are, unfortunately, at war and need to keep our docks well-guarded," Serpentis explained, "I will have a guard escort you to the morgue to retrieve the cadavers."

"Perfect," Shain said through a forced smile.

How am I supposed to find answers with an armed escort? This mission is going bad quickly.

"Serpentis, I am Doctor Scelerat. I have been asked by Dr. Mongoo on Sasori 2 to pull some needed medical files. Will you be able to take me to the medical archives so I may retrieve those?" The doctor handed a computer chip to Serpentis.

Serpentis took it and inserted into a small handheld device and, after reviewing it, handed it back. "Yes. Would you like to take care of that before your pick up?"

"Due to its urgent manner, yes, I would."

Serpentis made a couple of clicking noises and a brown toad-like creature stepped up next to them. "Natter Jack will escort you there before taking you to level 15 for the cadaver pick-up. May I have the remote to your U-Slates?"

Shain was still in a daze, wondering about the exchange between Serpentis and the doctor, but he quickly snapped back when Serpentis extended his claw. "Of course," he said, handing over the remote.

As they followed Natter Jack towards the elevators, he whispered to Dr. Scelerat, "What just happened?"

"I was afraid you actually had no real plans on how

you were going to get the information you seek. I made my own plan, which included forging documents from their chief medical officer on Sasori 2. You're welcome." Mizu smiled as the elevator doors slid open and they stepped in.

"When we get back on the ship, I owe you a big kiss," Shain responded.

"You owe me more than that." Mizu winked as the elevator came to a stop.

The doors opened to reveal a large, white-tiled hall. "Level 39. Medical Archives are down to the left," Natter Jack croaked.

"Are you ready to get some answers?" Mizu asked as they started down the hall.

"I am," Shain responded as they approached a guard sitting behind a desk.

"Please sign in," the guard requested, handing them a clipboard with a webbed hand.

Shain immediately recognised the guard as Ikarian— the red, reptilian body, the horn in the middle of its head, the spikes peeking out of the collar of its uniform—and when their eyes met, the Ikarian seemed to recognise him.

"You! Why are you here?" the guard whispered urgently.

"You know who he is?" Mizu asked in hushed tones.

"Yes. And she knows who I am," the guard replied

just as Natter Jack joined them.

"Guard, I'll take them from here," the Ikarian informed Natter Jack.

"Very good. I will meet you two on level 15 within the hour," Natter Jack said as he headed back toward the elevators.

"You two, in the Archives, now!" the Ikarian ordered.

"Captain, is that your meat suit?" Mizu asked as they followed the Ikarian through the doors.

"Yep, and I'm guessing his brain is a her, and I'm wearing it's meat suit."

"You two are lucky you weren't discovered," the guard said, locking the door.

"So, who are you?" Shain asked.

"You don't remember, Minister?" the Ikarian asked.

"Minister?" Mizu interrupted.

"I don't know." Shain shrugged. "I remember escaping a Sasorian base. I remember that my brain used to be in your body. But the rest of my memories are like a black hole in my mind."

"I need to get you to Professor Varanidae immediately. He must have blocked out some of your memories. I'm sure he can unblock them now that you are back."

"Sure, but first I need all my medical files and journal entries," Shain said.

"You won't find them here. You are a high security citizen. The only person who can give you answers is the Professor."

"Where is this Professor?" Mizu asked.

"45th floor." The guard smiled as he unlocked the door.

The three exited the Archives and headed back to the elevators.

"So, is this your body?" Shain asked spreading his arms.

"Yes, and let me tell you, I'm turning myself on and it feels a little creepy," the guard admitted, chewing his lip.

"Do you have a name?" Mizu asked.

The guard pressed the elevator button and the doors slid open. "Oh, I'm sorry, I'm Svoboda."

"I'm Dr. Scelerat and, of course, you know Shain," Mizu said.

As the three stepped in and the doors closed behind them, Svoboda said, "Actually she is Minster Shaintilia."

They fell silent as the elevator started to rise.

"Are you trying to tell me I'm an Ikarian female?" Shain broke the silence.

"No, you're a human female now."

"Well, I'm a man trapped in a woman's body like you are a woman trapped in a male's body."

"No, I'm a woman who is now a male," Svoboda confirmed.

"Why do you not call yourself Shaintilia?" Mizu asked, intrigued.

"That name is on the Wanted Criminals list. So, I changed my name to Svoboda."

Shain started to feel overwhelmed.

"Can this Professor Varanidae change us back?" Shain asked, rubbing his temples.

"Probably, but you know that can't happen," Svoboda answered as the doors slid open to reveal a large lab.

Shain and Mizu looked around, amazed by the gadgets and gizmos. The medi lab was much bigger than Mizu's; there were four examination stations, computers, industrial walk-in fridges, and small cages. As they took in their surroundings, they didn't notice that Svoboda had slipped away.

"Shain, I think we shouldn't have come here," Mizu said, expressing her concern.

"Jury is still out on that one." Shain peered into a glass cage of mayhews.

"Minister Shaintilia! Sir, why are you here?" A deep voiced made them both jump and they turned to see a purple reptilian who appeared to have no neck and was wearing medical scrubs.

"Professor Varanidae, I presume?" Shain asked.

"Yes."

"You obviously know me, but I don't know you. I feel I should, but I barely even know who I am."

"You are the Minister of the Ikarian moon, Hachurui. You are wanted for the deaths of six hundred women and children," the Professor explained.

"What?" Mizu and Shain said in unison.

"A set up," Svoboda interrupted as he joined them. "The professor forgot the words 'set up'. This is why he switched our bodies and changed our identities."

"Oh, thank Fu Chasa. I'm not a killer." Shain exhaled in relief.

"I don't know if you killed those people or not. I hid you for the sake of the Ikarian people. There is war and somebody started it." Prof. Varanidae pulled a small blaster from his pocket, levelling it at Shain and Mizu.

"What are you doing?" Svoboda roared, reaching for his own blaster.

"You shouldn't have come. I was explicit in my instructions before you left," the professor sneered.

"He doesn't remember anything. We are here by coincidence," Mizu said, becoming flustered.

The professor laughed. "My good doctor, you don't know the minister like I do. He'd sacrifice you for his own good."

Svoboda stepped between them. "You're not Professor Varanidae. You're—"

Shain flinched as the blaster went off, wet liquid splattering across his face. Svoboda's body collapsed to the ground and Dr. Scelerat quickly dropped to her knees to attend to him.

Shain peered into the Professor's eyes. "Who are you? What is going on?" he shouted.

"I'm sorry you don't remember. You'll be mourned." The professor pointed the blaster at Shain's face.

"Wait!" Mizu shouted, distracting the Professor. "Shain, you never asked what race I was?" she said quickly.

"I always figured you were Delphinusian?" Shain said, wiping blood off his face.

"For the last time! I am not!"

Mizu screamed as her eyes rolled back into her head and two rows of razor-sharp teeth were revealed. She dived over Shain, tackling the professor to the ground, and sunk her teeth into his neck, savagely tearing off chunks of skin.

She could not remember the last time she'd had fresh flesh and blood roll down her gullet. Her eyes rolled back and saw the blood that was spread across the floor. The professor's blood dripped from her chin as she stood.

"Ah, you're a Selachimorphian," Shain said.

"Yes. No blowhole," Mizu responded as she remembered Svoboda's body on the ground.

Shain looked down at Svoboda's body. "How long until the brain dies?" he asked.

"It's a human brain, so usually six minutes. But it is in an Ikarian body, so maybe nine minutes."

"What if we froze it?" Shain suggested.

"Thirty minutes, maybe. But I don't have any way to freeze a body this big."

"We won't have to. Grab an organ carrier from that fridge," Shain said, walking over to a table of surgical implements and picking up a laser scalpel.

Mizu was confused but did what her Captain requested.

Shain looked down at his old body, watching as black blood flowed out of the blaster hole in Svoboda's chest. He took a deep breath, knelt down and said, "Rest in Peace, Minister Shaintilia. Whoever you are," before turning on the scalpel and removing the head from the body.

Mizu rushed over with the carrier and Shain placed the head in it. Mizu pushed some buttons on the side, locking it and freezing the contents.

The two looked at the mess each other was covered in, then looked around the floor.

"I am a little shocked they don't have security

cameras in here," Shain said. At that precise moment, the lab doors opened and several Sasorian soldiers blocked the entrance, weapons drawn.

"Did you two get lost?" Serpentis asked, moving into the room.

"It was self-defence. You can see that on the cameras," Shain replied.

"Yes, and that guard's death was by the professor's blaster. I saw the whole thing," Serpentis agreed.

"Then why the armed escort?" Shain asked.

"Oh, that. Well, it seems I have a wanted political fugitive standing before me, Minister Shaintilia."

"That's the Minister, headless upon the floor," Shain pointed out.

Shain could see the anger brewing in Serpentis' eyes. "I am not an idiot. I have your whole conversation recorded and archived...ready for your trial. So, if you are done with this childish game you are playing, I have an empty cell with your name on it."

"Okay. You got me, Serpentis. What about my crew?" Shain asked.

"They are free to go. There are no warrants on them, and the doctor killing the professor was, as you pointed out, self-defence."

"Good," Shain said, turning to pull out the cage of mayhews. "Would you do me a favour?"

"Would you like those delivered to your ship?" Serpentis asked.

"No. I would like you to pick them up." Shain smashed the cage to the ground, grabbed Mizu, and dashed across the lab.

Serpentis picked up one of the small, furry, mayhews and held it up close to his eyes. "This was your big escape plan? Throwing your lunch at us?" Serpentis chuckled as he looked into the creature's big eyes. Without warning the mayhew shot yellow gloop onto Serpentis and the other soldiers. In one simultaneous move, Serpentis and his men melted down into a puddle of liquid flesh. Shain watched as the creatures scurried away.

"Let's get out of here."

They ran from the lab and quickly made their way to the loading docks. As the elevator door opened, Shain saw Natter Jack standing in front of seven long crates.

"Let's play this cool," Shain whispered as they walked up to Natter.

"There you are!" Natter said, relieved. "You never met me at the morgue, and you weren't at the Archives, so I came down to the docks with your cadavers."

"And my people haven't loaded them onto the ship?" Shain asked.

"No. Your engineer refused to come out until you were present," Natter Jack explained. "Hey, why are you two covered in blood?"

"Covered in blood?" Shain questioned as he looked at himself, then over a Mizu. "Holy Fu-Chasa, we are!"

Natter drew his gun but, before he could say anything more, he suddenly started to shake and then collapsed to the ground.

Mnogo and RED looked down at Natter, still holding the shock sticks they'd used on him.

"Where have you two been? And who's blood are you covered in?" Mnogo asked.

"No time to explain. RED get those cadavers into the ship. Mnogo, grab Natter and throw him in our holding cell," Shain barked.

"We're taking the toad?" Mnogo asked, shocked by the command.

"I'll explain after we are in deep space. Now move," Shain said as he followed Mizu into the ship.

"I'll get the brain into a resuscitation tank," Mizu said as she headed for the med bay.

Shain darted off to the bridge and prepared for take-off.

Mnogo joined him as he was making his final checks.

"The toad is locked up," Mnogo said as he strapped himself into the co-pilot's seat.

"Cadavers secured," RED said as he joined them

"Very good." Shain flipped on the com. "Control. *Ménage A Quatre* requesting de-docking codes."

"*Ménage A Quatre*. We are awaiting approval from command. Please hold," a robotic voice responded.

"Control. Our refrigeration units are unstable and I have seven corpses that need to be delivered. Can we speed this up?" Shain asked.

"Please hold until we reach Commander Serpentis. It will be just a few moments. He has been paged," the voice responded.

"RED can you override the docking clamps?" Shain asked.

"Of course, I can. I can't override the exit doors, though."

Shain noticed a recreational cruiser leaving its dock. "Get the clamps off. I'll get us out."

"Mnogo, transfer as much power as you can to the rockets," Shain requested.

"Will do," Mnogo replied, and started to push buttons.

"Mizu, strap in," Shain said into his com.

"Ready to release clamps," RED informed Shain.

"Rockets at additional thirty percent," Mnogo relayed.

"On my mark." Shain watched the cruiser get closer to the spaceport's doors. "3...2...1... Punch it, RED!"

RED pressed a button and the docking clamps released the ship. Shain immediately started the engines and the ship blasted away from the dock and sped toward the large cruiser ship.

"Captain, you are getting really, really..." Mnogo started to yell as Shain pushed the steering bar forwards, dropping the ship under the cruiser. He hung the ship close to the underneath of the cruiser until it reached the end of the bay, then he pulled up on the bar, just missing the cruiser, and blasted through the exit doors into open space.

Shain continued at top speed until he heard Mnogo mutter, "Close."

"We are clear but low on fuel," RED reported.

Shain turned a switch and the ship slowed down. "Mnogo, find us a fuel station outside the rim. I don't want to worry about any search parties."

"Yes, Captain."

Shain got out of his seat and left the bridge.

Shain was in a daze, unsure how he ended up in his quarters, but he stripped the blood-covered jumpsuit off and placed it on the bed.

He stared at it.

His clothes were covered in blood, yet he had not spilled a drop.

Confusion and desperation filled his head, and sadness ran through his body. He dropped to his knees and cried. This was something an Ikarian simply didn't do, and yet there he was…on the floor, blubbering like an idiot.

Shain got up and walked to his shower. There, he really examined the body he was in. It was much softer than his, but also firm and muscular; Svoboda must have been a soldier. He was surprised by all the hair a human body had; he remembered Mizu complaining that a female human shouldn't be that hairy, but he'd just ignored her until now.

After his shower, he got dressed and walked down to the medical bay. There was a cylinder tank with a brain floating in it, hooked up to a series of wires.

Shain stared at it.

"It seems to have little damage. RED thinks he can build a body for it," Mizu said as she placed a hand on Shain's shoulder.

"Will it be able to give me any information about my past?" Shain asked.

"I don't know. Physically, it is alright. I don't know anything about its memories, and I don't know if it can function again. The professor's work was very complicated."

"She surprised me with the way she accepted her new self. She didn't seem to try to be a human. She just became

Ikarian," Shain said, placing his hand on the tank.

"She was brave," Mizu agreed.

"Shaintilia is dead on that lab floor. It's time for me to accept that I am a human," Shain announced.

Mnogo's voice came over the intercom. "Captain, we are approaching fuel base Ziodey."

"I'm on my way up," Shain said. He turned to Mizu, "I'm going to need your help. I know how to be human, but I don't know how to be a female."

"I'll be happy to help." Mizu smiled.

Shain left the medical bay and made her way to the bridge.

RED and Mnogo were seated at the consoles, and Shain slid into her seat.

She turned on the com. "Fuel Base Ziodey. This is Captain Shain Boga. *Ménage A Quatre* ready for docking instructions."

She smiled.

MARCUS COOK lives in Cleveland, Ohio with his inspirational wife and cat. Ever since he saw, *Star Wars* at the age of four, Marcus has loved science-fiction. He is also inspired by Timothy Zahn, Kevin J. Anderson, Kevin Smith, Luc Besson, Ernest Cline, and Elmore Leonard.

Marcus' stories have featured in *Burning: An Anthology of Short Thrillers*, published by Burning Chair Press in 2018, *Worlds*, published by Black Hare Press in 2019, and *Storming Area 51*, published by Black Hare Press in 2019.

He always loves to hear from his fans.

Bibliography
Deep Space, Black Hare Press, 2019
Storming Area 51, Black Hare Press, 2019
WORLDS, Black Hare Press, 2019

Contact
Facebook: @ReadMarcusCook

BOUND
By Adam Bennett

Elbie has been enslaved in the feritan mines for longer than he can remember. He used to dream of seeing the night sky, but he learned long ago that such dreams are a waste of energy. Will he survive to see the stars once more?

Elbie struck down hard with his pickaxe. The mighty blow did little to mar the rockface before him. He raised the pick for another blow and imagined he was striking down at the face of the newest site foreman. Elbie wasn't usually prone to hate; his time in the feritan mines had taught him that such emotion was a waste of energy. He'd need all he had to make it through another day deep beneath the earth.

He'd been down here for so long he no longer knew what the sun looked like. He had no memory of entering the mines, or anything before the endless clattering of his pickaxe. He raised the tool again and struck, chipping off a small segment of rock and revealing a dully gleaming sliver of silver metal beneath the rockface. Elbie reached out to brush away the rock surrounding the feritan.

It was a large vein by the looks of it. He'd need to be careful to work around the vein so he could extract the precious mineral in as large pieces as possible. Taking a step back from the jagged wall, Elbie raised his pickaxe and struck down hard above the vein, working to free the feritan.

Several hours passed before he'd exposed the entirety of the silver metal. It was several feet long, and as thick as his arm. He struck a final blow and the entire price fell free. He turned to retrieve his hand cart and saw there were a pair of foremen standing silently behind him. He wondered how long they'd been watching his careful work.

"That's a large vein. Well done. I'll bring a team to help carry it to the cart. We wouldn't want you to hurt yourself. There's still a long day of work to do."

Elbie didn't reply. He'd noticed that the other foreman, the one who hadn't spoken, was the new man on the site. The one who was easy with the lash. Elbie had watched him whipping miners who he felt weren't working fast enough. Elbie was no stranger to the lash. No one who lived in the feritan mines was. But whippings were usually reserved for miners who couldn't keep up with the rigours of the mine. This new foreman was different. He used the lash to emphasise his displeasure. He used it as punctuation. He used it for no reason at all.

Elbie broke his eye contact. There was no use provoking the man. Instead, he reached down to the enormously heavy vein of feritan and with a grunt lifted it to his shoulder. He settled the weight and took a slow, steady step between the stunned foremen. He carried the hunk of metal over to the cart and dumped it among the scraps and shards of feritan other miners had deposited there. He turned, strode purposefully back between the stunned foremen and took up his pick once more. He raised it on high, pictured the new foreman's face and struck down hard in the hole the vein had left behind.

Elbie lifted his pickaxe and, after a moment's pause, drove the sharp point down into the unyielding rock. He struck again, chipping free a small section. His shoulders ached, but without slowing he raised the pickaxe on high once more, steadied his aim, and brought the head down hard, sending a shower of sparks flying against his bare chest. A fourth, and fifth, and sixth blow yielded little more progress. A whistle blew and he lowered his half-readied seventh strike, lay the pickaxe against the rock wall, and reached for a small canteen partially hidden in the rubble nearby. Elbie drank deep, careful not to spill a precious drop.

The whistle blew faintly again, and he screwed the lid on tight, picked up his axe and went back to work. Down the line another miner stuck his pick deep into the stone wall. He struggled shortly to free the trapped tool before collapsing to the ground, exhausted. Elbie hefted his own pickaxe and struck down hard into the stone, paying no attention as one of the site foremen walked down the stone passage and drew a beamwhip from his belt.

Elbie had worked the mines for as long as he could remember. He had seen hundreds of miners collapse after a drink break, the first blow after their brief respite too much for their aching bodies. He had never seen a foreman yell or shout for a miner to get up after collapsing. They simply arrived, whip in hand, and began to lay down blows on the fallen slave until he took up his pickaxe and resumed work, or, more often, died under the lash.

For his part, Elbie continued his own barrage on the

stone and tried to ignore the pained screams of the miner. Against the odds, the man eventually made it to his feet, the lash still raining down. He took up his pickaxe and struck a futile blow against the wall, his pick head slipping and skidding uselessly across the rockface. The foreman struck him another few lacklustre blows, but soon shrugged, hung his whip at his belt, and walked off slowly down the stone corridor, whistling.

Elbie struck two dozen more essentially ineffective blows against the boulder before another whistle blew, this time louder and longer, signalling the end of the day. He set down his pickaxe, drank a deep draught from his canteen, rubbed inadequately at his sore shoulders, and lay down against the rockface to get a few hours sleep before the next shift began. He knew how to conserve his energy with the woefully small down time he had each day. He drifted off, painfully aware of the whistle that would come all too soon.

It seemed he'd barely closed his eyes when the whistle blew once more. He stood, took a small sip from his canteen, took up his pickaxe, and began to strike at the rock face all over again.

After a short time, the same miner who had collapsed under the strain the day before fell again. Elbie scanned the tunnel in either direction and, seeing no foremen, put his pick over his shoulder and walked down to where the other man lay.

He was a stocky, short man, all other features obscured by a thick layer of rockdust. Elbie crouched beside him and after a moment of searching, located the man's canteen. He unscrewed the lid and held it out for the panting man to take.

A wicked line of fire erupted across Elbie's back and he dropped the canteen, its precious contents spilling over the dusty tunnel floor. Elbie shouted, his voice raw from disuse. He stood and turned to find the new foreman standing before him, beamwhip raised on high. He struck down, lashing Elbie across the chest, adding a second burning line of excruciating pain to the one across his shoulders. The foreman pointed with the whip handle down the corridor to where Elbie's station was.

Elbie put his pickaxe back over his shoulder and walked back down the corridor, the screams of the downed man echoing behind him as the greedy lash began to fall. Something inside Elbie snapped, and he turned back to face the foreman and his cringing victim.

The foreman's back was turned as he lay down strike after brutal strike. The miner cowered beneath the fusillade of vicious blows. The man had no chance of rising to resume his work. Just beyond the miner's outstretched arm, Elbie could see the fallen canteen, the last drops of water spilling free. His time in the mines had shown him endless whippings, he'd seen many men whipped to death, but something about the spilled water was too much. Even a new foreman should know how precious it was below the surface.

Watching as if outside himself, Elbie strode back to the foreman and raised his pick on high. He twisted the brutal point sideways and with all the strength he could muster he brought the flat side of the tool down hard against the back of the foreman's head.

With a sickening crunch the back of the man's head caved in and he dropped to the ground, a puppet with the strings cut. The beamwhip fell from his twitching hands and with an electric zipping sound, retracted back into its handle. Elbie knew without further inspection that the foreman was dead, his head turned to mush by the heavy mining tool.

The grimy miner still had his hands raised to ward off the blows of the lightlash. He peeked out through his fingers and saw Elbie standing above him, bloody pickaxe hefted over his shoulder. He glanced down at the shuddering corpse and smiled a wicked, involuntary grin. He reached a shaking hand out for the canteen and took a small draught from what remained before screwing the cap on tight.

Elbie helped the man to his feet without comment. He pointed down the rockface towards the elevator shaft and the rest of the miners. A small curve in the tunnel had kept Elbie's attack from the view of anyone else, but another foreman could arrive any moment.

The miner staggered off down the tunnel and Elbie looked at the roof of the tunnel above him. He found what he was looking for after a minute of searching.

He crouched down beside the corpse of the foreman and used the man's shirt to wipe the sticky, concealing blood from the face of his pick. After the tool was satisfactorily clean, he took a grip on the man's belt and shirt and dragged him a few metres down the tunnel.

Returning to his pick, Elbie saw the hated lash laying discarded in the rubble. He'd seen miners try to take a lightlash from a foreman on a couple of occasions and he knew that the weapon was armed with some sort of scanner that verified the person holding it was allowed to do so. Anyone failing the verification was hit with a massive electric shock.

Using his pick to push the weapon towards its owner's body, Elbie soon reunited the pair. Looking up to the ceiling once more, Elbie spied the seam he'd found.

With a carefully aimed blow of his pickaxe, Elbie dislodged the support strut the held the seam in place and as a groaning and grumbling sounded behind him, he ran down the corridor, back to his station and the canteen stowed there. As he reached the small steel water bottle the roof behind him shuddered and caved in on top of the bloody corpse.

The support struts between him and the cave in held and the destruction was contained to the end of the tunnel.

The next few hours were spent clearing rocks to pull free the corpse of the foreman who had obviously been killed when the support struts above him gave out. He was a bloody mess, his body crushed and battered by tonnes of falling rock. The man was almost unrecognisable.

The entire arm was abandoned as unstable, and Elbie and the other miners were moved up into one of the higher arms to continue their work. Elbie never learned the other miner's name, but that didn't matter. He knew the man wouldn't last much longer, but Elbie had given him another chance to survive. It was the best he could do.

Elbie raised his pickaxe on high and struck down freeing a moderately sized vein from the rockface. He picked up the misformed cylinder of metal and hefted it to his shoulder. The cart was full, so he placed the vein on top and began to push it towards the elevator.

There had been no repercussions from his murder of the new foreman. It seemed that his improvised cave in had covered his tracks well enough. He didn't know how long had passed since then—A week? A month? Surely no longer than that—but he hadn't seen the other miner around for some time. The man might have been transferred to another arm, but Elbie knew better. He'd seen the same too many times before.

The end of day whistle blew long and true as Elbie was walking a new cart back from the elevator ready for the next load. He gathered up his canteen for a small swig before settling down to sleep among the rocks and rubble of his station, passing straight into a deep and dreamless sleep.

"Lambda Beta Fourteen Seventy Seven? Lambda Beta one four seven seven? Has anyone seen…"

In his half asleep haze, it took Elbie a moment to recognise his serial number. He cut the speaker off as he woke fully and opened his eyes.

"Here," he said, raising a hand and getting to his feet. His voice croaked. He hadn't spoken in…he had no idea how long it had been. Maybe since before the cave in.

"Come with me," an unfamiliar foreman said, turning back the way he'd come.

Elbie frowned, looked the other way for the foremen that usually looked after his crew. He decided that he couldn't disobey a direct order from a foreman so he followed along meekly, pausing only to pick up his canteen. The foreman led him to the end of the arm and opened the elevator door, gesturing inside.

Now Elbie hesitated. He was forbidden to leave the mine arm without the rest of his gang and all the accompanying foremen. It was his life to step on this elevator without authority.

The foreman seemed to realise his dilemma and smiled, "Come, I promise this is all correct and accounted for. There will be no penalty or repercussion for following me..."

Despite the smile, Elbie felt uncomfortable. After a final moment's hesitation, he stepped forwards and boarded the large freight elevator. The foreman followed, closed the door, and pulled the handle causing the car to jerk and begin to ascend.

From deep within the earth the elevator rose, reaching higher and higher towards the surface. Elbie held on tight as the elevator rocketed up the shaft. Were they going to the top? That was just fanciful thinking, Elbie knew. No miner returned to the surface until the day he fell under the lash.

Sure enough, some ten levels shy of the surface the foreman yanked the lever back level and the elevator shuddered to a halt. Legs wobbling, Elbie followed the foreman as he pulled the doors open and walked out into the brightly lit corridor. It couldn't rightly be called a corridor, Elbie realised. After a few metres of the rocky mining tunnel Elbie was used to, the walls and roof opened up to a great cavern, filled with miners and foremen milling between stalls and shops carved into the walls.

It was the Bazaar.

Elbie had heard of the Bazaar, but he'd honestly thought it a myth, some far-fetched tale as fanciful as Berigan the Bold or Alpha the Frozen Robot. Seeing it now with his own eyes, he wondered what other stories he'd heard could possibly be true. Next he would meet the Sultan of Skieer and dance among the poison butterflies of Trace. The foreman walked into one of the buildings carved into the rockface and Elbie followed.

Inside was a bar, tables and chairs carved from precious denhewood, a smudged red glass mirror on the back wall behind the stone bar that had been carved during the construction of the place. Most of the chairs were filled with foremen, laughing and drinking, shouting uproariously. The room went slowly quiet as Elbie walked in, every face in the room turning to look at him.

The foreman didn't break stride, continuing up to the bar and sitting at one of the free stools pulled up there. Elbie swallowed at the scrutiny, but eventually followed him and stood nearby. The noise started back up again, somewhat muted. The foreman gestured at a stool. Elbie froze as the barman shot him a glare. The foreman raised two fingers and the barman's eyes flashed in fury. He didn't say anything however, and after a moment returned with two small glasses with a thick black liquid inside.

Elbie sat finally, ignoring the glare he got from the angry barman and started to unscrew his canteen. The foreman put a hand on top and shook his head. He pushed one of the small glasses along the impossibly smooth stone. Elbie screwed the cap back on his canteen and reached for the glass. The foreman picked his own drink up, clattered it into Elbie's and swallowed the black mixture down in a single gulp.

Elbie touched the liquid in the glass, frowning as it clung to his fingertip. He made to put the glass back down but the foreman put his hand beneath and lifted the glass back up. "Drink. I found you sooner than expected and I thought… Drink your drink. That's an order."

Elbie shrugged and lifted the glass to his lips. He jerked his head back in imitation of the foreman and managed to swallow the entire thick mess in one go.

His throat burst into flames. He fell backwards off his stool and clattered to the floor. The room burst into laughter, diffusing the tension, but Elbie heard none of it.

His whole chest and face felt like they were melting, and the feeling was spreading through his body. He stood, fighting through the pain as it faded to a flaming discomfort and the room swam back into focus.

The foreman wore a huge grin and held two more glasses of the thick, vile liquid, one proffered to Elbie. "Drink up. Second one is better."

It wasn't.

Elbie kept his chair this time, but the fiery liquid burned through him again, blurring his vision and sending the flames racing along his arms and legs. He was sure he would set the denhewood stool beneath him afire.

As the room swam back into focus, Elbie reached for his canteen. As his fingers closed on it a hand slapped it from reach, sending it clattering to the stone floor behind the bar. Elbie looked up to see the bartender, his expression changed. "You don't want to do that, sonny. Trust me."

Confused Elbie looked around to see the foreman on his feet, arm outstretched only a moment behind the bartender. "What?" he said, sitting back down, the fiery haze clearing more.

"You can't mix keaquine fluid with anything else. You'll be fine, just don't drink anything else for half an hour." He turned to the barman. "Thanks, I needed this. Two more, and we'll be out of your hair...figuratively speaking…"

Elbie stood, shaking a little from shock and the effects of whatever keaquine fluid was, and walked around the stone bar to retrieve his canteen. When he returned, the foreman handed him a third glass, gulped his own down and turned to leave. Elbie followed suit and, after a moment of burning agony, shuffled unsteadily to catch up.

They returned to the elevator, and to Elbie's surprise, the foreman raised the lever again, and a few short moments later they arrived at the surface. The elevator ground to a halt and the foreman pulled the huge door aside.

Elbie couldn't remember ever being on the surface. He must have been here at some point. He hadn't been born below, but he couldn't remember arriving either. The fire inside him had faded to a dull ember, almost forgotten as he stepped out onto the grey blue soil of the surface.

Above him a tall dome held back the stars. Through the dome he could see a small blue sun above the horizon. Off towards the tiny glowing orb, a pair of ships sat waiting to take off to some distant unknown corner of the galaxy. The inky black rocks beyond the edge of the dome were open to the vacuum, the jagged, unforgiving landscape levelled and cleared only around the dome and the landing zone that held the pair of spacecraft. Elbie guessed he must have arrived on the asteroid in one of the ships, but he had no memory of the experience. Something deep inside him yearned to travel among the stars, something only half remembered after his years beneath the surface.

The black twisted wasteland outside stood in stark contrast with the interior of the great glassine dome. Inside, thick vegetation grew up to a series of short, squat buildings, grey-green leaves and grey brown trunks twisted and gnarled into an impassable thicket surrounding the clearing the elevator came up into.

The dozen or so buildings, carved laboriously from the rocky asteroid, stood stout and squat and stolid, scattered about the small clearing, perched among the vegetation. A hundred or so foremen walked quickly between the buildings, ignoring the majesty around them. Elbie couldn't believe what he was seeing. He'd thought the cavern with the bar had been spacious, but the sky was so impossibly huge, the great glass dome wondrously distant. How could these people scurry about with their heads down amidst such wonder?

The foreman who'd collected him from below didn't seem to notice either. He walked off towards a building adjacent to the elevator shaft and went inside. Elbie reluctantly followed, hesitant to let the endless sky from his sight after so long below ground.

Inside he was scrubbed clean, washed by a handful of attendants who removed the grime and dirt from his skin. They clothed him in clean, dark clothes and soon enough he was back beneath the great domed sky once more, the small blue sun having risen slightly higher into the sky and moved along the horizon a significant distance.

While Elbie was staring at the sky, the foreman had walked directly off to the building furthest from the elevator shaft, and Elbie had to run to catch up to him. It was so strange being clean and wearing nice clothes that he wasn't sure how to feel about the whole situation. They reached the building and made their way up the ramp to the second story entrance and went inside. This was the largest of the buildings in the clearing, the only one with a second story, boasting easily twice the footprint of any of the others.

Inside, a secretary motioned them through and they passed immediately into a second, larger room with sparse furnishings. The room wasn't empty, and Elbie was amazed to be confronted with a sectioner. He'd never met a sectioner in person and wasn't exactly sure what he was supposed to do.

"This is Lambda Beta Fourteen Seventy Seven, sir," said the foreman.

The sectioner waved a hand and smiled. "I'm sure you have a more common name that the other miners call you, yes?"

Elbie hesitated but figured it would be worse not to answer the sectioner's question. "Yes, sir, uhh… Elbie, sir." His voice cracked again, weak from lack of use.

"I see," he said. "Elbie, ahh yes, Lambda Beta. Very good. I suppose you have no idea why you are here? No, of course not. How could you? I told Phil to keep it from you, and he obeys me well. Will you do the same Elbie?"

"Yes, sir," Elbie said, unable to hide the uncertainty in his voice.

The sectioner laughed, "Well, you know the right words, even if you don't know what the hell I'm talking about. Did you know you have been mining feritan here on Fulsome Station for twenty years? That is some achievement. The storytellers of old would surely make a fable of Elbie the Endurant, or Elbie the Everlasting. Most of my miners don't last half as long. Remarkable. What is your secret?"

"My secret? Uhh… Sir?"

"The secret to how you have outlasted most of the miners you came in with by more than ten years. The last of your batch died six years back. The last of the batch that arrived after you died before even him. How is it you are still here?"

"Honestly sir, until you told me, I didn't know how long I'd been here." The fiery keaquine in his belly gave him courage he was sure he wouldn't have had otherwise. "Mostly I try to avoid being whipped to death."

There was a thick silence in the room, and for a moment, Elbie thought he'd gone too far. Then the sectioner burst out in laughter. "That is hilarious. Try to avoid getting whipped to death... Hysterical..." He shook his head, suddenly serious. "I have brought you here to find out what makes you so long lasting. We need men to last as long as the robots do, else this is all for naught. You are coming with me to Tyr."

Elbie was stunned. He couldn't get his mouth to work. Surely not... "Sir, you are taking me...up there?" Elbie looked up at the roof and the sectioner nodded. "And we're going to Tyr?" Another nod. "*The* Tyr? The planet where Saint Piotr unfroze Alpha? You're taking me to the home planet of Pope Farran? Why?"

"My, you are an impertinent one. Be careful. When we get to Tyr, you may find that questions are frowned upon. You will find the answers to your questions soon enough, I'm sure. For now, we must make haste."

The foreman, Phil, led Elbie to the door and they passed the secretary's now-empty room and walked back outside beneath the enormous vaulted sky. Phil walked towards a smaller building and went inside, Elbie following. Inside, he was fitted for a vacuum suit. Once he was zipped up and ready, Phil, sporting his own vacuum suit, led him from the small building towards the airlock between the great dome and the waiting spacecraft.

They climbed up and soon were joined by the sectioner, the secretary, several foremen and a dozen armed guards, ready to leave the dome behind.

A tray holding glasses full of keaquine fluid was passed through the crowd and Elbie took one and downed it, following the example of the sectioner and the others milling about. The fourth one was definitely better than the first, but it still wasn't a pleasant experience.

Phil turned to Elbie with a smile, "Your fabled Saint Piotr set off on his pilgrimage to Tyr nearly four thousand years ago. It took him a thousand years of sublight travel to arrive so he could search for the penitent Alpha. You are about to make the trip in under a month, thanks to the very feritan you've spent the last twenty years mining. I'll see you on the other side… If you live…" He reached up with his helmet, clipped it into place, and stepped into the airlock. Elbie followed suit, clipping his helmet to his vacuum suit.

A sharp hiss sounded inside, and soon he could feel air being circulated through the helmet and around the inside of the suit. He stepped into the airlock alongside the sectioner and the guards and the doors closed on the domed mining facility. After a moment the opposite doors opened to the vacuum of space.

The walk to the spacecraft was only a few hundred metres, and Elbie and the others made the trip in less than a minute. The airlock to one of the spacecraft was open and they all climbed inside. After being cycled through, Elbie followed the example of the others and took off his helmet. He made his way to one of the seats and strapped himself in.

Within ten minutes the craft was ready for takeoff, and Elbie sat strapped to his rotating seat stressing about the journey. What had Phil meant by 'if you live'? Was this going to be a dangerous journey? Was there a high likelihood of something going horribly wrong? The journey from Earth to Tyr had taken Saint Piotr a thousand years to complete, all the while suspended in an outdated stasis chamber. When he'd arrived, the entire galaxy had been through the robotic uprising. The Tyr he'd landed on had not been anything like he'd expected. What would be there when Elbie arrived? What were they expecting to find from him? How had he lived so long beneath the mines while countless men died around him?

A rumble ran through the spacecraft and Elbie reflexively clutched at his armrests, strong miner's fingers digging deep into the plush upholstery. The ship moved beneath him and he let out an involuntary squeak. He was about to make a six hundred light year journey in less than a month. The very thought was sickening.

With a jolt, Elbie was thrown back into his chair, the gravitational forces of the ship's acceleration away from the asteroid and its mining facility pressing him into the chair that spun to face him in the direction of thrust. And like that, he was starward bound. Black tendrils began to creep into his vision and his breathing grew ragged. Just as he thought he was going to pass out, it was all over. The seat righted itself, and the sectioner and his secretary unclipped themselves from their chairs and began to make their way about the cabin.

Elbie remained seated, the shock of takeoff taking time to wear off. After twenty years in the dark, he was free, sailing among the stars. As he unsteadily unclipped himself from the restraints and stood to walk about the spaceship that would be his home for the next month until he arrived on Tyr for whatever was awaiting him, Elbie made himself a promise: he would return to Fulsome Station one day. He would return, and free the men from the yoke of the mines. He didn't know how, he didn't know when, but he would return, and he would make a name for himself for something more meaningful than being able to live through hell for longer than anyone else. He would return and the storytellers wouldn't speak of Elbie the Everlasting, or Elbie the Endurant.

They would speak of Elbie the Emancipator.

Seven billion years ago an O Class star exploded in the distant reaches of the Virgo Supercluster. Over the course of eons, particles of the star's dust spread through the universe until finally a series of them coalesced in New South Wales, Australia during the mid eighties. Thus was born the author and publisher **ADAM BENNETT**. His writing shows his yearning to return to his rightful home among the stars, a wish he will achieve, even if he has to wait until the heat death of the universe.

Bibliography

SCIENCE FICTION DOUBLE FEATURE: Phosphorus & Into The Eye, Zombie Pirate Publishing, 2019

FULL METAL HORROR 2: A Bloodstained Anthology, Zombie Pirate Publishing, 2019

WORLD WAR FOUR: A Science Fiction Anthology, Zombie Pirate Publishing, 2019

WITCHES VS WIZARDS: A Fantasy Anthology, Zombie Pirate Publishing, 2018

PHUKET TATTOO: Crazy Tales of Far Away Places, Zombie Pirate Publishing, 2018

FULL METAL HORROR: A Monstrous Anthology, Zombie Pirate Publishing, 2018

Relationship Add Vice: A Thrilling Mashup of Romance and Crime, Zombie Pirate Publishing, 2017

The Collapsar Directive: A Science Fiction Anthology, Zombie Pirate Publishing, 2017

FLASH FICTION ADDICTION: 101 Short Short Stories, Zombie Pirate Publishing, 2019

Connect
Blog: thoughtlesslibricide.wordpress.com
Facebook: @adambennettauthor
Twitter: @zombiepiratepub
Website: zombiepiratepublishing.com
Goodreads: goodreads.com/author/show/1201029.Adam_Bennett

ASCENSION
By Umair Mirxa

Twelve Goddesses. A Thousand Women. Six Viking Space Vessels. Earth's Most Legendary Male Warriors, Resurrected for Battle.

Aphrodite rearranged the front of her *peplos*, allowing its slit to fall open and reveal one long, luscious leg as she crossed it over the other. Bare from hip to ankle, it tapered smoothly down in all its glory to a daintily carved foot which swayed to a rhythm known only to her, even as she looked about herself with a sigh and a huff of exasperation. She had rarely, if ever, been so insulted. Of course, there was the time she had been forced to marry her ugly half-brother. It was not a memory, however, on which she cared to dwell. Slowly and firmly,

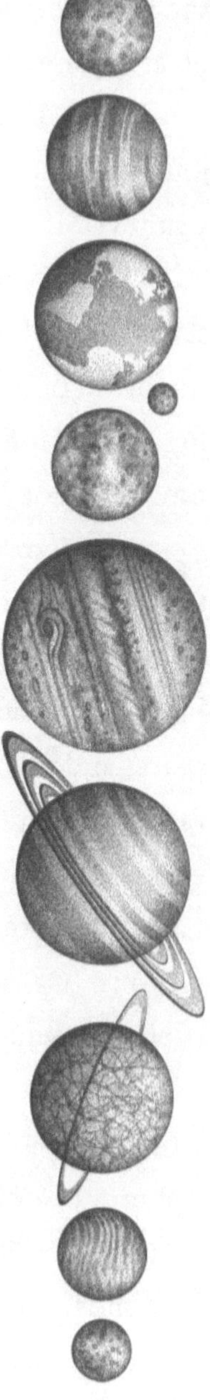

she folded her arms below her ample bosom, and glared up at her sisters, standing to either side.

"I still do not understand why we had to take this journey," she said with a sulky pout. "No. Do *not* roll your eyes at me!"

"How many times do you need it explained to you, sister?" asked Artemis, trying visibly hard to retain a modicum of patience, even as she struggled to maintain her composure. It would not do to have tempers flaring, especially not when no one could go anywhere.

On Olympus, and on Earth at large, the sisters had been able to give each other a wide berth as and when necessary. For nearly three years now, however, they had been confined to a vessel hurtling through deep space, and it had meant they had been forced to spend rather more time in each other's company. They had, each of them realised—and quite soon after leaving Earth too—they did not particularly care for the pleasure. Of course, none of them were, or ever had been, renowned for their forbearance.

"I simply fail to grasp why we would turn around when we were already halfway to our destination," said Aphrodite, looking out the porthole at the distant stars. "A place, I might add, we have sought after for three long and barren years. Three *years!* Now, at last, we find it, and you decide to go back to where we started."

"You *know* why we have to go back," said Artemis, exchanging a frustrated look with Athena. They had been having the very same arguments with their unruly sister, again and again, for days now.

The first few weeks following their departure from Earth, the three sisters had rendered themselves hoarse shouting and screaming at each other. Accusations, both true and wild, had flown. Plates, the food on them, and goblets full of wine and ale had been thrown. The vessel itself, and everyone on board, had trembled as threats were made, tears were shed, and things were yet left unsaid.

"Do you think, sister, the inhabitants of this planet we have decided to call home will simply allow us to rule over them?" asked Athena.

"Well, they should," said Aphrodite petulantly.

Eventually, as the weeks had turned into months, and perhaps driven together by their near constantly hostile sister, Athena and Artemis had managed to develop an affable truce. Aphrodite, however, had refused to relent, and had spent most days grumbling and complaining about one thing or the next. It had become so they had banished her from their own vessel, and exiled her, in turn, to four of the five other ships.

Without exception, the crews and captains had all begged for her to be returned soon thereafter. The

Egyptians had suffered her for two weeks before Sekhmet had threatened to tear her apart, limb from annoying limb. Even the Norse had only tolerated her on their ship for six weeks.

Amaterasu had sent her back on the third day with the point of a *ko-naginata* aimed at her back.

"Do not be silly, please," said Artemis. "You imagine they will yield without battle and abandon their way of life only because we show up, uninvited, and ask them for it?"

"No," admitted Aphrodite grudgingly. "I doubt they would."

"No," said Artemis. "Not even your charms are quite so powerful."

One of the biggest reasons for Aphrodite's constantly sour mood was the apparent failing of those very charms. No one, not one single soul on these travesties the Norse called ships, had shown even a passing interest in her. Not the Valkyries or the Amazons, nor the Berserkers or shield-maidens. They had scarce spared her a second glance, except of course for when she had thrown one of her famous tantrums.

However revolting she may have found the fact, Hephaestus *had* at least desired her. So had every god and goddess, man and woman she had ever met, including Ares, Hermes, Dionysus, and even the great Poseidon himself. Her beauty, famed as it was, had nevertheless seemed to hold no allure for the crew aboard Athena's fleet. She had never before been denied for quite so long, and the fact had been driving her insane. It had been more than a thousand days now since she had last had sex, and it was not for a lack of trying either.

Her sisters were chaste virgins both, so she had begun by attempting to seduce the other goddesses. Every single one of them had refused her advances. Sekhmet and Amaterasu had even had the nerve to be so offended they had threatened to kill her. The latter's consort, Ame-no-Uzume, had since refused to even look at her. Thoroughly insulted, and more desperate than she had ever before been in life, Aphrodite had turned her attentions to the crew, only to be met with utter and disastrous failure and rejection.

"Well," said Aphrodite sullenly, and in no mood to relent. "I wasn't planning to *seduce* the aliens."

"We shall need warriors and weapons then, yes?" said Artemis gently.

"Do we not already have warriors enough?" exclaimed Aphrodite, choosing to ignore Artemis' growl of frustration. "There are Amazons on board here with us, Valkyries and shield-maidens on the Norse vessel, and Onna-Bugeisha and *kunoichis* with the Japanese. You even brought along six score of Earth's most legendary male warriors, resurrected only so they could die in battle for you. How many more could you need?"

Her sisters had admittedly given her their reasons before, and more than once. Aphrodite, however, couldn't care less in the moment. She wanted off the accursed vessel she had been trapped on for years now. There was the hope, deep in her heart, of the crew being more amenable to her seductions once their journey was complete. Moreover, and though she would never willingly admit to it, she *had* been looking forwards to being intimate with a dozen aliens or two. Maybe more. She thought she would decide once she had laid eyes upon them.

"There are more than just warriors on the moon," said Athena quietly. "For years now, I have sent there every woman I could who has ever been wronged at the hands of men such as our father and brothers. There are scholars and scientists in the colony. Minstrels, scribes, and storytellers. Farmers, healers, smiths, and artisans skilled in every craft you could imagine. A thousand women, and we shall need every single one of them if we are to succeed in our quest for a new home."

Aphrodite's retort was interrupted as a pair of voluptuous Amazons entered the cabin and bowed deeply to the three sisters before turning to Athena.

"The Earth's moon has been sighted, my lady," said

the redhead. "We shall be landing presently."

"Thank you, Myrina," said Athena, and then turned to Aphrodite. "Come, sister. It is time to answer your questions, and to address all your complaints."

Aphrodite huffed, and then let out a long sigh. The Amazons had left without even looking at her. She let the slit in her dress fall back in place, and stood. For what good were the delights she had to offer if they were not appreciated?

The idea to find a new planet had sprung forth from Athena's mind, much as she herself had been born from the head of her father, Zeus. Seeds for it had first been planted the night Poseidon had raped, on the steps of her very own temple, one of her dearest, most cherished priestesses.

Athena had arrived, far too late, in answer to Medusa's prayers, only to find Poseidon vanished, and the poor girl, half naked, lying broken and ravaged near the temple doors. The sight of her had brought home for Athena the realisation that women, for as long as they stayed under the yoke of men, would continue to endure violent injustices.

She had carried Medusa inside, and hid her away

from the world. Over the next few months, as she nursed her priestess back to health, Athena had pondered her plan. Her first thought had been to carve a new, matriarchal nation on Earth.

It was an idea borrowed from her sister, Artemis, who had created a secret enclave near Thebes in Boeotia. The reservation protected all manner of beasts and animals from those who would hunt them for sport. Even Athena had only recently learned of its existence when Artemis had appointed their nephew Aristaeus, son of Apollo and Cyrene, guardian over the sanctuary.

Yet nations, no matter how strong and powerful, or carefully hidden, were prone to invasions and conquest. The city of Themyscira on the coast of the Black Sea, home to the Amazons, was the perfect example. No. What was required was a place that women could call home. A safe haven where they would not suffer at the hands of men. The more she thought about it, the more Athena had realised such a sanctuary could only exist on an entirely new world.

The fear of betrayal foremost on her mind, if only through a careless word let loose at the wrong time and in the wrong place, Athena set about executing her plan with utmost care. Tentatively, she shared her thoughts and ideas with Artemis, and was quite pleased to find her agreeable. She was taken aback, however, when Hestia adamantly refused to leave behind the world of men. Even more astonishing for Athena was the split moment Aphrodite took to make her decision.

"You speak of women wronged, sister," said Aphrodite, raising one delicately arched eyebrow in response to Athena's surprise. "Tell me then, who has been wronged more than I? Was I not forced by our father to marry my half-brother, and spend an eternity in misery?"

The opportunity to recruit goddesses not of Greece had presented itself to Athena when Amaterasu had taken ill and she summoned a dozen of them from around the world to Japan. It had been easy to convince the *kami* once it was revealed she was being poisoned slowly by her own brother, Susanoo. Her consort, Ame-no-Uzume, had been only too willing to accompany her beloved wherever she went.

Bastet and Sekhmet had joined the cause soon after, and brought Hathor along. Sól, though she had refused to go herself, had helped Athena recruit Freya, Idunn, and Skadi. Lastly, Amaterasu had enlisted Inari Ōkami. No further goddesses desired to leave Earth but Athena's ranks were quickly reinforced by hundreds of women, from all over the planet.

Even as her plans took shape, and progressed at a near alarming rate, Athena could not help but worry.

The search for a new, utopian planet - one inhabitable by humans and suited to what she had in mind - could, and ultimately did, take years. She took council with Artemis, and unbeknownst to anyone else, the two sisters established a sanctuary on Earth's moon.

Aphrodite stepped outside the vessel, ecstatic at the chance to truly stretch her legs, and stopped dead in her tracks. She heard Artemis chuckle as she stood in a stupor at the sight before them - rapidly blinking her eyes, trying to make them believe.

"Well, what do you think, dear sister?" asked Athena. "Do you still believe we were wrong to take the detour?"

A thousand women, from a hundred nations, stood rank upon rank, cheering their arrival. Beyond them were griffins, battle unicorns and war horses, elephants, lions and wolves and panthers, and a host of cattle. Yet Aphrodite had eyes for but a single person. Medusa had run up, kissed Athena on both cheeks, and was now engaged in a deep, animated conversation with Artemis as if they were old friends.

"I had imagined her a monster, slain years ago by Perseus," she whispered to Athena. "Was she always such a remarkable beauty?"

"Oh, there was a monster beheaded by Perseus but it wasn't Medusa," replied Athena with a rare chuckle. "It was a myth I propagated for her protection, even as I sent her here. Do you see Lamia over there? I did the same for her. Do remember, sister, before you try to charm them, that I would go to most any lengths for these women. I see you are taken with them, and thus I beg of you, do not give me cause to protect them from you."

"I know well what they have endured, my sister," said Aphrodite coldly. "If you knew me at all, you would know I would gladly die before I see them to harm."

"All is well, then," said Athena. "Come. We must prepare to depart. Now we have everyone and everything we need, I would not tarry here overlong."

The six ships in Athena's fleet were Norse raiding boats to look upon, rendered titanic and able to travel through space by Freya's magic. The Greek, the Norse, the Japanese and the Egyptians each commanded one, with the human women divided among them. The fifth ship carried the men, and the beasts of war and agriculture, the cattle, and the siege weaponry. An elite force of Amazons, carefully chosen by Athena herself, guarded the sixth.

"What are you hiding on yonder vessel?" asked Aphrodite. "It is the one ship I have not been allowed on since we first left Earth."

"Oh, just the odd trinket or two," replied Athena. "A few things we might need only if we are quite unfortunate."

The planet they had chosen to colonise, and named Hestia in honour of the goddess of hearth and home, was tiny compared to Earth. It had but one continent, though it was densely populated in most regions. The native inhabitants, while civilised for the most part, had not quite achieved the same advancements in technology as Earth.

It had been one of the primary reasons Athena had decided in its favour. She had only a finite number of warriors, with little to no chance of recruiting more, and she could ill afford to suffer large casualties at the hands of a more advanced civilization.

Furthermore, the weather on Hestia appeared to be idyllic, and early scouts had reported of large, fertile tracts of land, and a seemingly inexhaustible supply of fresh water from numerous lakes and rivers. By all accounts she had received, they had truly discovered the utopia she had first envisioned. Now all that remained for them to do was make a home out of it, and avoid the mistakes of men in the process.

Athena's fleet landed in the northern ocean, and dispatched smaller boats to scout the shoreline. There was a small period of concern when they saw one boat drop anchor, and tarry a while at the mouth of a bay. Soon, however, the boats all returned safely, and delivered their reports.

"Why did you drop anchor?" asked Athena, her voice laced with anxiety. "What did you see?"

"Nothing to warrant concern. I simply wished for more than a passing glance at the land," replied Artemis. "Oh, it is perfect, sister. Once we have settled here, I shall build a city on it to rival the grandest on Earth."

"Lay to rest, for now, any plans for the future. We must look to the present. What news from the shoreline?"

"A few fishing villages, a hamlet or two. Nothing more. No ships. The closest city is best estimated to be at least ten leagues inland."

"Prepare for battle then, sister," said Athena. "For you shall be my general, and command our forces on the ground. See the Amazons and Valkyries ready, and ask Sekhmet and Bastet to join you."

"So, let it be done," said Artemis with a wide grin, one only the call of battle could inspire.

The conquest for planet Hestia began, as most conquests are wont to do, with a simple raid on a quiet, bright afternoon. Bastet and her scouts had discovered a tiny hamlet, inhabited by a people most queer. They had managed to capture and bring back with them a prisoner, one the cat goddess claimed was a representative specimen of his species.

Athena studied him with Freya, Hathor, and Amaterasu. Their captive had but a single eye in the centre of his forehead, with a horizontal slit for a pupil. Red-skinned, muscular, and seemingly agile, he had paws for feet, and three-inch long talons for nails extending from his fingers and toes. He was naked except for a loincloth strapped around his waist, and the bush of green on his head was the only evidence of hair on his entire body.

Once he had been secured at camp, Bastet joined the band of Amazons, Valkyries, and Berserkers led by Artemis and Sekhmet in a raid on the hamlet. For all their fearsome appearance, the native inhabitants proved inept at battle. The few fighters they had were massacred in one fell swoop, and the rest of the population was quick to surrender. Athena's forces now had a base of operations on Hestia.

A fortnight was spent establishing the settlement and erecting such temporary fortifications as could be raised with limited time and resources. Athena did not, however, let her people rest idle. They could not afford a prolonged war with the natives, and yet she did not wish for senseless, brutal massacres. She would fight such battles as were necessary, and hope to establish terms of peace thereafter, for therein lay her people's only chance of survival on an alien planet.

Scout missions were sent out in rotation east, west, and south. Hunters, foragers, and scientists, escorted always by warriors, familiarised themselves with the land, and its flora and fauna, at all hours. Scribes were set to record all events and instances, no matter how small or insignificant. Smiths, bowyers and fletchers went to work, forging and repairing armour, swords and axes, and bows and arrows. The *kunoichis* were sent to infiltrate the larger cities, and assassinate threats as and when they deemed such acts necessary.

Artemis and Sekhmet, frequently joined by Skadi and Bastet, continued to lead skirmishes, and soon began to meet with organised resistance. They encountered a larger settlement of the red-skinned people, and met them in pitched battle on the outskirts of their village. The natives were routed yet again, and Athena's forces gained further ground in their advance.

Any local inhabitants captured were put to work,

teaching the invaders their culture and languages, helping them find food and provisions, and providing labour to further fortify conquered pieces of land. Slowly, and with each new skirmish and battle, the number of prisoners grew. Further native species were fought against and captured.

Bastet and Sekhmet, along with the Onna-Bugeisha defeated a large group of three-eyed, three-legged green giants with bark for skin. Artemis, the Amazons, and a band of shield-maidens led by Lagertha forced a company of ebony-skinned dwarves into retreat, and then survived an ambush by a battalion of tall, red-headed and bronze-skinned warriors who rode gigantic wolf-like creatures into battle.

The first of Earth's warriors to die in battle on Hestia fell during the ambush. Two shield-maidens were slain by arrows in the first assault, and a third was ripped apart by one of the monstrous creatures. The beasts were also responsible for the two Amazon deaths, as they slashed the women open from neck to waist with their claws. In acts of bravery worthy of legend, Artemis and Lagertha had yet contrived to lead their company back to camp, carrying all five of the fallen, and had even managed to take two prisoners.

The ambush, they learned from their prisoners, was

carried out by warriors from Yvilyan - the capital city of the grandest nation on all of Hestia, its people most noble and proud. Yet, they did not pose the most immediate threat to Athena's forces.

Yvilyan's warriors had but answered the call from Quixar to help defend it from the invaders. Athena brokered an agreement with the prisoners, allowing them their freedom if they would act as ambassadors of peace to their own city. Once they had departed, Athena commanded her army to march on Quixar.

The two armies met on the plains before the city's gates. A motley assembly of all the different races which inhabited Hestia were gathered together to defend their homeland. The invaders, not much different in their composition, were fighting for the hope of a new home.

Athena sent two Amazons as envoys to sue for peace, and received but their severed heads in return. Her wrath, in that moment, was terrible to behold.

The battle, when it began, was fought furiously and to the detriment of both armies. Warriors fell quickly on each side, and yet the natives were hopelessly outmatched. They lost ten of their own for every human life they took, as inch by inch, they were forced to retreat. Even in the throes of her rage, Athena found herself admiring their courage. For in the face of overwhelming odds, they yet refused to easily yield ground.

It was a pity, she thought, to lay waste to the lives of such brave and noble warriors. She had, however, already lost more than a hundred of her own people, and the battle had to be brought to a quick end before further losses were suffered.

"Release the automatons," she commanded.

A dozen mechanical dragons flew into battle, followed by bronze Colossi, and the Colchis Bulls. Next, she unleashed all the beasts of war she had brought, and let forth the Valkyries, each of them riding a pegasus. Every single native warrior outside the city's walls was slaughtered. Athena's forces gained the hill overlooking the city, entrenched themselves on top of it, and surrounded the city.

All those who had fallen in battle were carried from the field and prepared for funeral rites in the encampment. *The battle has taken a heavy toll*, thought Athena as the final count was presented to her. Four-and-seven-score of her warriors had been lost. She vowed to do all in her power to prevent further bloodshed as she stood over the fallen and prayed for their souls.

The siege lasted three days. On the morning of the

fourth, a delegation came forth from the city. Its leaders had realised no help was forthcoming and had wisely chosen to spare their people deaths from starvation. They climbed up the hill to the human camp, laid down their weapons at Athena's feet, and negotiated terms of surrender.

Hathor, as the city was henceforth to be known, would now and forever belong to the women who had come from Earth and to their descendants after them. Its new name had been chosen in honour of the goddess Hathor, the mistress of the stars, who had first discovered the planet, Hestia.

Anyone who did not wish to live under its new rulers would be permitted safe passage from the city. Of those who desired to stay, women and girls would be welcome within the city proper, and allowed every religious, social, and cultural freedom. All men and boys, from both Earth and Hestia, would live in a village to be built outside the city walls. Women who so desired were free to live among them as companions and wives and were encouraged to mate across species.

The ambassadors were treated, while scribes drafted the agreed upon treaty, to a celebratory feast of such delicacies from Earth as had survived the journey and the war. They seemed to delight in all they partook of, except the wine, over which they gagged most miserably, and thereafter looked at it with utter distaste.

Soon, the treaty was ready and signed by all twelve Earth goddesses, and the six local ambassadors who departed momentarily to relay the news to their people.

"We shall mark this day," said Aphrodite, joining her sisters as they stood on the ridge overlooking the city, watching the delegation make its way down the hill. "Every year, on its anniversary, we shall remember our fallen, and celebrate our glorious victory."

"No, sister," said Athena, her sombre eyes looking past Aphrodite to gaze solemnly at the four-and-seven-score warriors who lay wrapped in shrouds in the field beyond. "We shall commemorate our fallen and remember this day in our hearts, but we shall not celebrate it."

"Why ever not?"

"It will forever be a reminder of their shame to those who have lost today," said Hathor gently, coming up beside Athena.

"For as long as we flaunt our victory here, there will be no possibility of peace," said Athena. "If we wish to prevent further war and bloodshed, and desire to build here a world different from the one we left, then we must avoid the mistakes made on Earth."

"Wise words, sister," said Aphrodite. "How then, do you think, should we begin our new lives here on this planet?"

"Oh, I have a few ideas," said Athena with a smile. "Of immediate import is to bring the city to order and make certain we have provisions enough to provide for our people in the days and months to come. We yet know next to nothing of this planet's weather, its seasons, or what harvest we might expect."

"There are those among us who can bring their powers to bear," said Amaterasu, joining them with the other goddesses. "I can make the sun shine, or not, for as long as it is required. O-Inari Sama and Freya can render any patch of soil fertile, and of course, Artemis can provide as much game as necessary."

"I wish to build an acropolis on this hill," said Athena. "A stronghold to which we can retreat if required but also a keep wherein we preserve the knowledge, past and future, of our people."

"Oh, I can see a paved road from the acropolis to the city," said Idunn. "It shall be lined with twelve and three score apple trees on each side to commemorate our fallen."

"Well, our plans seem made," said Artemis with a wide grin. "For myself, once all is set to order, I should like to take a portion of our people and build a city anew on the land I espied when first we arrived on this planet."

"So, let it be done," said Athena. "It is the dawn of a new day, a new life for all of us. Let us put to rest those who died so we could live, and then drink ourselves into a stupor in honour of their memory."

"So, let it be done," repeated Aphrodite to loud cheers from the rest of the goddesses.

Aphrodite made her way through the citadel, cursing Athena for its labyrinthine design as she found herself repeatedly lost, and in front of the wrong doors, again and again. She had woken up late, in a mood, and had almost decided to not attend court but to lie in bed all day long. Moments later, however, it had occurred to her that a lazy morning was scarcely worth the grief she would certainly thereafter receive from her sisters.

She had risen, therefore, graceful as ever, from her bed, performed her morning ablutions, and dressed with as much haste as she could bring herself to muster. The crimson robes she chose to wear for the day were the most sultry in her possession. They clung to her form in manners most sinful, with a deep neckline which displayed her bosom in tantalising fashion, and a long slit down the left side which she could manipulate for her seductive ventures as and when necessary.

At long last, she came upon the door she wanted, and was pleased to see every head turn in her direction as she entered the courtroom. Slowly, and with a pronounced sway to her hips, she weaved her way through the crowd, and ignored the annoyed looks sent her way by Artemis as she took her seat next to Athena. Ambassadors from the eastern city of Yvilyan, as the natives called it, arrived ten minutes later.

Messages had been sent back and forth between Hathor and Yvilyan for weeks, negotiating terms for a trade agreement set within a more comprehensive peace treaty which the embassy had now come to officially sign. It would bind the two cities together and secure Hathor on all frontiers.

There were six delegates, four female and two male. Each of them was tall and muscular with long, red hair, green eyes, and bronze complexions. They were all dressed in near identical robes of deep, dark blue, and were the most beautiful creatures Aphrodite had seen since her eyes had alighted upon Medusa on Earth's moon all those months ago.

A wide smile appeared across Aphrodite's face as she feasted her eyes. The woman on the far left, she thought, was particularly gorgeous. She was pleased now she had chosen to attend after all, even as she hatched dreamy plans for how she would corner her prey alone during the revels to follow the tedious business of state.

Even more delighted with her choice of dress, she rearranged the front of her *peplos*, allowing the slit to fall open and reveal one long, luscious leg as she crossed it over the other. Bare from hip to ankle, it tapered smoothly down in all its glory to a daintily carved foot which swayed to a rhythm known only to her.

UMAIR MIRXA lives and writes in Karachi, Pakistan. His first published story, 'Awareness', appeared on Spillwords Press. He has since had stories accepted for publication in anthologies from Zombie Pirate Publishing, Blood Song Books, Black Hare Press, Iron Faerie Publishing, Clarendon House Publications, and Fantasia Divinity Magazine & Publishing.

He is a massive J.R.R. Tolkien fan, loves everything to do with mythology, fantasy, and history, and wishes with all his heart that dragons were real. When he's not writing, he enjoys reading novels and comic books, playing video games, listening to music, and watching movies, TV shows, and football as an Arsenal FC fan.

Bibliography
ANGELS, Black Hare Press, 2019
APOCALYPSE, Black Hare Press, 2019
BEYOND, Black Hare Press, 2019
Blaze, Clarendon House Publications, 2019
Curses & Cauldrons, Blood Song Books, 2019
DEEP SPACE, Black Hare Press, 2019
Divinity, Iron Faerie Publishing
FLASH FICTION ADDICTION, Zombie Pirate Publishing, 2019
Galactic Goddesses, Fantasia Divinity Magazine & Publishing, 2019
MONSTERS, Black Hare Press, 2019
Of Kami & Yokai, Fantasia Divinity Magazine & Publishing
Poetica, Clarendon House, 2019
Summer's Splash, Fantasia Divinity Magazine & Publishing
Tempest, Clarendon House Publications, 2019
UNRAVEL, Black Hare Press, 2019
Waters of Destruction, Fantasia Divinity Magazine & Publishing, 2019
Winds of Despair, Fantasia Divinity Magazine & Publishing, 2019
WORLDS, Black Hare Press, 2019

BLACK HARE PRESS

ZOEY XOLTON is an Australian Speculative Fiction writer, primarily of Dark Fantasy, Paranormal Romance and Horror. She is also a proud mother of two and is married to her soul mate. Outside of her family, writing is her greatest passion. She is especially fond of short fiction and is working on releasing her own themed collections in future.

Bibliography
ANGELS, Black Hare Press, 2019
APOCALYPSE, Black Hare Press, 2019
BEYOND, Black Hare Press, 2019
Curses & Cauldrons, Blood Song Books, 2019
DEEP SPACE, Black Hare Press, 2019
EERIE CHRISTMAS, Black Hare Press, 2019
JIBBERNOCKY, Black Hare Press, 2019
MONSTERS, Black Hare Press, 2019
STORMING AREA 51, Black Hare Press, 2019
UNRAVEL, Black Hare Press, 2019
WORLDS, Black Hare Press, 2019

Connect
Website: www.zoeyxolton.com

WELCOME TO THE VOID
By Zoey Xolton

The Void beckons the bold,
Whispering their names
It summons them to valiance.
To charter the stars,
To risk life and limb,
Beyond the known edges of the world.
Stars burn and galaxies collide,
Black holes crush all into oblivion.
The Void is as beautiful
As it is unforgiving.
Forsake air, forsake gravity,
The forces of eternity are against you.
Yet the brave will look ever skyward,
Wondering, curious.
What lies in the deep bowels of space?
Friend? Foe? Nothing?
Only a few will ever know,
And fewer still will live to tell the tale.

DEEP SPACE

ACKNOWLEDGEMENTS

When we embarked on our Black Hare Press journey back in late 2018, we never envisioned the huge support we'd get from the writing community. We have been truly humbled by the number of submissions we've received (around 3,000 over eight publications!) and have loved reading every single one.

So, thank you to everyone who crafted tales just for us—from the tiny tales in our Dark Drabbles series to these monstrous beauties you have read here in Deep Space—we thank you from the bottom of our hearts.

To our families and friends, collaborators, random strangers who took pity on us, and everyone who has helped us on the way: we couldn't have done it without you.

And to you, our discerning reader, we and these twenty-one talented writers did it all for you. We hope you enjoyed these tales of weird and wonderful worlds and space exploration. If you did, don't forget to leave a review.

Thank you all, and see you next time.

Love & kisses

Ben Thomas & Dean Kershaw

www.blackharepress.com

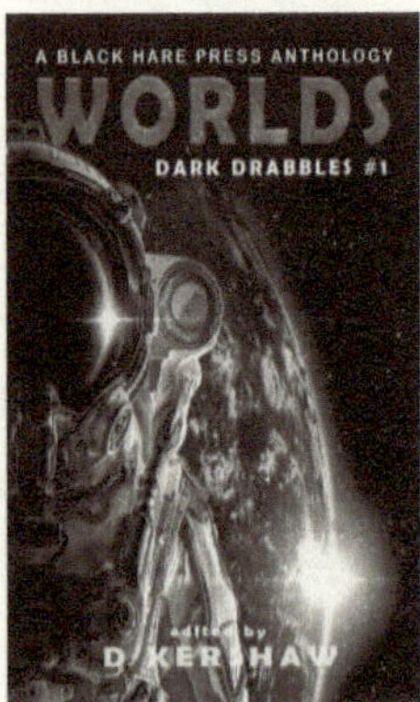
A BLACK HARE PRESS ANTHOLOGY
WORLDS
DARK DRABBLES #1
edited by
D KERSHAW

A BLACK HARE PRESS ANTHOLOGY
ANGELS
DARK DRABBLES #2
edited by
D KERSHAW

A BLACK HARE PRESS ANTHOLOGY
MONSTERS
DARK DRABBLES #3
edited by
D KERSHAW

A BLACK HARE PRESS ANTHOLOGY
BEYOND
DARK DRABBLES #4
edited by
D KERSHAW

A BLACK HARE PRESS ANTHOLOGY
UNRAVEL
DARK DRABBLES #5
edited by
D KERSHAW

A BLACK HARE PRESS ANTHOLOGY
APOCALYPSE
DARK DRABBLES #6
edited by
D KERSHAW

A BLACK HARE PRESS ANTHOLOGY
STORMING
AREA 51
SURVIVOR STORIES
edited by
BEN THOMAS
& D KERSHAW

9 781925 809220